HUNTER

ROSEWOOD HIGH #5

TRACY LORRAINE

Andy and Amelia

PROLOGUE

Poppy
Three years ago...

"Zayn, your turn," Ethan says, his eyes moving around the circle until he finds Zayn's excited dark eyes.

It's his birthday, he should be excited. Unlike me, who's been forced to attend a fifteen-year-old boy's party while ignoring the fact he doesn't want me, Ruby, or his sister here.

We stand out like a sore thumb among his football friends, but for some crazy reason Jada, Zayn and Harley's mom, seemed to think it was a good idea.

I roll my eyes at her naïve plans. At least Scarlett, their older sister, had the sense to argue and has hidden herself in her room.

The tension in the room ticks up a notch as everyone stares at the empty bottle that Zayn spins in the middle of the circle we're all sitting in.

All the girls around me, bar Harley, seem to hold their

breath in the hope of getting a chance at seven seconds in heaven with Zayn.

I try to keep my breathing steady in the hope of covering up that I'd also be more than willing to lock myself in the closet with Zayn.

He's hot, and I can't deny that I haven't had a crush on him since they first arrived in Rosewood last year.

It's just a shame he's one of Jake's football buddies. They might all only be sophomores, but I only have to take one look at the varsity team to see what they're going to be like in two years. Their egos and wannabe god-like personas are already growing larger than life.

I have no interest in getting tangled up with that. I'm not a popular girl, I'm not destined for the cheer squad or one of the sport teams. I'll just hide in the shadows while doing my thing and counting down the days until I can leave for college and finally take charge of my own life.

I let out a sigh, lost in thoughts of a future without the weight of my family weighing down on me. Being fourteen shouldn't be like this. I shouldn't be worrying about everyone else more than myself, but sadly it's my reality.

The bottle slows to a stop and my heart jumps into my throat as realization dawns that it could be about to land on me. I glance to Harley at my side and smile, imagining everyone's irritation—mostly Zayn's—should it land on his sister.

It misses her though, and when the bottle comes to a stop, it's pointed directly at me.

My eyes fly up in shock as I look up at Zayn.

"No. No fucking way," Jake, my cousin barks, his eyes narrowing on Zayn.

"Calm down, man. It's just some fun. Poppy, you're up for it, right?" Ethan looks at me expectantly.

"I... um..." I hesitate as all the sophomore girls' eyes drill into me.

"Just let him spin it again," Shelly pipes up, one of the cheer wannabes. "Zayn doesn't want to kiss a freshman anyway. She probably doesn't have the first clue about what she's doing."

I part my lips to argue, but really, she has a point. My experience with kissing is limited to an awkward lip press with Christopher back in junior high during a game of kiss chase.

"No second spins," Ethan spits, reiterating the rules that he laid out at the beginning of this stupid game. "You get in the closet or you forfeit, and I'm pretty sure none of you want to do the dares that I've got running around in my head." He smiles wickedly and Shelly pales slightly. I've heard all about Ethan Savage's dares, and so has everyone else in the room looking at their faces. "So..." He waves his hand between the two of us and the closet being used for this game.

My nerves quadruple to the point I worry if I'm going to be able to actually walk over there.

I push to stand, feeling the stares of everyone around me but no more so than Harley's shock and my cousin's death stare.

I manage to take two steps to where Ethan is now holding the door open before a hand wraps around my wrist.

"If he tries anything with you, tell me and I'll lay him out."

"It's fine, Jake. It's just for fun," I tell him, but I don't meet his eyes. The last thing I need him to see are my nerves and, dare I say it, excitement about this.

"It better be. You're worth more than any of this group has to offer." I don't miss the sounds of the rest of the team ribbing Zayn for having to kiss his little sister's friend, but I zone them out and focus on Jake.

"They're your friends, Jake."

"Yeah, and you're my family. The only decent one I got. I want the best for you, Popsicle."

I roll my eyes at his overprotectiveness, although I can't help but feel loved. It's something I don't feel all that often where my family is concerned. I think Jake is the only person who actually understands, who gets me. And for that, I'll forever be grateful.

"It's all good. You've got nothing to worry about."

He releases me, allowing me to slip into the closet.

I wait in the shadows for Zayn to join me while the hoots and hollers from his friends continue.

"Make sure she gives you one hell of a present, Hunter," someone calls, making me swallow down the lump of anxiety that's climbed up my throat.

It's only a kiss. I can do that. It's no biggie.

Right?

There's no doubt in my mind that he's only doing this because it's a game. There's no way in hell he'd ever willingly kiss me. I might have imagined what it would be like a time or two, but I suspect it never so much as crossed his mind, let alone in this capacity.

The door widens, allowing a sliver of light to illuminate me before it clicks shut, bathing us both in darkness.

My heart beats so wildly I swear he must be able to hear it. My hands tremble and my temperature spikes.

Every noise he makes sounds incredibly loud despite the fact I have blood rushing in my ears faster than I'm sure is natural as he closes the space between us.

"Poppy?" he asks, his voice sounding calm, like this is just an everyday occurrence for him.

I remind myself that it probably is. Jake, Zayn, and the others have girls hanging off them wherever they go. He's probably well-practiced in this sort of thing.

"Y-yeah," I whisper, hating that my voice cracks, showing my nerves.

The heat of his body hits mine. "Do you have any idea how long I've wanted to do this?"

His words throw me off for a second and it takes me longer than it should to register them.

"Y-you want to k-kiss me?" I sound pathetic and I kick myself for not sounding more confident.

"Yeah. There was no one else I wanted that bottle to land on. This is the only birthday present I wanted."

"Oh God," I practically whimper when his fingers find mine.

He steps into my body, pressing me back into the wall. I gasp at the feeling of his hard body against mine as his fingers tickle up my bare arm before he grasps the back of my neck.

"Ready?" he asks, his voice deeper than it was only moments ago.

My head spins as I fight to remember to breathe.

"Y-yeah, I—" I don't get to finish my thought because his soft, full lips brush mine.

At just that small contact, my knees go weak. He must sense it because his other hand lands on my waist. It feels huge as his touch burns my skin, causing sensations to swell within me that I've never felt before.

His lips stay on mine, unmoving for what feels like forever but in reality, it's probably not more than a second before his tongue teases at the seam of my lips.

I have no idea what I'm doing, but it doesn't seem to matter because my body seems to know what's expected of me and my lips part, allowing him entry.

If I didn't already know he'd had experience, then I did in that moment as he took control of the kiss. His tongue sweeping against mine.

My arms stay rigid at my sides as his fingers twitch at my waist, obviously wanting to move, but he never moves.

He kisses me like I've seen on TV, but it feels nothing like I imagined. I'm not nervous. Not self-conscious. I just let myself go and allow him to sweep me away.

All too soon, he places a chaste kiss on my lips and backs away from me. I miss him almost instantly, to the point I actually reach out for him, but despite my eyes having adjusted to the darkness, I don't manage to make contact with him.

"Poppy?" he asks again, his voice husky and rough, it does things to my insides I can't explain.

"Yeah?" I ask eagerly, desperate to hear it again.

"Don't repeat a word I said to you."

Lead fills my veins at his warning. I should have known he was lying.

I'm too devastated to respond, desperately trying to fight the tears that are already burning the backs of my eyes.

I thought he really meant it. That he's been thinking about kissing me like I have him.

Stupid, stupid girl.

He pushes the door open, the sudden light makes me close my eyes as a chorus of cheers erupts from the other side.

My heart sinks into my feet as I wonder how the hell I'm supposed to walk out of here with my head held high.

You're not, a little voice in my head says. *You just totally screwed up.*

The ruckus only gets louder as a victorious Zayn steps from the closet after his few seconds in heaven.

"So..." someone prompts. "Did she give you the gift you've been dreaming of?"

Before he answers, he looks back at me. I might be back in the shadows but he sees me and our eyes connect for the briefest moment.

"Nah, she's a frigid bitch." He walks away as his friends erupt in laughter and a couple of the girls descend on him, probably offering to do everything I apparently couldn't. All the while, I pray for the ground to swallow me up while continuing to hide in the shadows.

How long can I stay in here? Will anyone even notice?

1

Poppy

I rush out of the Hunter's kitchen with a drink in hand, ready to find Harley and Ruby to celebrate the New Year together.

Butterflies erupt in my stomach, despite all the crap in my life, this is an exciting moment. One year closer to finishing school. One year closer to taking control of my life. One year closer to leaving this place and everything I despise about it behind. This year we're going to become seniors, we get to start seriously thinking about our futures and what we want from life. I might not have it all figured out yet, but I know one thing. My future isn't here. There are too many memories and demons lurking in the shadows for me to ever want to stay.

But while I'm stuck here, I figure I'd better make the most of it.

I see a flash of Harley's bright red hair and I can't help but smile. At least I have a couple of good things in my life, my two best friends are definitely that. I have no idea how I'd survive this place without them.

The sound of the party around me begins to lessen as kids head outside, ready to watch the fireworks that are about to illuminate the sky.

I shouldn't have come tonight but despite my parents' obvious irritation that I was going to spend the night enjoying myself and they weren't, I packed a bag and walked straight out the front door. Most days I allow them to blackmail me into doing as they wish, tonight wasn't one of those nights.

I knew it was safe being here. It's mostly the seniors who are partying at the Hunter's, the majority of our junior class are elsewhere, thank God. It means that for once, I'm able to let my hair down and attempt to enjoy being a seventeen-year-old girl if just for a couple of hours, forget about the weight that presses down on my shoulders every other day of the year.

I'm almost at the door when a warm hand wraps around my wrist. The grip is hard, meaningful, and my heart jumps into my throat. A shiver of fear runs down my spine.

He's not here, I remind myself. *You're safe right now. He is not here.* It doesn't matter how many times I repeat those words in the millisecond I have before whoever has touched me makes themselves known, the fear threatens to swallow me whole regardless.

I kick myself for letting my guard down tonight, for allowing myself to think that I could have just one normal night. For once, just enjoy a party like everyone around me does without constantly looking over my shoulder, waiting for the devil to strike.

"You're looking hot tonight, Pops."

His deep, rough voice flows over me, and instantly my shiver returns, only this time it's not with fear.

Steeling myself, I lift my chin, ready to fight.

"Get your hands off me, Zayn."

I try to pull myself from his grip but he's holding too tightly. Before I've even had a chance to plan my next move, he's taken control and pulled me back until the cool of the wall bites into my skin.

He stares into my eyes and as always, I hate that he can see so deep.

"Why aren't you enjoying yourself like everyone else?"

"I... um... I am. See?" I lift my drink and tip it toward my mouth, only it doesn't meet my lips. Instead, it's taken from my fingers and pressed against his full lips in a heartbeat.

"That's soda," he states, his brows drawn.

"So?"

"Don't you want to let go, have a little fun? You're always so uptight."

I flinch at his words. I spend most of my life trying to cover up how I really feel, what's really going on with me. I really don't need him digging and finding the ugly things that I try to keep away from everyone else.

"Don't you want to have fun?"

"Who says I'm not?"

"Aside from the soda, your face."

My lips part to respond but I fear I have no argument.

"The others don't see it, do they?" His fingers lift and he tucks a lock of hair behind my ear, his touch burning all the way down to my toes.

"Don't see what, Zayn?" I snap. I shouldn't ask. I'm terrified to hear the answer, to know what he really thinks of me but that's the thing about my best friend's older brother. He affects me in a way that no one else ever has. It annoys the crap out of me.

"I don't know," he muses, staring deep into my eyes. "But I want to find out."

"Fuck you, Zayn," I spit.

"Now there's an idea. You think that'll help loosen you up a little?" His eyebrows wiggle in excitement as I will all of my muscles below my waist not to clench at the thought.

I told myself years ago that I wasn't ever allowed to lose myself in Zayn's smooth lines. He shattered my young heart all those years ago in that closet. I may never have forgiven him for that, but hell if I don't still dream about it. I tell myself that should the situation arise ever again that I'd tell him to go to hell, but I'm pretty sure I'm only lying to myself because even now, I can feel that kiss.

"Let me go," I damn near beg.

"Why, so you can go and pretend to be happy? Tell me how to make it better, Poppy. Tell me how to put a genuine smile on your face."

"Why do you care?" I ask, my eyes narrowing on his sparkling ones.

"I've always cared. I watch you, you know, when you're not looking."

"No," I argue, knowing that it can't be true. The thought of it being true and him discovering what I keep hidden is scarier than him admitting that he might actually care.

"These frown lines," he says, his finger gently running between my brows, smoothing them out. "I want to know what puts them there." His finger continues down over my nose until it connects with my lips.

I suck in a ragged breath as I watch his eyes follow its journey. It lingers on my bottom lip for a beat before pulling it out. His eyes darken as he sucks on his own bottom lip like he's imagining all kinds of dirty things.

I've seen the look on him before. Usually right before he makes a play for a cheer slut. But despite the fact I know that, it doesn't make me move. In fact, right now, with his scent filling my nose and the heat of his body seeping into mine, all it does is make me want to find out where he's going with this.

I don't need to look up to know we're alone right now, someone has turned the music down and all the voices that can be heard are coming from the garden.

I should push him away. Harley, or worse, Jake could see us and jump to conclusions. What I really don't need in my life right now is more drama. But as I remain locked in his stare, I'm powerless to move.

His hand wraps around the back of my neck, his fingers squeezing in the most incredible way.

"What keeps these muscles so tense, Pops? What are you hiding?"

My lips part to respond as he rests his forearm against the wall beside my head. He steps closer, completely surrounds me with his size and I feel like a little girl once again. I feel like I'm fourteen once more and about to experience everything I'd been dreaming about.

"Zayn," I warn as he slowly closes the space between us, the crowd from outside beginning their countdown to the New Year.

"Celebrate the New Year with me, Pops. Let's bring it in style."

He steps closer still. His hard, powerful body pressing mine back into the wall. His muscles meld with my softness and my knees threaten to give out.

Right as the first firework explodes, his lips connect with mine. His grip on my neck gets tighter and my lips part without any instruction from my brain.

You shouldn't be doing this, the little voice in my head screams. But I already know I don't have the strength in me to stop it. Not now that I can taste him, feel his tongue dancing with mine, feel his hardness pressing against my stomach.

Fuck, he actually wants me.

His tongue delves past my lips once more, searching mine out. This kiss is different to the previous one we shared.

There's no hesitation whatsoever. He knows what he's doing this time.

As he should, he's been with half of the senior girls according to the gossip.

"Oh God," I mumble against his lips, the realization of what I'm doing slamming into me full force.

Pressing my palms against his solid chest, I push in the hope of making him back up.

"Zayn, stop," I beg the second his lips part from mine.

Keeping my eyes on the fabric of my shirt, I fight down my need to pull him straight back to me.

I miss him already. It's crazy.

"You shouldn't have done that," I whisper, needing to at least attempt to tell him how wrong it was.

"Why?" His voice hits me exactly where I don't need it to. That combined with how ferociously his chest is heaving doesn't help my resolve at all.

"Because nothing good happens when we..."

"When we?"

I roll my eyes at myself, at the fact he needs me to say the words out loud. "When we kiss." I lift my eyes to him, needing him to know how serious I am.

"I don't have a black eye yet, do I?" he says, referring to what happened after that horrendous experience of our last kiss.

I might have wanted to hide in that closet for the rest of eternity but the second I heard Jake's angry growl and the girls start screaming, I didn't have a choice but to step into the light and watch as Jake rained hell down on Zayn's face for what he said about me.

"Give it time."

Our eyes hold, mine hold a warning whereas I swear his hold a promise, although I'm not entirely sure what he's trying to promise me. All I do know is that the tingles continue to race through me and my temperature doesn't decrease at all with his stare burning into me.

When the fireworks are over, the crowd starts to disperse and their chatter and laughter filter down to me. I know I need to move. I can't be standing here in this stare-off with Zayn when Jake or Harley emerges.

Thankfully, loud footsteps approaching us sound as I drag my eyes away from his dark and hungry stare.

I look up in time to see Justin clap his hand down on Zayn's shoulder. His eyes are wild and he sways a little on his feet. The guy's wasted.

I'm about to roll my eyes at the state of him when he says the words that rips the rug from beneath me once again.

"Sweet, man. I didn't think you were going to pull off your tag tonight. Right at the stroke of midnight, too."

My eyes widen as understanding washes through me. The team's little games aren't a secret around the girls of Rosewood High.

"What?" I ask, forcing the word out through the lump in my throat.

"Pop, it's not—"

"Don't lie to me, Zayn," I hiss back. "Tell me I wasn't a dare," I demand.

He swallows nervously but his lips remain sealed.

"Tell me," I damn near plead, not knowing how I'm going to deal with this again. The first rejection hurt like hell. But this time, it's so different.

That kiss, those few seconds of escape from reality, there's no way he can have any idea how much it meant to me, how much I needed it.

He gave me something that took me away, even if for a few seconds and now it's all crumbling around my feet once again.

"Pops, I—"

"No," I bark, shoving at his chest. "Don't *Pops* me. You're a fucking joke. You know that, right? The group of you are a fucking joke," I scream, briefly meeting Justin's eyes who doesn't so much as flinch at my volume.

Assholes.

Zayn takes a step back, his eyes still trained on me. Something akin to regret filling them but I refuse to acknowledge it.

Stepping past him, my arm collides with his, sending a pain right down to my fingers but despite my gasp, he doesn't react.

"I told you, nothing good comes from us kissing. It's time you realized that," I hiss at him before I storm past.

"And what if I don't?"

Shaking my head, I march from the kitchen and head toward the stairs.

What I really want to do is walk straight out of the Hunter's front door and leave this party and his games behind me. But where would I go?

Home?

I almost laugh to myself at the thought. I think I'd rather be Zayn's plaything, the pawn in his games, than being at home tonight.

I fly up the stairs, my legs burning as I take two at a time in my need to get away. I ignore all the doors until I get to the penultimate one and I swing it open.

The safety of Harley's room makes me sigh with relief. I slam it behind me, feeling the vibrations of the force I used before I throw myself at the bed.

I tell myself not to cry. Not to waste any more tears on that asshole, but it's not a fight I can win because the harder I try to keep them in, the more they insist on being released until I'm sobbing into Harley's pillow.

2

Zayn

"What the fuck, man?" I bark at Justin who stands staring at me like he didn't just fuck everything up.

"What? You won. You kissed your tag. What's the big fucking deal, that she didn't like it?"

I stare at him, my lips parted but unable to find any words.

He's right, this shouldn't be a big deal. I shouldn't care that she knows that it was a dare. I shouldn't have cared about the lie I told about her three years ago either. But I did, and I took the beating I deserved for it.

Things between Jake and I have never been the same since that night. I'd been in Rosewood less than a year and still trying to find my place within the team. Doing what I did was probably the biggest risk I've ever taken. If Jake didn't believe in my skills, he could have dropped me there and then. We might have only been sophomores, but he had the power, even back then.

I didn't lie to her that night. I had been thinking about kissing her. What fifteen-year-old boy in their right mind wouldn't. She was gorgeous. But not in the same way as the girls I hung around with. She was effortlessly beautiful. She hardly wore any makeup, she didn't need it. Her light brown hair had a natural curl and her gray eyes captivated me. There was so much innocence within them, but at the same time wisdom, the kind of wisdom that only came with experience, but I had no idea what that was. As far as I could tell, she had a good life. She lived with her parents and younger siblings and she'd formed a fast friendship with my sister. But there was more to Poppy than she let on and I was desperate to unearth whatever it was.

I've wanted a repeat of that night ever since. Not that she'd ever let me anywhere near her. She became distant to the point it pissed me off and instead of being concerned like I should have been, my automatic response was to be a dick.

I have no idea why she just kissed me like she did. I don't deserve it.

"Get out of my fucking way," I snap, pushing past Justin with such force that his drunken ass hits the floor. He cries out behind me, but I don't give a shit. The only thing I can think of right now is getting a drink. The new year has only just started but I'm already wishing for a do-over.

This is it. The best year of my life. Senior year. We've won both the division and the state championships. We're the fucking best team this town, our school, has seen in a really long fucking time. We're living the life. We have parties every weekend and more girls than we know what to do with. Mom ensures that I have everything I could ever want. So why do I feel like something is missing?

———

"Zayn!" My name being screamed from somewhere in the house drags me from my sleep. "Zayn."

"Oh fuck," I grunt, rolling onto my back, keeping my eyes firmly shut. Afraid that if I open them the light will burn them from my sockets.

My head pounds a steady beat as my stomach crashes about.

How much did I drink last night?

I think back to swiping a bottle of whiskey from Mom's drink cupboard while everyone else was forced to drink the beer she'd allowed us for the night, and I took myself to the only place I knew no one other than my sister would be able to find me. The treehouse.

We were too old to really make use of it by the time Mom moved us here, but it still comes in pretty handy. Mostly for me when I've had enough of all the female hormones running around my house being forced to live with three women.

New Year's Eve—or New Year's Day—I guess, and I was hiding like a pussy in a treehouse. It wasn't exactly the start of the year I'd imagined.

"Zayn Alexander Hunter, get your ass out here right—" The sound of my door flying open and then a loud gasp sounds out. "Oh my God." There's movement before she speaks again. "Get yourself decent, see your guest out, and then meet me in the kitchen. You have some work and a hell of a lot of groveling to do, my boy."

"Ooooh, someone's in trouble," a sickly-sweet voice comes from beside me, finally forcing me to open my eyes.

I take in the blonde who's half-asleep in my bed in only her underwear.

"Shut the fuck up, Laurie. What the hell are you even doing here?" I ask, having zero memory of even talking to her last night, let alone inviting her into my bed. Granted, it's not her first visit, but still.

"You brought me, said you needed to see the New Year in with a bang." She winks. "If you get my drift."

"You need to leave."

"But—" she starts, her hand skimming over my stomach until she's cupping my junk. She might think my morning wood is because of her, but she'd be bitterly disappointed. I have no idea if anything actually happened with her last night, but if it did, it certainly wasn't memorable. Not like a certain kiss.

"No, Laurie. It's time for you to go home."

I throw her hand off me and push from the bed. My head spins, forcing me to reach out for the wall until it clears.

"When I get out of the bathroom, you'll no longer be here." Reaching down, I swipe her dress and shoes from the floor and throw them at her.

"You're an asshole, you know that?"

"I've been called worse. You know where the door is."

She huffs in frustration, but I ignore it as I swing the door shut behind me and turn the shower on. The good thing about being the only male in the house is that I managed to snag one of only two rooms in this house with an en suite.

I grab the mouthwash and freshen up before resting my hands on the cool basin and hanging my head.

That was a dick move I pulled last night. I poured salt into an already pretty painful wound where Poppy is concerned.

I tell myself that receiving anything other than her hate would be weird anyway, and without looking at myself, I drop my boxers and step into the shower.

When I finally get down to the kitchen, desperate for the biggest mug of coffee I can find and maybe a blunt if I can unearth any, I discover Mom sitting at the island surrounded by empty bottles, crushed Solo cups and discarded cigarettes.

I wince at the sight but with last night's whiskey still flowing happily through my veins, it doesn't affect me as much as I'm sure it should.

"When I told you that you could have a party, I trusted you to keep it under control." Her voice is calm, cold even and it sends a shiver running down my spine.

"Sorry. People turned up with more alcohol and things went a little crazy."

"Crazy. The house stinks of weed, Zayn. The one thing I forbid in this house."

"I know. I'm sorry."

"You will be. I hope you don't have any plans today because all of this," she says, gesturing to the devastation. "Is all yours to fix. By the time I get back this afternoon, I expect it to be back to normal."

"Where are you going?" I ask, walking to the coffee machine.

"I'm taking your sisters for a spa day."

"Brilliant," I mutter. Scarlett may have been elsewhere last night, but Harley was here and enjoying the party, surely she should help me clean up.

"Oh no, don't even think about it," Mom warns as if she can read my thoughts. "We'll be out of your way in half an hour. Poppy is just packing her stuff up so I can take her home."

"Great." Thoughts of how Poppy and I left things last night leave a bitter taste in my mouth—worse than the lingering taste of the whiskey I can't shake.

"I suggest you start in your den. There are bodies everywhere."

She shudders as she says the words, hands me her mug and glides from the room.

Rolling my eyes, I rinse her mug out and place it into the dishwasher.

So much for a New Year's Day workout with the guys later today then.

I do as was suggested and head toward my den. I don't need to open the door to know what I'm going to find inside. The smell of weed and teenage boys lingers in the hallway.

"Rise and shine, motherfuckers," I shout, turning the spotlights on and hitting the button to open the blinds. Grunts and groans sound as bodies begin to stir to life. "Unless you planned on spending your day cleaning this house from top to bottom, I suggest you get your shit together and fuck off."

At the threat of cleaning up, everyone jumps into action.

Twenty minutes later and Justin is the last to leave as I begin sweeping the room with a trash bag in hand.

So much for being a fucking team. They were all more than happy to fuck shit up last night, but they have no interest in the consequences.

It wouldn't have been like this at the beginning of the school year. Jake, Mason, and Ethan would have stayed to help. Even a few weeks ago, Shane would have been here tidying up the mess they helped make the night before. But now they've all got their girls, they've got more important things to worry about than sorting this place out.

I'm in the kitchen getting a new bag when footsteps thunder down the stairs. Female voices fill the room and when I turn around, I find a smug Harley and a sheepish-looking Poppy standing in the doorway.

"Regretting it, yet?" Harley asks, her eyes flicking around the bottles and cups still littering the counters and floors.

"Fuck off," I grunt, ripping my eyes away from the two of them. Poppy might not have looked up at me but that doesn't mean she won't and I don't have it in me to see the hatred in her eyes, not yet at least.

"Jeez, you clearly didn't get a kiss at midnight," she mutters absently.

I fight not to react, but my spine goes ramrod straight.

Spinning back to them, I find Poppy staring daggers into me, begging me not to say anything. And I won't, not about that at least.

"That's where you're mistaken. Laurie only left a few minutes ago. Mom caught us in bed together."

I watch as all the color drains from Poppy's face and her lips purse in anger. I want to say there's some jealousy there but mostly, I think she just wants to cause me pain.

"I'm not sure that should be something to be proud of," Harley announces to the sound of Mom coming to join us.

"Ready to go?" she asks Harley before the three of them turn and disappear from my sight. Although I don't miss the "have fun" that Mom calls out to me.

3

Poppy

My stomach twists to the point I think I might puke on the Hunter's tiled floor as Zayn proudly states that he had a bedmate last night.

It's not news to me. I watched them both stumble inside as I made a trip to the bathroom before I finally fell asleep last night.

The jealousy, the anger that swelled within me like an angry beast was almost enough to force me to follow them and pull that hussy away from him.

But I couldn't. It wasn't my place. And as much as I sometimes want to pretend that there might be something between us, just to allow myself a few seconds where life might not be quite so shit, I know there's not. It's all fantasy, a game, where Zayn is concerned.

He's already proved to be a compulsive liar and last night was just another example of the shit that falls out of his mouth. It makes me wonder how much of it the cheer sluts fall for.

"Are you okay, honey?" Jada asks when both she and Harley take a step to leave, but my feet root me to the spot.

"Oh um... yeah. Just tired."

"Let's get you home so you can sleep it off." I hear the warning in her voice loud and clear. She hates that her baby is now a part of Zayn's senior year parties. But with Harley being a cheerleader now, she can hardly stop it. Especially when all she's done is encourage her youngest child to join the squad.

"What happened to Ruby?" Jada asks once we're backing out of the driveway.

"Um..." Harley hesitates. "I think she might have gone home with a friend."

Jada's eyes find her daughter's in the rearview mirror and then narrow in accusation.

The last thing I saw of Ruby last night was her dancing with one of the guys after I ran away from Zayn. After that, the only thing I know is that she didn't spend the night in Harley's room like we'd planned.

I cast a glance at Harley who just shrugs at me, clearly not knowing where she disappeared to either.

The little bit of concern I'd been feeling about our best friend grows even more. I really don't need anyone else to worry about in my life but she's changed recently and I fear she's on a one-way street to self-destruction if she's not careful.

The conversation in the car falls silent and I rest my head back, watching the passing scenery. I don't want to go home. But where else am I supposed to go?

"Here you go, honey," Jada says as she pulls up outside my house a few minutes later.

"Thank you," I say sadly. "Call you later?" I mutter to Harley before pushing the door open.

"Sure."

"Have a great day." I put as much excitement into my words as possible but they still fall very flat. I may have turned down the invitation to join them, but really, I'd love to. A day of forgetting about everything and just enjoying the relaxation and pampering, I can't even imagine what that must be like at this point.

"It's not too late to join us," Harley asks hopefully.

"I can't. I've got stuff..." I trail off, not wanting to go into details.

"I know. Have a good one."

I wave them both off and watch as their car disappears down the street before sucking in a breath and turning toward the house.

My stomach drops the second I push inside the front door. It's in silence with only the sound of Cooper's crying ringing through the house. My stomach drops, I knew I shouldn't have gone last night.

I drop my bags and make my way through the rooms to find where everyone is. We're lucky, I guess, we've got a decent house on the boundary between the rich and poor side of town. On the outside, it might look like we're a normal, happy family. But inside tells a very different story.

"What the hell?" I bark as I swing the living room door open to the sound of Cooper's cries getting louder.

His face is beetroot red, his little fists clenched in anger as he tries the only way he can to get attention.

Running over, I scoop him up from his bassinet and cradle him to my chest. His cries lessen but they don't stop. I discover why when the smell hits me.

Mom and Dad are passed out on the couch. Neither seems to be aware that he was crying or that I've even entered.

Reaching down for one of the cushions that are falling from the couch, I launch it at the two of them.

Mom mumbles something, but she doesn't wake.

"You two are a fucking joke," I spit. "They shouldn't have allowed you to be parents."

I take Cooper to the kitchen to make him a bottle before carrying him up to his room so I can change him.

With him cradled in my arm, I give him his bottle that his chubby little hands eagerly reach for while I check on the other two.

Austin and Sofia are in Austin's bedroom playing some shooting game that is way too old for them. I want to tell them that it's not appropriate, they're only eight and six, but what else would they do? Life in this house is hell, they're just trying to make the best out of a bad situation.

They glance up at me when I enter, but they're not surprised to find their older sister and not their parents checking up on them.

"Have you two eaten?"

"I made toast," Austin says, ripping his eyes away from the screen once again.

"Are you sure playing that with Sofia is a good idea?"

He looks back at the screen with a sigh.

"We're not babies," Sofia snaps before going back to killing someone who jumps out on the screen.

"Can you play car racing or something?"

"We'll change it up in a bit," Austin agrees, looking at his little sister who's busy maiming some guy. "Did you have a good night?"

"It was great," I lie. They're not stupid, they know that our lives, our parents, aren't normal but they don't need me making it any worse. I want to show them that better exists. That they don't need to settle for the bullshit hand we've been given.

"I'm going to finish feeding Cooper, then shower. If you need anything, just shout."

They both nod, once again lost in the violent game playing in front of them.

"Where are they?" Austin asks, making the ball that's already formed in my stomach grow larger. I wish there was something more I could do for them.

"In the living room." *Just stay up here,* are the silent words spoken between us.

"Okay."

"I'll make you some lunch in a little bit. Please, change the game."

They agree and I leave them to it. Maybe I should be more insistent but the last thing any of us need is for the three of us to fall out.

I sit myself and Cooper in the chair that faces out over the balcony in my room that overlooks our unkempt yard and then the rich part of town beyond.

Jake's old trailer is tucked at the bottom of the yard. I've spent hours sitting here wishing that I could move into the old, damp thing now that he's gone.

I used to feel sorry for him, stuck down there on his own. But as the years have gone on, I've found myself craving that musty trailer more than I should. If it weren't for my brothers and sister, then I think I'd have moved in already, but I can't do that to them. Who the hell knows when Mom and Dad would have got their shit together and fed them if I didn't show up when I did.

He guzzles down the bottle in record time before almost instantly drifting off to sleep.

I rest my head back, wishing that I could now curl up in bed and catch up on the sleep I missed out on last night like any other normal teenager. But I can't. I have people relying on me.

Once he's fast asleep, I carefully place him in the travel crib I have in my room and begin stripping out of my clothes.

Probably the only good thing about this house and my fucked-up parents is that I snagged the master bedroom, seeing as I'm basically the parent under this roof.

I used to feel bad for them. Dad hurt his back years ago and has, apparently, been unable to work since. I'm not entirely sure that is true seeing as he and Mom seem to be able to make more babies than they can look after and he's able to get about and play with his beloved beat-up cars all day long. As far as I can see, he's just a lazy fuck who doesn't want to get a job.

Mom works, sometimes. But it's about as sporadic as her moods. In the past, I've begged her to go to a doctor and get checked out. I swear she's got something that could be stabilized with the right medication, but she point-blank refuses, telling me that she's fine and that it's nothing a little weed won't fix. I beg to differ.

Overall, I fucking hate my life. And after being forced to spend every day here over the holidays, I'm more than ready to get back to school where I can at least get a little reprieve from my responsibilities. Although, life at Rosewood High isn't any more pleasant at times.

Not being at school means I don't have to face the devil who roams the halls and tries to make my life a living hell.

I always thought he'd get bored when I didn't react to his abuse when it started, but he never did.

It just gets worse.

And after all these years, I have a feeling that it's not going to stop until I break.

Or he kills me.

Right now, I honestly have no idea what's going to come first.

———

"You ready for this?" Ruby asks two days later from the driver's seat while Harley spins around so she can study me as I drop into the back of Ruby's car.

"One step closer to senior year, right?" I mutter sadly. They both know that I hate school or more so life in general, but neither know the whole truth, the dark secrets that I keep hidden.

They know my home life is shit and that my parents mostly check out on their duties, and they know that he—Preston Hellburn—likes to try to make my life as hard as possible but they have no idea just how much effort he puts in when they're all busy enjoying themselves.

"You look tired, P."

"Cooper cried almost all night."

"Jeez, your parents really need to figure out how to look after a kid."

I agree. It's not like I can argue with that point. Only while I'm sure they're thinking that it was his crying from their bedroom that kept me awake, the reality was that I was the one up soothing him, trying to calm him down so that Austin and Sofia also didn't have a ruined night sleep.

Thankfully, Harley and Ruby get lost in cheer talk and the upcoming season and championships.

I smile as they chatter excitedly, and pride swells within me for what they've both achieved. I might have no interest in any extracurricular activities, especially those that involve sports, but even I know how hard they've worked to be chosen for the varsity squad already.

As we approach Rosewood High a shiver runs down my spine.

I've got a year and a half, then I can get out of here. I can hopefully manage to secure a place at college and disappear to the other side of the country. Guilt nags at me that while I do that, my siblings will be left behind to fend for themselves. I hate it, but this is my life, I shouldn't be stuck here because of my parents' irresponsible decisions.

There are kids everywhere when we pull into the parking lot.

Harley and Ruby jump out, more than ready to get started on the new semester, whereas I move with a little less enthusiasm.

Eyes move over to the three of us. It's normal. Ruby and Harley have been appointed into Rosewood royalty with their squad places. That uniform means that everyone now wants to be their friend in order to improve their own social status or they just want to fuck them so they can brag.

I'm used to that kind of behavior. I've dealt with it for years.

I'm related to the king of Rosewood after all. Jake Thorn *is* Rosewood High. The girls all want him, the guys all want to stand beside him, and everyone bows at his feet seeing as he led the team all the way to the top last year.

And no one wants to be Jake's little bitch more so than Preston.

He might have things that Jake never did. The money, the mansion, the daddy who gives him whatever his black little heart desires, but he's missing one big thing that he's desperate for.

Respect.

He might think he's a little version of Jake hanging out with his JV teammates and playing the part of being important, but the reality is that no one likes him. And if someone were to take away his skill on the field, they'd drop him faster than he thinks is even possible.

He spends his time forcing people to grant him the position as the leader of the junior class but really his rule is all about fear.

Everyone is scared of him. He's a loose cannon. One

minute he can be completely normal, just your average school kid, and the next he's like the devil incarnate.

My skin prickles as we walk inside the building and toward our lockers.

He's here, I know he is. But then, I expected it. Since Jake and the Bears won the championship, his reign of terror has stepped up a notch.

He wants to be captain next year and for some fucked-up reason, he thinks I can convince Jake to give it to him.

What he doesn't seem to realize is that Jake would never listen to football advice from me, or anyone for that fact. He has his own opinions and ideas for his team and his word goes. He's not going to care what his little football-hating cousin thinks.

I roll my eyes at myself and the whole situation. If it weren't so insane, I might care more but at this point, I figure I just need to put up with him. One day I'll walk away from this place and never have to look him in his dead eyes again.

"Ew, what the fuck is that smell?" Harley complains when I open my locker.

My own stomach turns as it hits me, and I almost puke on my feet.

"I have no idea," I admit, my watery eyes landing on a lunch bag on top of the books I left here over the holidays.

They both lean in closer to get a look at what's causing the stench.

"Maybe I left my lunch here," I say with a shrug, knowing that it's not true but I may as well try.

"What the hell were you going to eat, a dead bird?" Ruby deadpans.

Her suggestion of a dead animal makes me heave as I remember walking out to feed Smidge, Austin and Sofia's rabbit, a few days before we finished school for the holidays to find the cage open.

I shouted at them for not closing it properly the last time they played with her, which only made them cry harder and for me to feel like the worst sister in the world.

But it wasn't them.

My stomach turns over.

Motherfucker.

My hands tremble with the realization that he's been at the house. In the past, everything he's done, any interaction between us has been at or around school. He's never once sought me out at home before.

The sweet faces of my siblings run through my mind. I can't let him anywhere near them.

"Well, whatever it is, you need to get rid of it. It's stinking up the entire hallway."

I look over my shoulder to see people starting to look this way with their lips curled in disgust.

"Great." Reaching inside my locker, I hold my breath as I pick up the bag and bring it closer.

"Oh my God, that's vile," Ruby mutters, covering her face with her hand.

I can't argue. It's repulsive.

Right as I turn to hotfoot it outside to the nearest trash can, I spot him.

He's standing right in the doorway—of course he is—totally blocking my exit with a smug smirk playing on his lips.

Kids around us seem to stop talking as they look between the two of us. It's no secret that there's no love lost between me and Preston. Unlike most of the kids around me, I'm one of the only ones who doesn't go running when he so much as looks at me.

When I said that I've refused to back down over the years, I mean it.

Preston Hellburn is no better than me. So what, his daddy has money and he lives in one of Rosewood's biggest houses?

I don't care that he can throw a football better than most. To me, he is just a person. A rotten one at that, and there's no way I'm cowering to him just because he thinks he deserves it.

Holding my head up high and with the possible remains of our beloved pet rabbit in the bag I'm holding, I walk toward him.

Predictably, he doesn't move.

"Excuse me." There is no politeness to my tone. It's cold, harsh, exactly the way he deserves to be spoken to.

"Make me." His voice is low, ensuring no one else would be able to hear.

My teeth grind as he stands before me unmoving, totally unfazed by my presence.

The air crackles between us, pure hatred firing off.

There's movement behind me, but I don't look to see what's going on. I soon discover who's joined us though because Preston smiles down at me. There's no happiness in it, I don't think this guy has ever been happy, it's full of malice and abhorrence. But only a second later, he steps aside and allows me to pass.

"Everything okay?" a familiar voice booms down the hallway. I want to feel relief, but I don't. The last thing I need is Jake getting involved in this. Preston is trying to use me to get to him. I refuse to allow it to happen.

"Of course. Poppy was just taking out the trash."

He nods to his little pathetic group of followers and they all take off in the opposite direction, allowing me to run outside and dump the bag.

As I run for the bathroom, the vile scent lingers in my nose. Slamming the door back against the stall, I drop to my knees and heave.

No one bothers to check that I'm okay. I'm not sure if that's because the smell is clinging to my clothes and skin or just because they don't care. Either way, it's nothing new. I like living my life mostly in the shadows.

The only people I really expect to follow are Harley and Ruby, but they've got their own lives now, they hang out with the team and squad. And I'm more than happy for them to go off and do that. I have no intention of joining that crowd.

I know the three of us are unlikely friends with them craving the cheer spotlight and me hiding, but our friendship runs deeper than our hobbies. I don't know what it is but it's there and it means everything to me. It's why I'm not worried about their rise to fame within the Rosewood hierarchy. They won't forget me.

I wipe my mouth with some tissue and flush the toilet. I might have lost my breakfast thanks to that prick but I don't feel any better.

Tears burn my eyes as I think about what he did, but I refuse to cry. He doesn't deserve any kind of reaction from me, let alone my tears.

I wash my hands and wipe at the smudged makeup under my eyes before squaring my shoulders and preparing to walk back out there. No one else will have a clue as to what happened back there.

But I know.

And he knows that I know, and that thought is terrifying. If he's willing to sneak into my house and murder our rabbit, what else is he capable of?

I always knew he was unhinged. Well, he wasn't as a child. He was just like the rest of us then the accident happened and it totally changed him. He might have lost his mother that day but it was like he gained a personality transplant.

He turned cold, evil, selfish. He suddenly wasn't happy with his life and he needed to be the best, be the one everyone else was jealous of.

I couldn't understand it then and I still can't to this day. I'm fairly sure I never will. I just need to focus on school coming to an end and getting away from it all.

Am I running away? Maybe.

Thoughts of my future drag me down as I pull the door open and step out with the intention of heading straight to first period.

I don't look up, I don't want to see if I'm the subject of everyone's attention. Sadly that means I also don't see the person whose chest I walk straight into.

4

Zayn

"Is Hellburn still giving Poppy grief?" I ask Jake as we turn the corner and stumble across them having a stare-off at the other end of the hallway.

"That guy's a fucking asshole," Jake mutters, his eyes drilling into the wannabe football captain.

His intentions aren't a secret, and if they're meant to be then he needs to remember that Jake and the rest of us hear everything that happens in this place. We have ears everywhere.

Although, we don't need those ears to know that he has some kind of issue with Poppy.

When I first started here, I thought that he just wanted her. But as time has gone by, things have changed.

"Should we..." I trail off, not really wanting to look like I care. Jake's still not heard about New Year's Eve but I know my time is limited. I'm surprised no one's snitched me out yet.

"Why do you care?" Jake snaps, although his stare doesn't leave the guy stopping his cousin from leaving.

"Because like you said, he's an asshole. What is that smell?" I mutter as we walk farther down the hallway.

The second Jake speaks, the entire hallway falls silent. I'm sure that more than a few of the spectators right now would pay good money for Jake—anyone really—to take out Preston fucking Hellburn.

He stalks off with his little gang of pussies before Poppy takes off running. Everyone else is too distracted to notice the speed she leaves at, but I see it.

"Hey, girl. What was that about?" I ask, sliding up to Ruby and resting my forearm on her locker.

Her cheeks are red long before she even looks up at me. "Poppy had something in her locker. Can't you smell it?"

"In her locker?"

"Yeah. Good holiday?" she asks, changing the subject from her friend.

"Uh, yeah. You?"

"I missed you," she admits, running her hand up my chest.

"That right? Because rumor has it that you spent time with Rich on New Year's instead of me. That hurts, baby."

She shrugs. "It wasn't anything like that. He's not you." Her lips curl in a salacious smile but it doesn't affect me like it usually does.

We're distracted when Chelsea makes an appearance and demands that both Harley and Ruby get their asses to the gym.

"Look out, Queen Bee is back," I call after her, earning me the finger over her shoulder.

"You got a death wish, man?" Shane asks, coming to stand next to me.

"Nah, if we get her angry, you're the only one she's taking it out on."

He thinks for a second.

"You're welcome."

He laughs and I can't help but let it affect me. It's good seeing him so happy, even if he shocked the hell out of the entire school by deciding that not only was Chelsea his girl but that he'd already gotten her pregnant.

"How're things?" I ask, wrapping my arm around his shoulder and walking us toward our own lockers.

"Oh yeah, you know. Standard shit with a pregnant girlfriend while in senior year."

"I still can't get my head around that."

"You and me both, man. I'm going to be a fucking dad. Like, I'm going to be responsible for someone else's life."

A shudder runs down my spine at the thought. Most of us can barely look after ourselves right now, let alone a kid.

"Any news from your old man?"

"Nah, he's still holed up in New York. He can fucking stay there for all I care. My kid doesn't need him as a grandad."

"Damn right, not when he'll have us as uncles."

"You think it's a boy?"

"Hell yeah, you're so having a little football player."

The others descend on us and our conversation comes to an end.

The guys start reliving their breaks, but as they talk about what they got for Christmas and the drama their families had, I can't get one girl out of my head.

"I'll see you later, man," I say, slapping Shane on the shoulder and walking away from them as the bell rings for first period.

I don't head for class, instead I go for the place I suspect Poppy might have run to.

I hover outside the girl's bathroom wondering if I should just barge in and find out if I'm right. But I don't need to because it seems luck is on my side.

The door opens and a defeated-looking Poppy emerges. Her eyes remain locked on the floor as if she's too afraid to even look up.

Moving closer, I expect her to see me, but she doesn't and instead crashes straight into my chest.

"Shit," she mutters, going to take a step back to go around me. Still her eyes remain on the ground.

Reaching out, I grip on to her upper arms, holding her in place.

"Poppy?"

Painfully fucking slowly, she lifts her head to look at me.

"Fuck." My heart constricts as I see the tears filling her eyes. "What did he do?"

"It's nothing," she whispers, averting her gaze.

"Bullshit," I spit, a little too harshly seeing as she flinches in my arms.

"Just let me go, Zayn." She fights in my hold, but I only tighten my grip to stop her.

"Talk to me."

An unamused laugh falls from her lips as her haunted gray eyes once again find mine. "Talk to you? That's a joke right?"

"No, if he hurt—"

"He didn't hurt me, Zayn. He doesn't have the power to hurt me. He's no one."

I open my mouth to respond but discover I don't have any words.

"Can I go now? I really don't want detention on the first day."

Without thinking, I release her and she immediately slips past me.

"If he does anything, you tell me. I'll fucking end him."

She turns to me, walking backward for a few seconds. "Why? You clearly hate me as much as he does."

Before I can respond to tell her that her words are bullshit, she's gone.

"Fuck," I bark.

"Mr. Hunter, you should be in class," Miss French, our guidance counselor says when she spots me in the empty hallway. I nod at her and head in the direction of my math class.

I don't see Poppy for the rest of the day, although that's not unusual. At times, I wonder if she's a ghost because despite being friends with my sister, who I can't seem to get rid of now that she's been added to the varsity squad, her best friend seems to vanish into thin air.

I don't have the same luck with Preston the prick because he's the first player I see the second I step into the locker room after school for our conditioning session.

He looks up when he realizes he has company and our eyes hold.

"What's up, Hunter?" he asks with a fake ass smile on his face. He really is a fucking snake.

"I don't know. It all depends on whatever that was with Poppy this morning."

"That, pfft," he says with a wave of his arm. "She wants me. Won't get the message that I'm not interested. I mean, she's not exactly my type. She's not even ho—"

I have him pinned up against the lockers before he manages to get that final word out.

"What the hell, man? I was trying to let her down gently. Ain't no one touching Thorn's cousin, I got that memo."

My forearm presses against his throat until his eyes widen in surprise.

People around here seem to forget that I'm not one of them, not originally. I didn't grow up with money, huge houses, and privilege like some of the kids walking these hallways.

I grew up in Harrow Creek. And that place is about as opposite as you can get from everything that Preston has experienced in his pathetic little life.

He might think I'm no threat but he needs to reconsider because while I might look like the fun, gives zero fucks about life, member of the team, he needs to remember that I was trained to fight at a very young age and with one mistake I will take him down.

"You stay the fuck away from her."

He splutters like he's fighting for breath but it's all for show, I'm not pressing that hard. Not yet.

Just as the door swings open, I release him and watch as he sags back against the lockers.

"I'm fucking watching you, Hellburn."

I don't stick around to hear his response, instead I step up beside Jake.

"Everything okay?"

"Yeah, just having a little chat with our boy."

Jake glances back over his shoulder and a smile curls at his lips at what he finds.

"That motherfucker isn't getting my team."

"I get that, I do. But who else is gonna have it? He's the best QB we've got by far once we fuck off."

"I dunno, I'm just hoping someone appears from out of nowhere."

"Amalie is turning you into a dreamer, man," I say with a laugh.

It's a well-known fact that his girl has softened his jagged edges just a little but hoping for a miracle seems a little far-fetched, but I guess crazier things have happened. And just to prove a point, both Ethan and Shane join us talking about something to do with their girls. Who'd have thought it.

5

Poppy

"This is pointless. I don't fucking get it," Harley whines, pushing the textbook across the counter until it crashes to the floor.

"You're looking at the big picture. You need to break it down," I say, hopping from the stool and going to collect the offending textbook.

"I just don't get it. I fucking hate math."

"Stop putting so much pressure on yourself." I bend down and my fingers brush the cover right as his words stop me dead.

"Well, this looks like a fun study session." I can practically hear the smugness in his voice.

I stand, smooth my skirt down and walk back to my seat.

"What do you want, Zayn?" Harley snaps. "Just because Mom has made you her bitch for the week, it doesn't mean you get to harass me instead of being out with your little team."

"My little team? You mean our championship-winning team?"

"By the end of the year, the squad will hold the same title."

"The squad with a pregnant captain. Right." Zayn rolls his eyes as Harley tenses beside me.

"Just because she's pregnant, it doesn't mean she can't lead us," she argues.

I'm used to their bickering and as usual tune them out and reopen the textbook to the section we were working through.

I might not hear the words they're saying but I'm very much aware of the deep rumble of his voice, and even more so when he walks over and stops beside me. His body heat burns into my arm as he leans over to look at what we're doing.

"I'm sorry, can I help you?" I snap, my eyes widening at his intrusion of my personal space.

"I don't know, can you?"

"Zayn, stop being a prick. We're trying to work."

"From what I heard, Poppy is working, you're having a bitch fit about it. You want a study buddy who knows his way around numbers, Pops?"

"No, I'm good."

"See, you're not wanted. Now fuck off. Doesn't Mom want you to clean the toilets or something?"

His eyes drill into his sister but while she's distracted, his fingers tickle up my bare arm.

Goose bumps erupt at his touch and I have to fight not to visibly shudder.

"Harley?" Jada's voice filters down to us from where she's working in her office. "Did you forget my coffee?"

"Shit," she mutters. "Yeah, hang on." She hops down and goes over to the coffee machine.

"While you're there, I'd love one, thanks," Zayn says,

walking around behind me and planting his ass on the edge of the stool Harley just vacated.

"I'm not your slave. You're the one doing the time, you should be the one doing it."

"Quit bitching and make Mom's coffee. You know she gets cranky when she hasn't had enough."

"I heard that," Jada calls.

"You were supposed to."

"That gardening isn't going to do itself, boy," she reminds him.

"Yeah, yeah, I'm going. Slave driver," he mutters, but it's with a smirk on his annoyingly handsome face.

"She that pissed about the party?" I ask, although instantly regret it when he turns his eyes on me.

"The party, no. She gave me permission for that. The mess, the damages, and the illegal substances, she's not so thrilled about."

"I can't believe you thought it would be okay," Harley adds.

Zayn shrugs, his eyes still holding mine captive while she finishes up and leaves the room to deliver the coffee.

"You ready to talk yet?"

"Nothing to talk about," I whisper, looking down at the textbook once more, not able to look at the serious expression on his face. I'm worried he'll see just how much I'm lying because the truth couldn't be any farther from the words I just muttered.

"Riiight." He reaches out again, his knuckles brushing down my upper arm.

My eyes close as the sensation washes through me but I refuse to react. I know what he's trying to do. He's trying to manipulate me just like he did New Year's Eve so that he can get what he wants.

"I've spoken to him." His admission makes me forget all

about my reaction to his touch and my eyes fly to his once more.

"You what?"

"I spoke to—"

"Yeah," I interrupt. "I'm not fucking deaf. Why would you do that? This has nothing to do with you."

"He hurt you, Poppy." His brows pull together in concern.

"He didn't. I told you, he doesn't have the power."

"Which is why you ran to the bathroom crying?"

"I wasn't... that wasn't..." I straighten my back, hating how vulnerable I sound right now. "This has nothing to do with you. I need you to back off."

"No."

"No?" I ask, my brows almost hitting my hairline.

"No," he enunciates slowly. "I'm going to find out what you're hiding," he warns, making my stomach turn over with dread.

"Just stop, Zayn." Stupidly, I reach out and rest my hand on his forearm. Electric bolts shoot up my arm at the contact and I quickly pull it away again. I shouldn't react like this to the guy who continually hurts me. "You have no business diving into my life. You're worried about him hurting me, then maybe you'd be better off looking in a mirror and thinking about how you've done the exact thing."

I drop to my feet, pushing the stool out behind me but unfortunately, he does the exact same thing and we end up almost chest to chest. The heat of his skin burns mine as his scent only gets stronger, although I can't deny it's a relief from the dead animal smell that's still coating my senses.

"I'm sorry, Pops."

"No," I say, holding my hands up in defeat. "I'm not even going there. It's done, it's in the past. You mean nothing to me, Zayn. Nothing."

I take a step back, clumsily tripping over the stool in my need to get away from him.

"You don't mean that," he warns, the edge of hurt in his voice making my steps falter.

"Don't I?"

"Not that there was anything there in the first place, but we're done, Zayn. Stay out of my life and my business." I storm from the room and almost collide with Harley, who's leaving Jada's office.

"Whoa, is there a fire in the kitchen?"

"No, just your brother. Grab your stuff, we're continuing in your room."

"What did he do?"

"Nothing worth talking about."

I spin on my heels and race up the stairs while Harley grabs her things.

"I'm done with homework," she announces, dropping the pile of books on her desk, flopping back onto her bed beside me and grabbing the TV remote. She turns it on and starts channel surfing.

"That's due tomorrow."

She sighs. "Why can't I be smart like you, Zayn, and Letty?"

"You are smart, Har. You just keep running straight into a brick wall and shutting down. You need to look at it from a different angle."

"I am, I'm not doing it." I glare at her. "Don't give me that look. I can't do it."

I hate that she's struggling with this. "Why don't you speak to Mrs. Harrington tomorrow before class, see if she can help before you miss this deadline?" I suggest, hoping our teacher will be able to show her a different trick that might make it all align in her head.

"Maybe I just... I want to be like you, you just get all this stuff."

"Trust me, Har, you really don't," I mutter sadly.

"How are things with your parents?"

At her reminder, I pull my cell from my pocket and check the time. Austin and Sofia will be back from their after-school club soon, I really should get going.

"They're... their usual disaster."

"You know the offer still stands if you need it. There's always a place for you here."

"Thank you, I really appreciate it. But I need to be there."

"They're not your responsibility, Pop."

The weight I'm all too familiar with presses down on my shoulders as she talks. She knows I do more than I should for my family, but she doesn't know the depth of it. Since Mom took a nosedive a few months ago, I haven't even invited anyone back to the house for fear of what they might witness.

"I know, but they need me. At least until Mom sorts herself out." I know I'm only lying to myself. If she was going to do anything, she'd have done it by now. "I should go."

"I'm sorry, I just—"

"Trying to help, I know. I really appreciate it," I repeat. "But Austin and Sofia will be back soon. I'd like to be home."

She nods sadly. "Can I drive you?"

"Nah, it's okay. I need the walk."

Before I climb from the bed, both mine and Harley's cell phone beeps simultaneously. It can only be one person.

"It's Ruby," I say when Harley doesn't instantly reach for hers, probably thinking the same as me. "Wants to know if we're up for a trip to the mall this weekend?"

"Ugh, I wish. We're at Dad's this weekend."

"Can't you cancel?"

"Nope. We did that the last two times and we barely saw him over the holidays."

"Fair enough. I'll tell her we can't." I start typing, but Harley stops me.

"You should go."

I let out a sigh. I want to, but while Ruby might have Christmas money to blow, as usual, I have nothing.

"Yeah, maybe."

I tap out a response that I'll let her know, leaving Harley to reply with her own excuse later.

Pushing from the bed, I grab my bag that I dropped on the end and swing it over my shoulder.

"See you in the morning?"

"You got it. We've got double practice after school though, so you might need to find another way home."

"Okay, will do." I open the door but look back before stepping through. "Har?"

"Yeah," she asks, dragging her eyes from the TV.

"Have another go at that homework, yeah. Maybe ask Zayn for help?" I suggest, much to her annoyance.

"We'll see."

It's not until I shut the door behind me that I discover that we have an audience.

"Ask Zayn what?"

I don't bother looking at where his deep voice comes from, instead I take a step toward the stairs.

"Poppy, don't do this."

"She needs help with her math homework, okay?" I snap, needing him to get off my case.

"She won't accept my help. I've tried."

"So, try harder. She's beating herself up about it. Thinks she's not smart."

"But she is." His confidence in his sister makes my footsteps falter at the top of the stairs and I do something really, really stupid. I look back.

My eyes almost bug out of my head when I find him

topless with his skin covered in droplets of water.

My lips part as I take him in, I'm powerless but to let my eyes roam. I know I shouldn't, that I'm opening myself up to all sorts, but I can't stop it.

"It started raining," is all he says.

"Okay great. That's great," I say in a rush before dropping down to the first step in my need to get away from his half-naked body.

It's not the first time I've seen it, but I'm pretty sure it's the first time we've been alone while it's happened.

"Where are you going?"

"Home?"

"H taking you?"

"No, I'm walking."

"Give me five and I'll take you."

"Um... no, it's okay."

"Poppy, it's pouring, you'll get soaked."

"It's just rain, Zayn. It's hardly going to kill me."

He raises a brow, waiting for me to comply. I really, really don't want to but then I glance out of the window and see the monsoon style rain pounding at the glass and my resolve starts to crack.

Before I know what's going on, he has my arm in his grip and he's pulling me toward his bedroom.

"No, Zayn. I can't—" He looks back at me, his dark eyes cutting off any argument that's on the tip of my tongue about why this is a bad idea.

He continues forward until we're through the door. He kicks it shut behind us before I find myself backed up against it.

"Zayn, stop. Please," I beg, looking anywhere but at him.

He doesn't say anything, he just stands there staring at me. His chest heaves as his breath tickles down my neck.

"What do you want?"

His breath catches slightly at my comment, but it still takes him longer than necessary to respond.

"I don't think you really want my answer."

"Okay, great. So don't tell me, just let me go."

"I can't."

My eyes find his and I gasp at the hunger I see staring back at me.

"C-can we j-just go, please?"

His teeth sink into his bottom lip and all I can think about is how good they feel against my own. But nothing good ever comes of that happening.

"Take me home now or I'm walking," I threaten.

After a beat, he backs up but his eyes don't leave me. Instead they run the length of my body causing my temperature to spike and an ache I'm not all that familiar with to erupt in my lower stomach.

"That's a shame. You look good in here."

His words bring reality back and I rip my eyes from his to look around his room.

It's painted black with silver features and where I thought it might look dark and depressing, I find I actually quite like it. It suits him.

His hands drop to his waistband and my heart begins to pound harder in my chest.

He pops the button and pushes the wet denim down his legs.

"W-what are you doing?"

"Getting changed. I'm soaked," he says innocently, still keeping his eyes on mine as he kicks off his pants.

He stands before me in just a small pair of very tight boxer briefs and a smirk. Smug fuck knows exactly what he's doing.

As do I.

"Whoa, Jake keeps you on the team looking like that. I

thought he only wanted players who were in prime condition."

His lips purse and his already ripped muscles tighten. It's in that moment I realize my mistake.

He takes a step toward me and I press my back harder into the door.

I shouldn't be here right now, and he really needs to put some more clothes on.

"I can assure you, Poppy. They don't come more... *prime* than me."

"Get dressed, Zayn." The quiver in my voice betrays me, and damn it if he doesn't miss it.

"You sure?" His eyes take another leisurely trip around my body and I can't help feeling like I might as well be wearing as little as he is from the heat in his eyes.

"Y-yes."

His eyes narrow but he doesn't come any closer. Instead he spins and opens his closet, dragging fresh clothes out and thankfully tugging them on.

"Is that why you turned Preston down? His physical appearance."

I tense at the mention of his name but I refuse to let him ruin any more of this day.

"Oh yeah, because it has nothing to do with his stellar personality."

Zayn snorts a laugh as he drags a shirt over his head. "You got that right, the guy's a class A prick."

"You had no right to talk to him today."

He looks back at me over his shoulder, his eyes saying so much more than his lips are.

"I can't not care, Poppy. He doesn't get to walk around tormenting you."

"Just leave it. If I need your help, I'll ask for it."

"No you won't."

"You're right, I won't. Shall we?" I ask, wrapping my hand around his door handle and pulling it open.

It's still raining when we get outside, although it's lighter than it was when he first pointed it out.

I hesitate at the passenger side of his truck, not really wanting to be in an enclosed space with him but knowing that he's going to leave me very little choice.

"You need a hand?" he asks, glancing at me from over the hood.

"N-no. I'm good."

Every single muscle in my body tenses the second I settle in his passenger seat, the entire car smells like him.

He turns the engine over and the car rumbles to life, the vibrations do very little to relax me as he pulls out of his driveway and heads toward my side of town.

The silence between us grows heavy as it stretches out.

"Harley said you're at your dad's this weekend," I blurt in the end, needing to break the tension.

"Apparently so."

"You like going there?"

He glances over at me. "You ever been there?"

"Uh... no."

"Then you really couldn't understand how much I really dislike going there."

"Oh. You want to see your dad though?"

"Sure, I just don't need the bullshit that goes along with it."

"Bullshit?"

"It's nothing." His words piss me off. If it were nothing, then he wouldn't have said it.

"Nothing?"

"Yeah. Just like what's going on with you is nothing. Like how we are *nothing*."

I look over at him and for a second he looks back at me, his eyes narrowed.

"Why do you look so shocked? You said it, not me."

"I know... I just..."

"Just..." he prompts, trying to get me to talk.

Thankfully, my house comes into view in the distance.

"Just nothing. Thanks for the lift."

I push the door open and slip down until my feet hit the ground.

"You know where I am if you need me."

I nod at him and slam his door shut.

As I walk to the house, his stare burns into my back but I refuse to turn around.

He should have no effect on me, and I need to work harder at stopping it from happening.

6

Zayn

y fingers grip the wheel, turning my knuckles white as I watch her walk into her house.

My need to follow her is all-consuming, but I know I can't. I might not know all that much about her but I know that there's a reason Harley hasn't visited her house in a few months. Harley tried to pass it off with it being because Poppy's mom had a baby, but I fear it's more than that. The shadows within Poppy's eyes point toward more than that.

There's movement in one of the rooms before she appears with a baby in her arms.

My body tenses for a beat at the sight and my lips twitch into a smile as she runs her hand over the baby's head.

As if she can feel me staring, she looks up and right at me.

Her eyes harden instantly. Our contact holds for a few beats before I throw the car into reverse and head out before she starts thinking things she shouldn't about me.

I'm not interested. I don't want her, I'm just... intrigued... concerned. *Captivated*, I push that final thought from my head as I speed back toward home and Mom's punishment of gardening jobs now the rain has stopped once again.

———

By the time Mom calls me to say dinner is ready, I'm more than ready to give in. Coach is working us hard knowing that he's going to be sending us all off to play college football soon and then spending hours on my hands and knees tending to Mom's beloved flowerbeds means I'm exhausted.

"Feel like maybe taking a shower first?" Harley complains when I join the two of them in the kitchen.

My stomach growls as the smell of Mom's lasagna and garlic bread hits my nose. The rest of the team headed to Aces after our session for burgers. I'd have more than happily gone with them, but I knew Mom would make my life not worth living if I bailed on my 'time'.

Walking over, I rub my muddy fingers over her cheek while she squeals and slaps me.

"Where's Letty? She left us again already?" I ask, noticing the absence of my older sister once again.

"Yep, she's gone to a friend's for a few days before the semester starts."

"Anyone would think she doesn't want to be here."

"I wish you weren't here," Harley mutters, walking over to the sink so she can wash her face.

"What am I going to do with myself when all three of you are at college?" Mom muses.

"Guess you should have thought about that before popping us out one after the other."

"Zayn," she says on a sigh.

"What? The lack of time between the three of us is all the

evidence we need to know that you and Dad did get along at one point."

"Can we not talk about your father please and just enjoy a meal together?"

"Sure." I pull out a chair and go to sit.

"Your sister has a point. Go clean up."

Rolling my eyes at her, I walk back out of the room to do as she suggests.

Mom changed when we moved here. Hell, she changed before that but it seems even more intense here.

After living a life with nothing and having to fight through every day back in Harrow Creek, she suddenly wants to appear perfect all of a sudden. Although I have no idea who she's trying to impress with all this.

Back in the day she wouldn't have batted an eyelid if Dad or I turned up covered in dirt and oil for dinner, she was just glad she was able to put food on the table.

But now, it's all about appearances.

She got herself some qualifications, a flashy well-paid job and everything changed in what felt like the blink of an eye.

Suddenly, we weren't trailer park kids with two parents who argued just as much as everyone else in that place, but we were packing up our stuff and moving to a fancy town and leaving one of our units behind.

When I return with clean hands, the atmosphere in the room is heavy, my fault for bringing up Dad and our past. Mom seems to think we left all that behind, but while we might no longer live there, that place will always be a part of our past, our story. She needs to embrace it instead of just running away from it.

"So how was school?" Mom asks tensely as we eat.

Harley chats away about bullshit girl stuff and the cheer squad while I stuff my face.

"I hear you're struggling with your math homework," I blurt.

"Is that true, Harley? I told you that if you're finding it challenging that I'll get you a tutor."

"No, no. Everything is fine," she seethes, while giving me a death stare.

"Zayn is in charge of washing and cleaning up. Harley, I expect you to go and work on that math homework." Mom stares between the two of us as she places her utensils on her plate and carries it over to the sink. "I'll be in my office."

Harley waits for her to leave before she starts.

"Was that necessary?"

I shrug. "Just deflecting her wrath away from me."

"You deserve it."

"I beg to differ."

"How'd you know about my math homework anyway?" she asks, crossing her arms over her chest.

"Poppy told me."

"Poppy? When the hell did you see Poppy? She left a while ago to go—"

"Home. I know, I took her. Nice of you to let her walk in the rain, by the way. Finished?" I ask, taking her plate and getting started on the cleaning.

"She was adamant."

"Well she let me take her."

"That had better be all you did."

"What are you suggesting?"

"You need to stay away from her."

"I think that's for me to decide, don't you?"

"She hates you after what you did to her."

"Pfft, that was years ago, Har. Anyway, she didn't seem all that bothered on New Year's Eve."

"Wait... what?"

"Huh?" Keeping my head down, I smile to myself. There's not much I love more than winding up my little sister.

"You just said something about New Year's and Poppy. What did you mean?"

"Don't know what you're talking about."

The dish towel that was on the counter whips across my back. It stings but I'm not going to let her know that.

"You're such a pain in the ass," she mutters, walking to the door.

"But you love me anyway," I call to her as she runs up the stairs.

Her returning growl makes me laugh.

I know I shouldn't have said anything. I'd put everything I have on the fact she's gone straight up to her room and called Poppy for the details. I have a feeling that might not be the last time I see Harley tonight.

And I'm right because not an hour later does my bedroom door fly open and she marches in with her hands on her hips.

"You kissed her. Again?"

"Ah, come in, why don't you. You know, it was a good thing I wasn't mid-wank."

"Ew." Her face screws up unattractively. "Why would you even... so gross."

I stare at her, waiting for her to get to the point.

"You kissed Poppy on New Year's Eve?" she screeches.

"Keep your voice down, Har. I don't need the whole street knowing."

"That had better not be because you're ashamed of it."

"Keep your panties on, Har. It was a game, we kissed, end of."

Her chin drops. "Are you really saying this to me?"

"It's the truth. Would you rather I lie?"

"I know the truth. Poppy told me the truth."

"Did she?" I smirk.

"Did she tell you how she was like putty in my hands?"

"You're a fucking dog. Stay away from my friends, Zayn. I mean it."

"Too late, lil' sis. I've had a taste of both."

"You fucking..." She flies at me, her arms flailing around as she tries to hit me but she's no match for me and in seconds I have her wrists in my grasp and her pinned to the bed.

"You really want to do this?" I ask, thinking of all the fights she's lost against me over the years.

"Fuck you, Zayn. Stay away from my friends."

"I try, Har. I really do," I lie.

"Pig," she shouts, fighting to get away from me.

After a few seconds, I release her and push her from the bed. She lands on the floor with a thump.

"I fucking hate you," she seethes, picking herself up and smoothing her hoodie down.

"Aw, I love you too, Har-Har," I say softly, using the name I used to call her as a kid.

Her lips purse and her tiny fists clench. I just about refrain from laughing at her. If she's trying to look menacing then she needs to try harder.

"You need to learn to fight. Maybe that's what we could do this weekend. Hell knows there are enough kids in that hellhole that could use a punch or two."

"You want to teach me to fight?"

"Sure, why not? You should be able to look after yourself. Impressing an attacker with your cheer moves isn't going to get you out of trouble."

She raises a brow.

"Did you want anything else?"

"No. Just..."

"Stay away from your friends. I'll see what I can do."

I wink and she groans as she storms out of my room as fast as she entered. Just to be a bitch, she leaves the door open.

7

———

Poppy

"So…" Ruby says, her gaze trained on me as we place our trays down on the table we've just taken over in the window of our favorite diner in the mall. "A little birdie told me something interesting yesterday."

I don't need her to say anything else, I already know the words that are about to fall from her lips and I'm already groaning internally. I guess my hopes for Harley to keep the gossip to herself was a big ask.

"You kissed Zayn!" she all but squeals, earning us a few unimpressed stares from the others around us.

"Yes," I mutter. "I'd been tagged, so he was just seeing it through."

"And you kissed him knowing you were a tag?"

"No, I had no idea. I kissed him because… I'm an idiot."

She rolls her eyes at me. "No, you kissed him because you'd heard how good he is."

"Trust me, knowing that every other girl in school knows just how good he is, is not the reason I did it."

"So why did you?" she asks, focusing her attention on her lunch.

"Because... I don't know. It was a serious lapse in judgment, that's all I know."

"Really? You're sticking with that lie?"

"It's not a lie, it shouldn't have happened."

"Oh, so you haven't been craving a repeat ever since his fifteenth birthday?" She raises a brow.

"No, I haven't."

"That's just bullshit and you know it."

"Why are you so keen for me to kiss him? I thought you wanted him for yourself."

"Meh," she mumbles around a mouthful of food. "I'll have him to play with if you don't want him."

"You have already *played* with him," I remind her.

"Not really. It was mostly Laurie, I was just... in the room."

"But—" I start to argue, remembering a little too well how she described that night to us after the event.

"I may have exaggerated a little."

"A little?"

"Yeah, I mean, I kissed him. Touched a bit. But nothing really happened."

"But you want it to?"

"Not if you want him."

"I don't want him," I argue.

"So he's not the one you fall asleep at night thinking about then?"

I damn near spray her with the soda I've just taken a sip of. "No, no, I do not." *Big fat lie.*

"Sure. And I'm guessing you're going to try to tell me that you haven't thought about that kiss after the event, what could have happened had it not come out that you were a tag, what might have happened if he took your hand and led you up to his bedroom."

My cheeks burn with the truth but despite the fact I know she can see it, I still insist on trying to plead my innocence.

"No. It was just a kiss. I wasn't going to... you know."

"Fuck him?"

"Shush, Ruby. People can hear you."

"And? It's okay to talk about sex, you know."

"Oh yeah, and when exactly did you decide that?"

She pales at my question and I mentally kick myself for going there.

Ruby was probably the most innocent out of the three of us, and that was saying a lot seeing as Harley and I are pretty innocent. But then *he* barreled into her life and in just a few short days, he changed her. Gone was the sweet and innocent Ruby, and in her place was a girl who wanted to do anything to help rid her of his memory.

It took us weeks to get her to talk, for her to tell us about her stepbrother's visit and the things that went down between them. I can't really blame her for wanting to erase it, but I'm not sure suddenly working her way around the football team like the other cheer sluts is the best way to go about it.

"Shit, I'm sorry."

"It's fine," she argues, but the quiver in her voice says otherwise. After she told us about what happened, she made us promise never to talk about it again. She wanted to forget he ever existed. I got it, although I'm not sure that locking it all up in a little box is the healthiest way to deal with it but she was adamant that it was over and that he was gone for good, so we had no choice but to do as she asked.

"So?" she asks, turning this back on me.

"So what?"

"You want him, right?"

I sink down in my chair and blow out a breath. "No."

"But—"

"No, there are no buts. I don't want him. The kiss was a mistake. Nothing further will happen. Got it?"

"Hmmm," she mumbles, irritating the hell out of me.

I want to continue arguing my point but something, or more like someone outside the diner window catches my eye and a shiver runs down my spine.

I didn't see a face, but I don't need to. I know when he's close. I feel it. I fear it.

"Are you okay? All the color just drained from your face."

"Oh... uh..." I keep my eyes out of the window, desperate to prove to myself that I'm just being paranoid. "N-nothing." I cringe at my use of that word. It seems to be one I'm using all too much recently.

"O-okay," she says. When I glance over, I find her looking the way I was but she clearly doesn't see anyone she recognizes either. "I'm thinking we finish up here and head back to where we first started. I want to try that dress on."

"Sure, whatever you want."

"Are you sure you don't want to get anything while we're here? I feel bad just shopping for me."

"No, I'm good. I got a ton of new stuff for Christmas." Another lie.

"Okay, well if you see something you like, make sure to stop."

"Of course." I cringe as I say the words. It wouldn't matter how much I might like something, it's not like I have the money to buy anything.

I need a job, but how do I get one of those around school, trying to ensure I get my grades high enough for a scholarship, and being the only reliable person my siblings have.

I'm distracted from my thoughts as Ruby pushes her empty tray away and lets out a very unladylike burp.

"Whoa, no wonder the team can't keep their hands off

you," I say with a laugh.

"You done? I need to get my shop on."

"Yeah, let's do it."

We clear away our trays and rejoin the crowds in the mall. The January sales are in full swing and it seems that it's not just Ruby who decided that today would be the perfect day to grab some bargains.

As we walk, I can't ignore the feeling that I'm being watched. My skin prickles as my heart picks up pace a little.

I look around as inconspicuous as possible but once again, I see no one.

I've been on edge since the first day back at school and the unexpected 'gift' that was in my locker. Preston might not have approached me since, he chose to torment with his silence instead of his presence, but I know that doesn't mean he's forgotten me. He's just planning his next move. I can only hope that his need for blood has been sated with Smidge.

My stomach turns once more as I wonder what evil things he might have done to our beloved pet. I still pray that whatever was in that bag wasn't him, but I know I'm only lying to myself.

I follow Ruby into the store she wanted to return to and glance around in the hope I don't see something I fall in love with because that would suck even harder than just not being able to afford anything.

I glance over my shoulder every now and then, but every time the coast is clear.

Chastising myself for allowing him to get in my head when he's probably nowhere near me, I rush to catch up with Ruby where she's heading toward the dressing room with an armful of dresses she's collected as she's made her way through the store.

"You trying anything on?" she asks, looking back to find me right behind her.

"Nah, nothing is catching my eye." For once that's not really a lie, I've spent too much time worrying about whether I'm being watched or not to really look at anything that was in front of me. "I'll wait here."

Resting back against the wall, I watch as she closes the door behind her.

I pull my cell from my pocket and find a message from Harley asking if we're having fun and explaining that she's not because Zayn has insisted on teaching her to throw a decent punch all weekend.

I'm so lost in our conversation that I don't feel someone walk up to me until the very last minute.

Thinking I'm in the way, I move to stand straighter so they can pass but instead of doing that, two large hands land on my arms and I'm practically thrown into the dressing room next to Ruby's.

Picking me up, Preston pins me against the wall with his hand around my throat.

"Poppy? Was that you? Are you okay?" Ruby shouts, although it's muffled by the small space she's enclosed in.

Preston's dead eyes bore down into mine, warning me not to say a thing. As if I would. The last thing I want is for anyone to know about this.

"Yeah, it wasn't me. One of the shop assistants dropped something."

Thankfully, the dressing rooms in this store are little rooms with solid doors. Should we have been in ones with curtains, I'm sure Ruby would have just stuck her head out to see what's going on.

"What the hell—"

My words are cut off when his other sweaty hand clamps down over my mouth.

I suck in ragged breaths through my nose but it's not enough as my chest heaves and my heart races in panic.

"Don't talk."

He leans in close before a low, evil laugh falls from his lips.

"You really think you're something, don't you?"

I try to shake my head but his hold stops me from moving.

"When are you going to realize that you're nothing?"

Nothing, there's that word again.

"Your friends only put up with you because you make them look even more attractive than they already are."

I moan against his hands, my body thrashing about in the hope of fighting him off. It's wishful thinking but I refuse to do nothing.

"Just because you're Thorn's cousin, you seem to think you've got it all. Well, let me tell you, little girl." He leans right in, the stench of weed and stale sweat fills my nose and my stomach turns over. "You're nothing. And I'm going to prove just how pointless you and your pathetic little life is."

His hand releases my throat and I gasp, dragging in as much air as I possibly can.

My relief only lasts a few seconds though because his fingertips begin to trail up the inside of my thigh.

"No, no," I try to cry against his hand as I attempt to curl in on myself.

"Fight, go on. It'll only make it more fun for me."

I want to scream, cry, hurt him but in those few moments as his fingers get closer to their final destination I just freeze in fear.

I don't want his dirty, murderous hands on me. Tears burn my eyes and I blink wildly in an attempt to keep them in. I don't want this motherfucker to see me cry.

"Do you know what pointless girls are good for?" He pauses as if he actually expects an answer from me. "Being ruined. Used and abused until they're no good for anyone else."

Noooooo, I scream in my head as he lifts my skirt up and his fingers slip under the edge of my panties.

Please God no, don't let my first experience of this be with him.

Please, please, please.

"Pops?" Ruby shouts.

My eyes go wide as his hand stills.

"Do not fucking scream, or I will hurt you."

"Y-yeah?" My voice is rough, panic-stricken, and I have no doubt that if she could hear me clearly she would instantly know that something was wrong.

"Could you go and get me that red dress in a bigger size. I think they made this with a nine-year-old in mind or something."

"Y-yeah sure. H-hang on."

My eyes remain locked on his as I wait to see what he's going to do.

"This isn't over," he warns, causing a shiver to run through me knowing that this is going to happen again, only worse next time.

I got lucky that he cornered me somewhere where really, he couldn't do much to me. But next time, he could plan something a little more private where no one would find us, or interrupt.

My stomach turns, bile burning my throat as he steps away from me and removes his touch.

He opens the door for me and without so much as a look back, I bolt from the small room. It's not until I'm in the main part of the store that I actually breathe again.

After what feels like a long time, I locate the red dress in question and grab what she needs before hesitantly heading back for the dressing rooms.

"Rubes," I call while wiping at my eyes. I didn't cry but I have no doubt my fear is written all over my face.

I glance to the dressing room, the door is still open and I have no idea if he's still inside, waiting for me to come back.

My entire body shakes violently as I think about him pulling me back in to finish what he started.

"Thank you," she says, poking her head and an arm out to take the hanger from me. "What's wrong?"

She doesn't even have to look at me and she knows something is up.

"I... uh... don't feel well. I think I'm going to need to go home."

"Oh shit, okay. Let me get dressed and we'll go."

"It's okay, I can call an Uber or something," I argue, not wanting to ruin her day.

"Don't be stupid. I'll just get this and try it on at home. Let me get dressed and we'll go."

"Okay," I whisper, not really having the energy to fight with her. Plus, if I'm honest, I don't really want to go anywhere alone right now, even getting in an Uber seems like a risk I don't need to take.

The moment she shuts the door, I step forward and poke my head into the dressing room he dragged me into, needing to know if he's still there.

I breathe a sigh of relief when I find it empty. There's no evidence that anything happened and it's so unbelievable that I almost start to wonder if I imagined it. Although I know it's only wishful thinking because the fear, the disgust I felt as he touched me still feels very, very real.

Faster than I thought possible, Ruby is dressed and ready to go. She quickly buys what she wants and we head out to the parking lot.

"How are you feeling?" she asks once we're on the road and heading back toward my house.

"Sick."

"Do you think it was something you ate?"

"I don't know. I just... I just want to curl up in bed." *Where I'm safe.*

8

Zayn

"Oh God, is she okay?"

The rest of my sister's conversation has mostly passed me by, it's been full of cheer bullshit and high school gossip but that one question piques my interest and I lower my own cell so I can attempt to eavesdrop.

"Why would she lie?"

Sadly, no matter how hard I try, I can't hear who's on the other end. From the cheer chatter, I assume it's Ruby.

I shift on our dad's rock-hard couch, the one I actually used to think was comfortable as a kid and try to get closer.

"Shit, yeah. I'll call her in a bit and check in on her."

The subject changes and I'm forced to wait until she finally hangs up to find out what I want to know.

"You should have just asked me to put it on speakerphone if you wanted to listen so bad," she sasses the second she lowers the phone from her ear.

"What's wrong?"

"Why do you care?"

"You sounded worried."

Her eyes narrow at me but she must decide to put me out of my misery.

"You're a pain in the ass. Something happened with Ruby and Poppy when they were at the mall."

Dread fills my stomach but I fight to keep the reaction off my face.

"What happened?" My voice is hard and clipped, and Harley doesn't miss it.

"Poppy got sick at the mall. Ruby had to take her home." She shrugs like it's not a big deal but that's not how it sounded on the phone.

"But you said she was lying."

"Ruby doesn't know that. She just felt like something was off. Poppy was fine one minute then not the next. She just said it was weird."

"And you're not worried?"

"Of course I am, and I'll call her when you stop with the twenty questions. Jeez." She rolls her eyes at me before lifting her cell and tapping at the screen.

Not wanting to look more interested than I should be, I push from the couch and go and check on the dinner that Dad's left cooking while he's disappeared off somewhere.

I wanted to go home from the second we got here Friday night, but now I have even more reason to leave.

Poppy being ill, or whatever, shouldn't be my issue but for some reason, I can't help thinking that it is.

Preston's smug as fuck face appears in my mind. I'm probably jumping to conclusions but after what happened the other day, I can't help but think that he's involved in this somehow.

I don't trust him at all and he's clearly after her for some reason. It makes me wonder if this has always been as bad as it seems to be and that she's somehow managed to keep it quiet all this time.

I stir the bolognese Dad's made. It's Harley's favorite and he makes it every single time we've come as if it makes up for the shithole we have to stay in with him. It does very little to mask that this place is crumbling around us, but I guess it does make it smell better.

By the time I get back, Harley has ended her short call.

"So?"

"Are you going to really pretend that you weren't listening?"

"Hearing your side isn't all that helpful." I don't even bother trying to deny it, we both know that I'm guilty.

"She's got the stomach flu. Hit her all of a sudden in the store. She's fine. Just sleeping it off."

Harley believes every word she just said, I can see it in her eyes. Unfortunately, Poppy's excuse for her weird behavior isn't sitting right with me.

The rest of our time with Dad drags, all I want to do is pack our stuff into my truck and drive us both back to Rosewood. Once we're finally able to leave, I gun the engine out of the trailer park, kicking up the gravel behind us and head for home.

"What the hell is up with you?" Harley mutters next to me. "Got a cheer slut on a promise or something?"

"Shut the fuck up, Har." I don't need to look at her to know that she's rolling her eyes at me. "Would you even want to know if I did?"

"Absolutely not. Just want to know how loud I need to turn my music up when I get home."

"Well, as far as I know, one isn't waiting for me naked on my bed."

"Good to know. I'd appreciate it if it stays that way too."

"Mom will be home. I'd hardly arrange that knowing she's there."

"Wouldn't put it past you."

"Wow, really have low expectations of me, huh?"

"What do you expect? I hear all the things you all get up to."

"Right, and I know all the things the squad gets up to but do you hear me accusing you of all that shit?"

"Have I kissed both of your best friends?" she asks, her voice hitching a few decibels. "No, exactly. I've gone nowhere near any member of the team."

"Yeah, because you all think they're pricks."

"Well, there is that. But even if they weren't. They're your friends, Zayn. There's like some unwritten rule about that shit."

"I must have missed that one when I did the test."

"You're a cock. Why either Ruby or Poppy went anywhere near you is beyond me."

"You love me really."

"Only because I have to. Most of the time I don't like you very much."

"If it makes you feel better, I'll give you a free pass to kiss one of the guys."

"If it makes me feel better? Fucking hell, Zayn."

"The offer is there if you want it."

"Wow, I really appreciate your permission. Now which loser should I choose to exchange saliva with?"

I shudder at the thought of her kissing any member of the team, but I have kinda asked for this.

"I can't promise I won't lay him out after, be warned."

"You can take the boy out of the trailer park," she mutters as we leave the place behind us in the darkness it belongs in.

Ignoring her, I turn the music up and try to keep my thoughts of what might have happened in the mall earlier out of my head. The last thing I need is to jump to conclusions.

It's dark by the time we get back. As usual, Mom is in her office working but as ever, I don't hold it against her. She's worked damn hard to get where she is. She studied and got her degree behind Dad's back because it was something she always wanted but never had the chance, and then she landed herself a kickass job here which has allowed her to have the life she's always dreamed of. I'm proud of her for pursuing her dream. Most people's dreams in Harrow Creek just shrivel up and die. There aren't many who manage to do what she's done.

"Have you both done all your homework?" she asks after begrudgingly asking about our weekend.

"Uh..." Harley hesitates.

"Get upstairs and get it done, young lady."

"I'm going, I'm going."

"And you?" Mom asks, turning her hard stare on me.

"All done, although I want to read over a report I've written."

"That's my boy." She squeezes my shoulder in support before I follow Harley up the stairs to unpack and get ready for a new week to start, or at least, that's what I allow them both to believe.

I sort my stuff out before changing and sneaking back out. It's not a hard task seeing as both Harley and Mom have locked themselves away.

I close the front door as quietly as I can and jog to my car.

By the time I pull up at Poppy's house, I've almost convinced myself that I'm crazy and turn back around. But even still, something has me climbing from my car and heading to her front door.

Before I can talk myself out of it, I lift my hand and knock.

There's movement inside, a baby crying and other kids

shouting so when a harassed-looking woman pulls the door open, I can't say I'm surprised.

"What?" she barks, looking me up and down.

"Uh... is Poppy here?"

"She's in her room." She's gone before I even get a chance to ask where that might be.

Hesitantly, I step inside and close the door behind me. I glance around. The house is a mess, there is stuff everywhere, and the shouting and screaming continues.

Locating the stairs, I head up, leaving the chaos behind me with a wince.

The first two rooms are clearly the kids' rooms followed by a bathroom all of which are as messy as the last.

The next door is closed and something tells me that it's the one. Rapping my knuckles against the chipped paintwork, I wait to see if there's going to be a response.

"Come in," a quiet yet familiar voice calls.

Sucking in a breath, I twist the handle and push the door open.

She's in bed facing away from the door as I first walk inside and close the door behind me. But when I don't say anything, she twists around.

"What's—Zayn?" Her eyes go as wide as saucers as she stares at me. She sits bolt upright in bed as she blinks a few times. "What the hell are you doing here?"

I close the space between us as she shifts up the bed, keeping the sheets to her chest.

"Are you okay?"

"Uh... confused, mostly. Why are you here?"

I run my eyes over the small amount of her I can see, looking for evidence that she might not be okay.

"Zayn?" she prompts when I don't respond.

"What happened at the mall?"

The limited amount of color that was on her face drains

away, leaving her ghostly pale. My stomach drops, that's all the confession I need to know my instincts were correct.

"I-I wasn't feeling well."

"Bullshit, Poppy." I drop down onto her bed and slide a little closer to her. "Tell me what really happened."

Her eyes bounce between mine before they drop to the sheets.

"Poppy?" I reach out, my hand landing on her upper arm and she flinches away. "Pops?"

"He was there, okay? He cornered me. Said some things, did some things. I just needed to leave, so I said I was sick. Happy now?"

"Happy?" I ask incredulously. "How could that possibly make me happy?"

She shrugs, pulling the sheets up higher in an attempt to hide from me.

"Damn it, Poppy," I snap, wrapping my fingers around her sheets and tugging them away from her. "Stop hiding from this."

Fuck.

My eyes drop from her eyes to her body that I've revealed. She's wearing a thin white tank and a pair of panties, leaving inches upon inches of smooth skin on display.

Her breath catches as she notices what's got my attention and she reaches out to take her covers back.

"No," I bark. "No more hiding. Not from me."

"I don't have the energy for this. You need to leave before my parents catch you."

"Your mom let me in. She sent me up here. I don't think she cares."

My words don't seem to be news to her. "Of course she doesn't."

My brows pull together as I study her. There's so much

more to Poppy than meets the eye and the more I learn, the more it's confirmed that most people see straight past it.

Kicking my shoes off, I move closer, sitting on the sheets so she can't use them to hide behind. I'm not leaving this room until I get some truths out of her.

"What did he do to you, Poppy?"

"It's nothing." Her words infuriate me and by the widening of her eyes when she looks at me, I think she can tell. "Just forget it, Zayn. You shouldn't be here."

"And yet, here I am. Let me help you." Reaching out, I run my knuckles down her bare upper arm. She shudders, her skin pricks with goose bumps and her eyes shutter slightly.

"Zayn." I think it's meant to be a warning but it falls a long way from the mark.

"Did he hurt you?"

I hold her eye contact and shift a little closer still, her floral scent getting stronger and making my mouth water.

"N-no."

"Did he threaten you?"

A bitter laugh falls from her lips. "That's all he does. You don't need to get involved in this."

"And yet I am, and I won't be leaving until you tell me what happened."

"Fine," she huffs. "He followed me into the dressing room and... yeah." Once again she looks down at the bed, unable to hold my stare.

"Poppy," I say softly. "Did he... did he touch you?"

"Please don't do this, Zayn," she begs. The brokenness in her voice guts me.

"I'll fucking kill him if he so much as laid a finger on you."

"Can you leave, please?"

"No," I bark and she startles at my tone.

Reaching out, I take her chin between my finger and thumb and force her to look at me.

"You need to tell me what he did."

"I don't need to tell you anything."

"Fucking hell, Poppy. Stop covering for that motherfucker. I just want to help."

"You can help by staying out of it."

"But—"

Her eyes drop to my lips briefly before she cuts me off. "No buts. Please, just leave it. He's full of threats, I'm not scared of him."

"Which is why you ran away claiming to be ill?"

"I just needed to get away. Everything was just too much."

"What else is going on? What are you keeping from everyone?"

"It's just life, Zayn. Sometimes it's shit, but you've just got to carry on."

"That's bullshit, Poppy."

She shrugs, sadness oozing from her. Sadness that I wish I could take away.

Without thinking, I lean toward her.

"Zayn, what are you doing?" she whispers, but she doesn't stop me or pull away as I slip my hand around to the nape of her neck and press my forehead against hers.

"Making your life a little less shit."

"No, we... we can't..."

"Says who?" My lips brush hers as I wait for her to stop arguing and accept that this is about to happen.

"Nothing good happens after this... happens."

"Well, maybe it's time to change that."

My fingers grip her tighter as I brush my lips against hers once again, only with more insistence this time.

She remains as still as a statue for two seconds but the moment she feels my tongue run along her bottom lip, she caves, just like I knew she would.

She needs this right now, she just doesn't know that she does.

Her lips part and I greedily push my tongue past them in search of hers. A quiet moan rumbles up her throat as I deepen the kiss.

Just like the previous two times, everything around me vanishes and the only thing I'm aware of is her. It's a heady feeling and one I haven't been able to find with anyone else. It's addictive and I can only imagine how good it might be if we were to ever take it farther than just a kiss.

"Zayn," she moans when I kiss across her jaw. Her head falls back, allowing me the access I want to her neck. I brush my lips across the smooth, taut skin, feeling the thundering of her pulse just beneath the surface.

My tongue sneaks out, licking a line back up before I suck on her skin.

"So sweet," I murmur against her.

"Oh God."

Shifting on my knees, I lower her back to the bed, never moving my lips from her.

"You need more?" I ask, half expecting her to tell me to go to hell, so I couldn't be more surprised when she agrees.

"Make me forget, I don't care how."

I pause with my lips against her pulse point, waiting for her to start laughing and push me off, but she doesn't. Instead her chest continues to heave beneath me.

Sitting up, I stare down at her. Her tank is not far off being see-through, her pert nipples obvious beneath the fabric. It's pushed up around her waist, showing off the smooth skin of her stomach and her hips are covered in a lace edged pair of pink panties.

"Z-Zayn?" I hate the hesitation in her voice, she thinks that I've stopped because I don't want to give her what she needs, but she couldn't be farther from the truth.

"Shit, sorry. You're just so... beautiful."

A self-deprecating laugh falls from her lips. "I appreciate that, but I look a hot mess."

My eyes find hers. Yes, they're red from crying and she's got makeup smudged down her face from the tears she's shed. But I don't see any of that. I see the hunger, the need in her gray depths. I see her cute freckles that I know she hates and tries to hide with makeup. I see her full, pink lips and her shy little smile. I see her sinful curves that I crave to touch, to feel against me.

"Want me to prove you wrong?"

"Sure, if you think it's possible."

There are a million things I could say to her, to try to convince her of, but she wouldn't believe a word of it, so instead, I stick with actions.

9

Poppy

His lips crash down on mine once more and I forget about everything, all the reasons why this shouldn't be happening, and I just lose myself in his kiss. He makes it too easy to push real life aside and just focus on him.

It's dangerous. Too dangerous. But after the day I've had, it's more than welcome.

If Preston is serious about what he started today in that dressing room, then I may as well make the most of what Zayn's got to offer before Preston takes whatever it is he thinks I owe him.

His lips leave mine once more in favor of kissing down my neck. Butterflies go wild in my belly. I've never had a boy in my room, let alone one on top of me while I'm half-naked but hell knows there's no way I'm stopping this now.

Something coils tightly inside, telling me that things are

only going to get better and I'm more than happy to find out just how good it's going to be.

His lips brush over my collarbone and the swell of my breasts.

His heated eyes find mine. Something crackles as our connection holds.

"You want me to stop, just say the words." His hot breath races across my sensitive skin and makes me shiver.

"Okay," I breathe, unable to find my voice while he's looking at me like I'm something precious. It's as incredible as it is unnerving.

He nods once before crawling down my body a little but he stops when his mouth is right above my breast. His eyes remain on mine as he closes the space between us and flicks my nipple with his bottom lip.

A bolt of lust shoots straight to my core and my thighs clench as heat spreads throughout my body.

"More?"

"More," I confirm, my fingers twitching to reach out and touch him.

He does the same again, only this time he doesn't stop at just a gentle touch, instead he lets his teeth graze me. My reaction is the same as before, only stronger.

"Oh God."

He smiles as I moan, my hips grinding against his inner thighs where he has me pinned to the bed.

"Fucking hell, Poppy."

"What?" I ask in a rush, thinking I've done something wrong.

"I want you so fucking bad right now."

"Really?"

"You underestimate yourself too much. You're beautiful..." He places a kiss along the neckline of my tank before tucking his finger in the fabric and pulling it down a little. "Sexy..." Kiss. "So fucking sexy." He pulls the fabric lower exposing my nipple but I can't find it in me to care as his eyes hold mine, showing me just how much he means the words that are falling from his lips. "And I can't get enough."

"Oh shit," I cry before covering my mouth with my hand when I realize just how loud I was. There is a houseful of people below us. Any of them could walk in at any moment and here I am laid out with Zayn's lips wrapped around my nipple. "Fuck." I have no idea if I'm cussing because of reality or the sensation of his tongue lapping at me.

He moans as he continues licking and kissing across my breast until he exposes the other one and gives it the same treatment.

"More, Zayn. More." I have no idea what I'm begging for, all I know is that I need whatever more is more than I need my next breath.

"You got it, baby."

He slides down the bed, pushing the fabric around my stomach up so he can kiss me until he hits the edge of my panties.

"Zayn?" I ask, pushing myself up onto my elbows to watch his descent. "Are you..." I trail off, not really wanting to ask in case I'm wrong and he's not about to do what I think he is. My cheeks flame red. He glances up at me with a wicked smile playing on his lips and a naughty glint in his eye.

"If you want me to."

"Um..." I murmur, biting down on my bottom lip. "No one's ever..." I fall back into the bed, flinging my arm over my eyes as I die of mortification.

Zayn's well... Zayn. Hotshot member of Rosewood's champion football team, all-around sex god and one of the boys all the girls dream about, and he's here, looking up at me like I'm the only girl in the world and offering me something that I never thought I'd experience with him, despite the number of times I've fantasized about it.

"Hey," he says, peeling my arm away from my face. "What did I tell you about hiding from me?"

I keep my eyes averted, but he moves so I have no choice but to look into his.

"You have no idea how glad I am that no one ever has." His voice is rough and my breath catches.

"You really want to…"

"Stop talking, Poppy." His fingers brush my lips. "You know full well that I never do something I don't want to."

"I know but—"

"Ah ah," he says, tapping my lips once again. "Just lie back."

He kisses down my body once more and just like last time, I watch his journey, fascinated by how he looks with his lips pressed up against my pale skin. Once he's past my hips, his fingers tuck inside my panties and he waits for me to lift a little to help him out.

I suck in a breath and close my eyes as he lowers them. I don't need to see him to know he's staring down at me, I feel it burn my skin.

"Look at me," he demands, and I'm powerless but to do as I'm told.

I rip my eyes open at the same time he wraps his fingers around my ankles and parts my legs.

His eyes hold mine as he settles himself between them before he drops to his stomach, his eyes zeroing in on my center.

I fight to keep my eyes on him, my embarrassment over his closeness to my most intimate part almost too much to bear.

"So beautiful. I bet you taste so damn sweet too."

I'm suddenly so glad the first thing I did when I got home was to shower.

His fingers brush me, parting me before he leans forward.

"Oh holy... fuck," I groan as his tongue gently licks at me. It's so gentle, so sensitive, just so... everything.

I want to demand he stops yet beg he continues. My head spins as my fingers twist in the sheet beneath me.

My back arches as he does it again, my hips lifting from the bed.

He chuckles, and it sends vibrations up my spine that only adds to the sensations.

Draping his arm over my stomach, he pins me to the bed to stop me from getting away before continuing.

"Zayn," I cry when it all gets too much. My hand reaches for him and my nails scratch at his scalp as I try to get more.

I need more. I need to discover what it is I'm chasing.

I just need... "Shit," I gasp as one of his fingers begins circling my entrance.

All of my muscles tense as something intense builds inside me.

"Please, please," I beg, needing to shatter. I've got myself off before when my curiosity got the better of me, but it was nothing like this, nothing quite so consuming and so... intense.

The world around me vanishes, we could be anywhere on the planet right now and I wouldn't know it, even less care about it. The only thing that matters is the sensations racing through my body and the ache in my core that's going to explode.

His fingers slide inside me, stretching me open but the small bite of pain only adds to what he's doing.

"Oh my God," I scream a second before I crash.

Something within me shatters into a million pieces as my body convulses on the bed beneath him.

But he never stops. His tongue, his fingers, they both keep moving, drawing every last drop of pleasure from me.

"Shit, Zayn that was—"

"Poppy?" a little voice calls from the other side of the door a beat before the handle rattles.

"Fuck," Zayn barks before practically dropping to the floor at the other side of the bed.

I wrestle with the sheets and just about manage to cover up my almost naked body by the time Austin's little head pokes inside my room.

"Hey, bud, is everything okay?" My voice is high-pitched yet rough at the same time and I cringe at hearing it.

"Uh... are you feeling better? It's just Mom and Dad have gone out and..."

"They've gone out? Where's Cooper?"

"With us. He's okay, he's sleeping."

"Jesus," I mutter under my breath. "Did they say how long they were going for?"

He shakes his head. "We haven't eaten."

Of course they fucking haven't. "I'll be down in a bit and I'll see what I can find for you."

"Thank you." He ducks back out of the room and I fall back to the bed, blowing out a long breath of frustration.

It seems Zayn managed to rid the tension from my body for all of five seconds.

Zayn, shit.

I twist to the side of the bed where he vanished to see him rising to his feet.

There's concern written across his face and I fight the need to hide, knowing what he just heard, but there's more than just that. There's hunger and it makes everything inside me clench.

"You need to go," I say in a rush before he gets a chance to make this situation any worse.

He studies me for a beat before dropping down so his nose is only a breath from mine.

"This time, I'll do as you ask. Next time might be a very different story."

My heart jumps in my chest. Next time? He thinks there could be a next time.

"This isn't going to happen again."

"You going to try to tell me you didn't enjoy it?"

I close my eyes, not needing to see the smirk that I know will be playing on his face.

"This shouldn't have happened, Zayn. You shouldn't have..."

"Kissed you, touched you, *ate you*." His voice is so low, so dirty and suggestive that I can't help but squirm.

I flinch when his hand wraps around the back of my neck and my eyes pop open in surprise.

"This is happening again, Poppy. I need more, and I know you do too. Now go look after your family before I'm forced to start asking more questions, like why your parents just fucked off leaving you in charge of three hungry kids with no warning." I panic, assuming that he heard Austin, which of course he did..

"T-things are complicated."

"Aren't they always." He drops his lips to mine, his tongue pushing inside until it tangles with mine. My breath catches when I realize that I can taste myself on him but he doesn't stop, hell, nor do I.

By the time he pulls back, I'm a panting mess again.

"I'll see myself out."

"Make sure they don't see you."

"You underestimate me, Poppy."

With one last kiss, he stalks toward my door but stops and turns back before walking through it.

"You need me, you know where I am. I won't let that motherfucker hurt you, Poppy. All you've got to do is say the word."

"T-thank you. But it's okay. Everything is okay."

His eyes narrow, he doesn't believe a word of it, and rightly so, but thankfully, he pulls the door open and silently steps into the hallway.

What I really want to do is curl up into a ball and try not to cry myself to sleep as I obsess over every second of today, but I can't.

I've got people relying on me to feed them and keep them alive.

I give myself thirty seconds before I stuff everything about today in a box, close the lid and fling the covers off me. The sight of my almost naked body threatens to bring it all back, but I push it down. I'll do what I've got to do, then I'll let myself drown.

Thankfully, I find a frozen pizza at the back of the freezer, so I throw that in the oven and make both their packed lunches for tomorrow while it cooks.

As Austin said, Cooper is fast asleep in his bouncy chair while the two of them watch some awful-looking kid's show that has them both in hysterics every few minutes. The sound of their joy and laughter makes my heart ache. At least they're not as affected by all this as I am.

I rest my ass back against the counter and wonder where all this is going. The life we're living under this roof isn't sustainable.

I'd hoped that when my aunt returned a few months ago that it might help fix things. But her appearance did nothing for Mom, her inevitable departure however sent her on a downward spiral.

She used to have good days, good weeks. I could be normal some of the time. I'd have friends over, sleepovers even, knowing that Mom was going to just be... well, a mom. But she got pregnant again and, I shake my head, everything just went to shit.

She's up and down so fast it gives me whiplash. She and Dad are either at each other's throats or giving us all a show that we never need to see. It's... exhausting, and unless they seek out the help they so desperately need, I can't see them getting better anytime soon.

The movement of a shadow out in the garden catches my eye and has my heart in my throat, but when I look, it's just a tree blowing in the wind, the leaves catching the brightness of our outside light.

I tip my head back and blow out a slow stream of breath. Things can only get better, right?

"Is it ready, we're starving," Sofia says, racing into the kitchen and almost colliding with a bar stool.

"Yes, go and get your brother and I'll dish up."

"Yess," she squeals. "Austin, dinner!"

"Shush, you'll wake Cooper." Although as the words leave my lips, I wonder if that would probably be for the best, he should be awake right now if I have any chance of having a decent night's sleep.

Once they've eaten, I tidy up and let them carry on watching TV with strict instructions that they're to turn it off and come to bed the second the program finishes. They agree and thankfully, I know I don't have to worry about them doing as they're told. The one good thing in all of this is that they're incredibly good kids. Although, I fear that's because they see too much, understand too much and know that I'm not the one they should be giving grief to. That would be our absent parents.

I walk back upstairs with the sound of their laughter filling my ears. It makes a part of me feel lighter, but it's not enough.

The fear I felt in that dressing room earlier is still clinging to me along with the confusion over Zayn's visit.

Closing my bedroom door behind me, I pull my clothes off as I make my way to my bathroom and turn the shower on.

I'd already had one when I first got home. The only thing I could smell was him and it turned my stomach knowing that he was that close. That he touched me, that he almost...

I gag, the thought too much to take.

He almost took exactly what he wanted and I have no doubt that next time he'll be more successful. He wants to break me, hurt me, and doing that might just be the way to do it.

I don't want him breathing the same air as me, let alone touching me.

It's why I let Zayn do what he did. On any other day, I probably wouldn't have allowed it to happen.

Wouldn't you? Like you stopped him kissing you?

But the thought of it being him who touched me first, who gave me that before Preston can taint me with his own evil touch, well... it spurred me on. More than it probably should.

The water is barely warm when I step under it, but I don't notice, I'm too lost in my own head.

I think back to the evil intentions in Preston's eyes in that dressing room and a shudder runs through me. He was serious, I have no doubts about that, if Ruby hadn't had called, I have no reason to believe that he wouldn't have taken exactly what he wanted. Sick fuck.

He has girls falling at his feet on a daily basis. What's wrong with one of them? Why can't he take it out of one of the sluts who think they can use him to take a step up the Rosewood ladder?

My thoughts flick back to Zayn. Why was he even here? It doesn't take a genius to figure out that it's come from Harley, but why does he care?

I told him we were nothing, yet he turned up here anyway and helped me forget, despite the fact I barely told him anything like he demanded.

Confusion swells within me and tears burn my eyes. I

don't want to cry over that entitled prick. He doesn't deserve a reaction from me but as the tears spill over, I accept that I can't stop them, can't stop myself from feeling when he constantly pushes me.

My hands tremble as I realize that I'm probably going to have to see him tomorrow... both of them. How am I supposed to look either of them in the eye and pretend like my entire world isn't currently crumbling around my feet?

My back hits the wall and I slide down until my ass hits the floor.

The barely warm water continues to rain down on me until it turns icy cold, but still I remain curled up in a ball wishing the water would wash me away with it.

10

———

Zayn

"Where have you been?" comes from the kitchen the second I close the front door behind me.

My heart jumps into my throat and I feel like a naughty little boy again. I may have snuck out earlier but it wasn't because I'm not allowed, more that I didn't want to invite any questions about where I was going.

Turning left, I step through to join Mom where she's sitting at the island with a glass of wine.

"I just went for a drive to clear my head."

She nods in understanding.

Pulling open the refrigerator, I grab a can of soda and join her.

"I'm sorry, Zayn."

"What for?"

She lets out of a long sigh. "For dragging you all into this thing between your dad and me."

"It's okay, you don't—"

She cuts me off before I get to tell her that I understand. "It was never meant to end this way. I wanted a better life for all of us, I had no idea that he was going to act the way he did."

"Mom," I say, reaching out for her hand. "You don't need to do this. His reactions aren't your responsibility."

"I know, but I see the look on your face every time you come back from that place and I hate it. I never wanted to build a life there, I certainly didn't want to bring my kids up there. I had a plan, a plan for a better life but..."

"I know, Mom." She's told me this story before, and although I appreciate the truth, it doesn't change anything. Our family is still broken, we're here, he's there and the three of us are in between the two of them like punching bags waiting for the next hit.

Mom was supposed to go to college, the first in her family, she was all ready to go and then she met Dad. They fell in love, she got pregnant with Letty and that was it. She ended up with the trailer park life that she's always despised. Soon she had three young kids and no way out.

I remember the look that was always on her face when I was a kid. She was miserable. It didn't take an expert to see that she was depressed but she was stuck in hell.

She was a good mom, she did everything she could for us, but it wasn't enough for her.

We had no idea she'd somehow managed to start studying but when I found out, I was so proud of her. I still am now. She had a dream, a dream of a better life and she found a way to make it happen, something many people are never brave enough to do. She had no idea that Dad was going to kick off like he did and refuse to be a part of her future.

His decision still shreds her, I can see it in her eyes. As much as she likes to curse him out, I know she still loves him. Sadly, I think the two of them have just changed too much over the years, they want totally different things and I think it would take a miracle to ever fix it between them.

"Did you have a good time with your dad?" she asks after a few moments of silence.

"Uh... it was... fine." She gives me a sad, knowing smile.

"I'll never regret what I did. Seeing the three of you here, knowing that you have the world at your feet, it means everything to me."

"I hate going back there," I admit. "It's so... depressing."

"You don't need to tell me that."

"You're amazing, Mom."

A smile curls at her lips at my words. "Anything for my babies. Now, are you all ready for school tomorrow?"

"You know it." I wink at her.

"Any college will be lucky to have you next year." She squeezes my hand before I stand from the stool.

Now that I've turned my applications in, I'm trying not to think about it. I know my first choice, I want it so fucking badly, but I know that there's nothing I can do now. I just have to sit and wait for that letter to drop through the door that's going to decide my fate.

"Thanks, Mom."

I leave her to it and head up the stairs. Music comes from Harley's room and my hand twitches to knock, to find out if she's still struggling with that math homework, but the memory of what I did tonight stops me.

She'll never forgive me for going after Poppy after warning me to stay away. That's just the problem though. I can't. And knowing that she's being tormented by that motherfucker makes me want to protect her even more.

My fists curl as I picture him standing before me looking like the fucking weak ass pussy that he is.

Harley was right, you can take the boy out of the trailer park, but the trailer park is always in the boy.

People around here might not see me as that, most of them don't even know what my past consists of. All they care about is that I can play ball. They have no idea about the dark side of me I keep hidden. We might have left that place four years ago, but I'm not sure it'll ever leave me. Especially when we keep getting dragged back. Just one more thing to look forward to once college starts, although the thought of Harley going alone into the pit of vultures scares the shit out of me.

My room feels cold and empty as I step inside and close the door behind me. I want to be back in her room, feel the heat of her skin, hear the soft moans she made as I worked her toward orgasm. But I know she was right to kick me out. I shouldn't have even been there in the first place.

I pull my shirt over my head, her scent filling my nose as it moves, and I groan. I was so fucking hard for her as I gave her what she needed to escape. But that was just it, it was about her, not me, and I've walked away with the bluest balls known to man.

Dropping my pants, I crawl into bed, but her scent lingers and before I can stop myself, my fingers wrap around my length and I work myself to my own release with images of her laid out before me filling my mind.

———

I'm already worked up and on high alert before I even take a step into the school building the next morning.

My need to teach that fucker a lesson for whatever it was he did to her at the mall is almost all I can think about.

I scan the faces as I make my way down the hallway toward where her locker is. A few people try to stop me and a couple of the cheerleaders join me, clinging to my arms like they belong there. I don't shake them off like I probably should. I figure that if my entire attention isn't on that prick when my eyes land on him then it's probably a good thing.

I don't have to take too many more steps before he emerges in front of me with his little posse surrounding him.

He oozes entitlement and it makes my muscles pull tight in disgust. So what, daddy has a lot of money, it doesn't stop him from being a total fucking asshole. He seems to think he's untouchable, that daddy can cover up or buy off whatever shit he gets himself into, and to be fair, it might have worked up until now. But he's not encountered me before and there is no way he can drop a few hundred bills to make me forget what he's doing.

He scans the hallway, staring down his nose at the students around him until his eyes lock on mine. He startles slightly before his jaw clenches.

My lips curl into a smile, but it's anything but friendly. The stupid motherfucker doesn't even have the sense to look a little afraid. He's clearly already forgotten about our little chat in the locker room last week. Probably all the fucking pills he pops frying his brain cells.

Our eyes hold for a couple of seconds but someone more interesting at the other end of the corridor catches his attention.

I don't need to look to know who it is. I can see it in his eyes. He looks like a lion who's just spotted his prey.

I take a step toward him, glancing at the girl who's holding his attention. The sight of her makes my breath catch.

Her light brown hair is pulled back from her face accentuating her cheekbones and full lips. Something stirs within me as I remember just how her lips taste but the dark circles around her eyes are a stark reminder of the reality of why I did what I did last night.

I still have no idea what Preston did or how bad it was, but the ball of dread in my stomach tells me that my worst suspicions might just be correct.

Poppy was different last night. Her kiss was different, the way she reacted to me was different. She was desperate for me to make her forget, and that was because of what he did.

Her eyes catch mine and her steps falter, that is until she looks away from me and finds Preston. Then all the color drains from her face before she looks to the floor and makes quick work of getting to her locker.

Not wanting to give her the attention she clearly doesn't want, I walk toward him instead, despite the fact my body screams to go to her.

I don't stop until my shoulder slams into his.

"What the fuck, man?" he barks as all his crew stop and stare at me as if I'm about to lay him out right here in the middle of the school. It's tempting, I'll give them that but I'd hate to give him the satisfaction of watching me getting carted off by Hartmann when we're caught.

"Watch your fucking back," I warn, my voice low so none of our audience will hear.

A deep growl rumbles up his throat. "Fuck you. I do what I like."

My fists clench with my need to hurt him, it takes all my self-restraint to keep my arms at my sides and walk away from him.

His evil laugh hits my ears and I almost change my mind. Glancing over my shoulder, I find him staring right at Poppy who's still as white as a sheet at the other end of the hallway.

It's all I need to tell me that he's not going to give this up easily and that if I want to help her, free her from his twisted game, then I need to up the ante.

———

By lunch my muscles are still pulled tight and I'm still on high alert waiting to see or hear that the douchebag has done something else.

I don't usually listen to the senior class gossip, let alone the junior gossip but today I hear everything, and when Harley and Ruby come to join the cheerleaders at lunch, I listen to every word while the JV football team occupies the table beside ours in their need to be us.

Preston is noticeably absent from his group almost all of lunch. The rational side of me says he's probably just with a teacher or in the gym or something, but the other part of me says that he's with her.

My blood turns to lava as I think about him touching her, about him forcing her to do something.

My fist slams down on the table before me, making the lunch trays rattle and everyone to stop talking and stare at me.

"You all right, man?" Justin asks, his eyes boring into me.

"Yeah, I just... fuck. I'm outta here."

Without waiting to hear what any of them have to say, I push from my stool, all but throw the tray and its remaining contents into the trash and storm out of the gym.

If Poppy isn't with my sister and Ruby, then there's only one place she'll be. I march toward the music department.

The looks on the music geeks' faces are a picture as I pass them on my mission to find her. If I weren't so agitated about his suspicious absence, then I might be entertained by it.

I might not make a habit of coming to this corner of the school but I know where to look. Sadly, I don't make it to the practice rooms before I stumble across the one person I really didn't want to see right now.

"Zayn." Preston nods, his pretentious, asshole smirk plastered across his face.

"What are you doing here?" I seethe.

"Visiting a friend. What about you, I didn't have you down as a music fan."

"Fuck you."

"Now, now, I was only being friendly."

I don't bother responding, I push past him, my legs moving even faster than before, my need to find her even stronger.

He watches me go, I feel his stare burning into my back but I refuse to turn around and give him the satisfaction of knowing that he affects me in any way.

Looking through the window of all the practice rooms, I search for her but I come up empty. It's not until I look through the final small window that I find her defeated form slumped over a piano.

My chest constricts that he was down here doing God knows what with her while I was sitting in the cafeteria with the team.

I don't bother knocking, I just push the handle down and shove the door open.

Her entire body flinches with the sound but she doesn't turn around, she doesn't do anything.

It's almost like she's given up, lost her fight.

It fucking kills me.

"Poppy?" My voice is soft, quiet, in the hope of making her relax.

"What do you want, Zayn?"

"Are you... are you okay? Did he..."

"He did nothing. You should leave."

I hesitate, not knowing whether I should do as she asks or what I want to do.

"Why do you keep insisting on pushing me away?"

"Because it's the right thing to do. You don't owe me anything, Zayn. You have no reason to keep poking your nose into my life." Her words cut but I refuse to allow her to know it.

"What if I want to?"

A sad laugh falls from her. "Why would you want to?"

"Why wouldn't I?"

Walking over, I come to a stop beside the piano and look down at her. She rushes to wipe the tears from her eyes before she looks to the other side of the room in an attempt to hide from me.

"Poppy, what did he do?"

"He did nothing," she cries, standing from the stool and once again turning her back on me. "He did nothing, he means nothing. All of this has nothing to do with you. Just go back to your team and gaggle of cheer sluts and leave me alone."

Closing the space between us, I place my hand on her waist. She tenses but she doesn't immediately push me away.

"Zayn," she sighs. It's so quiet, so broken that it makes something inside my chest physically hurt for her.

I spin her to face me and gently push her up against the wall so she can't escape too easily.

"Talk to me, Poppy. Please. Let me help."

"There's nothing you can do."

"That's shit and you know it."

She still refuses to meet my eyes and I hate that she's hiding from me. Lifting my hand, I tuck my finger under her chin and force her to look up.

I swallow down the curse that wants to explode from me when I see the tears filling her eyes.

"He was here?"

She nods.

"Did he hurt you?"

"Not physically."

"Hurting you in any way isn't going to work with me, Poppy. How long has it been this bad?"

She shrugs and it pisses me off that she can try to brush this under the carpet like it's nothing.

"He's just a stupid boy, playing stupid games."

"You really believe that?"

"What did he do at the mall?" I try again, still desperate to know the truth.

"Enough," she barks, her eyes narrowing at me, a little of her normal fire returning. "This isn't your fight."

"It shouldn't be yours either. Why haven't you told anyone about this?"

"Why bother? What are they going to do about it?"

"What about your parents?"

"Pfft." She rolls her eyes and it's like she's thrown fuel over the fire that's crackling away in my belly.

"This is bullshit. He's not going to get away with this."

"No, Zayn. You need to stay out of it. This is my battle, not yours."

Her small fists grip on to my shirt and pull me closer.

"Please, Zayn. Don't do this. Don't get involved."

Our noses are only a breath apart, her scent fills my senses and her heat burns my skin.

"Poppy," I groan. "I can't help it." I have no idea what exactly I'm admitting to, but it doesn't really matter because the second my lips brush hers, all thoughts fall from my head.

Her muscles lock up for a beat and I start to think that she's going to push me away, but instead of doing that she releases my shirt, and she slides her palms around my back and drags me closer until the length of my body is crushing hers against the wall.

My fingers tangle in her hair, allowing me to tilt her head to the side to deepen the kiss.

Her tongue meets mine, her kiss as desperate as mine.

With my hand gripping her waist, I pour everything I'm feeling into the kiss. The anger that she's being treated this way, my frustration that she won't just tell me the truth, my need to do something about it, to make it go away, to make her life easier.

"Zayn," she mumbles against my lips as her hands flatten against my stomach to create some space between us.

"Stop fighting it, Pops."

"I'm not fighting anything. We can't do this."

"You're the only one who thinks that way."

I press myself harder against her ensuring that she feels exactly what she does to me with just her kiss.

My lips trail down her jaw.

"I'm not sure your sister or my cousin would see it that way."

"Fuck them. This isn't about them."

She shudders as I suck on the sensitive skin beneath her ear.

"No, Zayn. Stop."

Her words are like an ice-cold bucket of water poured over me, and I immediately step back.

Her brows draw together as if she's confused by me doing as she said but she soon recovers.

"You need to go."

"Why is it so hard for you to let me help you?"

"Because I don't need it."

"Okay, so... tell me what he was doing here. What did he say to you?"

"The usual shit."

"Fucking hell, Poppy." I lift my hands to my head in frustration and tilt my face to the ceiling. "Do you really need to make it so hard?"

She doesn't respond.

"If you don't start talking, I'll just assume the worst. I'll be forced to think that when he accosted you yesterday that it was so he could put his hands on you. Is that what he did?" A thought hits me and my stomach turns over. "Did he? Did he touch you? Is that why you let me last night?"

The small amount of color that was in her face drains away.

"I'm going to fucking kill him."

"Zayn, no. It's nothing like that."

"You're fucking lying. Just tell me the truth."

"Keep your nose out of it."

"No," I seethe, closing the space between us once more. My eyes boring into hers and begging for her to confess while hers pleads with me to stop.

"I don't need you or anyone else fighting my battles for me. Preston is a douchebag, we all know that, but I can handle him."

"But—"

"No, Zayn. There are no buts here. Leave it the hell alone."

"I can't promise you that."

"You don't have a choice."

My brows rise as I stare at her.

"Fuck this, Poppy. I'm not going to stand by while that prick treats you like you're worth nothing."

Stepping away from her, I storm toward the door before ripping it open.

"But what if I am?" Her voice is so broken that I almost step back inside and close the door, but I know I can't. She doesn't want me here.

"If you think that, then you've already let him win."

The door clicks closed behind me as I walk away from her. Regret sits heavy in my stomach but it's not as insistent as my need to go and find Preston and show him what I really think of him.

Anger surrounds me like a dark cloud as I make my way

through the school. Kids litter the hallways, but one look at me and they pale slightly.

"What the fuck is wrong with you?" Jake asks when I pass him where he's got Amalie backed up against her locker. It's not unlike the move I just played on his cousin.

Something stirs within me, but I push it down.

"Nothing," I bark, successfully proving that there is something wrong.

I crack my knuckles, my need to hurt someone starting to get the better of me.

"Coach has fucked off somewhere. The gym is empty if you need to..." He trails off, his eyes dropping to my hands.

Without saying another word, I blow down the hallway and toward the locker room.

There are a few kids getting dressed, ready for next period but none of them are brave enough to stop me as I make a beeline for the gym, or more specifically, the punching bag that's waiting for me.

The second I see the red leather, I launch myself at it as if it's Preston himself.

My roar of anger fills the empty space around me as I plow my fists into the leather, wishing that it was his face.

11

Poppy

I might be almost at the end of my last class of the day, but my head is still back in that practice room at lunch. The last person I expected to stumble across when I walked inside with the intention of hiding for an hour was Preston.

And it wasn't just Preston, because he had Annie, a JV cheerleader, pressed up against the wall and was grinding into her like it was what she needed to keep her alive.

I went to leave, not wanting to ever see that, but the second he saw me, a sinister smile curled at his lips and he demanded that I stay and watch.

I should have walked straight back out, but his increasingly scary behavior meant that I couldn't help believing that his threats are more than just words these days.

When he tells me that I'll be next and that I will enjoy it, I have no doubt that at least the first part of that statement is true.

A shudder runs up my spine as I remember.

The things he said as he touched her, the way he compared how she was enjoying what he was doing to how I reacted the day before.

The way he spat at me that I was broken, useless. Nothing but a tease. Frigid. The way she giggled as if his words were a hilarious joke she couldn't get enough of.

All of it turned my stomach, and the final one brought back memories of a certain birthday party that needed to stay locked in the box I've shoved them in.

Even now I can hear his words like he's whispering them in my ear.

It shouldn't have affected me, but I couldn't help succumbing to the tears when he finally dragged her out. Thankfully, it was before he actually fucked her with me in the room.

I'd felt ridiculous allowing his vile words to hurt me but I couldn't help it. I only have so much tolerance for his shit.

When the door opened once more, I was convinced it was him coming back to take more from me, to attempt to make me bend to his will like that slutty cheerleader who moaned like a whore every time he so much as glanced her way.

It was pathetic. Both of them were pathetic.

I was expecting him to be in my last class of the day, so when our teacher kicked things off and his desk was still sitting empty, I was more than relieved not to have to spend the hour feeling his hateful stares burning into my skin.

Everything is normal, well as normal as Rosewood High ever is, until the boy himself bursts through the door only a few minutes before the end of the day. Only he doesn't look like he did earlier because he's covered in blood. Not that it seems to bother him.

A collective gasp sounds out around the room and he stands proudly, displaying his injuries to his loving crowd.

"Jesus, what happened to him?" Amalie mutters beside me.

"Christ knows, he had it coming though." As I say the words, realization hits me.

He did have it coming, and from someone I warned not to do anything.

He wouldn't. Would he?

As the chaos continues, I slip out of the room after muttering to Amalie that I'm going to use the bathroom. Our teacher doesn't even notice I leave, he's too busy attempting to deal with Preston who is lapping up the attention of all the girls who are offering to be his personal nurse. I try not to gag at the thought.

Just before I turn the corner, I feel his hate-filled stare trained on me.

Glancing back over my shoulder, I hold his eyes for a beat. They're cold, it's not unusual, but I can't shift the fear that snakes around my entire body.

This is not going to end well for me. Preston doesn't take well to being threatened, and I can imagine even worse to being attacked.

Leaving him behind, I turn right down the hall instead of left toward the bathroom.

I might be wildly off the mark here, but I follow my gut all the way down toward the boy's locker room. The trail of blood that I follow sure makes me think I'm on the right track.

Hesitating outside the door, I wonder if I'm about to make a massive mistake but then I think back to my warning about leaving this be, and my anger that he's ignored me forces me to swing the door back and go marching in.

My lips curl as the smell of sweaty boy fills my nose but I don't let it put me off as I march through, past the lockers and benches in the hope of finding the person I'm looking for.

The water that was running cuts off and my heart jumps into my throat as realization of what I'm doing hits me.

Walking inside here is probably the most spontaneous thing I've ever done. Preston isn't wrong when he tells me that I'm boring. I can't help wondering how much of that is actually his fault. I spend most of my life trying to stay away from him, which means avoiding most parties and all other social events that most kids at Rosewood High live for.

I continue forward until I find one person with his back to me. Water droplets cover his wide shoulders and run down his back, soaking into the towel that's wrapped around his waist.

I see no evidence that he was the one who made such a mess of Preston, but I don't need to see any, I know.

He turns and I suck in a deep breath as I prepare for him to see me.

"Jesus, Poppy," he barks, his eyes going wide and his chest swelling as he sucks in a sharp breath. "What the fuck?"

Squaring my shoulders, I take a step toward him. "Funny, because I was going to say the exact same thing to you."

"I don't know what you're talking about. Shouldn't you be in class?"

"Shouldn't you?" I quip.

"I was... eh... working out."

"Were you?" Closing the space between us, I lift my finger, running it none too gently over the emerging bruise around his eye. "Treadmill fight back, did it?"

"Poppy," he warns.

"Don't *Poppy* me." Dropping my hand to his, I grip his fingers and lift his hand so I can look at his knuckles. "I told you to fucking leave it," I shout, throwing his hand back down with as much force as I can muster.

"Yeah, and I told you I couldn't."

"So that makes it right?" I seethe.

"Trust me, Pops. Nothing about this is right."

"How many times do I have to say it, Zayn? This is not your fight. It's not your place to get involved."

"Really? So how else are you planning on making him stop?"

"I... uh..."

"Exactly. And what's going to be next, huh? You might refuse to tell me what he's doing but I know it's bad. I can see it in your eyes, Poppy. I can see the fear, the sheer terror whenever he's close, whenever someone so much as says his name. You don't have to deal with this. You don't deserve this."

"Don't," I warn as he takes a step toward me, crowding me with his large frame.

It's bad enough that he's standing there in just a towel with nothing but water trailing over his bronzed, taut skin. I watch one droplet as it runs down from his collarbone, over his chest and drops down to his abs.

Fuck.

My eyes lock on where the towel is tucked around his waist, knowing that he's naked beneath.

My teeth sink into my bottom lip as I try to imagine how it might look and wonder how easy it would be to pull it from his body.

"Go on, if you want to."

My eyes fly up to his, shocked that he's responding to my thoughts.

"W- what?"

"You're staring at the towel as if you want it to disappear, so make it."

"N- no, that's n- not..."

"No?"

He steps forward and I'm forced to take one back to stop his body from brushing up against mine.

"What are you doing in here, Poppy?"

"I... um... I had a feeling that you'd be here and I... uh... wanted to..."

He takes another two steps and I find myself once again caged between him and the wall.

"You wanted to... continue what we started earlier?"

"What? N- no. I wanted to shout at you, tell you that you're totally out of order for doing what you—"

He swallows my words as his lips cover mine and his tongue plunges inside my mouth.

"Zayn," I mumble, wanting to fight but finding my body getting sucked into his and losing myself once again to his kiss.

This has got to stop, I think to myself as my hands land on his shoulder blades before running down his back until they hit the fabric of the towel.

His thigh pushes between mine until I find myself grinding down against it. Pleasure explodes from my core as his hand cups my breast over my shirt and squeezes.

"Oh God," I cry, my head falling back against the tiles behind me.

"Let go, Poppy."

His lips trail down my neck before his tongue licks all the way back up.

"I'm so mad at you," I tell him, unwilling, even now, to let this go.

"Good, let me make it up to you." His voice is deep and gravelly, and it does funny things to my insides.

Every muscle in my body locks up tight as he pushes his thigh harder against me, the first tingles of my release begin when there's a loud crash at the other side of the room.

"Hunter, you still in here?" a familiar voice barks.

"Y-yeah, man." Zayn pulls back from me, his eyes wide in panic as realization hits me.

I need to get out of here right freaking now.

"You seen Hellburn? Some lucky son of a bitch got the chance to rearrange his face."

Jake's voice gets closer as I look around, trying to figure out how to get out of this.

Zayn looks toward where he's going to appear from, allowing me to slip from between him and the wall. Before he's even noticed, I run. Fast.

12

Zayn

I take a huge step away from Poppy and run my hands over my head as I try to figure a way out of this. If I thought I'd done a number on Preston, then it'll be nothing compared to the beating Jake will give me for touching Poppy.

It's not until he appears around the side of the lockers, his brows pulling together as he looks at me that I glance to the side.

Where she was just a few seconds ago, writhing against the wall, is empty.

"What the—" I mutter to myself under my breath.

"Is everything all right?" he asks suspiciously. His eyes running the length of me. "Oh fuck, were you jacking off? Fucking hell, man."

"What? No, no. I was not—" Glancing down at myself, I find my still semi-erect cock tenting the towel. *Fucking hell.*

Jake's brow rises in suspicion.

"I had a girl in here," I admit.

That interests him more than the thought of me getting myself off because he starts to look around as if she's going to appear. I really fucking hope she doesn't. I have no idea where she's gone but I can only hope it was out of the other door.

"Oh yeah?" he asks suspiciously as Mason, Ethan, and Shane appear behind him.

"What's going on?" Ethan asks, looking between the two of us.

"Hunter says he had a girl in here," Jake joyfully informs them as the rest of the team make their way inside. "Well it's either that or he was beating off to the smell of your sweaty boxers," he says to Ethan.

"Fuck off," I grunt.

"I see no girl here, Hunter. I could, however, do with my underwear back though."

Flipping them all off, I march over to where I abandoned my clean clothes and drag them on ready for Jake's conditioning session.

"So you're not gonna tell us who you convinced to spend last period in here with you instead of in class?"

"Nope," I say, earning a round of moans from the four idiots who are still grinning at me. "Why do you all look so excited about this? Jealous or something?"

"Fuck yeah, locker room hook-ups with our girls is the best. This one time Rae snuck in and—"

"No time, Savage. Fantasize later about your girl."

"No need. While yours might have vanished into thin air, almost like she doesn't exist, I live with mine." He winks before dragging his shirt over his head and pulling another from his locker. "My days to fantasize are long over, man. You should try it."

"Who'd have thought it, Ethan Savage whipped by one five-foot-nothing pocket rocket."

"Believe it, bro. Hell has indeed frozen over."

The four of them fall into easy conversations about their girls as we change and I can't help feeling a little jealous. Now, I'm not saying I want Poppy as my one and only, but shit, the four of them sound so fucking happy it's almost enough to make me reconsider my ways.

Our session is... fine. Preston eventually arrives having cleaned himself up a bit and mostly pulls his weight while everyone else looks at him like he's lost his mind. I'm beginning to think he probably has. Out of all the girls at school, why mess with Poppy. He should know that it'll only end one way—with Jake Thorn breathing down his neck—so why bother? What's he getting out of this?

Jake's session is hardcore and I can't help but wonder if it's for Preston's benefit. Jake might not yet know what's going on, but he already dislikes the prick as much as the rest of us, so putting him through his paces while he's clearly in pain is an afternoon's entertainment to both of us.

Once he's finished, he sends us back to the locker rooms to get showered and dressed. The second I step inside, all I see is her backed up against the tiled wall, her head tipped back in pleasure, her lips swollen from my kiss and her soft mewls for more.

My cock swells once again, my need to finish what we started getting the better of me.

I'm in no rush to go anywhere. The guys all talk about heading to Aces, but the only place I want to go is wherever she is. I wonder if she's going to be at my house again with Harley, but then I think of the events of the day and I suspect she'd have made every excuse not to. Harley would have been in cheer practice, does that mean Poppy is hanging around somewhere on her own waiting?

My eyes flick to Preston where he's drying off after showering and a little of the fury I felt earlier swirls in my stomach.

Feeling my stare, he looks over. His lips thin in frustration. I know he hates that I got the better of him earlier. But I think he's beginning to understand that he's underestimated me.

He shakes his head as if what I did earlier and my reasons for it mean nothing. I take a step toward him, more than happy to teach him another lesson, but a hand lands on my shoulder.

I look to my right to find Shane standing there with his brows drawn together.

"What the fuck has gotten into you?"

"Nothing," I mutter.

"Tell that to your knuckles. Don't even think about lying to me about this."

"Fine, but not here," I say, knowing that Jake is only a few feet away.

I trust Shane, he's been a good friend over the past couple of months and hell knows I need to talk to someone about this.

He nods once and continues getting dressed.

The second we're both ready, we blow out of the locker room and toward the parking lot.

Music blasts down the hallway from the gym where the squad are practicing and it brings back earlier thoughts as to whether she's here somewhere waiting for a lift from Ruby.

Pulling my cell from my pocket, I find her contact and shoot her a message. It's a long shot, but I can't help myself.

Zayn: Are you still in school?

It's read instantly, but no reply comes.

Lifting my hand to my head, I rub my palm over my short hair.

I want to fix this. I want to make Preston leave her the fuck alone and I want to do things to her that I really fucking shouldn't, but I can't help thinking that both of those things have disaster written all over them.

In just one afternoon, I had beaten the shit out of Hellburn and I've almost gotten Poppy off in the locker room. Where the hell is this going next?

The fact I haven't already been dragged into Hartmann's office surprises me. I touched him on school grounds. If I were smart about this—and clearly, I'm not—then I would have waited until after our session this afternoon. Organized to meet him somewhere neutral, not have a fake note sent to him pretending that Coach wanted to meet him before the last class of the day. It was stupid and I need to be smarter where he's concerned if I'm going to do anything about getting him off Poppy's back.

"So?" Shane asks as he follows me to my truck and falls into the passenger seat.

"Ugh," I complain, dropping my head to the headrest behind me.

"Hellburn had it coming to him."

"Agreed. But why today, what's happened?"

"You gotta keep this to yourself, man."

He nods. I don't even need to ask, I know it goes without saying.

"He's bullying Poppy."

Shane's eyes go wide. "Poppy? Poppy as in Jake's Poppy?"

"The one and only," I say, something I'm not sure I like swelling in my chest at the thought of her.

"Fuuuck. Has that prick got a death wish?"

"I'm starting to wonder if he has, yeah."

"Jake doesn't know—"

"Obviously," Shane adds.

"I don't think anyone really knows. She's kept it well hidden but I fear this might have been going on for a while."

"Right. Okay," he says as he digests what I'm saying. "So what are we going to do about it?"

I glance over at him, my lips curling at his need to help with this.

Shifting in my seat a little, I think for a second.

"I have no fucking clue. He needs to be taught a good fucking lesson, though."

"More so than you did today?"

"You saw the smirk on his face all afternoon. He was fucking loving it."

"He just wants the attention. Probably his reason for going after Poppy in the first place. That guy craves the spotlight and he's desperate to fill Jake's shoes next year."

"Not gonna happen."

"We know that. Jake and Coach know that. But apparently he never got the memo."

"Fucking hell," I sigh.

"You gonna tell me the rest of it, or just leave me guessing."

"The rest of it?"

I glance over to find his eyebrow raised as he stares at me.

"Chelsea and I saw you New Year's Eve, man. You might not have claimed victory on that tag, but I know you won." His eyes sparkle with delight.

"Fuck." I run my hand down my face, scratching at my jaw.

"This is more than fighting for Poppy's honor because of Jake, isn't it?"

"I... I just... fuck."

"Oh, bro. You are so fucked." He chuckles.

"That's it, laugh it up."

"I'm sorry, it's just nice to focus on someone else's drama for a little bit."

"How's Chelsea doing?" I ask, desperate for the conversation change.

"She's good, man. She's got a little bump going on, it's pretty awesome." His eyes go all soft and sappy, and as much as I want to rib him for it. I just can't.

"I'm happy for you, man. Maybe a little freaked out for you, but happy nonetheless."

He laughs at me before his face turns serious once more and he looks over at me.

"Nice try, by the way. What about Ruby?"

"What about Ruby?"

"I thought you wanted her?"

"Nah, she's hot, but it's just casual fun between us."

"Does she see it that way, she seems pretty keen, man."

"Yeah, yeah she does." I think back to the last party where Ruby and I fooled around, I remember the sadness in her eyes every time she looked at me. It was like she was disappointed that I wasn't someone else. I know Harley is worried, she said that something had happened with a guy last year but I don't know the details, but she was never interested before whatever that was. Now, it's like she just needs an escape. I was always happy to provide that service. I figured it was better me than some of the other guys who might take things too far.

Ruby might act like she's playing it easy, but I see the barriers she's built up around herself. She doesn't really want to be one of the cheer sluts, she's just lost and trying to find where she fits in life now.

Shane raises a brow but he doesn't push any further.

"So the girl in the locker room earlier was Poppy then, I assume."

"Yep, she stormed in to rip me a new one for getting involved with Preston."

"She told you to leave it alone?"

"Sure did. I rearranged that fucker's face anyway."

We both let out a sigh, probably both thinking of the mistakes I've made already.

"You should listen to her."

"That's just the thing, she won't tell me anything. I think... I think it's bad, but she won't admit it. Just keeps trying to brush it under the rug."

"Then maybe stop trying to force her, just—"

"But what if something happens?"

He shrugs. "You want to help her, support her, then you just need to be there. Do as she asks and stop trying to be the hero that she doesn't want."

"Fuck me, Shane. Where'd all this sensible advice come from?"

"I'm about to be a dad, I need to start figuring shit out."

Silence fills the car for a beat as I think about what he just said.

"Thanks, man. I needed that."

"Anytime, and if shit gets really desperate, I know a couple of girls who can help with all the advice you might need."

"Please, don't..."

"Tell anyone about this?" He guesses when I trail off. "No worries there. I've been on the end of Thorn's fists, not a place I want to be again, I can tell you that much."

"Great."

"You need to tell him."

"Doesn't that kinda go against your previous advice to just be what she needs?"

"Uh... fuck. Yeah, I guess it does. Okay then, well. How about just watch your back. When he finds out you're banging his cousin he's going to be after your balls."

"I'm not banging her."

"But you want to, and you always get what you want, so..."

The squad emerges from the building in front of us and

the pair of us watch as Chelsea starts looking around for Shane.

"Go get your girl, man."

"You don't have to tell me twice. Call me if you need me."

"Sure thing."

He climbs from the car and I watch as he pulls Chelsea into his arms and drops his lips to hers.

Maybe that kind of life isn't so bad, having a girl who looks at you like you're the most incredible human on the planet.

Taking his advice, I throw the car into reverse and back out of the parking lot, only I don't head home. I go in a different direction.

I park my truck out on the street and walk around the huge bushes that hide her house from the main road.

There are cars parked in the driveway but the house seems to be in silence, that is until I hear voices and kids' laughter from the back yard.

Walking around the side of the house, I come to a stop on the corner when I find her running around playing soccer with her two younger siblings.

"Goal," she squeals, running around with her arms above her head and high fiving her little sister in celebration. Her little brother sticks his tongue out at the two of them while stealing the ball and hurtling toward a makeshift goal that consists of two rocks at either side of the grass.

Poppy is just about to take off after him when she stops and looks over her shoulder. Her eyes find me almost immediately and her lips part in shock.

13

Poppy

The familiar shiver that I'm being watched runs down my spine and fear wraps around my chest.

With my breath stuck in my throat, I turn around, praying that he's not here. That he's not watching me while I play with Austin and Sofia. Life here is already hard enough without him forcing his way in and ruining that as well as my school life.

But when I look over my shoulder, he isn't the one I find watching me. Instead I find the one person I haven't been able to get out of my head since I ran from the locker room a few hours ago.

Our eyes lock and another shiver runs down my spine, but it's not the same one as only a few seconds ago. There is no fear, just anticipation, hunger.

My lips part to say something but the reason I went into the guy's locker room in the first place slams into me.

He ignored me about Preston and took matters into his own hands. The exact opposite of what I asked him to do.

Schooling my features, I square my shoulders and walk over to him while Austin and Sofia play behind me.

I pass Cooper who's fast asleep in his bouncer, pacifier firmly in place, and don't stop until I'm right in front of him.

"What are you doing here?"

He swallows almost nervously before his tongue licks across his bottom lip. The move isn't intentional, I don't think, but hell if it doesn't affect me. I know what those lips are capable of and it causes heat to pool between my legs at the thought alone.

"I... uh... came to apologize."

"To apologize?" I ask, my brows almost hitting my hairline.

"Why do you look so surprised?"

"I just didn't think you had it in you."

"What, to admit when I'm wrong?"

"Yeah, something like that."

"Poppy, I—"

A bloodcurdling scream from behind me stops his words.

I spin around and run before I've even realized what the issue is.

"Shit," I spit when I find Sofia curled up in a ball on the asphalt that runs down to the trailer at the bottom of the garden. "Are you okay?" I ask, dropping to my knees beside her and attempting to check her over.

Her sobs break my heart. "M-my k-knee."

I look down and find it grazed with grit and fluff sticking to it. Blood trickles down her shin and starts to soak into her white sock.

"Let's get you inside and cleaned up."

I'm just about to reach for her to carry her inside when she moves from the ground. I look up to find Zayn with her in his arms.

"It's okay, I've got her. Lead the way."

I glance down to Sofia to make sure she's okay, only to find her staring up at him as if he's some kind of superhero or something.

I roll my eyes and mumble to myself. Great, he's got another girl after him and this one's only six.

"It's a magical power. I can't help it," he says with a smirk.

He takes off for the house before I even have time to consider what the state of the inside might be like.

The second we step into the kitchen, I cringe. The air is permeated with the weed my parents have been smoking all day while we were at school and the room looks like a tornado has run through it. It's a million miles away from what Zayn's house ever looks like. Well aside from the weed, that's one rule he tries to break as often as possible.

He coughs not long after stepping inside before turning to look at me. "Should these three be in here?" he asks with genuine concern on his face.

"Probably not, but there's not a lot I can do about it," I say sadly. I want to pretend that I don't know what he's talking about and kick him out so he doesn't have to witness the disaster that is my life but it's a little too late now.

"Fair enough." He places Sofia down on the edge of the island before looking down at her knee. "You're being so brave," he says to her in the softest voice that does things to my insides. "You got a first aid kit, Pops, or are you just going to stand there staring?"

"Oh uh... yeah, sure."

I run back outside so that I can collect Cooper before rushing toward the bathroom.

"Out of the way then," I demand once I'm back with the box in hand.

"I can do it."

"It's okay, you really don't—" My words falter when my eyes meet his.

"Just get her some chocolate or something. We decided that she deserves it, right, Sofia?"

"Yes," she says with the widest smile. My heart drops because I don't think I've seen that much excitement on her face in months.

He must sense my dejection because as I turn, he grabs my forearm. "You're a good sister, Poppy." His lips curl into a smile but I can't find it in me to return it. Instead, I pull the cupboard open and pray that there's some chocolate in there somewhere.

By the time I've finished rummaging around and thankfully managing to find something, Sofia is giggling behind me, her injury long forgotten.

I have no idea what Zayn is doing but to be honest, I don't really care. The noise is like music to my ears.

"So do you think you've got another match in you?" he asks.

"Yes!" she squeals. "Boys against girls." Before either of us can say anything, she's off the counter and running back outside where Austin still is, practicing his dribble.

"She's sweet," Zayn says softly as we both watch her run back outside.

"Yeah, they're good kids."

"What's going on here, Poppy?"

I sigh, desperately wanting to keep my secrets close, but Zayn has witnessed just a small part of our lives now, I can hardly lie or try to keep it hidden. "Not a lot, to be honest. Our parents are..."

He turns to me, his brow raises as he waits for my answer.

"Well, they've pretty much checked out."

"Shit, Poppy."

"Please, don't. It's fine. I've got it all covered."

"Maybe so but—"

"Please," I beg. "Just leave it."

"Come on you two," Austin shouts.

"Go on, I'll grab Cooper."

Zayn stares at me for a few seconds too long, making me wonder what he really sees when he looks at me before taking off for my little brother. He may be a football player but in a second he has the ball away from Austin and is showing off his skills.

"I hope you're not trying to impress me, Hunter."

"Me? Never." He winks, and I can't help but laugh as Austin sets about explaining the rules of our backyard soccer game.

We run around like we have no cares in the world as we battle it out to be able to call ourselves the winners. Austin and Sofia laugh more than... well, I can't even remember when they last enjoyed themselves this much. And I can't deny that I'm actually having fun too, especially every time Zayn gets a little too close or decides to go in for a dirty tackle.

"Whoever scores next are the winners then it's bath time," I say despite the fact we're all loving life right now, reality is only so far away and it's a school night.

Sounds of Austin and Sofia's complaints fill the air.

"Can Zayn stay for dinner?" Austin asks, already becoming attached to his new teammate.

"I'm not sure—"

"I'd love to, lil' man," he says, totally interrupting me.

"Are you sure?" I ask quietly when he walks past me to get the ball.

"Yes, now come on. You've got a game to win."

"Oh please. It's so ours."

His lips curl into a smirk. "Here lil' man, get ready." He kicks the ball to Austin before reaching behind his head and pulling his shirt off.

My eyes drop to the skin he reveals. It ripples as his muscles flex beneath.

I'm still lost in my daze as Austin kicks him the ball and he skillfully dribbles it past me, kicks it back to Austin who scores the winning goal. Sofia comes to a stop where she was chasing him in an attempt to stop him and stares at me.

"Poppy," she sighs with a roll of her eyes.

"S-sorry," I mutter, irritated with myself for allowing the sight of Zayn's naked chest to render me useless.

"Looks like we win, lil' man," Zayn says, high-fiving Austin who looks up at him like he's God's gift to soccer.

"Bath time, you two. Go and get sorted and I'll be up in a little bit."

They both complain but as always, they do as they're told.

Zayn's eyes are trained on me the entire time making my already increased temperature spike.

"Those were dirty tactics."

"Oh baby, if you want dirty, I can give you dirty."

I want to laugh but his stare is so intense as he closes the space between us that I can't.

My stomach somersaults as his scent fills my nose and the heat of his body seeps into mine.

Reaching out, he tucks a lock of my hair behind my ear.

"You could have done the same thing," he whispers.

"Take my shirt off in front of the kids, oh yeah, why didn't I do that?" I sass.

"I have no idea because it was all I could think about."

He leans forward to claim my lips but I manage to get my fingers between us so when he touches me, it's not my lips he finds.

He growls in frustration but doesn't force the situation. "Why not?"

"Look up."

After a second, he does as he's told.

"Little shits." He chuckles quietly, confirming what I already knew. Both of them have run upstairs and pressed their noses against the window to watch us.

"Okay, well, I guess I'll just have to wait until they go to bed. What time does that happen exactly?"

"It doesn't matter. I'm still mad at you."

"I know. I was hoping to show you that there's really no need." He moves his lips to my ear. "You already know that I can make you feel so good. And I think we've got unfinished business from earlier."

I manage to catch the groan that threatens to rumble up my throat but I'm powerless to stop my thighs squeezing together.

"I need to go and make sure those two don't drown. You really don't need to stay for dinner."

"What if I want to?"

"Why would you?" I ask, but I don't mean for the words to come out loud.

"Many reasons."

"Put your shirt back on, no one needs to look at that," I say as I back away from him.

"Are you sure about that? Something tells me that you need to do more than look."

Fucking hell.

"You can walk away as much as you like, Pops. You know that I'll just keep hunting you down."

"Keep an eye on Cooper," I call over my shoulder.

I shake my head as I make my way into the house and up the stairs.

The TV booms from the living room where my parents are but I don't even bother looking. Experience tells me that they're not coming out for a while.

By the time I get upstairs, Austin is already out of the bath and Sofia is on her way into it. I hurry her up knowing that

Zayn could be downstairs and seeing all kinds of things I really don't want anyone seeing, but without insisting he leaves—which I already know he won't do—or ignoring what everyone else in this house needs, there's not a lot else I can do right now.

I leave them both to play around in their bedrooms before stopping off in my room to change my shirt after running around the yard for the past few hours. After pulling a tank over my head, I go back to see what trouble Zayn might have got himself into.

I'm not even at the bottom of the stairs when I hear his voice followed by giggles and coos.

What Is he doing? I smile to myself as I get closer and am able to make out the words.

"Where's the bunny?" Giggle. "There he is." More giggles.

My heart swells at hearing that little laugh.

I come to a stop in the doorway, cross my arms over my chest and lean my hip against the frame as I watch the two of them.

Cooper is still in his bouncer, but Zayn has lifted him onto the table in front of him so they can play.

"Where's the bunny?" Zayn drops the stuffed toy out of sight while Cooper's face lightens up with amusement before Zayn magically makes him reappear again. Cooper laughs like it might be the most incredible thing he's ever seen and I start to wonder if I actually agree with him.

He must be able to feel my stare because after passing the bunny back to Cooper, Zayn turns his dark eyes on me.

Something crackles between us the second our eyes lock and it makes my breath catch.

"H-having fun?" I stutter, needing to fill the silence between us.

"Yeah, he's pretty cool, this one."

Zayn's eyes drop from mine to where I have my arms

folded under my breasts. They darken and his lips part as he takes in my cleavage.

Dropping my arms, I walk over to them.

"Yeah, you're pretty cool, eh, Coop?" His eyes brighten as he looks at me, the way I'm sure they should when he looks at our mother.

There's a loud crash from the living room and I startle, Zayn's eyes immediately zeroing in on the door.

"It's our parents," I mutter, needing to wipe the concern off his face, not that the truth is likely to do that.

"What are they doing in there?"

I shrug. "Getting high? Wasted? Both? I don't know, I've stopped worrying about it."

"Poppy, I—"

"Please, Zayn. Don't. I know how it sounds... how it looks, trust me. But please. No one knows about this. Even Harley doesn't know how bad it is."

Conflict passes across his face.

"You can't live like this, Pops."

I jump when his fingers brush mine, but instead of pulling away like I should, I allow him to pull me into his side.

"What other choice do I have?" I ask when I finally find my voice.

His lips part like he might have an answer but he soon closes them again.

"If I tell anyone about the reality here, we'll all end up in the system. At least if I can wait until I'm eighteen then—"

"Then you should be getting ready to go to college. You shouldn't be doing this."

"Someone has to."

Our eyes hold, his full of concern and worry as the sound of footsteps pound down the stairs behind me.

"What's for dinner? I'm starving."

"Who wants pizza?" Zayn announces, pulling his cell from his pocket and proceeding to order delivery.

"No, you don't have to…"

"Please, Poppy. Just let me help."

I open my mouth to argue but my stomach beats me to it and growls loudly.

Zayn raises a brow at me, and I forget any fight I might have had.

We have a quick debate about toppings and after discovering that all of us agree that pineapple does not belong on a pizza, Zayn places the order and I set about getting us drinks.

"You've got the choice between water or… water," I say, looking in the cupboard in the hope of finding some juice but coming up empty.

"Do you know what? I was just thinking that I really fancy some water."

His smile knocks me for six and I have to fight my need to walk over and plonk myself on his lap so I can show him just how much what he's doing right now means to me.

I clear my throat after a second or two. "W-well that's a relief."

I grab four bottles of water and some plates and place them all on the table before going to make Cooper's bottle.

"How'd you learn to do all that?" Zayn asks, nodding at me as I place it in a bowl of cold water in the hope it cools faster.

"Just picked it up, I guess. I watched with those two, and when you don't have many choices, you just figure it out." I drop the bowl in front of me, and lower myself to the chair beside him.

His fingers almost immediately find mine under the cover of the table. Unable to look away, I stare into his eyes as he shakes his head at me.

"What?" I ask, a shy smile twitching at my lips.

"You're a little bit incredible, do you know that?" he whispers while Austin and Sofia bicker about something on the other side of the table.

"I'm just doing what needs to be done."

Our connection holds and for a minute or two, I swear it could just be the two of us in the room. Everything else fades as so many things pass between us, despite the fact no words leave either of our lips.

My thighs clench as he runs his eyes down my body, once again hovering on my cleavage.

"I like this top. You really should have worn it while we were playing earlier."

"Oh yeah?"

"You might have had a better chance at winning."

"I'll remember that for next time," I whisper but my breath catches when I realize my mistake.

Why would there be a next time? Zayn is hardly going to want to come and hang out with my kid brother and sister again.

He could be at Aces right now with the team, with any member of the squad grinding down on his lap and whispering slutty promises in his ear. Why would he want to be here?

Cooper growls in his seat, telling me that his patience for the bottle is waning.

"What's that look for?" Zayn asks, his hand resting on my waist, and I reach over him to take Cooper out of his seat.

I still as the heat from his hand burns through the fabric of my tank.

"N-nothing. Do you... want to feed him?"

"Me? You think I can?"

"Of course, he seems to love you."

Zayn's stare on me is intense, I feel the tingles it creates right down to my toes.

"Okay then. Sure. I've never fed a baby before."

"It's easy," Sofia pipes up. "I do it all the time." While she might be proud of her skills, a familiar sadness passes over Zayn's face to what I feel.

"You're a great big sister, Sof." She beams at my praise as I lift Cooper and place him in Zayn's arms.

My fingers brush his abs and chest as I release Cooper and his eyes fly to mine. Surely he didn't feel the same spark I just did when I touched him.

Our eyes hold for a beat before Cooper complains that we're taking too long.

Ripping my stare from Zayn, I collect his bottle, check the temperature and pass it over.

I give Zayn a couple of quick tips but Cooper is so hungry that he doesn't allow Zayn to hang around.

Sitting beside him, I look at the two of them. He looks so natural sitting there holding a baby.

"Maybe you should let Shane and Chelsea come around to babysit one time, they sure could do with some practice," he says with a laugh.

My stomach twists uncomfortably at the thought of inviting others here. He must see my panic because when he turns to look at me, he winces.

"I didn't actually mean..."

"I know," I say, reaching out and placing my hand on his forearm.

Sparks shoot from the innocent touch and our eyes lock once more.

"Do you ever get to go out? Get to be... normal?"

"I came to your party at New Year's."

He nods, probably casting his mind back to all the other parties I haven't been at.

"And I went to one of Ethan's a few months ago."

"Pops," he sighs.

"They're not really my thing, it's not a big deal."

"It's not just parties though, is it? It's hanging out with friends, it's going to Aces, the beach, the arcade. Anything."

"Please... don't." He doesn't need to tell me all of the things that I miss out on, although I don't think he really appreciates right now that it's not just because of these three monsters that I don't do all those kinds of things. Even if I didn't have kids to look after, I wouldn't be there because I don't want to see *him.*

Thoughts of Preston are like having a cold bucket of water thrown over me.

"What's wrong?"

"N-nothing." Thankfully, as I push my chair out to escape from his assessing stare, the doorbell rings.

I race to the door, desperate for a little air, but equally hoping that my parents stay put in the living room. I might not be all that happy about Zayn pushing his way into my life— my home—but it's somewhat bearable while they're hiding.

Austin and Sofia's faces light up as I carry the pizza boxes into the kitchen. The scent of the tomato sauce and melted cheese making my stomach growl even louder.

"When was the last time you ate?" Zayn asks with a laugh when he hears it over the kids' excited chatter.

"Er..."

"Shit, don't answer that."

I nod, lowering my head so I don't have to meet his eyes. He's already learning too much without being able to read my thoughts like I know he's able to.

I sit back and allow the kids to take their fill before I even reach for a slice. It's the way it always is—the way it has to be.

"Come on, I ordered plenty," Zayn encourages as he continues to bounce Cooper gently now he's back in his seat with a full belly.

"I know, I just..."

"Eat, Poppy. You need to look after yourself as well as these three for once."

I do as I'm told, mainly because I don't want to start an argument in front of Austin and Sofia, but also because I can hardly deny that he's right.

I just about manage to keep my growl of appreciation down as I take my first bite, although from the heated stare I feel from beside me, I get the idea he's aware of my reaction.

"Good, right?"

"So good," I mumble around my mouthful.

Zayn keeps Austin and Sofia entertained throughout dinner like a pro. It makes me wonder what experience he has with kids, it's hardly from Harley seeing as there's barely a year between them.

"Okay, you two need to get upstairs and get ready for bed."

"Ohhh, but it's still early."

I smile at the two of them. "You have an hour to watch TV or play. But I expect you to both be in bed and ready for sleep in an hour."

They roll their eyes at my bossiness but after rinsing off their plates they both do as they're told.

"They're good kids," Zayn says as their footsteps get quieter.

"They really are. I'm going to take him to my parents," I say, nodding at a sleeping Cooper before lifting him in his chair and walking from the room.

"You shouldn't have to do all this," he says again as I walk back into the kitchen with empty hands. Both Mom and Dad were awake, they watched me place their child in front of them although it doesn't fill me with much hope.

I walk past where he's still sitting at the table and come to a stop at the sink, blowing out a frustrated breath. I shouldn't feel guilty about leaving Cooper with his parents, but I do. He should be their responsibility, not mine. But that's not how things are in this house.

Pushing his chair out, he comes to join me at the sink to do the cleaning up.

"I know, but it is what it is."

"What's the real issue with your parents?"

My muscles tighten and he doesn't miss it.

Putting his dishtowel down, he moves to stand behind me. His fingers brush against my shoulders and he pushes down into my bunched muscles.

"Oh God," I moan, my arms falling limp at my sides as I immediately start to relax.

"Talk to me, Poppy," he breathes in my ear, sending goose bumps racing across my skin.

"Dad hurt his back at work years ago, says it's too bad to do anything other than drink himself into a coma, apparently. Mom... I don't really know. She had postnatal depression with both Austin and Sofia but managed to beat it. Although she's always been very up and down. Then she had Cooper and it's like she's just checked out. She knows there's something wrong but she refuses to seek help, says we can't afford it."

"Fuck."

I shrug. It's my life, not much I can do about it.

"All this shouldn't be on your shoulders."

"What am I supposed to do about it? Go to social services and watch as we're all taken away?"

"I..." He hesitates. "I don't know." His voice is sad and I hate that it's because of me. I shouldn't be dragging him, or anyone else, into this. It's why I've kept everyone at arm's length since Cooper was born, hell, I was doing it long before that, I just don't think I'd realized it. "I could talk to my mom. See if we can get yours some help."

"She won't accept it," I say, full of confidence.

She refused when both Austin and Sofia were born and I

have no reason to believe that she'll be any different now. She's fallen even deeper into her blackhole this time. I doubt she can even see the light.

"I'm so sorry, Poppy."

His hands drop to my waist and he spins me around before stepping into my body.

"It's not your fault." The words are so quiet, I doubt he even hears them.

"No, but it still sucks."

His eyes hold mine captive, rendering me useless.

"Tell me how to make it better."

"You can't, I—"

His fingers press against my lips. "I don't mean everything. I'm not a miracle worker. I just mean right now. What do you need right now?"

My lips part. One single word dancing on the tip of my tongue, desperate to fall out but as scared as I am to admit it, I'm equally terrified of what will happen next.

Zayn's already shown me just how good he is at making me forget. If any more were to happen, I'm not sure I'd be able to give it up again willingly.

"Say it," he encourages. "I need to hear you say it."

I bite down on the inside of my lips, fighting my need to jump into his with both feet and fuck the consequences.

"Y—"

He nods, a small smile twitching at his lips.

"You."

I barely finish the word before his lips are on mine in a bruising kiss.

His hands drop to my thighs, gripping them, he lifts me into his body before lowering my ass to the counter. He pulls me right to the edge and wraps my legs around his waist as his tongue dances with mine.

His fingers twist in my hair, tilting my head to the side so he can explore more of my mouth as his hands drop down over my shoulders, brush over my breasts and come to a stop on my hips, pulling our bodies tighter together.

He grinds into me and I gasp, ripping our lips apart, as an intense sensation washes through me.

"You feel that?" he mumbles against the corner of my jaw.

"Y-yes," I whisper when he does it again. The hard length of him is impossible to miss as it continues to drive me crazy.

"You do that to me, Poppy. Every fucking time I look at you."

"Oh God," I moan when he does it again, his fingers digging into my ass.

"You always have."

"Zayn." I want to tell him to stop, to stop using these lines to get what he wants, but his name falls from my lips as a plea instead.

"Forget it all, Poppy. Right now, none of that matters. This, this is all that matters." He runs his tongue up the length of my neck and my entire body shudders in pleasure.

"U-upstairs."

"You sure?" he asks, suddenly sounding like the sensible one out of the two of us. He pulls back to look into my eyes. "I need you to know that this isn't why I came. Well, not really."

I shake my head at the boyish smirk on his face.

"Sure it wasn't."

14

Zayn

Just as she's about to laugh at me, I slide her from the edge of the counter and carry her toward the stairs.

"Do you think they even know you have company?" I ask, although when she tenses in my arms, I immediately regret it.

"I don't really care. Pretty sure they don't either." Her lips land on my neck, the soft brush of them cut off what I was going to say. "You can do all kinds of things and they'll be totally none the wiser," she whispers in my ear.

"You're playing a very dangerous game here, Poppy," I warn, my voice low and rough, showing just how much I need her.

"Oh yeah, why's that?"

"It's like you're challenging me to ensure you make enough noise to alert them to the fact I'm dirtying up their daughter."

"Hmmm... what did you have in mind, Hunter?" she practically growls in my ear.

"Well," I say, my hands gripping harder onto her ass. "It seems that I've already captured my prey, all that's left to do is feast on her."

"Oh God," she whimpers as I walk us through into her bedroom.

We both glance over at the closed bedroom doors when the sound of kids squealing sounds out.

"They're fine. Plus, I put a lock on my door."

I pull back and look at her with a smile on my face.

"Hoping I was going to come back, were you?"

"A girl can dream. Or, I'm sure I could have found another willing friend."

"Absolutely not," I snap. "Just me. Only me," I growl, making her shudder.

"O-okay," she agrees as I kneel on the edge of her bed and lower her down. "Don't you have to be home or anything?" she asks as I hover over her, our noses almost brushing.

"You trying to get rid of me now I've got you here?"

"No, no," she says in a rush. "I was just..." She trails off as I sit up and pull my cell from my pocket.

"I've got nowhere else to be." I let her watch as I turn it off and throw it down on her bedroom floor. "No one else exists apart from you and me, baby." I wink before reaching behind me and pulling my shirt off.

I look down at her after the fabric has passed my face and find her biting down on her bottom lip as her eyes roam across my body, much like they did earlier.

"Thought you might want a closer inspection."

"Zayn, I—" She looks up at me with wide eyes like she's just been caught with her hand in the cookie jar.

Reaching forward, I take her hand and in mine and lift her

fingertips to my stomach, gently brushing them over my muscles.

My cock swells from her simple touch and I bite back a groan at having her hands on my naked skin.

"Take your fill."

I stop moving when her fingers hit my waistband and her eyes once again meet mine.

She's a virgin, I know that from my previous visit, and while I don't care if we do no more than kiss, I can see in her eyes that she's freaking out about this.

I drop forward once again, sliding my hands up her thighs and to her waist.

"We don't have to do anything you're not happy with. I didn't come here to steal your innocence, Pops," I whisper in her ear before running my tongue around the shell and biting down on her lobe.

"No?" she moans. "Why'd you come then? Surely it wasn't to play dad to my siblings."

"I came to apologize. To tell you that you were right."

"I was?"

"Yeah." I don't stop kissing her. My lips trail down her neck until I brush them over her collarbone and down to the swell of her breasts. This bit of skin has been driving me crazy since she returned wearing this shirt before dinner. "I should have listened to you instead of going after..." I trail off, not wanting to say his name and ruin the moment. "I need you to take the lead, in more ways than one," I say, looking up at her.

Her lips are parted as she drags in rapid breaths and her usually light gray eyes are dark and full of hunger.

"Tell me what you want, what you need."

Her leg curls around my back before she flips us over.

"Oh-oh." I chuckle. "Like that, is it?"

"What? You think you can always be the one in charge?" she asks with a smirk.

Stretching my arms out, I rest my hands behind my head and lie out beneath her.

"I already told you, take your fill, baby. I'm all yours."

She blushes harder as her eyes drop from mine, down my body to where my cock is quite clearly tenting my pants. It's so fucking cute and totally not what I'm used to with the cheer sluts.

"I-I haven't..."

"I know," I say, reaching forward and lacing her fingers with mine so I can tug her down on me.

Her chest presses against mine and a growl rumbles up my throat as her lips find mine once more.

As we kiss, she gets braver, her hand starting to explore across my chest and stomach.

"Fuck, Pops. You're driving me crazy," I groan when she kisses across my jaw and starts down my neck.

"Yeah?" She looks up at me, her eyes wide in amazement.

"Yeah. Your touch is addictive."

I can see that she wants to argue, but she doesn't, instead, she sucks in some courage and continues kissing down over my chest.

Her kisses are so light, so teasing that my entire body locks up with need.

Reaching down, I thread my fingers into her hair, not to control her movements but because I can't stand not to be touching her.

"Jesus, do you have any idea how hot you look right now?" I ask as I watch her lick across the indentation of my abs.

My cock strains against the fabric of my pants, desperate for some action but I meant what I said a few minutes ago. We only take this as far as she's happy with.

I mean, I shouldn't even be here in the first place, so I may as well try to do something right.

She moves down until she kisses along the edge of my waistband.

"Poppy," I moan, damn near desperate for what could come next.

She pauses and sits up a little.

"Zayn, I—"

Sitting, I cut off her words with my lips. My hands run up her thighs and slip under the fabric of her tank.

"Oh God," she moans when I take her breasts in my hands and squeeze gently. Her lips leave mine as her head falls back.

"So beautiful," I whisper against her neck.

I push the fabric of her shirt up, waiting to see if she'll lift her arms for me. After a beat she does and I throw it across the room.

"Zayn," she moans as my lips trail over her breast and my teeth graze her nipple over the lace. "Off."

Sliding my hand around her back, I flick the clasp of her bra, not needing to be asked twice to remove it.

The second it clears her body, I drop my lips to her exposed skin.

"Shit," she gasps when I suck her rosy pink nipple into my mouth. "Shit, shit, shit," she chants, making me smile.

"You taste so good."

"Umm... you too," she moans as I continue.

"You want me to make you come?"

"Oh God," she cries, her fingers gripping on to my shoulders as I pull her hips down so I can grind into her.

"You feel how hard you make me?"

"Yeah."

"My cock is desperate for you."

"Zayn, shit."

I don't say it because I'm trying to convince her to go further, but because every time I say something dirty, the blush that already covers her cheeks and neck spreads lower and her grip on my shoulders gets tighter. She's so close already and I've barely touched her.

"You gonna come like this? Or do you want more?"

"More, please. More."

Flipping us, I immediately reach for the button on her pants and pop it open. She lifts her hips as I tug, helping me pull them from her body.

The moment they're off her feet, I run my eyes up her almost naked body. The only thing covering her is a white scrap of cotton.

Her chest heaves, catching my attention, her breasts are covered in my bite marks causing something possessive to wash through me.

Poppy is mine. No matter what fucking happens after tonight, no other fucker is getting their hands on her.

She. Is. Mine.

Fuck what Harley thinks. Fuck what Jake will do to me. She's it for me.

"Zayn?" Her voice is quiet and hesitant, and I realize that I've been standing here too long without doing anything while she's practically naked.

"Shit, sorry. I'm not... fuck," I bark when panic washes across her face. "No, no. It's all good," I say in a rush, opening the fly of my pants and pushing them down my legs to prove to her that I'm not going fucking anywhere.

"Oh," she breathes, her lips forming an O as she runs her eyes down the length of me. "So you're not... regretting this then?"

"Fuck no. I was just thinking..." She looks at me expectantly, but I can hardly tell her what I was just thinking, she'll run a fucking mile, I'm sure. "Shit, it doesn't matter."

Kicking off my shoes and pants, I drop to my knees at the end of the bed, and after wrapping my hands around her thighs, I tug her so her ass hangs over the edge.

In seconds, her panties are on the floor and my face is between her thighs.

When I glance up at her, she's staring down at me with total fascination in her heavy-lidded eyes.

"So fucking sweet," I mutter before dropping lower and pushing my tongue inside her.

She cries out as I press the pad of my thumb to her clit and circle until she's scratching at my head and crying out my name as her release consumes her.

"Jesus, shit," she pants, lying back on the bed trying to catch her breath. "I think that was better than last time."

"Yeah?" I ask, crawling up the bed and smiling down at her happy face.

"Yeah. I think I could do that all day," she admits.

"I'm sure we could skip a day and do just that." A darkness passes through her eyes at my mention of school. "Next time Mom is out of town, I'm going to lock you in my room and make you come over and over and over." I trail my fingers up her stomach before circling her nipples and making her squirm.

"Sounds like the best day ever. But what about you?"

"What about me?"

Her eyes flash down to my very tented boxers. "You need..." She hesitates and I can't help but smile at her shyness.

"Yeah, but when you're ready."

"But what if I want to?"

I run my nose along the length of hers. "Like I said, all yours whenever you want."

She bites down on her bottom lip, in deep thought.

"I... I need to have a shower."

"Oh." I laugh. "That's it, is it? You get yours and kick me out?"

She swings her legs off the side of the bed and nervously walks toward a door at the other side of the room.

It makes me smile that she wraps her arms around herself in an attempt to cover up yet only minutes ago I was up close and personal with her most intimate place.

"No, I was wondering if you wanted to..." She trails off, looking over her shoulder as she kicks the door open to her en suite.

"You want to know if I want to watch as water runs over your naked body?" I ask, my brows almost in my hairline, wondering if she thought there was any way I'd ever refuse an offer like that.

"Um... yeah."

"In a fucking heartbeat, Pops."

I'm off the bed and in front of her before she's had time to blink. Wrapping an arm around her waist, I pull her flush to my body, loving the feel of her hot, naked skin against mine.

"Maybe we'll add showering to our list of things to do on our day off."

"I'm not sure. You haven't shown me how good it can be yet."

"Oh, Poppy. What are you doing to me?"

I walk her backward into the room before releasing her so she can turn the water on.

When she turns back around, her breath catches at finding me bare before her.

Her eyes latch on to my solid length and she sucks her bottom lip into her mouth, making it twitch in anticipation.

"Something you can work with?"

Her eyes fly to mine, realizing that she's been caught staring.

"I literally have no idea," she whispers, backing into the walk-in shower.

"I'm sure you'll be just fine."

I stalk toward her, a smirk playing on my lips as she bumps against the tiled wall.

Water rains down on both of us as we stare at each other.

"How did we end up here?" she asks, although I'm not sure if she's talking more to herself than she is me. Her arms are still locked around her torso and I hate that she's trying to hide.

"I think it started with me fucking up and needing to apologize." Reaching out, I pull her arms from her body.

"Ah, that's right. Your stubborn ass never listens."

"I'll do anything you want me to right now," I admit, caging her in with my forearms and pressing our bodies together.

"So I just need to get naked and tell you not to fight my battles for me?"

"I'll never stop fighting your battles, Poppy. If someone hurts you then—"

"Stop," she says, placing two fingers to my lips. "Not now. Right now, let's forget everything but—"

"Fuck," I bark as her fingers slip between us and wrap around my cock.

"Okay?"

"Oh, baby. You have no idea."

My eyes shutter as she grips me a little harder. She hesitates, and not wanting her to stop, I drop my arm, wrapping my hand around hers and slowly guide her up and down my shaft.

"Fuck, Pops."

Our eyes remain locked and I watch as hers darken before me.

"You like that?"

Her lips part. "M-me? Shouldn't I be the one asking you that?" She tilts her head to the side.

"Your eyes are so dark right now." I drop my gaze down her body. "Your nipples are begging for my touch. You're wet for me, aren't you, Poppy?"

"Zayn," she whimpers.

"You want to feel me again, don't you?"

She shakes her head. I know she's lying but what I really don't expect is what comes from her next.

"There's something else I want to try more." She bites down on her bottom lip and seductively looks at me through her lashes.

"Oh yeah? What's that then?" I ask, leaning toward her until our noses are touching and my lips are just a whisper from hers.

She hesitates, before lowering herself down the wall.

"Fuck, Pops," I groan at the sight of her.

"I-I don't know," she whispers when she's at eye level with my cock.

"Trust me, as long as you don't use your teeth, you can't do anything wrong."

Releasing my hand, I rest the other against the wall to keep me upright as I wait to see what she's going to do.

She continues moving her hand, that alone is enough to have me racing toward release faster than I should, but the sight of her, the way she unknowingly licks her lips, teasing me for what might come next, drives me fucking insane.

Her eyes flash up to mine, indecision fills them.

"It's okay," I whisper, my hand threading into her hair ready to gently pull her up.

She's not ready for this, I've already pushed farther than I should. Hell, I probably shouldn't have even come here in the first place, let alone touched her again.

Just as I'm about to get her to stand, she leans forward.

"Fuck," I bark as the softness of her tongue hits me. She licks the tip, our eyes remaining locked. My fingers fist her hair as the sensation washes through me.

With her hand still moving slowly, she leans forward and

does it again, and again before she gets brave and wraps her lips around the head and slowly sucks me into her mouth.

"Holy fuck, shit," I groan, my head falling back and my eyes closing so I can focus on what she's doing.

She can only suck me in her mouth twice before my balls start to draw up, telling me that this is going to be over sooner than I want it to be. Hell, it could go on forever and it wouldn't be long enough.

15

Poppy

I close my lips around him, and his taste explodes in my mouth.

He groans above me, and when I run my eyes up his torso, I find his head tipped back in pleasure.

Lust shoots straight to my core knowing that I'm the cause.

What he's done to me the last two times has been nothing short of mind-blowing and knowing that I can give him a similar experience has me craving more.

It's wrong. He shouldn't be here, and he really shouldn't be in the shower with me, but I could hardly send him away when he had that wicked glint in his eyes.

My life is beyond shit, as he's quickly learning, and he's fast becoming my secret guilty pleasure. Hell knows I deserve to enjoy myself every now and then.

He said it himself earlier that I deserve to have some fun, act my age, well look at me now doing what all the others are.

I push away thoughts of the others who've already been on their knees before him and focus on the now. The past, the future, anything outside of the room doesn't matter.

"Poppy, shit. I'm gonna come," he warns, his voice deep and gravelly.

His cock twitches and I panic. Pulling back from him, I watch as his hand covers mine once more and together, we finish him off. Hot spurts of his cum land on my chest as he growls out his release.

The second he's finished, he reaches down and pulls me up from the floor.

The water immediately begins to wash the evidence of what just happened from my body, but that doesn't stop him from reaching out and running his fingertip where he marked me.

"I think that means you're mine now," he muses, his eyes locked on the spot.

"Oh yeah? I'm sure all your cheer sluts might have something to say about that."

His eyes fly to mine, his brows pulling together. "I don't give a shit about them, Pops. Being with them..." He hesitates before wrapping his hand around the back of my neck. "Being with them is nothing like this."

The length of his body presses against mine, his already semi-hard cock presses against my stomach once more.

His nose grazes mine before his lips capture mine and his tongue plunges into my mouth.

"I'm fucking addicted, Pops," he whispers into our kiss.

———

After another orgasm each, we finally clean up and wrap ourselves in towels. Well, I wrap myself in a towel, the small ones we have barely cover any of Zayn. Not that I'm complaining because his body, shit... it's captivating.

I watch his muscles ripple as he dries off, my mouth watering for another taste of his skin.

"Pops," he warns when he turns and finds me staring. "Keep looking at me like that and we're never leaving your bedroom ever again."

"I'm pretty sure people would miss you if you did that."

He doesn't miss what my words imply and sadness washes over his face.

"People would miss you too," he says, stepping up to me and cupping my cheek.

Emotion clogs my throat and burns the back of my eyes.

"Not as many as you."

"Stop, please. You make it sound like you're worthless."

I shrug, hating that it's Preston's words that come to mind when he says that.

"Sorry," I whisper, looking away from him, ashamed that I allowed my insecurities about this out.

"Don't hide from me, Pops. And believe me when I tell you that you are not worthless. You're incredible. What you do here, it's amazing. Don't ever allow anyone to make you believe you are anything less than you are."

Tears pool in my eyes at his words.

"Aw, shit. I didn't mean to make you cry."

"I'm okay. Thank you, Zayn. For... everything."

"Oh, Pops. You are more than welcome."

Chemistry crackles between us like it always does and the temptation to let it consume us once again is almost stronger than I am, but I know it's time to let reality back in.

"You should go," I whisper as he leans in to kiss me.

"What if I don't want to?"

"Zayn, your mom will wonder where you are."

"I'll tell her I'm staying at a friend's. She won't care." He drops his forehead to mine, his dark eyes holding mine captive, begging me to agree, but I know I can't.

Shaking my head slowly, I force the words out that I really don't want to say. "We can't. You need to go."

"It was worth a try, huh?"

"Yeah, and I wish things were different."

"Me too, Pops. Me too."

He pulls me to him for a sweet kiss before he releases me, bends down to pick up his discarded boxers before walking back to my room as naked as the day he was born. It is one fine sight.

"Are you staring at my ass?" he asks with a laugh.

"Damn right I am."

He chuckles and the sound makes me feel a little lighter once again.

"Zayn, what are we going to do about Harley and Jake?"

I stand leaning against the bathroom doorframe while he gets dressed.

"Right now, we do nothing."

"So, I'm now your dirty little secret?"

A smile plays at his lips. "Hell yeah." He winks, making me laugh.

"Don't worry about everyone else, Poppy. Just enjoy it for what it is."

"Okay," I agree, although the word tastes bitter on my tongue. There are so many questions I want to ask him about this, about what we now are—or aren't—but I can't. I don't want to be one of those girls.

"I'll see you tomorrow, yeah?"

I nod, desperately trying to keep my sadness from my features that he's about to leave.

"Remember, if you need me, if that prick tries anything, just call me. I've got your back, Pops. Whatever you need."

"Thank you," I breathe.

"Anytime."

He gives me another knee-weakening kiss before pulling open my door and slipping through it.

A long sigh falls from my lips and I sag back against the wall as images from our time together tonight flash through my mind.

My cheeks heat and my temperature spikes as I think about the things we did. So much for telling myself I wasn't going to kiss him again. I think I've well and truly shattered that promise to myself.

As I push from the wall and drop the towel that was covering me, I realize that I don't even care. This evening has been the exact escape I needed and for the next few hours I'm going to enjoy the high Zayn left me with. Tomorrow, however, is a different story and I have a feeling I'm going to feel very different about it.

After pulling on some pajamas, I go and check on Austin and Sofia, who as predicted, are both fast asleep in their beds.

The living room door is still closed when I get to the bottom of the stairs and there's no crying coming from inside, so I decide against dropping myself back into real life already. After I get myself a bottle of water, I head back up to my room in the hope of having a full night's sleep without Cooper keeping me awake.

My cell dings as I close my door behind me and I rush over.

My heart leaps when I see Zayn's name staring back at me.

Zayn: I can still taste you.

My cheeks burn at his dirty words.

Poppy: Who says I can't say the same thing?

A smile pulls at my lips as I hit send. I feel all kinds of naughty right now. Crawling into bed, I wait for his response.

Zayn: Fuuuuuck. I'm coming back.

Something explodes in my belly at the thought. I want to say it's panic that he's going to do so, but really, I think it's just excitement that he might ignore my need for him to leave.

Sadly, he never reappears but that doesn't mean we don't spend the whole night sending suggestive messages back and forth.

By the time I turn my light out and close my eyes, my head is full of all kinds of ideas for what I want to do to him the next time I see him, and I soon find myself dreaming of some of those very things.

The next time I wake, my skin is covered in a sheen of sweat and I have a very vivid image in my head of what Zayn was doing to me in my slumber.

Knowing I need to put all of that behind me, I throw the covers back and plod to my bathroom.

Everywhere I look, I see him. Standing with his hand resting on the wall in the shower, with my tiny towel barely covering his body. His presence is ever-present and by the time I'm ready for school, I'm damn near desperate to get a look at the real him instead of just the image in my head.

"Where's Harley?" I ask, dropping down into the passenger seat of Ruby's car when she pulls up out the front to get me.

"Ugh, running late. Bad hair day or some crap. She's going to drive herself."

"You have a good night?" I ask, although I instantly regret it because I might open up the conversation about my own. I don't want to hide things from Harley and Ruby, but I can hardly tell Harley about what happened, and I don't want to put Ruby in a position where she has to lie to Harley.

"Yeah. We went to Aces and hung out for a bit after practice and then I had a ton of homework to do. That math assignment is killer, right?"

"Right," I agree. "What about you?" She glances over at me briefly when she pulls to a stop at an intersection. "Wait, hold that thought. Is that a hickey on your neck?"

Lifting my hand, I immediately cover the spot she's staring at.

"Um..."

"Poppy," she warns, her eyes narrowing at me because she's forced to focus on the road once more.

"It's nothing."

"Bullshit it is. Who gave it to you?"

"I'm not talking about this."

"Oh, hell yes you are."

"Oh my God, was it Zayn?"

"What? No," I protest a little too harshly.

"Fuck. It was. OMG. OMG. Give me all the details right now."

"Ruby," I groan. "It's nothing. Really."

"Anything between you and Zayn is not nothing."

"Look," I say, turning to her. "You know as well as I do the drama from anything happening between us could cause."

"Didn't seem to bother either of you last night," she mutters, her voice full of amusement.

"Ruby, please. This is serious."

"As serious as a hickey." She giggles. "Did you give him your V-card?"

"No," I mutter.

"Girl, why not? I have it on good authority that you couldn't give it up to anyone more... skilled."

I groan at her words. "Maybe because of that."

"Don't do that, Poppy. You're better than all of them and you know it."

"Do I?"

She pulls into her usual space in the school parking lot and turns to look at me.

"Enough, okay. I don't need a lecture. Last night was..." I trail off, trying to come up with a word to describe what it was that doesn't make Ruby think I'm as desperate for a repeat as I am. Her brows rise as she waits. "A mistake." Her lips part to argue and I rush to beat her to it. "A mistake that doesn't need to be discussed or repeated."

"But—"

"No buts. The conversation ends here and we don't speak of it again, and you certainly do not repeat it to Harley." I pin her with a look that I hope communicates how serious I am about this.

"Okay fine. But we need to do something about that hickey if you don't want Harley asking about it herself. Come on."

I follow her to the bathroom where she does a much better job than I did at covering the red mark with concealer. It probably has something to do with the fact she can afford to buy decent makeup, whereas mine is the cheapest stuff I can find at the store.

"There, as good as new," she says, checking out her handiwork.

"Thanks, Rubes."

"Anytime."

Harley still hasn't arrived when we get to our lockers and switch out books, although I do however get that familiar shiver running down my spine.

Looking over my shoulder as discreetly as I can, my eyes immediately lock on to a cold pair that turns the blood in my veins to ice.

His lips curl into an evil smirk as he watches me.

"You are mine," he mouths, making fear claw itself around my chest.

Ripping my eyes from his, I stare into the darkness of my locker as I fight to not react.

My cell dings, dragging my thoughts from his warning. Hope fills me that it might be Zayn wishing me good morning but when I wake my cell up and see an unknown number, that fear begins to grip me once more.

As far as I know, he doesn't have my number. But somehow, I know that this is him. I have no idea how, but I do.

Hesitantly, I swipe the screen and open up his message.

Unknown: Someone's being a naughty girl…

My heart thunders in my chest as I wait to see what's going to come next.

But it doesn't. Not immediately anyway.

I start to relax, thinking he's just trying to wind me up but then it dings again, and dread fills me.

Opening it once again, I gasp as I find a photo of Zayn and me in my yard last night. It's from after our game of soccer when he almost kissed me.

Fuck.

Pocketing my cell before Ruby looks over, not that she's likely to see as some of the squad have descended on her, I turn back around to where he was only moments ago, only this time, he's not there.

I look around the hallway, but he's nowhere to be seen.

My heart thunders in my chest as I think about him knowing what we've been up to. Up until now, he's never had anything to bargain with. I've never had secrets, well, aside from my home life, so he's never been able to use anything against me.

Until now.

If he goes to Harley, or worse, Jake, then shit is going to hit the fan.

Fuck, fuck, fuck.

I look around in the hope I spot Zayn. I need to warn him, but him or any of the team are nowhere to be seen.

"Ready for chemistry?" Ruby asks, dragging herself away from the squad.

"Uh... yeah, can't wait."

"Are you okay? You look really pale."

"Yeah, I'm good. Let's do this."

Ruby threads her arm through mine and together we make our way toward our first class of the day.

My skin prickles as we move, telling me that although I couldn't see him, he's still watching me.

Well, this day certainly went to shit faster than I was hoping for.

16

———

Zayn

"Zayn," Mom bellows the second I close the front door behind me. All the good feelings I had running around my body instantly vanish with the tone of her voice. "Get your ass in here right now."

I already know I'm in the shit before I look at her, I can tell by her tone. I'm sure there could be a number of things that could have pissed her off, but I've got a suspicion this afternoon might have just caught up with me.

I round the corner and her murderous eyes land on me instantly.

"You've been suspended," she spits.

"Fuck," I mutter, running my hand over my head.

"Yeah. *Fuck*. Principal Hartmann said you beat a junior up for no reason."

"It wasn't for no reason, Mom. I'm not a monster."

Her brows rise. I know I'm not totally innocent and that

life before our move to Rosewood was a little different from what it is now. Fighting in Harrow Creek was a daily occurrence but since moving here, I've mostly managed to keep my nose out of trouble.

"Hartmann said you tricked him out of class and attacked him in the locker room. Is that right?"

"Yes," I sigh, walking toward her and jumping up on the opposite stool. "He's not a good person, Mom. He more than deserved it."

"Well..." She blows out a breath. Mom knows that I've always been honest with her. If I've fucked up, I've confessed. I've never hidden anything from her, so I know that she wants to believe what I'm saying, but at the same time she wants to rip me a new one for my actions. "That may very well be true. But this isn't how you go about it."

"He's hurting someone I care about. I couldn't sit back and ignore it."

Her eyes narrow at my admission. I've never, ever mentioned anything about caring for someone before. I've never even had a girlfriend that she's met. Never wanted one. So I understand why she's shocked.

"Anything you need to talk about?"

I think of Poppy and everything she's forced to endure because of her shitty parents, let alone Preston.

I know that I should probably tell Mom. She could help, she would help. But I've already gone behind Poppy's back once today. I refuse to betray her twice.

"No, I'm good. I know I shouldn't have done it, Mom. But something needed to happen. I refuse to sit back and allow him to hurt someone."

"Someone you care about," she reminds me, as if I need it. I can still taste her, feel the heat of her body against mine. "Anyone I know? The girl from your bed the other morning by any chance? I didn't recognize her, but then most of your friends are normally clothed when I see them."

"Mom," I groan, rolling my eyes. "No, it's not her. It's... no one, it doesn't matter."

She narrows her eyes at me, instead of saying anything, she reaches out and squeezes my hand.

I'm about to get up and walk away when her voice stops me.

"I trust you, Zayn. You've got a good head on your shoulders. If you say it was necessary, then I believe you, but you can't go around doing this. It's senior year and you've got too much to lose."

I nod, standing from the stool.

"We've got a meeting with Hartmann first thing, and you've got to pick up work from your teachers."

"Great."

"You'd better work your ass off here this week, boy."

"All week?" I ask.

"Yep. All week."

I groan as I walk away, stopping at the refrigerator to pull out a soda before going to my room.

Well, this day really has gone to shit.

Sure, I was kinda expecting it. But it doesn't mean it sucks any less.

My need to tell Poppy has me reaching into my pocket for my cell as I climb the stairs.

My thumb hovers over the keys, but I realize that I can't tell her this yet. I'm suspended because I was trying to protect her from Preston. If I'm not there, then... *shit*. Mom's right. I really didn't think this through.

Ignoring my need to tell her, I go down a different route with my message. Hopefully one that will make her smile, remind her just how incredible tonight was before she finds out the truth tomorrow.

———

Morning rolls around all too quickly.

"Why aren't you ready for school?" Harley snaps at me when I join her in the kitchen.

"Didn't Mom tell you? I'm suspended."

Her eyes open amusingly wide. "No. Why?"

"I beat the shit out of Preston."

"That was you? How didn't I know this?"

"I'm sorry that the first thing I did after wasn't to go running to my little sister to tell her," I mutter, going for the coffee machine. Although, I already know that caffeine isn't going to be enough right now.

"Fuck off. Why'd you hit him?"

"Why not? That guy is a class A prick."

"Agreed but it's not like you to go around swinging your fist because you feel like it, well, not here anyway."

"It just did, okay? I'm going back to bed."

"Don't forget our meeting," Mom says, breezing into the kitchen. "I've had to move my entire day around for this, so make sure you're ready."

"I'll be ready," I call down to her.

We're almost at school when the first class of the day is about to start. I haven't heard anything from Poppy, so I can only assume that she's not heard the gossip yet. That's not overly surprising seeing as she keeps her head down and tries to avoid almost everything that happens in that place.

Just before Mom parks, I drag out my cell and send her a simple message. I probably should say more, but I have no idea how to explain what I want to say to her.

Zayn: I'm so sorry.

I stare at the screen for a minute, but it never shows as

read before I'm forced to get out of the car and walk beside Mom to listen to Hartmann rip me a new one.

To be fair, the meeting isn't as bad as I thought it might be. And I can't help but wonder if that was because Hartmann also wanted his chance to punch Hellburn in the face. I wouldn't put it past him. It's no secret that Preston's father donates a hefty check to the school once a year, allowing Preston to act like a douchebag because he thinks his father owns this place.

Entitled prick.

I allow Hartmann to give me his speech about how he expects his students to behave, let alone members of our successful team. Blah, blah, blah.

My fist clench and my teeth grind with my need to tell both Hartmann and Mom just what a prick Preston really is, but without breaking my promise to Poppy again, I can't. All I can hope is that he fucks up soon before anyone gets hurt, and shows himself for what he really is.

Thankfully, my teachers have already delivered me a stack of work, and by the time we leave his office, I've got enough to keep me occupied for a month, let alone four days off school.

"Well, that wasn't so bad," I mutter as Mom and I head out to the parking lot.

"Zayn," she breathes. "You're suspended. How is that going to look to UCLA?"

"They won't care, Mom. Kids get suspended all the time. I've got a solid GPA, plus football. This is nothing."

"I hope you're right," she mumbles, unlocking the car and ripping the door open.

"They've probably already made their decision anyway."

"How are you so calm about it? Don't you want it anymore?"

I shake my head. "Of course I want it." UCLA has been my dream for as long as I can remember but I try to keep levelheaded about it. I've worked my ass off, written what I hope is a stellar application. All I can do now is wait. If it's meant to be then it will be, if not, there are plenty of other incredible colleges out there.

"Well, could you at least look a little bit anxious about it. I think I'm feeling it for the both of us."

"Everything will be fine, Mom." Reaching over, I squeeze her hand.

She nods before backing out of the space ready to kick my ass out at home so she can head to work.

A week of sitting at home on my own. Not exactly my idea of fun but then I guess this is meant to be a punishment. Even if that motherfucker did deserve it.

17

Poppy

Zayn: I'm so sorry.

My brows pinch as I stare at those three little words. Dread starts to fill me as I try to think about what he's sorry about.

Sorry about last night? About what we did?

It was all a joke, wasn't it?

My temperature spikes as anger swells within me. My stomach turns over and I have no choice but to push my chair out behind me as I run to the bathroom to save me from puking all over my desk.

By the time I push into the stall, the feeling has subsided, although the anger is still burning strong.

Tears sting my eyes as I think about everything he gave me yesterday. How light he made me feel as he took me away from the stress of my life.

"You motherfucker," I scream into the silence of the bathroom as I finally give in to the tears.

When Ruby bursts into the room she finds me curled up in a ball on the floor, still crying.

"Jesus, Poppy, are you okay?" she asks, dropping to her knees beside me.

"Y-yeah. I'm sorry. I don't know what came over me." I risk looking up and all I find in front of me are a pair of knowing eyes.

"Something to do with this maybe." She passes my cell over. The screen is now blank but from the look on her face I'm assuming she saw what made me run.

"What's he done?"

"I... I don't know," I admit.

"So why are you in here crying if you don't know what he's done?"

"He regrets it, doesn't he? Do you think it was just a dare like New Year, a game like his birthday?"

"Uh..." Ruby comes to sit beside me, our shoulders touching as she reaches for my hand. "I'm sure it wasn't."

"I need to find him," I say with renewed enthusiasm as the idea of going and ripping him a new one for treating me like this hits me.

"Y-you can't," Ruby says, her grip on me tightening.

"Why can't I?"

"Haven't you heard the gossip?"

I look at her with raised brows. "When do I ever listen to the gossip?"

She rolls her eyes at me. "He's been suspended for punching Preston's lights out. Any idea why he did that, by the way?"

"What? Why didn't you tell me this sooner?" I bark at her.

"I thought you knew. You clearly spent most of last night with him. I assumed he told you."

"Jesus, Ruby." I push from the floor and grab a paper towel to clean up my face with.

"What?" she asks innocently. "So that makes everything better now that you know he's been suspended for fighting."

"Well, no." But it sure gives me a better idea as to why he's sorry. I don't need to remember the smirk on Preston's face earlier to understand why he looked so fucking happy.

Jesus. This is a fucking mess.

"You need to talk to Harley about this, Jake too."

"Yeah," I agree.

"Come on, you ready to get back to class?"

"Yeah," I say sadly, already regretting running out like that. I've just made myself an even bigger target by acting like a complete nutcase. My MO is to keep my head down at every opportunity and try to blend as much as possible in an attempt not to give him any more ammunition to come at me with.

The second we both step back into class, all eyes turn on us—well, me—including the teacher.

"Everything okay?" she asks me, her brows pulling together in concern.

"Yeah, I'm sorry, I just felt a little..." I trail off. "I'm good now, thank you."

She nods at me, although the concern doesn't leave her face.

Ruby retakes her seat but the second I turn away from Mrs. Pritchard, *his* eyes pin me to the spot. An evil smile curls at his lips before he blows me a kiss and raises a brow.

Fear snakes around me and for a second I wonder if I'm about to run back out of the room. But I swallow it down, rip my eyes from his and march back to my seat to continue with the lesson.

I unlock my cell when Mrs. Pritchard is distracted once more and find another message waiting for me.

Zayn: If he tries anything tell me and I'll be there in a flash.

My fingers squeeze my cell.

If he tries anything, does Zayn not know Preston at all? Of course he's going to try something.

My cell vibrates in my hand once more. Expecting it to be him, I quickly wake it back up but the unknown number I find staring back at me turns my body to ice.

Unknown: While the bodyguard is away, Preston gets to play…

My muscles tense and I hate myself for reacting. His stare burns into my back, I don't need to turn around to know that he's smiling in the knowledge that he's getting to me.

Locking my cell, I shove it into my pocket deciding against replying to Zayn or being forced to read anything else from Preston.

His attention never leaves me and the second the bell to the end of first period rings, I stuff my books into my bag and practically run from the room.

I almost collide with Amalie as I make my escape down the hallway.

"Whoa, something on fire?" she asks, looking me over.

"Sorry, just excited to get to gym," I lie.

"Are you okay, you look a little terrified?"

"Yeah, I'm good. Honestly."

The rest of the school thankfully descend in the hallways and any chance we had of having a conversation comes to an end.

"I'll see you later, yeah?"

"Sure," she says, but I hear the concern in her voice.

When did I stop becoming so good at hiding how I was

really feeling? *Probably about the same time you let Zayn put his hands on you, again.*

Locking down the little voice in my head, I march toward the girl's locker room, thankful that Preston isn't going to be anywhere near me.

"Ah, you decided to show your face then?"

"Ugh, yeah. I had such a hair nightmare this morning," Harley complains, running her hand over her bangs.

"Looks perfect to me."

"It should after the amount of time I spent on it. I could really do without volleyball right now, it's going to ruin it."

"I'm sure you'll still look stunning, Har."

"Whoa, you look a little too lively today. You knocked back a few Red Bulls or something this morning?" she asks when I instantly start getting changed as if I'm actually looking forward to what's to come.

"No, just feeling a little pumped."

I still when her hand lands on my forearm. "Are you okay?"

"Yes," I snap. "I'm fine. Your mom pissed then, or what?" I ask, hoping to get the heat off me.

"Pissed doesn't really cover it. I didn't know why she was in such a mood when I got in last night though. I only found out this morning. I thought she was going to blow a fuse though, and I don't think it helped that he spent most of the night out avoiding her."

My cheeks heat and I keep my back turned to her and I continue changing into my gym clothes. "Have you spoken to him about it?"

"Nah, not really."

"So you don't know why he did it?"

"No, but does anyone really need a specific reason to hit Preston? I would, given half the chance, he's a dick, and he treats you like shit."

You don't even know the half of it.

"Come on, girls. You can spread the gossip at lunchtime," Miss White shouts, clapping her hands together in the hope we speed up a little.

Volleyball helped to release a little bit of the tension that was pulling at my muscles, but it didn't last because the second I walked into every other class I had for the rest of the morning, his cold evil eyes followed.

When the bell rang for lunch, I ignored my empty stomach and instead took myself to the library. The music rooms are usually my sanctuary, but after yesterday, I don't feel safe going there. I need to do something out of character to throw him off, so the final aisle of the library away from everyone else is it.

I drop my bag to the floor before lowering my ass to the ground and tipping my head back against the books and closing my eyes for a beat.

The sound of others filter through the air, but no one is anywhere near me, thank God. I just need a few minutes of not looking over my shoulder, of wondering when he's going to strike. There's no if, it's just when and I want to be prepared for when it happens.

Each minute ticks by as if it's an hour.

I wish I had a car, so I could get away from it all then. I could go to the beach. Walk along the sand and feel the waves against my feet. I can't even remember the last time I did that. Or I could drive up to the cliffs where we used to go for picnics when things were relatively okay and just watch the clouds.

Anything other than being here like a sitting duck waiting for the inevitable.

My cell dings and I reluctantly pull it from my pocket. I pray that it's Zayn. He's sent a couple more since I ignored his messages this morning. But I haven't even opened them. I have no idea what I'm even supposed to say.

It was easy last night, he left me on a high and our banter was easy. Today with the weight of the world pressing down on me, I have no idea what to say to him.

Only when I look at the screen, I find it's not him and my stomach sinks into the pit of my stomach.

Unknown: Come out, come out, wherever you are...

My cell trembles in my hand as I stare down at his words.

I fucking knew he'd be looking for me.

The temptation to get up and run out of the school is strong, but I refuse to let him win. He will not break me.

I don't unlock my cell for fear it might open the message and show him I've seen it, instead I shove it to the bottom of my bag. My hand hits a packet as I do so and I find a smashed up cereal bar that I spend the rest of lunch nervously nibbling on.

He's not in my final classes of the day, and I almost begin to breathe normally again knowing that I'm going to be able to lock myself at home soon and try to put this day behind me.

Not having Zayn here shouldn't make any difference. I'd managed all this time without him having my back, but only a few days after he figures out there's something going on and I'm already relying on him.

It's pathetic and I chastise myself over and over before the final bell of the day rings out.

I'm stronger than having to rely on a boy to protect me.

The second the bell rings, I sweep my books from the desk and run for my locker. If I didn't have books in there I needed for tonight's homework then I'd run straight out the doors and not look back, well, not until tomorrow.

Both Ruby and Harley have practice, so unless I want to risk hanging around for a bus, my only option is to walk.

Shifting my bag up higher on my shoulder, I set off.

Every car that passes has me on edge, but almost an hour after I set off, I drag my tired legs up our street.

"Hey, good day at school?" Mom asks as I push through the front door.

I do a double take when I find that she's actually showered and dressed today.

"Uh... yeah... it was... fine." A lump crawls its way up my throat at my lie.

As I stand before her, all I want is for her to be a normal mom and for her to pull me in for a hug and tell me that everything's going to be okay.

But that's not my reality.

"You been somewhere nice?" I ask, dropping my bag to the bottom step and heading for the kitchen to find some food.

"We went to the store for some supplies."

Thankfully, I've got my back to her so she doesn't see me roll my eyes at her need for supplies. They sure aren't the same kind as other parents make an effort to go out for.

"Does that mean we have food in the house?"

"Don't be so cheeky, young lady."

"Cheeky?" I ask, astonished. I spin to her and take in her irritated expression. "Oh my God, you're serious, aren't you? Unbelievable," I mutter to myself. "Well seeing as you believe your words, how about you parent your own children when they turn up from their after-school club tonight."

"Why? What are you doing?"

"I don't know. Maybe I'll go out and get drunk like every other kid at school gets to do while I'm babysitting your offspring."

Grabbing a bag of chips and a couple of cans of soda that are sitting on the counter, I storm past her and up the stairs.

I don't usually say anything to her about the disaster that our family is but I've just about had my fill today.

I slam my bedroom door so hard that it makes the entire

house shake before flipping the lock I installed after Zayn's first visit.

I didn't do it in the hope he'd come back, but as Austin interrupted us that day, I realized just how little privacy I get in this place and I stopped off at the hardware store and picked it up.

I throw the doors open to my balcony and kick my shoes off before launching myself on my bed and shoving my head into my pillow.

Today can go suck it.

18

Zayn

I stare at the unread messages with dread sitting heavy in my stomach.

He wouldn't have done anything, would he?

I tap my finger on the side, trying to decide if I'm just making a bigger deal out of this than necessary.

Poppy has clearly handled this to a point for a while now. This hasn't suddenly just started. But that doesn't do anything to settle the trepidation swirling around within me like a tornado.

I could send her another message, but if she refuses to read that one too, I'm in no better position, other than starting to look a little desperate. That's not really a look I crave, like, ever.

"Fuck it," I mutter to myself, shoving my feet in my sneakers and slipping from my room.

It's late, the sun has already long set and the winter wind whips around me when I step from the house.

I've spent all day working in the hope I could get everything done and emailed in so I can spend the rest of my impromptu days off doing something a little more fun. Although that's unlikely with all my friends and teammates spending their days in class.

I push my key into the ignition and turn the engine, my truck rumbles to life and I set off.

Mom's not here, she's out at some dinner with some colleagues and Harley has locked herself in her bedroom, probably fighting with some more math homework that she refuses to let me help with.

I'm at Poppy's house before I know it. The lights are on and unlike last time, I see her family all sitting around the table in the dining room like they're... normal.

It's an odd sight after everything I discovered here last night. Only, when I walk around the side of the house, I find that Poppy isn't with them.

Not wanting to interrupt, especially if she's not home, I walk around to the backyard and look up at her bedroom.

The lights are out but the curtains blow in the wind where the doors are open.

Spotting a ladder that's resting against the wall, I move it a little closer to her balcony and without a second thought, I climb.

My heart's in my chest as I throw my leg over the railing and step onto the balcony. This probably wasn't my wisest move, but I guess it's a little late now.

The room is cold and silent as I step inside. The light from the moon allows me to see the lump in the bed and as I get closer, I find that she's sleeping.

The sight of her in one piece settles something inside me.

As gently as possible, I sit down beside her. Unable to keep my hands to myself, I reach out and run my knuckles down her cheek.

Her eyelids flutter at my touch. She blinks a couple of times before she realizes she has company. She gasps, and fearing a scream is about to rip from her throat, I gently press my hand over her mouth, not wanting to alert her parents.

"It's okay. It's just me."

Her eyes focus after a beat and she relaxes, although she looks anything but pleased to see me.

"How did you get in here?" she whispers, looking to her locked door.

"I climbed. You should probably move that ladder in the yard, anyone could let themselves in here while you sleep." I drop my lips to her ear. "It might not end as pleasurably as my visit."

"You shouldn't be here." Her voice is all deep and rough from sleep and it makes my cock swell.

"But I am," I say, leaning forward and brushing my lips against hers.

"You need to leave," she breathes, although there's no strength behind it.

"What would be the fun in that when I could stay here and get you off instead?"

"I'm mad at you," she breathes, her eyes boring into mine.

"When aren't you?" Running my hand over her shoulder, I wrap my fingers around the back of her neck, my thumb stroking over the soft skin over her pulse point. It thunders beneath my touch, giving away how she really feels about my visit. "Stop fighting what you want, Pops."

"I told you not to get involved," she whispers. "Now you've been suspended because of it."

"It doesn't matter. It was worth it."

"Risking your future?"

"Jeez, you sound like my mom."

"Yeah, because I ca—" She abruptly cuts herself off.

"What was that?" I ask, my tone lighter than a few moments ago.

"Nothing."

"No, no. You were going to say something." My grip on her tightens a little.

"I wasn't going to say anything."

"I'm pretty sure you were about to admit that you care about me."

She huffs, making me laugh. "You're my best friend's brother. Of course I want you to do well."

"Oh, is that why. Not because of this." Closing the small amount of space between us, I crush my lips to hers in a bruising kiss.

Flicking the covers off her, I run my hand down her body.

"Zayn," she moans, arching into my hand. "You need to go."

"Your words might be saying that, but your body is telling me something else, Pops." I cup her breast, pinching her nipple through the thin fabric of her tank.

"No, Zayn." At her refusal, I pull back, my brows pinching together.

"What's wrong?"

"We shouldn't be doing this and you know it."

"But—"

"No, no buts. I'm doing what I should have done days ago. This can't happen between us. You need to leave."

My eyes bounce between hers, waiting for her to tell me that she's joking.

"You're serious right now, aren't you?"

"Yeah. I am."

I study her for a few more seconds before backing away. Her walls have come up, I can practically see them and I know I've got no chance of scaling them right now.

"What happened today?"

"Nothing, Zayn. You need to stop trying to protect me. Just go back to not even realizing that I exist."

"Pops. I've always known you exist."

"Well you had a funny way of showing it while you were whoring yourself around the cheer squad. Now get out."

"Fine." I push from the bed and back up toward the door. "I guess I still get to tell the guys that I got between your legs."

She gasps at my words and I immediately hate myself for making what was between us sound any less serious.

"Get the hell out, asshole." Her voice cracks at the end and my fingers twitch to reach out for her, my apology is right on the tip of my tongue but when she turns her back on me, cutting off our connection, I know I've got no choice but to do as she said.

I climb down and then take the ladder that made my entrance so easy to the very bottom of their property. The thought of someone else making use of it and letting themselves in while she's sleeping does not sit right with me.

With a glance back at her bedroom, I make my way to my truck.

I slam my palms down on the wheel in frustration. That wasn't how that was supposed to go.

I don't remember the drive home but the second I get home I run into someone I really don't have the energy for.

"Shouldn't you be grounded or something?" Harley asks, popping her hip and resting her hand on it.

"What the fuck does it have to do with you?"

"Wow, you're in a delightful mood this evening. Miss out on your daily cheer slut attention or something?"

"Fuck off, Har." I push past her and storm through to the kitchen and toward Mom's drinks cabinet.

"Mom will flip her shit if she finds you stealing from that."

I roll my eyes at the fact she followed me. Of course she fucking did, goody two shoes.

"Yeah, well, what if I don't give a shit. Go run along and tell her, see if I care."

Swiping a bottle of vodka, I slam my shoulder into hers and march from the room.

"Ow, that fucking hurt, asshole."

I don't respond. I've already said too much. Instead, I march toward my bedroom, slam the door and flip the lock to ensure she stays the fuck out of my business.

19

Poppy

My chest heaves and tears burn the backs of my eyes as I listen to Zayn climb back down the ladder.

Did I want to send him away? No, not really. But I also knew that I couldn't keep doing this.

Last night, he made me feel so incredible. With barely more than a touch, he made me forget everything.

It made today hit me harder than ever. I don't need that. I don't need to get lost in a boy.

I just need to survive.

I need to go back into the shadows, pretend that I don't really exist and get through the next eighteen months.

Once I know he's at the bottom, I climb from the bed and peer out of the curtain.

My chest aches as I watch him move the ladder. He's so

damn thoughtful. It makes me wonder if I just made a massive mistake.

But I didn't.

We can't happen.

There are so, so many reasons why anything further happening between us would be a bad idea.

I blow out a breath as he disappears from my sight and my shoulders slump in defeat. I've given up asking why I was dealt this life when I could have had an easy one that allowed me to hang out with friends whenever I wanted, to have any boy I wanted and to walk through school with my head held high. But I still can't help wondering why I got stuck with this shit.

Dragging my eyes away from the darkness outside, I push through my bathroom door. I've only taken two steps inside when I sense a person already in here with me. But I don't get a chance to scream because a sweaty hand covers my mouth and my back and head collides with the wall.

Pain spears down my neck from the force of the collision and my eyes immediately begin to water.

Cold devil eyes stare down at me.

"I didn't think you were ever going to join me, Pops." He uses the name that Zayn calls me, and my stomach turns over.

He heard all of that, saw all of that.

I swallow down the bile that threatens as I hold his stare.

My heart beats wildly in my chest as my body trembles in fear. I hate that he can probably feel it, that he knows I'm scared right now.

His eyes are wide, his pupils blown and he stinks of weed.

"It's a shame your bodyguard had to leave so quickly, I thought the two of you were going to give me a private show. I would say it's a shame, but I'm not sure I'd want his sloppy seconds." He leans in, his rotten breath filling my nose and turning my stomach once more. "I much prefer to be the first. He can pick you up after I've finished with you, if there's anything left."

I try to shout, scream, anything, but my voice is muffled against his disgusting hand and my body is frozen in fear.

"You know, I thought you'd at least try to fight. Has your boyfriend taught you nothing?"

"Fuck you." I spit into his hand, not that he can probably make it out.

"And here I was thinking you were waiting for me." He lifts his spare hand and cups my breast.

I try to flinch away from him but I've got nowhere to go, and I've got no hope of overpowering him.

The tears I desperately don't want to shed fill my eyes as his hand roams, moving to the other side and pinching my nipples until they react to his touch.

"No, no, no," I chant. "Please, no," I cry as he pulls at my tank with such force it rips, exposing my bare breasts to him.

"Oh, Pops. What have we got here?" His wild eyes drop to my breasts.

Slamming my eyes close, I turn my head away, not able to watch him looking at me with that hunger in his eyes.

"Look at me, Poore," he spits, using my last name.

My eyes fly open and I'm forced to watch as he rubs himself through his pants as he stares at my breasts.

"I wonder if you taste as bitter as I've always imagined."

I shake my head wildly as he licks his lips, sucking his bottom one into his mouth.

His fingertip circles my nipple and as much as I hate his touch, my traitorous body reacts to it, heat pools between my thighs.

I don't think I've ever hated myself and my life more in that moment.

Moving from my breast, he trails his fingers down my stomach until he finds the waistband of my shorts.

My eyes are wide as he teases the skin. He's really going to do it this time.

Finding my fight, my arms fly at him, my nails scratching at any bit of skin I can connect with.

"Fucking bitch," he groans when I manage to gouge a chunk of skin from his upper arm that's holding my mouth hostage.

His hand drops and he manages to take hold of both of my wrists and lifts them above my head.

His eyes run the length of me again before he brushes his cheek against mine. "Be a good girl and don't scream. Well, not until you're coming on my fingers anyway."

His words repulse me. "What the fuck is your problem? What do you think this is going to achieve?"

"Who says I want to achieve anything?"

"You want Jake to make you captain. I can assure you that this isn't the way to make it happen. When he finds out—"

"Which he won't," he warns.

"You won't be alive long enough to play a game as a senior, let alone captain it."

An evil smile curls at his lips.

"That's where you're wrong, little girl."

"I'm fucking older than you, asshole," I spit. "The only fucking baby here is you. You're fucking pathetic." I spit at him and he backs away a little in shock.

"Bitch," he roars, backhanding me across the face. "Know you're fucking place."

"My place is not being terrorized in my own home by a fucking psychopath." The last thing I want to do right now is have a conversation with him, but I figure that the longer I put off the inevitable, the more chance I have of either figuring a way out of this or someone interrupting him.

If I had normal parents, they might be likely to come and check on me, especially after how I spoke to Mom earlier but as it is, I'm sure she's already forgotten.

His growl makes my body tremble harder.

"I'm going to fucking ruin you. Jake won't have a choice but to do exactly what I want if he wants you alive."

"No one gives a shit about me. Haven't you noticed that during all your stalking?"

"Shut the fuck up. I didn't come here to have a conversation with you."

"Fine," I say, glancing around the room, my eyes locking on something that might get me out of this sooner rather than later. "Do your worst."

"I fucking knew you wanted me." His hand loosens on my wrists allowing me to slip one way while the other plunges into my panties. "Oh, baby. So wet for me."

I fight not to retch as his fingers graze my clit. While he's distracted, I reach out, grabbing the cup I keep my toothbrush in and with as much force as I can manage, I swing it toward his head.

"Motherfucker," he barks, stumbling away from me and thankfully removing his touch.

I sag back against the wall, but I can't allow myself to relax yet.

He looks back at me, blood trickling down the side of his face.

"Now get the fuck out of my house," I demand. "Before I scream for my parents and have your ass thrown into jail."

"Oh, baby. We both know your drugged-up parents don't give a shit."

I gasp. He knows.

To my amazement, he stumbles toward the door. "This isn't over, Poore," he spits before thankfully disappearing from the small room.

Stumbling back, I crash against the wall and slide down until my ass hits the floor.

My adrenaline runs out and I drop my head into my arms and sob. My entire body trembles with the fear I still feel with the disgust.

He was in here watching and listening to me with Zayn. He was waiting for me. Waiting to... I can't even allow myself to think about what his intentions might have been.

He knows about my parents, which means he probably knows that he could get away with almost anything without alerting them.

Suddenly, I think of the ladder that Zayn moved away from the house to stop people coming up and I jump to my feet. If that's gone then how did he get out?

I stand in the doorway to my en suite, my body exposed and stare at my open bedroom door.

He just walked straight through my house after that. What if someone saw him?

Without allowing myself to think about the answer, I race over, close my door and flip the lock again.

Pulling my ruined tank around me, I suck in deep lungfuls of air, trying to calm myself down.

Okay, so he touched me, he hurt me, but I'm okay. I'll be okay.

After closing and locking the balcony doors, I tell myself never to open them again and strip out of my clothes, dropping it all in the trash. I'll never be able to wear any of it again without seeing his evil eyes and feel his bruising touch.

I turn the shower on hot and step under, allowing it to burn my skin. To singe his touch from me, to banish his scent that's clinging to my skin.

Sinking down to the floor once more, I wrap my arms around my legs as silent tears drop.

I want to call Zayn. I want to feel his arms around me and

have his scent in my nose, reminding me that I'm safe, but as I walk from my bathroom, my body still trembling, I don't reach for my phone.

I sent him away for a reason. I need to be stronger than breaking my resolve only an hour later because Preston decided to pounce.

I'm in a daze as I pull on a fresh set of pajamas and crawl into bed. I curl into a ball and torture myself by reliving the events of tonight over and over.

Alarm bells should have gone off when Zayn mentioned the ladder, but that thing has been tucked alongside the fence for years, I just assumed he'd made use of it. I had no reason to believe that he was the second one to let himself in while I slept.

Thanks to my afternoon nap, it meant that I laid there tossing and turning for hours while being tormented by the memory of Preston's cold eyes and evil touch.

When my alarm went off this morning, I swear I'd only just fallen asleep. My eyes are still heavy and my muscles ache as I drag my ass toward my next class.

I haven't seen or heard from Preston, thank God. I know he's in school though. I've heard others talking about the fight he had last night and how the guy he fought is apparently fighting for his life in the hospital. I refrain from informing the gossips that it's all a load of bullshit. No one would believe me if I even tried.

He's still weirdly absent by the time lunch rolls around, but I know he's just in the shadows waiting somewhere, so just like yesterday, I take myself to the back of the library.

It's busier than the day before but I find an empty aisle and dump my stuff on the floor, ready to wait out the lunch break until I can go to class and then hide at home, with my doors locked tonight.

Pulling out my cell, I find a message from Harley asking if I'm coming to the cafeteria for lunch. I quickly tap out a lie that I'm still in class working on an assignment, before reluctantly opening the stream of messages I have from Zayn that I've been ignoring.

He starts off with an apology for last night, promising me that he'll back off, but also that he misses me. He tells me what work he's got to do today and explains how bored he is alone.

I debate replying. I might have sent him away last night but that doesn't mean I couldn't do with someone to talk to right now. But I don't get a chance to make a final decision because another message comes through, one from a number that fills the blood in my veins with ice.

Unknown: You can run but you can't hide…

A picture message follows, I stare down at a picture of me looking at my cell, much like I am now.

My head flies up in the direction he must have been in to take that picture, but there's no one to be seen.

"Fuck," I hiss to myself.

I make a snap decision.

Poppy: Are you still in the cafeteria? I'm done now.

Harley replies immediately to say they are, and I throw my bag over my shoulder and head out.

Safety in numbers and all that. Maybe hiding was the stupidest thing to do.

I spend the rest of the day looking over my shoulder, waiting for him to jump out of the shadows. But he never does.

Part of me is relieved. But the other part knows that he's just waiting for the right time and I wonder if it would be better to just get it over with.

But it seems he's not in any rush to continue what he started like he warned because the rest of the afternoon and the next day passes with nothing. Even his irritating messages stop.

As the hours pass, I become more and more jumpy, to the point I piss myself off.

When a note arrives for me not long before the end of my last lesson of the day from Miss French to remind me that I should be in a guidance counselor meeting, I don't think anything of it.

I can't deny that I've been avoiding having to sit down with her, and I've missed more than one appointment with my need to put off having to even consider any serious decisions about my future. I was hoping with application season in full swing that she'd have her hands full with the seniors and leave me alone for a little while to shove my head farther in the sand.

Sadly, it seems that's not the case.

I pack up my stuff and my teacher barely even looks up when I show him the note. With a sigh, I walk out of his classroom. No one else even spares me a second glance, they're either too busy with what they should be doing or lost in their own conversations with the people surrounding them while our teacher pretends to ignore them. Idiots.

Miss French's office is only a short walk and everyone else is in class, so I don't think to look over my shoulder as I make my way down the hallway. That is until a door opens behind me and a very familiar hand clamps over my mouth and an arm wraps around my waist.

I'm too shocked to scream, not that it would do any good. But seconds before I'm dragged backward into the storage closet, I manage to make use of my legs and start kicking in the hope of making contact and forcing him to let go of me before it's too late.

"Fucking bitch," he grunts as my heel connects with his shin. But it's not enough because the walls close in on me before the door closes and I find myself thrown up against the metal shelves that line the walls.

Pain shoots down my spine from where it connects with one of the edges before I fall to the floor.

A loud click sounds out in the silent space and my body begins to tremble.

There's only a single light bulb hanging from the ceiling that lets out a dim light, but it's enough to make a shadow fall over me when he stands above me.

"What do you want?" I snap, digging deep and finding some strength to fight him when all I really want to do is curl up in a ball and cry that I allowed him to get to me so easily.

"What do I want? I think we both know the answer to that question, don't we, Poore."

"It's not going to work. Whatever you do to me isn't going to make Jake give you his team."

"Maybe not, but I may as well have some fun trying."

"Fun? You think this is fun?"

"Oh, Poppy. You're the most fun I've had in a long, long time."

He crouches down before me, his cold eyes drilling into mine.

"Y-you don't look like you're enjoying yourself right now."

He smiles at me. It's so sinister and terrifying that it makes my stomach drop into the tips of my toes.

He's going to fucking kill me in here if I give him half a chance.

"What are you going to do to me?" I ask, my voice weaker than I'd like.

"We're going to play. Do you like to play games, Pops?"

"With you? No."

"Well," he says, reaching out and wrapping his hot fingers around my throat, lifting me from the floor as if I weigh nothing more than a feather. My back once again collides with the shelving and my head bounces off one, causing me to shut my eyes for a beat. "That's a real shame, because I really want to play with you. And do you know what? You're going to really enjoy it."

"No," I spit.

"Ah, but you forget. I remember how wet you were for me last time. How much you wanted me to get you off, how you craved my touch."

"Never," I hiss.

My arm flies up to hit him, but he's quicker, and I find myself trapped in his hold.

"We can do this the easy way, or the hard way. It's really your choice."

"I'm not playing your fucking games."

"Hard way it is then." My front is slammed against the wall, my cheekbone smarting from where it connects as he binds my hands with tape behind my back.

"Better. I'm not really into scratchers. I prefer to be the one dishing out the pain."

I tug at the restraints testing how tight they are but without a hell of a lot more force, I'm not getting out of them anytime soon. "You can't hurt me, Preston. You're nothing to me."

"You sure about that?" Before he's even finished the words,

the back of his hand forces my head to snap to the side. My eyes fill with tears as my already painful cheek burns with his slap.

"Fuck you. Do what you want to me. I'll make sure you never get your way. Jake will never let you have his team."

I'm spun around, my back once again against the wall as his hand squeezes my throat so hard it becomes harder and harder to suck in air to breathe, white spots start swimming in my eyes.

"I'm going to ruin you until he has no choice but to give me what I want if he wants you breathing," he snarls in my face, his teeth bared and spittle flying from his mouth with his anger.

I tilt my chin up in defiance, not willing to show him the fear that is wrecking my insides.

Everyone is in class right now. I could scream but really no one will hear me, it would be pointless to even waste the energy trying.

"Go on then. Break me," I hiss at him.

His eyes darken with his desire before his fingers reach for the waistband on my pants.

My stomach turns knowing that there's a very good chance he could succeed this time.

I look around for something to help, for a weapon but with my arms bound behind me, I have no chance of grabbing anything.

The fabric parts and he's just about to push his fingers inside the fabric when the door rattles and the handle moves.

My heart jumps into my throat as Preston's eyes meet mine.

I should scream, alert the person who's outside as to what's going on in here but no matter how hard I try to make the noise rip from my throat, his haunted stare and his ever-tightening grip on my throat ensures my lips stay firmly closed.

"Scream and I'll fucking kill you right now," he whispers, his voice low and menacing.

He removes his touch from my body and reaches behind him. I half expect him to pull a gun on me, but the sight of the smooth metal of a blade turns my blood to ice.

Thankfully, the person outside just mutters a curse before they must disappear.

"They're going to come back with a key," I state, my voice much calmer than the riot that's happening inside me.

"I'd better be quick then. How should I let them find you? Still coming down from the high you're craving or bleeding out from when you deny me?"

"You're a fucking psycho," I spit at him.

"And you need to be taught a fucking lesson." He closes the space between us, his scent filling my nose and making me want to retch.

He places his knife on the shelf and I have a split second to act or he's going to go through with one, or both, of his threats.

While he's distracted, I lift my leg with as much force as I can manage and slam my knee into his crotch.

"Fuck," he barks, releasing his hold on me in favor of clutching his junk.

As fast as I can, I run around him pulling at my restraints with all my might. The tape digs into my wrists, slicing the skin open I'm sure, but I don't stop until it's stretched enough that I can finally pull a hand free. Snatching my bag from the floor where it fell, I run for the door as he hunches over in pain.

"You fucking bitch. You're going to pay for that." I look over my shoulder just in time to see him drop to his knees.

If I were as sick as him, I might take some pleasure in his pain but all I feel is relief.

I flick the lock and run as fast as I can without looking back.

I ignore all the classroom doors and run to the exit.

My lungs burn as I make my way between the buildings until I'm in a dark alcove.

My chest heaves as silent tears stream down my cheeks.

Lifting my arms, I push my sleeves up to look at my wrists. I pull the tape that's still wrapped around one and drop it to the ground. My skin is red with blood starting to dry around the one I pulled free.

"Fuck," I bark, angrily wiping at my cheeks. I'm furious with myself for not even suspecting that attack.

The bell rings out in the buildings before the noise of kids starting to emerge from classrooms begins to get louder.

I take off without putting much thought into it. All I know is that I don't want to be seen and that I don't want him to catch up with me.

With the thought of him trying to follow me home, I turn in the opposite direction. The kids are still at school and Cooper is with a sitter this afternoon, so if he turns up there, he's only got my parents to deal with.

My legs carry me as fast as they'll go, my need to get away from school never stronger.

My muscles burn and my skin is flushed by the time I turn up a familiar street.

I shouldn't be here but I don't know where else to go, where else I'm going to be safe and to forget all about the last hour of my life?

I don't bother knocking, I never do, so it would be weird to start now. Plus, the lack of cars in the driveway point toward only one person being here.

I let myself in and after finding the kitchen empty, I head up the stairs.

Music hits my ears about halfway up, telling me that I'm heading in the right direction.

It's not until I wrap my fingers around the door handle that I begin to question why I'm here, but then the image of Preston staring down at me in that storage closet fills my mind and I know that I don't want to be anywhere else.

20

Zayn

I hear the front door close before footsteps race up the stairs, but despite the fact that Harley should be at cheer practice and Mom told me that she was in meetings all day, I don't really think much of it.

That is until my door swings open and I find a distraught looking Poppy standing there staring at me.

Her hair is a mess, her eyes are red-rimmed and there are tear tracks down her cheeks.

My heart jumps into my throat at the sight of her.

"Fuck, Poppy." I'm off the bed and in front of her before I've even realized that I've moved.

I take her face in my hands and wipe her tears away with my thumbs.

"What's happened? What has he done?"

Dread settles in the pit of my stomach. All of this is my

fault. I lost control and now I haven't been there to keep an eye on her.

She lifts up on her toes and brushes her lips against mine.

"Please, Zayn," she begs. Her hands slip under the fabric of my shirt, her fingertips brushing over my abs. The heat of her touch makes my cock swell. "I need this. I need you."

Her tongue licks across my bottom lip and my restraint snaps.

My fingers thread into her hair as I give in to her kiss.

Desperation pours from her as she clings to me, and as much as I know this probably isn't what we should be doing right now, I'm powerless but to give her what she says she needs.

My tongue sweeps against hers as she loses herself in my kiss. Her hands frantically explore my body before she wraps her fingers around the hem of my shirt and begins pulling it up.

"Off," she mumbles into my mouth.

Reaching behind my head, I grab the fabric and pull, ripping my lips away from hers for the shortest amount of time possible.

I forget about everything I should probably remember in these few moments. I forget about how she sent me away the other night, I forget about what she might have been through today if the look on her face is anything to go by and I just follow her lead.

Her fingers slip inside my sweats and before I know it, they're pooled around my ankles, her hand already beneath the fabric of my boxers, palming my ass.

"Fuck, Poppy," I groan, dropping my lips to her neck and nibbling on the soft, sweet skin. "Up," I encourage, pulling her hoodie up her body then throwing it behind me the second it leaves her body.

"More, Zayn. Everything."

I still at her words.

"Poppy, what's—"

My words are cut off when she presses her fingers to my lips. "Please. I need this. You."

"Fuck, what are you doing to me?"

I stand before her, both our chests heaving, our breaths mingling as our eyes remain locked on each other. She practically begs me not to stop, not to allow her time to think, while I desperately try to do the right thing. But my brain isn't winning in the thinking department right now.

"Please. Make me feel good."

My lips take hers once more in a dirty, wet kiss. Her nails rake down my back as I press her against the wall. Hitching her up, I wrap her legs around my waist, allowing me to grind into her.

I hiss in pleasure as the burning heat from her pussy surrounds my cock. "So good," I groan into her kiss.

"More."

Pulling her from the wall, I find the clasp of her bra and flick it open, ripping the fabric from her body.

My lips drop from hers and down to her neck.

"Oh God. Oh God," she chants as I kiss each of her breasts but ignore her peaked nipples.

Her back arches in pleasure, trying to give me more but still I resist.

"You wet for me, Poppy?"

"You should find out," she breathes, her voice deep and raspy.

Flicking the button on her pants, I push my hand inside.

Her eyes hold mine as my fingers part her and find her swollen clit.

"Zayn," she gasps when I press against it. "Yes."

I push lower, finding her soaked entrance.

"Oh God." I push two fingers inside her tight channel, my cock aching to feel just how hot it might be. "Oh God."

"That good?"

"Yeah," she pants, her eyes locked on where my hand disappears into her pants. Her head falls back against the wall as I circle her clit. "Bed, now." She says it so quietly, I'm not sure I've actually heard the words but as her hand wraps around my forearm and she tugs, I start to think it wasn't my imagination.

Lifting her into my arms, her lips find mine as I carry her over to my bed. The sheets are a mess from this morning, seeing as I had nowhere to go. I quickly sweep them aside before laying her down in the center.

I hesitate with my fingers wrapped around the waistband of her pants but with one nod of her head in agreement, I pull them down her legs, kissing down her torso as I do and finally sucking her nipples into my mouth. She thrashes beneath me, her nails scraping across my head and shoulders as I tease her.

"Zayn, please. I need to feel you."

"You don't need to ask me twice, Pops."

I kiss down her belly, dipping my tongue into her navel before pushing her legs wide and sucking her clit into my mouth. I lick at her, nip her and push two fingers deep inside her, bending them exactly how she likes it.

"Oh God, yes, yes," she chants as her muscles begin to clamp down on me and her body starts to tremble as her release surges forward.

Sucking harder, I push my fingers a little deeper and it sends her over the edge.

"Zayn," she cries as her body convulses.

I pull back once she's come down and stare at her on my bed. Her light brown hair is fanned out over my pillow, her cheeks are flushed, the desperation I saw in her eyes when she first arrived is long gone, completely replaced by heat. Her flush continues down onto her chest and I continue running my eyes down her curves.

"Zayn?" she asks, hesitation creeping into her voice.

I don't say anything, I can't. She's so fucking beautiful, and even better laid out on my bed.

Pushing my boxers from my hips, I crawl onto the bed with her, groaning when the heat of her skin hits mine.

"You're so beautiful," I whisper before sliding my fingers into her hair and crashing my lips to hers once again.

I settle between her legs, the head of my cock teasing her core, causing my desperation for her to skyrocket.

"I want you," she breathes into our kiss.

"Pops," I groan. "It shouldn't be me," I admit, kissing down her neck.

"Says who?"

"Fuck."

"You'll never get to take this back. This is kinda a one-time thing."

"I know," she says, her hungry gray eyes locked on mine. "I need it, Zayn. I need you."

Pushing up from her, I wrap her legs around my waist and take myself in hand, rubbing the head through her heat.

"Oh God," she moans as I tease her already sensitive clit.

"Are you on birth control?"

She shakes her head. "No."

Reaching for my nightstand, I rummage inside until I find a condom.

Her eyes burn my skin as she intently watches me rip it open and roll it down my length.

When I glance up at her, I find her teeth attacking her bottom lip, a small smile playing on them.

"Last chance to change your mind."

"Nope, not happening." Her eyes hold mine as I bend over her, I can see her determination in the gray depths. I probably should question it but right now with my cock lined up at her entrance, I'm not exactly thinking clearly.

"Please," she breathes. "Fuck me, Zayn."

"Jesus." I drop my lips to hers as I grip her ass in one hand and slowly push inside of her with the other. A moan rumbles up my throat as her heat engulfs me, and I'm forced to break our kiss so I can focus on the sensation and attempt to find my restraint. "So tight. So good," I groan, needing her to know how fucking incredible she feels.

A smile curls at her lips.

"More. Don't hold back."

"Pops, I—"

"You're not going to break me, Zayn."

"Fucking hell." I drop down once more, plunging my tongue into her mouth as my hips surge forward.

She cries out into my kiss as I push past her barrier before stilling.

"You okay?" She's gone as hard as stone beneath me and has tears pooling in her eyes. "I'm sorry, I'm so sorry," I whisper, wiping one that drops with the pad of my thumb.

"It's okay. Keep going, please. Make it feel good. Take me away."

She's said so many things since walking through my door that should make me question this, but I'm too lost in her to think straight.

Pulling out of her slowly, I slide back in, keeping our kiss at a similar pace.

It takes a few minutes but before long, her arms emerge from under my pillow in favor of running down my back.

"Okay?"

She nods, her hands dropping to my ass and pulling me tighter into her body.

I drop my lips to her neck as I up my speed, giving her exactly what she craves.

All too soon, the familiar tingles of my impending release start to race down my spine.

"Poppy," I groan. "You feel so good."

"Zayn," she cries, her already tight pussy starting to clamp around me.

"Are you going to come over my cock, Pops?" Just like I suspected, at my dirty words her muscles tighten even more. "You like it when I talk dirty to you, don't you?"

"Zayn," she moans, her back arching.

Sitting up, I change the angle, locking her ankles behind me in one hand and continue to thrust into her.

"Oh fuck," she cries when I press my thumb against her clit.

"You look so fucking hot right now with my cock inside you, baby." She thrashes about on my bed.

"Please, Zayn. I need... I need..."

"I know what you need, Pops."

I grind into her, hitting her deeper than before and after only three more thrusts, her entire body stills for a beat before she falls over the edge.

"Fuuuuck," I groan as she forces me over with her.

I keep moving until we've both come down before pulling out of her, tugging the condom off and dropping it over the side of the bed. I fall down beside her, wrap my arm around her waist and pull her into my side.

"Kiss me," I demand and without missing a beat, she turns her flushed face to me and offers up her lips.

We kiss for ages, just enjoying the feeling of each other's bodies pressed up against the other. My cock aches for another round, but that's not what this is about right now. I want to show her that I can take my time and treat her how she deserves, unlike how rushed we were when she first stormed in.

"I shouldn't have done that," I admit to her when we break

apart in favor of dragging some air into our lungs. Our legs are still tangled together and my arm locked around her body.

"Done what?"

"Took your virginity. Not like that. I'm sorry."

"You're sorry?" she asks with a laugh. "I'm pretty sure I asked you for it."

"I know but..." I push up on my elbow and look down at her, my hand lifting to the red mark on her cheek that has anger stirring in my belly. "Why did you come here, Poppy?"

Her body tenses, telling me that I'm right. Not that I needed any kind of confirmation, I knew it the moment she pushed the door open and I took advantage.

"I needed you."

"Yeah, I know." I can't help a smile tugging at my lips. "But why? You've ignored me since you sent me away and then this."

She breaks our eye contact. I hate that she still thinks she can hide from me.

"Poppy?" I ask, cupping her cheek and turning her face back to me.

She lifts her arm as if she's going to pull my hand away, but she doesn't get the chance because I find something that I've missed this far.

"What the fuck is this?" I lift her arm up in front of me, inspecting the welts and cuts around it.

She tries tugging it away but I'm stronger by far. "It's... it's nothing."

"Bullshit. What happened this afternoon, Poppy?"

"It's nothing."

"Stop lying to me." My anger explodes within me, my muscles twitch to get up and start pacing, do anything to try to expel my need to do something but I fight it and keep her in my arms.

"What good will it do? The last time you knew something

happened, you got yourself suspended. I refuse to allow this to ruin your future."

"My future. What about your present, Poppy?"

"It doesn't matter," she whispers.

"Like fuck it doesn't. You don't deserve any of this. Fuck." I throw myself back on the bed, my irritation at her being able to just brush it off like it all means nothing pisses me off beyond belief.

"Zayn, please. You've already done too much. Just trust me to handle it."

"Handle it?" I sit up, grabbing both of her hands and staring down at her red wrists. "He fucking bound you. What else did he do, Poppy?" Lifting my hand, I brush my thumb over the red mark on her cheek.

She shakes her head, still refusing to give me the answers I need.

"You need to stop protecting him," I snap.

"So what am I supposed to do? Tell the teachers? Hartmann? We both know that his daddy will make sure everything is swept under the rug. Or should I tell Jake and watch as he ruins his own future by going in all guns blazing like you did?"

I blow out a breath. "I don't know, Poppy. But you can't continue like this."

"He'll get bored eventually."

"No, he won't. We both know you're just lying to yourself. He won't stop until he gets what he wants."

"Not happening."

"Fuck." I drop my head into my hands. "He should not win. It's fucking wrong."

She climbs from the bed. "You think I don't know that? This has been my life for years, Zayn." She lifts her arms from her body in exasperation.

"Years?"

"Yeah, well... not quite like this. The past week or so, it's been worse. He's suddenly turned into an even bigger psycho."

"What's changed?"

She bends down, swiping her discarded clothes from the floor and begins dragging them on.

"You. You are what's changed."

I gasp, not expecting to hear her say that. I thought it was just that it's senior year and his time to shine was almost in touching distance.

"Because I beat the shit out of him?"

"No, Zayn," she breathes as if I'm an idiot. "He knows about this." She gestures between us.

"H-how?" I scoot to the end of the bed, not happy with the distance she's put between us.

"It doesn't matter. He just does."

"How, Poppy?" I ask, standing and stalking toward her until she has no choice but to back up.

"Just leave it. Coming here was a mistake. I shouldn't have —" Her words are cut off when she hits the wall.

Lifting my arms, I cage her in.

"How does he know, Poppy?"

"Fuck." She looks over my shoulder, unable to keep eye contact but I don't fight her on it, I know I've already won. "Where was the ladder when you climbed up it the other night?"

"Against the wall a few feet from your.... No, no, Poppy do not tell me that he—"

"He was already there. I just assumed you found the ladder where it's always been. I never in a million years thought you meant it was already up against my balcony."

"Where was he?"

"In the bathroom."

"Fuck," I roar, my knuckles connecting with the wall

beside her as she cowers away from me. "Shit, I'm sorry. I'm so fucking sorry."

I wrap my arms around her trembling body but she fights me.

"No, I need to go. I shouldn't have even come here in the first place."

"Poppy, please." My voice is bordering on begging but I don't give a shit. I can't have her leaving and putting herself in danger. "I'm not letting you walk out of here alone."

"Well, then I guess it's a good thing that you have no control over me, isn't it? I refuse to cower down to that prick."

"No, no," I shout. "He can't touch you again. He just fucking can't."

"Why, Zayn?"

"Because you're mine," I roar, my chest heaving as our eyes lock.

Her breath catches for a beat before she recovers from my admission.

"That's just it though, isn't it? I'm not yours, and I never have been. You haven't treated me much better than him over the years."

"I'd never hurt you, Poppy."

"Physically, no. But do you have any idea how many nights I've fallen asleep crying because of you?"

My lips part in shock.

"No, exactly. You have no fucking clue."

While I'm standing frozen in shock, she pushes her feet into her sneakers, rips the door open and disappears from my sight.

I made her cry herself to sleep?

"Shit, Poppy, wait," I cry, fumbling around for my boxers.

They're only halfway up my legs when I follow her out of the room and toward the stairs.

"Poppy, please, stop. Just..." I race down the stairs and find her with her back to me and her hand ready to open the front door and leave.

"You don't want me, Zayn. You never have. I'm just a plaything, a toy that you had some fun with when your friends weren't around. Let's not pretend there's any more here than there really is."

"No, that's not true."

"Well you just scored the ultimate win. All the way with your sister's best friend, that must get you some points with the team, right?"

"You think I... fucking hell, Poppy. It's never been like that for me." When I finally reach her and place my hand on her waist, she startles. But not allowing her to hide from me, I spin her to face me.

My breathing catches at the sight of her tear-filled eyes and the river of ones that have already spilled over running down her cheeks.

"Poppy. Fuck."

The second I pull her into my arms, her first sob erupts.

I drop my lips to the top of her head and hold her to me as she crumbles, hoping that I can at least help in a small way.

After a few long minutes, her breathing starts to even out but she still doesn't pull her face from my chest.

"Do you remember what I said to you in the closet that day?" I ask softly.

She nods but no words leave her lips.

"I meant them. There wasn't anyone else in the room that day I wanted to kiss more than you. I thought all my birthdays had come all at once when the bottle landed on you."

"But what you said after," she whispers.

"It was bullshit, Poppy. I shouldn't have said it. I regretted it the second the words fell from my lips, but as the entire team turned their stare on me, I just couldn't help it. I didn't know how to admit that I liked my little sister's best friend."

"You liked me?" She lifts her head from my chest and the vulnerable look in her eyes guts me.

"I've always liked you, Poppy." I brush my thumb over her cheek. "But I don't deserve you."

"You can't say—"

"I can say that," I cut her off. "Because it's true. You're so beautiful, kind, thoughtful. Innocent—"

"Was," she adds with a laugh.

"You still are, Poppy." I drop my lips to her head. "It's why I can't have you going out there and taking this on by yourself."

"I've done okay this far."

"You have, but you shouldn't have to. You should have told someone."

She shrugs. "So what do you suggest? You already agreed with what I said earlier."

I think for a minute. "You own a gun?"

"Zayn," she gasps, her eyes impossibly wide.

"It was a joke. I'm joking." *Kind of.*

"Okay, good. He might be a prick, but I don't want to kill him, Jesus."

"We'll think of something. Come on, let's go back upstairs before Harley catches us."

"You ashamed of me?"

"No, not even a little bit, Pops. I just thought that maybe you might want to tell her about this instead of letting her walk right into the evidence."

She nods. "Yeah, good thought."

Taking her hand in mine, I lead her back up to my bedroom.

21

———

Poppy

Zayn locked his bedroom door the second we walked back inside and after pulling on his sweats, we crawled onto his bed and he pulled me into his arms.

He found something to watch on the TV but even now, over two hours later, I'm not really sure what we're watching.

My head is still back in that closet with Preston breathing down on me.

Feeling Zayn's eyes on me, I turn to look up at him.

Harley still hasn't come home, nor has his mom, so it's easy to hide out in here like the real world doesn't exist right now.

"Stay the night with me."

My chin drops in shock as his dark eyes continue to hold mine.

"Oh my God, you're serious, aren't you?"

"Deadly. I want you safe, Poppy. He's already got himself into your bedroom while you were sleeping. What's next?"

A shiver runs down my spine because I really have no idea. He keeps telling me that he's going to ruin my life, but what exactly does that mean? My life is already pretty shit as it is. There's not really all that much he can destroy.

A thought hits me, making the ball of dread which seems to have taken up permanent residence in my belly grow larger.

"He's going to come for you."

Zayn's smile drops. "He's not that stupid," Zayn says with confidence.

"Well, I beg to differ. Everyone thinks going after Jake's cousin would be a stupid move, but it seems nothing stopped him going there."

"No offense, but he probably thinks he can overpower a girl. But if he's got any sense, he won't try anything with me."

"You make out like we should all be scared of you," I say with a laugh. "I hate to tell you this, but you're hardly scary."

"I know a few people who probably have a different opinion."

I narrow my eyes at him, begging him to explain.

"How much has Harley told you about where we came from?"

"That it was a trailer park." I think for a minute. "That's probably about it, other than she hated it."

"Yeah, well, she had a very good reason to hate it. Harrow Creek is not a good place. It's full of drugs, guns, and violence. You either accepted that kind of life or you got out. It's lawless, run by the guys who have the most money and power."

"Sounds like something from the movies," I mutter.

"Yeah, it pretty much is. I wasn't brought up like the kids in Rosewood were. I was taught to fight, to protect what's mine and defend until the end."

"So what are you telling me exactly?"

"You need Preston to go away, I can make it happen."

"Whoa, I thought we were joking about killing him?"

"With my own hands, yeah. But for the right price, I could find plenty of people who'd be more than willing."

"Fucking hell, Zayn," I breathe, pushing away from him and sitting up as his words settle into my head.

I look back at him, and it's almost like I'm seeing a different person for a moment.

"You ever kill someone?"

"Poppy." He laughs, sitting up with me and taking my hand in his. "We left when I was fourteen. Mom worked her ass off to ensure we all got out before it was too late. So no, I've never killed anyone, thankfully, I never had the opportunity. But if we stayed much longer, I'm sure it would have been inevitable."

"Jesus."

"When you don't have money readily available, people will go to all kinds of extremes to look after those they love."

"I get that."

"I know you do. More than most."

I blow out a long breath. "He's not going to go away, is he?" I drop my head, allowing myself to accept those words for the first time.

"No. Not unless he gets what he wants, and even then, he's such a prick that I wouldn't put money on it being over."

"I don't want to kill him, Zayn."

"I know you don't, baby." Goose bumps race over my skin at his name for me. It makes me feel much more secure and happy than I probably should. "Those are extreme measures."

"Jake won't give him the team," I state.

"I know. We need another way, because you're right about his dad's money and influence, he'll make sure nothing sticks."

"This is a mess."

"We'll sort it out." Wrapping his arm around my shoulder, he pulls me back down to the bed with him. "I meant it, Pops. Stay with me tonight."

"I can't. I have the kids to look after."

He brushes the hair from my face and stares into my eyes. "Then let me stay with you."

"Your mom will freak. You've already been suspended."

"Then let me hide you in here with me." He rolls on top of me, dropping his lips to my neck. "Just think of the fun we could have."

I giggle like an idiot as he tickles up the sensitive skin of my neck with his tongue.

"Okay, okay. But I need to go home, see what state my parents are in. If they can look after the kids, then yeah, I'll stay."

"Come on then," he says, jumping from the bed.

"Excited much?"

"I just want you to myself."

"You mean you want me naked again?" I raise a brow in his direction where he's busy pulling on a clean shirt and hiding his toned olive skin from me.

"Something like that." He winks, making me shake my head at him.

"Come on then but be prepared to be disappointed. My parents aren't known for being reliable."

"I've got a good feeling."

Zayn holds my hand the entire drive to my house and to my surprise, I find Mom in the kitchen being normal again.

"What's all this?" I ask, very aware that Zayn insisted on following me into the house. I'm not sure if it was to protect me or because he was worried I might lie to get out of spending the night with him. Truth is, just the thought of falling asleep with his arms around me fills my entire body with tingles.

"Just cooking dinner, is that so weird?" Mom asks, her face actually looks shocked that I've commented. I guess that just proves how far gone she is.

"Yeah, it is. I'm going to stay the night at Harley's, is that okay?"

She looks over my shoulder, her eyes narrowing on Zayn.

"That's not Harley," she states.

No shit. "Zayn's just giving me a lift because Harley is still at cheer."

She nods, accepting the lie that fell flawlessly from my tongue. I guess when you have absolutely no respect for the adults that are supposed to care for you, lying comes easily.

"Okay, great. Go for it," she agrees before turning her back on both of us as if we've already left the room.

"Great, thanks," I mutter, rolling my eyes at Zayn the second I turn to him and find his concerned stare on me.

He follows me up to my room and stands with his back pressed against the door while watching me collect a few things I'm going to need.

"Mom's working late," he says after a long stretch of silence. "Says to get our own dinner."

I look over my shoulder at him staring down at his cell. Walking over to where I dropped my purse when we first walked in, I dig mine out, praying there isn't a message from *unknown* waiting for me.

Thankfully, the only people who've sent me messages are Harley and Ruby. Guilt swamps me that I'm doing all this behind Harley's back. I tell myself it's to protect her. It was at first, the fewer people involved in this shit with Preston the better, but now... I glance up at Zayn who must feel my stare because he looks up and flashes me his megawatt smile. My tummy clenches with desire and my, although tender, core aches to feel him again.

Somehow, I manage to rip my eyes from his and look back down to my cell.

There's a message from Ruby telling me that Harley is going back to hers to work on an assignment we were all given earlier and asking if I want to join them.

"Harley is at Ruby's. They want to know if I want to join them."

I look up just in time to see a sexy smirk pull at one side of Zayn's lips, "Perfect," he says, pushing from the door and stalking toward me. "An empty house means I can make you scream."

A whimper falls from my lips as his hand wraps around the back of my neck and heat heads south of my waist.

"What if I want to go hang out with my friends? Tell them all about what I've done today."

"Oh? And what's that exactly?" he teases.

"That I lost my V-card to an insanely sexy senior."

"Insanely sexy, huh?"

"Some would say so."

"Some?"

"Ruby for one."

"There's nothing between me and Ruby, Pops."

"I know. She told me."

"So did you want to go and tell your friends all about my cock, or would you prefer to feel it again?"

"Zayn!" I squeal, swatting his shoulder playfully. "Your sister definitely doesn't want to know about your cock."

"Hmmm... I guess that decision's made then," he says, nuzzling my neck and breathing me in.

"I can't get enough of you, Pops. I'm pretty sure I've been addicted since my fifteenth birthday."

"Don't," I beg.

"Don't what? Tell you the truth?"

"If I find out you're lying, Zayn, I'll never forgive you."

"Trust me, Pops. I never wanted to walk out of that closet that day. I was so fucking hard for you."

My cheeks heat and I tear my eyes away from his.

"Don't pretend you're embarrassed. I know for a fact that you like my dirty words."

My lips part to argue but then I remember just how hot they made me feel while he was inside me and I realize that I can't.

"Hurry up and I'll be able to prove my point sooner rather than later."

"You don't need to prove anything. I remember," I admit.

"Hmmm, me too."

Zayn bites down on his bottom lip as his eyes track down my body, turning my temperature up a notch instantly.

"You're going to ruin me, aren't you?" I shove down the feelings that that word threatens to drag up. This has nothing to do with that asshole, and the only ruining Zayn is going to do is going to be very different from his threats.

"Nah, baby. I'm going to fucking consume you."

"Oh God."

"Hurry up." He swats my ass before dropping down onto the end of my bed and resting back on his elbows, his eyes locked on me.

"Okay, I'm good. Let's go."

"Finally." I watch as he reaches down and rearranges himself in his sweats before standing, although his rearrangement didn't do much to cover his hard-on.

"Issue?" I ask, quirking a brow at him.

"Yeah, I'm in a room alone with you," he says it like it should be obvious. "Don't tell me that if I were to push my hand into your panties right now that you wouldn't be wet."

I shrug, fighting the smile threatening to spread across my lips.

"I thought we were going?" I walk toward the door but am

abruptly stopped when his palm slams down on the wood from behind me before I get the chance to open it.

His lips brush my ear, his breath tickling down my neck as his palm skims down my spine before his fingers disappear under the waistband of my pants.

"Zayn," I gasp.

"I need the answer, Pops." His fingers part me before one digit pushes inside me. He groans as if he's in pain.

"Glad you know now? Did it help your little issue?" I ask, looking over my shoulder at his pained expression.

"I should bend you over right here and fuck that smart mouth right out of you."

Fuck, how is it he's even hotter when he talks to me like that?

"You could. Or you could wait until we're locked back in your room with no chance of interruptions."

"Let's go." He takes my bag from my hand before lacing his fingers through mine and all but drags me from the room.

I shout a bye to my mom, but I don't hear her say anything in return. I hate that I feel guilty about leaving my brothers and sister with them, but I can't help it. I should feel confident that their mother is going to look after them like she should, but I don't.

Zayn throws my bag in his trunk before holding the passenger door open for me.

"Ah, he can be a gentleman."

"What's that saying? Gentleman in the street, freak between the sheets."

"Oh my God, you're insufferable."

"You love it." He leans in and steals a quick kiss before closing the door on me and jogging around to the driver's side.

"What do you want for dinner?"

"Uh..." I hesitate, thrown off by his sudden subject change. I really thought he was going to race home and feast on me.

He glances over after backing out of my driveway and I can only assume he can read my thoughts because he says, "Oh, don't worry, that will happen after."

"Oookay. So... Chinese?"

"Chinese it is."

We swing by a takeout place and pick up dinner before Zayn continues driving in the opposite direction to his house.

"Head Point?" I ask when he pulls up into the deserted cliff edge parking lot. "Isn't this where kids come to hook up?"

"You haven't been here before?" he asks, pulling a box of noodles from the bag and passing them over to me.

"Do I need to remind you that I live a very different life than the football god and the cheer sluts he usually spends time with?"

"I love that you're not them. It's refreshing."

"So how many of them have you spent time with up here?"

"The team? I don't swing that way, baby." He winks, flashing me a wicked smile.

"Nice try. You know that's not what I meant."

"A couple," he mutters before stuffing a load of noodles into his mouth.

"Well, I guess that's better than the entire squad."

"Hey," he mumbles around his dinner. "I'm not that bad."

"Oh really?"

"Hell yeah," he says after swallowing. "Savage used to be way worse than me."

"And look at him now," I say with a laugh.

"Yep, pussy whipped motherfucker."

"Is it so bad?" I ask, finally starting to dig in.

"Nah, they all make it look pretty fucking awesome, if I'm honest. I've never seen any of them happier."

"That's nice. Jake deserves it after everything."

"They all do. None of them have had it easy."

"Being a kid is tough, huh?"

"You can say that again."

"Says the boy in the huge house with all the money and one of the kings of Rosewood High?" I tease, knowing that he has his own issues beneath how his life might look.

"Or the boy who's been in love with his sister's best friend for like, forever, and not able to do anything about it?"

I damn near choke on my noodles as his words register.

"I mean, you know what I mean. I wanted a repeat of that kiss for a long time," he says in a rush, trying to cover up his previous words.

"Right. And here I was thinking you hated me."

"Never, Pops. I just hated how much of a fucking tease you were. Always at the house wearing short skirts, flashing about everything I couldn't have."

"Now I know you're lying. You never looked at me twice."

"That's what you thought."

Zayn relaxes back, clearly happy that I don't say anything about his accidental admission, not that I think he really meant it. He turns on the radio and the soft sound of some singer I've never heard of fills the small space around us.

"This is nice," I say, looking out over the horizon where the sun is starting to descend, turning the ocean a gorgeous orange color.

"It's not just for making out up here, you know."

"Oh really. I'm disappointed. I was hoping to tick off make-out session with a Rosewood Bear at Head Point off my bucket list."

"Oh? Well, now when you put it like that, I'm sure something could be arranged."

22

Zayn

"I like seeing you like this," I say, watching Poppy where she's resting back in the passenger seat with her feet up on the dash and a small smile playing on her face.

"What's *this* exactly?" she asks, turning to me, a line forming between her brows.

"Relaxed."

She sighs, looking back out to the ocean. "It doesn't happen all that often and I already feel guilty about it."

"Stop," I say, reaching over the center console and lacing her fingers with mine. "It's okay to forget it all for a few minutes."

"But what if Mom doesn't feed them? What if they stay up too late?"

Reaching over, I lift her from her seat and settle her so she's straddling my lap.

"I love how much you care, but they'll be okay. Your mom

has cooked, they have food. And if they go to bed too late, does it really matter? They'll be a bit tired tomorrow and probably have an early night to make up for it.

"They're good kids, Pops. You're an amazing sister. It's okay to have a night off."

"But—"

I press my lips to hers to cut off her words.

She smiles at me but lifts her hand and tugs my arm down.

"Harley is going to hate me when she finds out I've been going behind her back."

"So tell her."

"And Jake?"

"Yeah, we can tell him too."

"You're serious enough about this to tell Jake and risk the consequences?"

"What's he really going to do? Try to give me a black eye and a couple of broken ribs? I've handled worse, I'm sure I'll cope."

Her lips twist as she thinks.

"Talk to me, Pops. Tell me what's going on in that head of yours."

"Can we... can we deal with Preston first?" She wants to say more but slams her lips shut, stopping her from saying it.

"Of course, if that's what you want. What else?"

"I'm just worried..."

"Worried about..."

"That once all this is over and he's no longer a threat, that you won't want me. That this is all just a game."

"You need to stop thinking like that. None of this is a game, Poppy. I want this," I say, cupping her face in my hands and rubbing her cheeks with my thumbs.

"I want you. I've wanted you for a long time. You're not just my little sister's best friend. To me, you're so much more than that."

"Zayn," she breathes, tilting her head to the side.

"Whatever you want to do, just tell me. I'll follow your lead. If you want me to be your dirty little secret, then I'm happy to be. If you want to stand on the school roof and shout it for everyone to hear, then I'll stand right beside you."

Her eyes flood with tears at my words.

"And here I was thinking you're an asshole."

"Oh, baby. I'm still that. You just bring out my softer side."

Bringing her face closer to mine, I brush my lips against hers.

"Now, tell me. Are you ready for your first make-out session with a Rosewood Bear at Head Point?"

"So ready."

"Good, me too."

Dropping my hands, I wrap them around her hips and pull her closer until the heat of her core is right over my cock and her breasts brush against my chest, making my hold on her tighten as her tongue pushes past my lips to find mine.

We make-out for hours as the sun descends around us.

By some miracle, no other cars join us but that doesn't mean they won't.

"Zayn," she moans, kissing across my rough jaw and down onto my neck as her hips grind down on me.

"You gonna come, baby?"

"Hmmm," she groans.

"Sit back," I instruct and she does so without questioning me.

With a little space between us, I can just about push my hand inside her pants.

I find her wet and ready for me, and in record time, she's coming on my fingers.

"Better?" I ask when she sags against me, an exhausted mess.

"You could say that."

"We should head back before the others do."

I lift her back into her seat and start the engine.

"But..." She glances down at my crotch where my cock is trying to punch through the fabric of my sweats. "Don't you want..." Her face drops as if I'm refusing her advances.

"More than I could explain. But we're on borrowed time here. Someone else will pull up and I don't want anyone seeing anything of you they shouldn't."

"O-okay."

"You can make it up to me once we're home."

Her smile knocks me for six when I look over at her. How the fuck did she agree to this? I don't deserve her, that's for fucking sure.

Thankfully, the driveway is still empty when we pull up so we're able to grab some drinks and lock ourselves in my bedroom without being caught.

We might have been lucky tonight, but I know that time's not on our side. There's no way we're going to be able to sneak around with Harley's room right down the hallway. Tonight is going to have to be a one-off. Somehow, I'm going to have to trust that Poppy is going to be safe without me and allow her to go home.

My fingers twitch to reach out to some of my old friends from Harrow Creek to come and deal with Preston once and for all, but something tells me that she'd never forgive me if I were to do something like that. I have to follow through on my promise to allow her to do it her way. As much as it pains me. Putting a bullet through the motherfucker's head is too tempting.

"Here, wear this," I say after rummaging through the closet.

"What is... oh, really?" she asks nervously, and when I look up, I find her staring at the red fabric in disbelief.

"Yes, really." I walk up to her and grip on to the bottom of her hoodie, pulling it up and over her head. Her bra goes too, revealing her pert, rosy pink nipples to me.

"Zayn?" she asks, as I stare down at her body.

"I changed my mind." I pull my jersey away and drop my lips to her breasts.

"I'm not here to be your plaything," she snaps but I know she's teasing. Something tells me that she'd be more than happy to comply. "Give me that." She reaches forward to where I pulled my jersey behind me and tugs it from my hand and over her head.

I take a step back and look at her. I can't even complain that she's covered up her tits because she's standing before me wearing my fucking number. I shake my head, as if I can't believe I'm actually seeing it.

My cock swells at the sight.

Mine. All fucking mine.

"Do you have any idea how hot you look right now?"

"Me?" she asks, pointing at herself in disbelief, but she's got a naughty glint in her eye that makes my temperature increase a few more degrees.

"Yeah, you."

She takes a few steps back. "You want me to stay like this?"

"Yup. You're mine now." As I attempt to close the distance between us, she steps back once more. The tension crackles between us as she teases me.

"So you wouldn't want me to remove these?" she asks, her hands going to her waistband.

"Hell yeah." I watch with a smirk as she kicks her pants from her legs.

"And what about these?" she asks, hooking her thumb in her black lace panties. "Would you want me in *just* your number, Hunter?"

My mouth goes dry at that thought alone. The sight of her long legs sticking out the bottom is fucking incredible but knowing her perfect little pussy is beneath, bare for the taking. Fuck.

"Every fucking day, Pops. Take them off."

"While you're fully dressed? I don't think so," she sasses, dropping her eyes down my still fully clothed body.

In record time, I'm standing in just my boxer briefs, her eyes feasting on my skin.

"Better?" I ask, attempting to get close to her again.

"For now." She laughs and it makes my heart constrict.

"Fuck, I can't get enough of you." I press her body up against mine and slip my tongue past her lips, desperate to feel her against me once more. My hand slips under my jersey to palm her ass and she moans into our kiss.

Without warning, she drops to the bed, her face in line with my cock.

"I think I owe you one." She winks.

"I'm not counting, Pops."

"That's a shame, because I am." Her fingers wrap around the waistband of my boxers and tug. My cock springs free, making her tongue run along her bottom lip, her eyes locked on mine.

"I'm pretty sure you couldn't look any hotter than you do right now."

"You sure about that?"

She leans forward and sucks my length into her mouth, her heat surrounds me and almost makes me lose my damn mind.

"Fuck. Yeah. Okay." I thread my hand into her hair but allow her to take control as she sucks me deeper and deeper.

I just let out my release, my heart thundering in my chest when the front door slams and feet run up the stairs.

Poppy looks up at me with wide, panicked eyes.

"It's okay, I locked the door."

Dropping my hands to her waist, I throw her up the bed.

Her hand slams over her mouth as she lets out a shriek of surprise. That is until her entire body tenses as a knock on the door sounds out.

"Zayn?" Harley calls.

"Yeah."

"I've got work from your teachers."

"Leave it out there," I grunt, desperate for her to just go away.

"What are—fucking hell, are you jacking off again?" she asks, her voice higher pitched than normal.

Poppy rolls into my side, shoving her face into my chest.

"Yeah, could you knock again and pretend to be the maid coming in to polish my—"

"You're fucking sick," she screams before she runs to her room and the slam of her door makes the walls shake.

The second we know it's safe, Poppy barks out a laugh.

"Pretend to be the maid?" she manages to get out through her laughter. "Please, for the love of God, tell me that you don't have a maid, let alone one that polishes anything of yours."

"We have a cleaner, but I wouldn't let her anywhere near me with her feather duster, don't worry."

"You're a nightmare," she says, falling back down into my side and snuggling close. Her bare leg drapes over my waist and I can't help but to trail my fingertips over the smooth skin.

"What?" I ask innocently. "It got rid of her, didn't it?"

"Yeah, and probably scarred her for life."

"She'll cope. She can consider it karma for the fact she now crashes all my football parties in her slutty little dresses."

"Oh, because you haven't been torturing her for years? Did you ever think she does those things out of karma to get back at you?"

"Huh..." I think back over our childhoods and all the things I've done to torture her over the years. Poppy probably has a point. "Nah, that can't possibly be the case. I've been the most awesome big brother ever."

"Sure," she says with a laugh, tapping my chest gently.

"Maybe you just need a reminder of how awesome I am."

I roll her onto her back, settling myself between her legs and capturing her lips to cut off any argument that might have been about to fall from her lips.

We hibernate in my room all night. Harley doesn't bother knocking again but I do slip out to see Mom to reassure her that I've done all my work and got the extra Harley collected for me once she came home.

She looks at me weirdly the entire time, as if she suspects something and it makes me nervous that she's about to race up to my room. But she doesn't say anything and after a few minutes, she allows me to go back up to my girl.

"Poppy?" I whisper when I return and flick the lock once more before finding my room empty. My stomach bottoms out for a second that she's run the second I've left her alone.

I only have to wait a second before she emerges from my bathroom with a plume of steam billowing out behind her.

"You've got a bath," she states, running her eyes down the length of me.

"I do. I never use it though, so eat your heart out."

"Oh, I was thinking you could use it tonight."

A smile curls up at my lips as my brain catches up with her plan.

"You know, I was thinking that tonight was the perfect night to christen the thing." I walk toward her and gather her up in my arms.

"Shit," she gasps, running her fingertip gently down my neck. "I didn't realize I left a mark."

A smile plays on my lips.

"What?"

"That explains why Mom looked at me suspiciously."

"She knows?"

"I doubt that. She probably just thinks I snuck someone in this afternoon."

"Which you did," she helpfully points out.

"Hmm... so I did. She's not going anywhere either."

23

Poppy

I wake with a happy smile on my face as I open my eyes and find I'm laid on Zayn's naked chest and with his arm protectively wrapped around my waist.

I have no idea if he's awake or not but I can't help running my fingertip around the lines of his stomach that the sheets reveal.

Each time I make contact, his muscles bunch and I smile.

"Hmm... I could get used to this," he says into my hair before dropping a kiss to the top of my head.

The move takes me back to relaxing in the bath with him last night. There was no point where he didn't have some kind of contact with me and as time went on, I craved it more and more.

He rubbed the tension from my shoulders, gently cleaned around my sore wrists and peppered kisses up my neck while he played my body to perfection. I'm not sure I've ever felt so relaxed as I did in his arms last night.

I blow out a slow breath, this might feel incredible right now, but we both know it's not going to turn into a regular thing.

"Skip today. Stay here with me," he says, his fingers wrapping around my hair and tugging gently until I have no choice but to look up at him.

"I can't, Zayn. It won't do any good. I've just got to hold my head high and carry on."

"Are you going to tell me what he did yet?"

I shake my head. If I tell him any of the details about Preston accosting me, it'll just make him angrier than he already is, and I'd hate for him to end up hurt because he was fighting for me.

This is my fight. My problem. I refuse to allow anyone else to get in the middle. It's exactly why no one else knows just how bad things are.

"Just tell me one thing. Did he... has he touched you?"

"No." It's a half-lie, and it tastes bitter as it passes my lips, but I know I can't tell him the truth. He's barely holding it together as it is where Preston is concerned. I can't do that to him. "I should get ready for school."

I push from him and swing my legs over the bed.

"Wait," he says, his hand wrapping around my wrist, preventing me from standing. "I'm not letting you out of this bed until I feel you coming around my cock."

His lips trail down my spine, sending goose bumps racing across my skin.

"Well, if I have to," I concede and fall back onto the mattress when he encourages me to do so.

———

After a short argument that I ultimately lost, Zayn drives me to school once I've sent a message to Harley and Ruby to let them know that I'd make my own way.

That hardly ever happens, so I know for a fact that they're going to have questions for me the second I step foot on Rosewood High soil.

We waited until everyone else had left the house. I thought it was just so we wouldn't get caught but Zayn pointed out the moment that we were in the car that it was mostly because he didn't want me in school and anywhere near Preston for a second longer than necessary.

I swooned, hard. But no matter how protective he is about me, I think we both know that it's not going to stop him. If Preston wants to get to me, then he will.

The parking lot is almost empty of students by the time we arrive seeing as the bell for first period has already rung.

"If I get detention then it's all your fault."

"You're hardly late. Come here." He leans over the console and crashes his lips to mine.

"I will be if you continue doing this," I mumble against his lips.

"I'll miss you."

I can't help but laugh at him.

"What?"

"Nothing, just wondering where bad-boy Hunter has gone, is all." I wink at him and reach down for my bag.

"Oh don't worry, baby. He's still here. I might even unleash him on you later." That promise has more desire than probably necessary coiling around my lower stomach. "Last chance to skip with me. Empty house..."

"I can't, but I really appreciate the offer."

"I'll pick you up later, yeah?"

I nod, thinking of the place he told me to meet him after school to give us less of a chance of being spotted.

"Okay, now go. Your cleaning lady might be waiting."

He laughs as I climb from the car, close the door behind me and make my way to the building.

The closer I get, the harder my heart beats. I look around, praying that no one is watching us and I'm almost at the doors when movement behind a tree off to my right catches my eye.

My footsteps falter as I keep my eyes on whoever is clearly hiding.

I take one step up to the building when he emerges. My entire body turns to ice at the look in his eyes. His warning is even more stark than normal.

"You're done," he mouths. Fear explodes within me, and I rush to get into the building to be surrounded by other students.

"Where the hell have you been?" Ruby asks the second I drop into my seat beside her.

"Sorry, family shit," I mutter, refusing to look at her, knowing that she'll be able to read my lie.

She studies me as I pull my books out and flip my textbook to the page the teacher has written on the board, ready to go.

"Family shit, huh?" Before I can respond, her finger tucks into the neck of my hoodie and she pulls it away from my skin. "Feel like telling me the truth this time?"

"Fuck, Rubes."

"Little morning hook up, I like it." She winks and I groan.

"Can we not, please?"

"Not what? Talk about how a certain player is rocking your world in the back of his truck?"

"Yeah that," I mutter as the classroom door opens and Preston strolls in like he's not almost ten minutes late. Our teacher doesn't so much as look up at him. But then I guess that's the kind of thing you expect when your father pretty much owns his ass. It's a harsh reminder as to why I'm not sitting in Hartmann's office right now explaining everything that Preston has done.

Lowering my eyes before he spots me looking at him, I stare at the desk in front of me, praying that all of this will just come to an end without anyone getting hurt sometime soon. Sadly, I can't see how that's going to happen. He's not just going to give up now. Senior year, and what he thinks is rightfully his team, is almost in touching distance.

Thankfully, that's the last time I'm forced to be in the same room as him. He was supposed to be in my class before lunch, but his chair was tauntingly vacant. It has me on high alert, expecting something to happen that would drag me from the room and right into his hands.

The interruption I'm expecting happens almost twenty minutes before the end of my final class. I was beginning to think that I was going to escape and be able to run to Zayn's car and to safety very soon. But the second the classroom door opens and Principal Hartmann steps into the room, my heart falls into the pit of my stomach.

I don't know how I know that it's got something to do with me, or that it's my name that's about to fall from his lips, but I do.

"I'm so sorry to interrupt," he says to our teacher. "Miss Poore, could you please come with me?"

Harley shoots me a concerned look from the other side of the room. I force a smile onto my face and try to play down the panic that's beginning to rise within me.

As predicted, she threw question after question at me about my absence this morning, along with my refusal to hang out last night. I used Mom as an excuse, but I think, despite her being a disaster parent, that my excuse is starting to run out of steam. The time to come clean is coming, before they dig and find everything out themselves.

I collect up my stuff and follow Hartmann out of the room

and all the way to his office. He doesn't say a word, which in itself is concerning. He always has something to say.

When I step into his office, I'm greeted by two police officers and a woman in a suit.

"Poppy, please take a seat."

I do as I'm told, but mainly because I'm so confused, my brain too busy trying to figure out what's happening to consider defying him.

"Poppy," he breathes, as if he's using the time to find his next words.

A million and one thoughts run through my mind about why I could have been dragged in here. I've seen all the films, usually it's when the girl gets told her entire family was killed in a car crash and her life is about to change forever.

My breathing starts to increase as I stare at Hartmann, wishing he'd just spit it out.

"I'm sorry to have to tell you but your home was raided this morning and your parents have been arrested for possession of illegal substances."

"Oh my God," I sigh, falling back into the chair, my hand coming up to cover my racing heart. "Everyone is alive? The kids?"

"Y-yeah. Everyone is alive," he confirms, looking from me and to the woman behind me.

"Good. That's g-good," I stutter, trying to process what he did actually tell me now that I know I'm not about to attend five funerals as an orphan.

"Hey, sweetie. I'm Bea, I'm a social worker, and I've been assigned to you and your siblings throughout all of this."

"Hi," I say shakily. She's got perfectly straight blonde hair and light blue eyes, so light that I almost think they could be fake.

"I know this must have come as a shock."

I nod, although really, is it? Mom and Dad have been

doing all sorts in our house for years. The smell of weed that permeates the air most days isn't the half of it. I guess the reality is, that this was going to happen eventually.

"Where are my brothers and sister?"

"Cooper is with my colleague, she's fantastic with babies, he's being well looked after. I was hoping that maybe you could come with me to pick Austin and Sofia up from school. It'll be a little less scary if they see a familiar face."

"Yes, yes, anything. What's going to happen to us?"

"Well," she says, her eyes still holding mine as a sadness washes through them. This must be the part of her job she hates more than any other. "We're going to need to find you all a temporary place to stay while the investigation is carried out. Then depending on what is found, you may be able to return home." She puts extra emphasis on the may, but it's pointless, I already know the outcome of this. "Or we're going to need to find the four of you a more permanent place to live."

I nod, accepting her words. They might not have just told me that everyone died in a car crash but even still, my world has just been flipped upside down.

"We're not going to be going home," I mutter sadly.

"What makes you say that?"

A bitter laugh falls from my lips. "They're guilty. Let's not talk with false hope. They're both addicts and shit parents." I slump down in the chair, suddenly feeling totally exhausted.

"Oh, okay. Well..." She looks to Principal Hartmann and then the two officers who are still standing exactly where they were when I walked in. "Shall we go and get Austin and Sofia? It will give us time to have a chat about what's to come."

What I really want to do is run. Run as fast as I can from this office, from this school, from the town and just make it all go away. But I can't. Just like before, my priority right now needs to be those three helpless kids who've just had their parents ripped from them, no matter how shit they were, I wouldn't wish that on anyone, which is why I've kept my mouth shut all this time.

"My car is in the parking lot. Is there anything you need to grab before we go?"

"Y-yes, I've got some books in my locker I need."

"Okay." She nods, pushing to stand and then holding her hand out for Hartmann.

"Poppy, take the time you need. We'll be here for you when you're ready to return."

"Assuming I'm not shipped halfway across the state?" I mutter, the reality of what's possibly about to happen slamming into me. This could be my last day at Rosewood High. It could be my last day with Harley and Ruby, with everything I've ever known.

Tears burn my eyes as Bea follows me toward my locker. I empty it out because, why shouldn't I? I may never see it again.

With a loud sigh, I push open the main entrance doors and make my way toward the Prius I'm directed to.

After dumping my bags in the trunk, I fall into her passenger seat.

"This isn't the end, Poppy. You could very well be back here in a few days and be able to return to some kind of normal life."

"Really? How many kids in this situation have done that before?"

She pales.

"Exactly."

"Before we start looking at other options. Do you have any family who might be able to help you all out temporarily?"

I think of Mom's sister, Jake's mom, and curl my lip up in disgust. Talk about out of the frying pan and into the fire. She fucked off sometime around Thanksgiving and we haven't seen or heard from her since. Something that I know Jake is more than happy about.

We've got no grandparents, or at least not any that would be interested. Dad's parents are both alive but they haven't visited us before so I can't imagine they'd jump at the chance of taking us all in.

"Dad has a sister. She lives in Maddison County. We see her a couple of times a year, she always brings us gifts. But her and Mom have never really gotten along, so it's kind of strained at best."

"Okay, do you think she'd help? I'd really rather not put you all into the system. This could be a very temporary thing."

"Bea," I sigh. "I appreciate your positivity. But please, can we cut the bullshit. This sucks. It really fucking sucks, but there is no way my parents are getting off scot-free here. They've been doing drugs and neglecting the four of us for years. Even if they do get out, you'd be stupid to allow us to return to them."

"Wow. That was... honest."

"Look," I say, keeping my eyes on the passing scenery. "I want my family together. I do. I'd love nothing more than to be a happy unit where our parents do what they're meant to and we all grow up with happy childhoods, but that is not the case. I've watched the kids miss out on so much over the years, and they deserve better."

"You've got a very mature head on your shoulders, young lady."

"Yeah, well that probably comes from basically being a mom for years. Can I just ask one thing?"

"Of course. Although I can only promise to do my best. A lot of things right now are out of our control," she says, almost as if she's sensing what I'm going to say.

"Please try to keep them together. They're family, they deserve to grow up together."

"And what about you?"

I shrug. "Do whatever, just focus on them."

"They're very lucky to have you, Poppy."

"I'd rather they had decent parents," I mutter sadly as I rest my head back and close my eyes.

Tears continue to burn my eyes, but none fall. I haven't got any for my parents. All I feel is fear for my siblings.

It's not until I see their school up ahead that it really starts to affect me. How are we supposed to tell two little kids that their parents are in prison and our lives are about to change forever?

"It'll be okay. Kids are more resilient than we expect. If they can see you being brave, they'll take strength and comfort from that."

I nod as I climb from the car when she does.

The next thirty minutes absolutely guts me. Seeing both Austin and Sofia's bottom lips tremble as we explain to them the best we can about what's going on and that, other than to go and get our stuff, we're not going to be staying at home for, well... possibly ever.

With them both huddled into my sides, we make our way out to Bea's car to go and find Cooper.

Bea's cell rings and she leaves us to get inside while she speaks to whoever is on the other end.

"Everything is going to be okay," I tell Austin and Sofia as I strap myself in and turn back to look at them.

"They're going to split us up, aren't they?" Austin asks, understanding this situation better than I hoped he would.

"I don't know, bud," I answer honestly. It's the best I can do for them right now. "They'll do everything they can not to let it happen."

Sofia remains deathly quiet although the sound of her shaky breaths fill the car where she's trying not to cry. I give

Austin a sad smile as he reaches over and takes her hand in his.

I turn away from them when I'm not able to be brave any longer. Watching them break, it's too much. They can do whatever they want to our parents, but I can't cope with watching my brother and sister fall apart because of them.

I wipe at my eyes, trying desperately hard to keep the tears inside so they don't have to witness me fall apart as well as each other.

"Good news," Bea says, dropping down into the driver's seat. I look at her, she's got a smile on her face but it doesn't meet her eyes, she knows just how shit this all is. "My colleague has been in contact with your aunt. She's willing to take you in."

"Really?" I ask, disbelief laced through my voice.

"Really. She's going to meet us at the office. Said she'll be about an hour and a half."

For the first time since I left Zayn's car this morning, a small trickle of hope races through me.

Auntie Trish is wonderful. There've been many times over the years when I've wondered why we couldn't have been her kids instead. She's got her life together and is married to a great guy, although the two of them never had any kids of their own, which I always found odd because she's always been fantastic with me and my siblings.

The drive to the office is short and I soon find myself running through an office when I spot Cooper in the arms of another kind looking lady.

"Coop," I squeal, pulling him into my arms and hugging him like I haven't seen him in years.

He coos at me and I'm unable to fight the tears any longer. With him still in my arms, I drop on the couch the other woman was sitting on and sob like I've wanted to do since those ominous words fell from Hartmann's lips earlier today.

I glance up at the wall, hoping to find a clock. It takes a few seconds for my watery eyes to read it but when I do, I discover that it's only been just over an hour since my life changed forever. It already feels like a lifetime ago.

Austin and Sofia come over and cuddle into my side as the two women watch us with sympathetic expressions on their faces.

"Are you guys hungry? Thirsty?"

"Yeah," Austin says, no surprise there, he's always hungry.

"Sandwiches okay?"

"That's perfect, thank you so much."

We're all silent as they both walk away chatting to themselves, probably about us and what's going to happen next.

They bring us a huge platter of food along with cans of soda and bottles of water, but as Austin and Sofia dig in, I can't bring myself to eat any of it. My stomach is in knots, I'm pretty sure I wouldn't be able to keep it down even if I did try.

The clock ticks by slowly as we wait for Auntie Trish to arrive but as the minutes pass, I begin to wonder if she was lying and isn't coming at all. That is until a panic-stricken voice fills the air around me.

"Where are they? I need to see them now."

I look up as Bea points over to us and Auntie Trish comes barreling through the door.

I stand with a sleeping Cooper against my chest as she wraps us both in her arms.

I break once more as her floral scent surrounds me.

"Oh Poppy, everything is going to be okay. You're all coming home with me and we'll sort everything out. I promise."

I pull from her embrace and look into her kind green eyes. "T-thank you."

"Oh, sweetie. I'd do anything for you all, you know that."

"I know but this is..." I trail off not really knowing what to say about it. "An extreme circumstance."

"Maybe so, but you're my family." She kisses my temple before dropping down and pulling both Austin and Sofia into her arms. "I can't believe how much you've all grown. I've got your favorite candy in the car," she whispers, and their little eyes light up for the first time since getting escorted into their principal's office earlier.

It takes a couple of hours, but eventually we are able to make our way to Auntie Trish's car and I discover that the reason she was late is because she stopped to get a car seat for Cooper. We finally manage to figure out how to get him in it securely before climbing into the front seats.

She turns to me, a somber expression on her face. "I'm so sorry, Poppy. I can't even imagine how you're feeling right now."

"I wish I could explain it. It's a weird mix of terror and relief." She reaches over and squeezes my hand in support.

"I know this is unbelievably hard. But Evan and I will do everything we can to make it as easy as possible."

"Is he okay with this?"

"Of course he is, sweetie. He loves you all as much as I do. Now, let's go and pack you all some stuff and head home."

I nod to her, rest my head back and close my eyes.

It's dark by the time we pull up to her home, but lights illuminate the front of the building. It's an impressive Victorian home painted in a soft mint green. The huge front porch is covered in bright flowers and is the kind of house that every kid draws as their dream home and almost every adult wants for their two-point-five kids.

I look back over my shoulder to find all three of them fast asleep.

"Poor things. I bet their heads are spinning."

Just as we open our doors to step out, Uncle Evan jogs down the steps and pulls Auntie Trish into his arms before turning to me.

"Poppy, I'm so sorry it got to this, but I'm so happy we can help." He wraps his arms around me in a giant bear hug and I'm hit with the scent of paint that always follows him around.

"Thank you so much. I can't tell you how much I appreciate you both doing this."

"Don't be silly. You're family. We always look after our own."

I think of all their visits, their arguments with my parents as they tried to support them to turn things around and I let out a sigh. I really need some sleep.

The three of us take a passed-out child each and carry them into the house.

We've only stayed here a couple of times in the past, but it's enough for us to already have allocated rooms.

"Cooper can stay with me," I say as Auntie Trish and Uncle Evan lower both Austin and Sofia onto the twin beds in the room they've shared in the past.

"Are you sure? I don't mind taking him to give you a break."

"If he wakes, he's going to want someone familiar."

"You're right. I'll get the travel crib from the closet."

I sit on the edge of the bed and she's back in a flash and setting up Cooper's temporary bed.

"Come and have a drink with us before you hit the hay," Auntie Trish suggests after we stand staring at a sleeping Cooper for a few minutes. Uncle Evan has already unloaded the car and the suitcase of clothes I packed for myself sits on the bed.

"Uh... sure."

After pulling the door too, I follow Auntie Trish down to their kitchen.

"What do you want? We've got most things."

"A soda would be great."

She nods and pulls one from the refrigerator.

She pours herself a small glass of wine and together we go and join Uncle Evan in the living room.

I curl myself into the corner of the sectional and sip at my soda as the tension begins to weigh me down.

"I'm sorry, Poppy. I don't know what to say to make any of this better," Auntie Trish says with a wince.

"You can't. Let's just call a spade a spade. This is all shit."

After her initial shock has passed, both her and Uncle Evan bark out a laugh.

"That, my dear, is the truest thing I've ever heard," Auntie Trish says. "Everything is going to be okay, though. After a good night's sleep, we'll get our heads together and make a plan."

"Sounds good," I lie. Nothing about this sounds good but it's the hand I've been dealt so I just need to deal.

After finishing my soda, I excuse myself to bed. I strip out of my clothes and pull on a tank and some sleep shorts and crawl into the bed.

Hugging my knees to my chest, I allow myself to break once more in private.

24

Zayn

I sit outside school where I agreed to meet Poppy after school for almost an hour before I finally accept that she's not coming.

I call her, message her, but I get nothing back and none of my messages even get read.

Dread fills my veins that he's done something really fucking dumb. But is he really stupid enough to do something during a school day? I'd like to think not but he's proving himself to be more and more unstable as every day passes.

I might not know the details of what he's done seeing as Poppy refuses to give them up, but I see the fear getting worse and worse in her eyes.

Climbing from the car, I jog around the buildings until I can look over the field where the guys are training.

Coach is nowhere to be seen as Jake runs the drills.

My eyes dart over each team member before they fall on Preston running up and down along with the others.

I narrow my eyes at him in the hope I'll get a clue somehow that he's behind this, but I see nothing.

I slip back into the shadows before I'm caught. The last thing I need is for my suspension to be extended because I couldn't follow a couple of simple rules.

Hoping that she just had second thoughts about me getting her, I climb back into my car and head for her house.

As I pull into the driveway, I find it sitting quiet. I look in the windows as I walk around and don't see anything untoward, although I can't shift the feeling deep down that something is wrong, very wrong here.

I try both the front and back doors, but they're both locked. Retrieving the ladder that I moved a couple of nights ago, I prop it up against the wall Poppy's balcony sits on and make quick work of climbing up.

Those doors are locked and her room looks like it did when we walked out last night.

"Where the hell are you?" I mutter as I climb down the ladder and once again hide it away.

I call her again the second I get into the car, but just like every other time I've tried this afternoon, it goes straight to voicemail.

"Motherfucker."

I sit in my car, my head spinning, trying to second guess that prick and what he might do with her. Anger burns in my belly. I know I promised her that I wouldn't take matters into my own hands again, but what the hell am I supposed to do now?

A little voice in the back of my head tells me that she's probably fine, that I'm jumping off the deep end right now thinking that he's done something. But I just can't shift the ball of dread in my stomach that's growing larger by the second.

My eyes flick to the clock. Jake's session is over. They'll be heading for Aces.

I slam the car in drive before I even really think about it.

In minutes I'm pulling my car up next to Ethan's and jumping out.

"Ah look, did mommy let you out, you bad, bad boy," one of the guys announces to the entire diner as I approach the team's table.

To my surprise, I find Jake, Mason, Ethan, and Shane all sitting with the rest of the team. Jake must see my shock because without me saying anything he replies with, "The girls have gone to the mall."

"O-okay. G-great. Could we... could we have a word?"

His brows draw together but he nods, sliding from the booth. I nod over my shoulder and he follows me out, but not before I lock eyes with Preston, who's sitting at the other end of the table.

The asshole smiles at me. Actually. Fucking. Smiles.

My fists curl with my need to beat whatever he's done to my girl out of him, but I can't. Not yet. It's going to fucking happen though. I'll just be smarter about it next time.

"What's up?" Jake asks when I come to a stop by the railing that stops us from walking directly down onto the beach.

"Er..." I hesitate, lifting my hand to rub the back of my neck.

"Zayn?" Concern covers his face, pulling his brows together and forming crease lines on his forehead.

Blowing out a breath, I just go for it. I deserve the beating for touching her anyway. "Have you spoken to Poppy today?"

"Uh... no, why?"

"Shit." I scrub at my jaw. "Things with Preston are bad, Jake. Like, really fucking bad. I don't know the details but he's after her. He thinks by using her, he can get to you and then you'll hand over captaincy to him or some bullshit."

He takes a step closer, listening to every word. "Go on."

"I was supposed to pick her up after school... a favor for Harley," I tag on, hoping it might make this just a little better. "She never showed."

"She probably just decided it was better than being in a car with you. She hates you, Hunter."

"Yeah." I squirm under his stare a little. "I know. But something's not right, man. She won't answer her calls, she's not even reading her messages. Her house is silent. She's just... gone."

He's silent for a moment. "You're really worried, aren't you?"

"Yeah. And I think you need to be too. He's got a fucking screw loose, I'm telling you."

"This why you beat the shit out of him, because you found all this out?"

I don't need to say the words, he can read them on my face.

"Why didn't you tell me?"

"She didn't want me to."

"Leading me to my next question, how the fuck do you know about all of this?" he quizzes, making guilt swirl around me like an angry storm.

"I overheard Harley on the phone with her, something sounded off so I started digging, asking questions. She's refusing to do anything about it... because of you."

"Me?"

"Yeah, she knows you'll fly at him for hurting her, and she's trying to protect you."

"Jesus, fuck," he says, running his hands through his hair and resting his back against the railing.

I follow his lead, my eyes moving to the diner window and locking directly onto a set I never want to look at again.

"He's a smug motherfucker. He knows."

"We need to be careful. Poppy has refused to go to Hartmann or the police, she knows that Hellburn's dad owns this place. He'll get any misdemeanors swept under the rug. If we want to get him, we need to be smart."

"What exactly are you suggesting?" he asks, glancing at me.

"I have no fucking idea, but we're going to destroy him."

25

Poppy

I barely get a wink of sleep. I spend the whole night tossing and turning, my imagination running wild about what could happen to us now, what my future might be like. Will my aunt and uncle keep us? Or is this just a stopgap to entering the system and Christ knows what will happen after that. We've all read the horror stories from those situations.

The sun is just waking up, but the kids are still asleep.

I heard movement not so long ago, which I assume was Uncle Evan going to work, but other than that, the house is silent.

I blow out a long breath and wipe my eyes. They're so sore from crying most of the night. Now the morning is here, I need to be stronger. This isn't just about me and my ruined life, it's about the kids. I need to be strong for them. Show them that there's nothing to be afraid of.

Feeling like I need to talk to someone, to hear a familiar voice, one who always makes me feel safe, I reach for my purse.

My cell phone is dead at the bottom, so after locating my charger and plugging it in beside the bed, I power it up.

I didn't even consider everyone else when all of this was going on yesterday, but when my cell comes to life, so do a stream of missed calls and messages.

Mostly from Zayn.

Fuck. Zayn.

He would have been waiting for me after school. "Shit."

I have message after message asking if I'm okay, wanting to know where I am, if I'm safe. Guilt swamps me that I didn't even think about him yesterday. I guess it's understandable given the circumstances but still, I feel awful.

But even still, I ignore his messages for now and focus on the one I want.

Hitting call on his name, I lift my cell to my ear.

It rings a few times before his sleepy voice croaks down the line.

"Poppy?"

"Shit, I'm sorry. What time is it?" I look around the room for the answer but find no clock. Pulling my cell away from my ear for a second, I find it's not even seven a.m. yet.

"It's okay. Where the hell are you? What's going on?" he attempts to ask calmly, but I hear the fear in his voice.

"Mom and Dad got arrested."

"Fuck. Where are you?"

"With Auntie Trish. The police and social services turned up at school. Thankfully, she agreed to take us all in otherwise..." I shudder, not wanting to think about the alternative.

"Jesus, Pops." I can imagine him rubbing his hand down his face in concern. "What's their address, I'm coming to you."

"It's okay, Jake. You've got school."

"Poppy," he warns, his voice low. It might scare other kids at school, but I know him better than that. "You need me, then I'm there. Send me the address," he demands once more.

"Okay fine. But we're fine, honestly."

"I don't care. I'm coming."

Tears burn my eyes and emotion clogs my throat at his need to come and protect us. This is why I never told him about Preston. I know he'd do anything, even at the detriment to himself, to ensure my happiness and safety.

"T-thank you."

"Aw, Pops," he breathes when he hears the crack in my voice. "I'll be there as soon as I can, okay?"

"Y-yeah. I'll tell Auntie Trish you're coming."

"Everything's going to be okay. I won't have it any other way."

I hang up the phone, engulfed by the silence of the house once more, but it feels that little bit easier to breathe now that I've spoken to Jake.

Squaring my shoulders, I leave my cell on the nightstand and rummage around in my bag for some fresh clothes and head for the bathroom and one very hot shower.

Auntie Trish and I are sitting on the porch watching the kids play when the rumble of an engine slowing down in front of the house has us both looking to the driveway.

Amalie's little red sports car pulls up before both her and Jake climb out. Amalie hovers a little, whereas Jake flies at me, opening his arms and embracing me in a huge hug. The exact thing I needed.

I bury my face in his chest, breathing in his scent and allowing it to ground me.

"It's going to be okay, Popsicle," he whispers, using the nickname I hated as a kid, but right now it feels like the most normal part of my life.

After long minutes, he finally releases me, although I don't get very far because he just tucks me into his side.

"Trish, it's good to see you," he says, nodding at my aunt. They've met a few times seeing as Jake has lived with us for years, but they've never really spent any time together seeing as they're not related.

"You too, Jake. And who is this young lady?"

"This is my girl, Amalie. Brit," he says, gesturing for her to join us. "This is Trish, Pops' aunt."

"Hey, it's so nice to meet you."

"Oh, you snagged a British, girl. Good on you, Jake." Trish laughs. "Can I get you all drinks? Coffee?"

"Please."

"We brought pastries," Amalie says, lifting a bag I hadn't noticed she was carrying. "We weren't sure if..." She trails off.

"I'll grab some plates."

As we sit down, Austin and Sofia finally notice that we have company and come running over to see Jake. In seconds they're each sitting on one of his knees and staring up at him like he hung the moon in the sky before driving over here.

We focus on the kids, laughing along with them, and ignoring the elephant in the room.

Auntie Trish brings out a tray full of coffee and plates for Amalie's pastries before telling us that she's going to leave us to it for a bit.

"Austin, Sofia, I'm going to make cookies, would you like to help?"

"Chocolate chip?" Sofia asks, jumping off Jake and following Auntie Trish.

"Can I lick the bowl?" Austin asks, trailing behind as if Auntie Trish is the Pied Piper.

"They're so cute," Amalie says, watching them disappear through the door.

"They're good kids. They don't deserve any of this." I sigh, staring down at Cooper who's happily sitting in his bouncer.

"What are you going to do?" Jake asks, sitting forward and resting his elbows on his knees.

"I would say wait and see if they get charged, but let's be honest, we both know they're guilty. Only an idiot would let them off."

"I know. Fuck," Jake barks, pushing to his feet and pacing back and forth across the porch.

Amalie reaches over and squeezes my hand in support.

"You can't stay here, Pops. You belong in Rosewood."

"I might not have a choice, Jake. I need to do what's best for them." I tilt my chin to the kitchen.

"I'll be eighteen in a few months, maybe Auntie Trish could look after them until—"

"We can," Jake shouts. "We'll take custody of them. We're old enough. Amalie has money, we've got a home."

"Jake, no. You're talking crazy. You can't do that."

"Why not? If it means you all stay together. If I get to keep the little family I have."

My heart swells for him. Standing before him, I wait for him to get to me and reach out for his hand to make him stop.

"As much as I appreciate everything you're saying. I can't let you do that. You need to be thinking about your future, college, Amalie. You don't need to be burdening yourself with my family."

"I just—"

"I know, Jake. Trust me, I know. These kids have been like my own for years. I know you're just as protective of all of us. But this isn't your fight. It's mine."

"Ours," he says, his lips twitching up into a smile.

He pulls me into his arms once more. I close my eyes for a

beat, accepting his support. When I pull them open again, I find Auntie Trish watching us in the window with a smile on her face.

"Come on, the coffee is getting cold."

We walk back over to join Amalie, who's been silently watching the exchange between us.

"How'd the cops find out?" Jake asks after a few silent seconds.

"Who knows. It was going to happen sooner or later. Since Cooper was born. It's just been a disaster."

"I'm so sorry I haven't been there."

"None of this is your fault. You've been starting your life. As you should have been. They treated you like shit for years, I never expected you to hang around and play happy families once you finally got out."

"I shouldn't have just left you there."

"I'm a big girl, Jake. I can look after myself."

Something passes across his face but he tucks it away before I get a read on it.

"What?"

"Nothing. It's nothing."

I narrow my eyes at him, but he keeps his lips sealed.

———

Jake and Amalie end up staying almost all day. We all play in the yard with the kids and just try to be as normal as possible.

They excuse themselves when the police turn up, along with Bea, to talk to both me and Auntie Trish.

I'm hardly surprised that the police want to question me, I did openly admit that my parents were both guilty in Hartmann's office. A story that I'm more than happy to stick to. This might be hell right now with our futures up in the air but life in that house with them wasn't exactly heaven. I can't help but wonder if we're better off without them, whatever might happen to us.

Auntie Trish assures Bea that we have a home here for as long as we need it and she finally leaves happy that we're all happy and safe with a promise to be back in a few days once there's more news about our parents.

Apparently, there's a high chance they'll be bailed before a trial but we're not going to be allowed to see them or even have contact with them. No issue for me with that, but I know that Sofia especially doesn't really understand all of this and is already wondering where her parents are. Austin, however, just seems to be taking everything in his stride.

"Evan is out at his monthly poker game tonight. I wondered if you were interested in a girly night once the kids are in bed?" Auntie Trish asks me after sending Austin and Sofia to run a bath and find their pajamas.

She made them both their favorite dinner, but we have yet to eat.

"We could order whatever you want. Have cocktails, virgin of course, I'm not sure supplying you with alcohol while the social workers are sniffing around is a good idea," she says with a laugh and a wink. "Watch some chick flicks. Talk..." The way she says talk makes my heart drop. What does she need to tell me?

"Yeah, that sounds great."

Together we go through the kids' usual nighttime routine, or at least the one I try to give them before Uncle Evan excuses himself for his night out and gives Auntie Trish a kiss to her temple.

They're such a sweet couple and so good with the kids that I can't help wondering once again why they don't have any of their own.

"So what's it going to be. Pizza? Chinese? Thai?"

"Chinese," I say without a second thought. I might have

only had some with Zayn two days ago, but I could eat it every night given the chance.

"Okay, here," she says, passing her cell over with a menu open. "Order whatever you like. I'm just going to change."

"But... how much..."

"Whatever you want, Poppy. No expense spared." With a soft smile, she disappears down to her room.

I order all my favorites before placing her cell on the counter and following her lead, replacing my jeans with a pair of sweats and a tank.

"Okay, here you go." Auntie Trish turns to me with a fancy looking cocktail in her hand when I return. "Margarita sans the good stuff."

"This looks awesome. You didn't need to go to all this effort though."

"Are you kidding. I usually spend poker nights alone watching crap TV. I'm thrilled to have a friend." She pulls me into her arms and kisses the top of my head.

We get ourselves comfortable on the couch as Auntie Trish pulls up Netflix and starts scrolling.

"Who do you fancy? We'll binge watch him."

I admit to my Zac Efron addiction and she immediately pulls up *High School Musical*.

"Wow, I haven't watched this in forever."

"So you like a blast from the past?"

"Anything a little newer with him a little... older?"

"Sure thing."

She flicks through until we agree on one I haven't seen before. We're only about twenty minutes in when the Chinese food arrives and we hit pause.

We lay all the containers out on the coffee table and sit crossed-legged on the floor.

"What's up, Pops?" Auntie Trish asks when she catches me looking at her.

"I just... I've never done this with my mom. It's nice. Normal."

"Aw, Poppy." She gives me a sad smile. "I'm so sorry."

"It is what it is." I shrug.

"I always wanted to do more. But it was never my place. Your mom and I, we've never got along. When my brother announced they were together, I was less than impressed. Crap, sorry. You probably don't want to hear this," she says, chastising herself.

"No, no. Carry on. I've lived with them all my life, but I don't even feel like I know them, if that makes any sense."

"It does. We've all known each other since school. Your dad and your aunt, Kate, were older whereas your mom and I were in the same year."

"Were they together in school?"

"No, your mom... she had another boyfriend in high school."

I nod, wondering why she seems to panic at that.

"This is so good," I say, focusing back down at the food in the hope of breaking the sudden tension.

"Poppy, I really mean it when I say that you can all stay here for as long as you need to. You know that, right?"

"I do. But I don't expect you to keep us forever. You've got your own life to get on with. The second I'm eighteen, I can get custody and get out of your hair."

"Is that your plan?"

"Yeah, I guess. I refuse to let them go into the system. So I guess it's down to me."

"Poppy," she says on a sigh and I know what's coming next.

"Do you think it's going to be that easy?"

"No, not at all." A sad laugh falls from my lips. "Nothing about any of this is easy. But I've been taking care of them for years. I'm more than capable."

"I know you are. I'm not doubting that. I just think that you need to be thinking about your future as well as theirs."

"It's fine. I'll get a job, find somewhere to live. I'm sure I'll figure it out."

"But what about college? What about a boyfriend, parties, and all the things you should be worrying about as you head into your senior year?"

"I don't feel like I've missed out this far." An image of hiding out with Zayn pops into my head and I remember just how incredible it had felt to have no responsibilities and just be a teenager for one night. I lock it down before I allow it to consume me.

That's gone. All of that is over.

Zayn's messages still taunt me on my cell. I know I need to reply, that he's worried about me. But right now, I don't have it in me to reach out. I just need to focus on my family, on our future.

"Evan and I have tried for almost fifteen years to have kids, Poppy," she says from out of nowhere. "We've done IVF, even a couple of adoption attempts, but it just doesn't seem to happen for us. This is why. If we'd had our own kids, then we wouldn't have been able to help like we can now."

"You really believe that?" I ask with a heavy heart. They'd have been the most incredible parents, and I hate that's been taken away from them.

"I believe that everything happens for a reason, yes. Poppy, I will do everything and anything I can for you and those three. I'd have done it for any child I was lucky enough to care for, but you're my family. There's no way I, or Evan, could turn any of you away."

Tears sting my eyes and my vision blurs.

"But your life, your job. We can't expect you to give everything up to suddenly become parents overnight because our own are useless."

"Poppy, it would be my honor to do all those things. I only work part-time at the college, they'll be flexible, I've no doubt. The schools around here are incredible. The neighborhood is fantastic. You could all be very happy here."

I look around the room we're sitting in. It's so homely, cozy. I know that what she's saying is true. But could I just up and leave Rosewood that easily?

"What about school?"

"I've got some contacts at Royal Maddison Prep. We could see about getting you in there."

"No, no. That's too much."

"Okay, well there are other options too. I just want you all to be happy, Poppy."

"I know. And I appreciate it more than you could know."

"Let's put the movie back on and forget about reality for a few hours. It'll still be there in the morning."

I nod, because sadly she's right.

26

Zayn

"Harley, Zayn," Mom bellows up the stairs. "You've got guests."

I'm up off the bed and flying down the stairs in record time. But when I get to the bottom, I don't find who I was hoping for.

"Hey," I say, looking between Jake and Amalie.

"Have you seen her?" Harley asks the second she rounds the corner and finds them waiting.

"Yeah."

"Come on," I say, directing everyone down to my den.

Everyone drops down onto the couches, but unable to sit still, I pace back and forth. Jake's eyes follow my every move. I know he's suspicious. Hell, I would be too if someone came to me about Harley or Letty and said the things I did. He suspects there's more to this than I admitted to. But where there may have been at the time, now I have no idea.

Poppy has been gone a day, I've sent her numerous messages and called almost every hour, but despite some of my messages being read, she's not responded.

"Her parents have been arrested for possession of drugs."

"What?" Harley shrieks, making me wonder just how well Poppy had covered all this up.

"Fucking hell. Where are they all?"

"With their aunt. She's good, they're safe," he says, pinning me with a look.

"That's good."

"What's going to happen? They'll get off, right?" Harley asks.

"No, I don't think so."

"But... shit. They're druggies? No wonder she stopped inviting me over. Jesus, it's like we've just fallen back into Harrow Creek," Harley mutters, making Amalie's brows pull together. I'm not surprised she's never heard of the place. I wish I hadn't.

"They're coming back though, right?"

"Honestly, I don't think so. Trish said they can stay as long as they need to. They've got no reason to come back without their parents."

"Uh uh, no way. This isn't happening." The three of us watch as Harley marches from the room like a woman on a mission.

"Where's she going?" Jake asks.

"No idea. I gave up trying to predict her years ago."

I fall down onto the couch and tip my head back, trying to process everything Jake's just said.

"What about..."

"Preston?"

"I've got guys watching him."

I raise a brow and Amalie laughs. "He thinks he's suddenly some gangster boss or something."

"Ignore her. If I start sniffing around, he's going to get suspicious. Ethan is going to try to talk to him, Mason too. See if they can sweeten him up. If he's doing what you think he is then I'm going to fucking end him."

"Be sensible. We don't need you in prison too," I mutter, leaning forward and dropping my head between my shoulders.

"You got anything else you want to tell me, Hunter?"

I look up at him and swallow nervously. His eyes drill into mine.

"No." I could tell him that Poppy and I had a thing. What's the point if she's not coming back here?

"Are you coming to Justin's party?" Amalie asks, trying to break the tension.

My lips part. My first reaction is to say no, to go upstairs and wallow like a pussy. But what good is that going to do?

"Yep, let me go get changed and we can go and get fucked up."

I walk out to the sound of them talking behind me, but I don't pay any attention to the words. Now the idea has been planted, all I want to do is go and get trashed and forget all this shit.

Justin's house is smaller than mine or Ethan's where we usually party, but it's plenty big enough for the team and the squad, and the few others that decide to gate-crash.

The second we arrive, Jake and Amalie head off to the left, I guess in search of their other couples while I march straight down to the kitchen.

There are bottles and Solo cups covering every surface. Ignoring the cups, I go straight for a bottle and then in search of the guys.

I find most of them in Justin's study where the speakers are with the majority of the squad grinding up against them. I look around, thankfully not finding my sister. Although I do lock eyes with Ruby.

Her chin drops before she stumbles her way over to me, clearly having already had one too many drinks.

"Where is she? Is she okay?" she slurs as she crashes into me with her need for answers.

Placing my hands on her waist, I steady her, looking down into her blown eyes.

I lean into her so no one else can hear me. "She's okay. Her parents have been arrested. She's with her aunt."

"Arrested?" she shouts, causing a few people to look over.

"Keep your voice down, Rubes. I'm sure she doesn't want everyone knowing."

"Shit. She's coming back though, right. You're going to go and get her."

My fists clench with my need to do just that.

"I can't do that."

"Why not? She belongs here. With you."

My lips part to respond but I'm too thrown by her last two words to form any of my own.

"You know…"

"Yeah, don't worry. Your secret is safe with me."

"Shush, or it's not going to be secret that needs keeping."

Threading my fingers through hers, I pull her from the room in the hope of finding somewhere quieter to have this conversation.

Dragging her into the dining room, I kick the door closed behind us before twisting the cap off the bottle of vodka and swallowing a generous mouthful. The alcohol burns my throat but it's exactly what I need.

"What do you know?" I turn on Ruby.

"Share and I might tell you."

Rolling my eyes at her, I hand the bottle over and watch her as she takes a shot.

"So?"

"I know you've been banging her. I know you've been sneaking around. And, I know that Harley has no idea." She smiles wickedly at me. "Oh, I also know something else..." She taps her index finger to her lips teasingly. "Oh yeah, that's it. She fucking loves it!"

"Jesus. You need to stop," I snap, snatching the bottle from her when she goes to have more.

"What happened, Ruby? You used to be the sweet one then suddenly..." I wave my hand at her. "You're a mess."

"Yeah, well, that's what happens when bad boys sweep in and shatter our innocent little hearts." My chin drops at her words. I assumed it was something to do with a guy, but I didn't know for sure. "What? You don't think you're going to do the same to Poppy? Bad boys never change, Zayn. They might pretend to for a while. But they always screw you over eventually."

"Who was it?"

"Ah, ah, ah," she says, pushing from the wall and stalking toward me. "It's too late to defend my honor now, Hunter. You had your chance with me. Now you're fucking my friend so you, my friend," she says, tapping my nose. "Are off-limits. To both my body and my secrets. Now..." She takes my hand and pulls me toward the door, or attempts to, seeing as she doesn't weigh much more than a feather, she doesn't get very far. "Let's go dance, knowing that we won't end up in bed together tonight. Although," she stops, running her eyes down the length of my body. It wasn't so long ago that I might have been affected by her heated stare, but now, after everything with Poppy, my cock just isn't interested. "I have it on good authority that you've got skills."

"Yeah, no more drinks for you."

I give into her and allow her to pull me back down to the

study and when she spins into my arms, I comply, because what she just said is true, nothing will happen between us.

Twisting my head to the side, I take another drink of my vodka as she grinds against me, but at no point do I offer her anymore. She needs to sober the fuck up before some other asshole decides they want to take advantage of her.

"Hey, I wondered when you were going to show," a sickly-sweet voice says as a warm hand brushes across my back before stopping on my bicep.

Ripping my eyes from Ruby, I find Laurie smiling at me seductively.

"Sorry, he's taken," Ruby slurs at her. "Go find yourself another player for the night."

"It didn't stop you from sharing before."

Regret fills me from that night. I shouldn't have touched Ruby, but I'm starting to learn that I don't have all that much restraint when it comes to my sister's friends, but I really shouldn't have gone near Laurie. She's a stage five clinger.

Laurie physically pushes herself between me and Ruby.

"Oh look, he's dancing with me now."

"Fucking hell," I mutter, finishing off my bottle in just a couple of huge swallows.

Laurie starts moving, her talons digging into the skin of my shoulders and her overbearing perfume filling my nose.

———

Groaning, I roll over onto my back but find my arm is trapped under something... fuck.

I sit bolt upright, rolling the person who was like a dead weight pinning me to the bed straight off the other side.

"Ow, what the fuck?" a croaky voice barks before a familiar head pokes above the side of the mattress.

"Ruby?" I ask, rubbing my eyes, trying to get them to focus

while I attempt to remember anything about getting home last night.

Glancing down at myself, I relax a little when I find I'm fully dressed.

"Well, that wasn't exactly the thank you I was expecting for getting you home in one piece and away from Laurie's grasp."

"Uh... what... um..."

"Oh, calm down," she says, climbing back onto the bed. "Nothing happened."

"Okay, so... why are you here exactly?"

"I took your advice and sobered up, while you got shit-faced. Then before you did something really fucking stupid like suck Laurie's face off, or worse, I made you leave."

"Okay, that's... g-good. But still, why are you here?"

"I wasn't intending to stay, I had a car outside waiting to take me home but you dragged me down with you, tucked me into your side told me how much you missed me and other similar soppy shit—I assumed you thought I was Poppy, whatever." She waves it off like it's nothing before continuing. "You passed out and I couldn't get out, so I thought fuck it and went to sleep while you were still muttering crap."

"Right," I say, rubbing my hand down my face. "Jesus, this is a mess."

"Nothing happened, Zayn. Poppy is my best friend, I'd never."

"I know. I know. I didn't mean that." Scooting back, I rest my back against the headboard and rest my arms over my knees as the incessant pounding at my temples continues.

"You need to talk to her," she says, copying my position.

"Yeah, well... she'd need to answer her cell for that to happen."

"Jake knows where she is. Go to her."

"Her world's just been turned upside down, Rubes. The last thing she needs is me storming in and making it worse."

"Who says you'd make it worse? She might be waiting for you." She turns to look at me and raises a brow.

"Why is this so hard?"

"Nothing to do with relationships is meant to be easy, Zayn. That's why they're so much fun." She smiles but it doesn't meet her eyes.

"You want to talk about it?" I offer, seeing as she's been my sounding board this morning.

"Nah. Unlike you two, it's hopeless even thinking about it."

"Okay, well. The offer stands should you need it."

"I appreciate it." She scoots to the edge of the bed. "You mind if I..." She gestures to the bathroom.

"Fill your boots. You want me to call you an Uber to get home?" I call before she closes the door.

"That would be awesome, thanks."

Ignoring all my social media apps, I pull up the Uber one and call for a car. I don't have the energy to deal with high school gossip and drama right now, not when I've got enough of my own going on.

Ruby emerges a few minutes later, looking a lot more put together than I feel.

"Your car will be here in a few."

"Walk me out?"

Thankfully, we don't see Harley, the last thing I need with the reminder of last night's alcohol running around my system is to try to convince her that nothing happened with Ruby.

"Thank you," I say, trying to sound as sincere as possible as she makes her way down to the waiting car.

"You too, you probably stopped me from making a huge mistake last night too."

A warning to take care of herself is on the tip of my tongue, but I swallow it down. She's already got a dad to give her those kinds of warnings, I need to butt out.

I wave her off as her car speeds down the street before walking to the kitchen.

"Really?" Mom asks, looking over my shoulder to where Ruby just disappeared.

"Nothing like that. Promise."

"I should hope not." She narrows her eyes at me, and I immediately feel like a kid again.

I make myself a coffee and sit up on the stool next to her.

"You heard about Poppy?" Mom asks. She stares at me as if she's trying to read my reaction for some reason.

"Yeah, sounds awful."

She continues to study me.

"What?"

"Harley asked me to get involved to see if I can help, maybe see if there's a way for her to come back to Rosewood to finish school here."

"Right," I say, letting her words settle as I sip at my too hot coffee.

"How would you feel about that?" She pins me with another look that has me wondering if she's not really asking the question she's making out to be.

"Um..." Something flutters in my belly at the thought of her being about to get Poppy back to finish school. I have no idea if that's what she'd want. But I can't imagine she'd be too thrilled at having to start over. I know I'm not happy about it, but it's not my life that's just been thrown into a tailspin. "I guess that's up to Poppy. No harm in asking though, staying at Rosewood High would make life easier for her, I'm sure."

Her eyes bounce between mine. "Okay."

"Okay?"

She nods and looks back to her tablet that she was reading before I joined her.

"Zayn," she calls out when I'm at the door. "I left something on your dresser while you were out last night that I found in my laundry. I know it doesn't belong to me or your sisters." She quirks a brow, a small smile playing on her lips.

"Uh… okay, thanks."

I walk away wondering what the hell she's playing at, I'm even more confused when I walk into my room and discover what I missed last night—not hard with how drunk I was—and this morning. Reaching out, I run my finger over the lace of Poppy's bra.

Looking back over my shoulder at my door, I wonder how much Mom knows. Is that why she was being weird asking me about Poppy downstairs.

I place her bra in my drawer and fall back down in the bed as both Ruby's and Mom's words from this morning swirl around my head.

27

Poppy

For some stupid reason, the first thing I did this morning was reach for my cell. Huge fucking mistake.

I'd hoped to find a message from Jake, Harley, Ruby, even another from Zayn so I knew they hadn't forgotten me already despite the fact I haven't replied to any of the previous ones yet.

The last thing I expected to find when I opened Instagram was my feed full of images of last night's party, with close-up photographs of Zayn with Laurie pressed against him.

Because looking at one image wasn't enough. I click on her profile and open each one. They're all selfies of them dancing, of their bodies pressed up against each other's, her lips pressed to his neck, his cheek, the corner of his mouth.

My stomach still turns over now as I think about it, my fists curling in the sheets beneath me. I was barely gone a few hours and he's already going after a cheer slut.

I don't know why I'm surprised. He's got a reputation after all.

I just thought, stupidly, that things were different. That he —we—were different.

Stupid, stupid, Poppy.

"Poppy, you've got a visitor," Auntie Trish calls down to my bedroom where I'm lying on the bed staring at the ceiling. I've got a million and one things I probably should be doing, but I can't focus on anything.

"Okay."

I swing my legs off the bed and pull my hair back into a messy bun. I washed it earlier and then had an afternoon nap with it wet, who knows what kind of mess it's in now.

I glance down at myself. Black sweats and an oversized gray hoodie. Yeah, I've never looked better. I roll my eyes at myself and head out assuming it's Bea or the police and I really don't give a crap how they think I look.

Auntie Trish's voice fills the air around me as I make my way toward the front door, but I don't hear another voice. So when I round the corner the last person I expect to find standing on the porch is the person who's been tormenting me all morning.

"What are you doing here?" I snap, marching over to where Zayn's standing.

"Uh... I think I'll leave you two to it," Auntie Trish announces, before spinning on her heels and walking toward me. "He's cute," she whispers in my ear as she passes.

"Hmm... shame he's a dick."

She gasps as Zayn's eyes narrow on me in confusion.

Nice fucking try, Hunter. I'm not falling for these games. I might not be in town right now but I see you and your manwhore ways.

"Pops," he whispers, the frown lines on his forehead deepening the closer I get.

"Don't. Don't Pops me. Not after what you've done."

"Me?" he asks, innocently pointing at himself.

"Do yourself a favor and knock off the act. It's not going to work on me, Hunter." I practically spit his last name.

"Oh, on last name terms are we now, Poore? And here I was coming to see how you were doing because I was concerned."

"Concerned? Oh yeah, you looked so concerned last night. Fun party, was it?"

"No, not really."

"You're such a fucking liar. I don't know what I was even thinking these past few weeks. It was a game, wasn't it? Some stupid pact with the team, see how far you can take things before you drop me from a great height."

"What the hell are you talking about?" He takes a step forward as if he's about to invite himself in.

Reaching out, I grab the door and close it slightly, shuffling forward so he has no choice but to stay out on the porch.

"I can't believe how easily I fell for it. I'm so fucking stupid. Was it *his* idea? Was that his way of ruining my life? He discovered my weakness and somehow convinced you to join in his sick and twisted games."

"Well?" I ask, throwing my arms up when he just stands gaping at me. "You win, okay. You fucking win," I scream as if the motherfucker is out there listening to this. "You ruined my life, well done. Everything's fucked. Congratulations."

Zayn's hand touching my forearm finally stops my rant.

"Pops, what are you talking about? I'm not playing any game. I've already told you that."

He takes a step toward me, his heat burning into my front through my baggy clothes.

"No, Zayn," I try to argue as he brushes his knuckles gently up my arm and wraps his hand around the back of my neck.

He drops his forehead to mine and I have to really fight not to give in to the pull I feel toward him.

It's been easier to ignore while I've been here, knowing there's so much distance between us but now he's here, now his scent is filling my nose and the heat of his skin burning into mine, my resolve is slipping.

"No, Zayn. I can't do this."

"Why?"

"Why?" I ask, a bitter laugh falling from my lips. "Maybe because you spent most of last night grinding against Laurie, and that's only what the camera caught. I hate to think what happened after."

"Nothing happened with Laurie, Pops."

"Try telling her Instagram that."

"It's just photos. She was drunk. I was drunk."

"Yeah, exactly. Are you going to try to tell me you remember the night?"

"I—"

"Exactly. You have no fucking clue. I should have known you'd never change."

"But—"

"No, Zayn," I bark. "I'm not interested. In case you hadn't noticed, my life is already in crisis right now. I don't need your drama and lies on top of all of that. Now, did you come here for anything else or are you done?"

"I—"

Before he gets another word out, I take a huge step back and swing the door closed. The entire house rattles with the force of the slam.

The second it's closed and I can no longer see him, feel his touch, tears fill my eyes before spilling over.

"Poppy," he shouts, slamming his fists down on the door. "Poppy."

Sucking in some confidence, I take another step back in an

attempt to stop myself from reaching back out, pulling the door open and falling into his arms.

I can't.

It's over.

My life as I knew it is over.

"No, you need to leave."

Spinning, I run full pelt to my room ready to lock myself inside and to spend the rest of the afternoon sobbing into my pillow, only I don't make it that far.

I'm stopped by a warm body before a pair of arms wrap around my shoulders.

"Shush now," Auntie Trish soothes in my ear as she holds me.

I have no idea how much time passes as I cry on her shoulder for everything that's happened in the last two days. But seeing Zayn, knowing that life is carrying on at home as if I was never there has reality slamming into me.

Rosewood is my home, it always has been. Who am I now?

I have no friends, no life, no future.

I'm just lost.

So fucking lost.

At some point she must move us because the softness of my bed hits my ass.

"I'm so sorry," I mutter, wiping at her soaked shirt.

"Poppy, it's okay. You have nothing to apologize for. I can't even begin to imagine how you're dealing with this right now."

I tuck myself back against her and she rocks me for long minutes as if I'm a kid. Which, I guess, I am despite the seriousness of the situation I'm trying to deal with right now.

"Do you want to talk about it... about him?" she asks after several long silent minutes.

Uncle Evan took the kids to the store a while ago to give them a change of scenery, so we've got the house to ourselves.

"His name is Zayn. He's my best friend's brother."

"Ohhh," she says with a knowing chuckle.

"He was very nice to look at. I'm not surprised you've fallen for his charms."

"He's not my boyfriend."

"No? He seemed pretty concerned about you, not to be yours."

"He didn't seem that concerned at a party last night. The evidence is all over social media."

"Poppy, you're a smart girl, I don't need to tell you how social media morphs things. It only shows you a small part of a story." Auntie Trish's voice holds a seriousness that only comes with experience, but then I guess that comes with the territory of being a student support advisor at MKU. I bet just a few of her issues stem straight from social media.

"I know," I mutter. "But seeing those images while I'm here." I blow out a breath. "It hurt, you know."

"I do, Poppy. I understand." She squeezes me tighter. "You want a giant mug of hot chocolate? I think I might even have some marshmallows in the back of the cupboard somewhere."

"That sounds really good."

She leaves me to sort myself out and after splashing my face with cold water, I risk a look out my bedroom window. The driveway where Zayn's truck was parked is now empty. My cell taunts me from the nightstand, but I ignore it. If there's anything on there from him then it's got the power to break me.

"I didn't think I'd miss Rosewood like I do," I admit once I'm curled up on the couch with a steaming mug of chocolate cradled in my hands. "I always thought getting away would be the best thing to happen to me, I know I didn't expect it to be with these circumstances but, I'm starting to wonder if maybe it wasn't so bad."

"I remember being exactly the same way when I was applying to out-of-state colleges. I thought getting out of

Rosewood would open up the world to me. Turns out, I'm a total homebody. I never even made it to the first day. I ended up at MKU, and look how far I've gone since. I still work there."

"It's a good college. I've looked at it with my friends," I admit.

"Yeah? Do you have any idea what you want to do?"

I shake my head. "My plan was to just get away, but I'm starting to wonder if that's what I want."

"If you could go back to Rosewood now, would you?"

"Yes," I say before I've even registered that I've spoken. "I mean, I don't know. Things with Zayn are complicated, then this whole other issue with another guy. It would be easier to just run away."

"But you don't want to do that, do you?"

I shrug. "Better the devil you know, I guess." I think of Preston and a thought slams into me. "Have the police said how they discovered all this?" I ask as innocently as possible.

"I believe they were tipped off by someone. But I only overheard that when they were talking to each other."

"Of course they did."

"Poppy?"

"It's nothing. It doesn't matter." It's the truth. If my life is going to be here now, then none of it matters. I no longer have to fear Preston and his ever increasingly dangerous games. He'll need to find another way to get to Jake because he's just lost his pawn.

It makes me wonder what his game plan was with it all. If he even had one at all. Is he just that sick that what started as a plan soon turned into something much more sinister? Unless he turns up here now, he's got no leverage with Jake. If it was him who did this, he's handed all his information to the authorities instead of using it to blackmail me.

"Are you okay?" Auntie Trish asks, studying me where I'm lost in thought.

"Y-yeah." I sigh.

———

The next few days pass in a blur. We have more social worker visits, more police visits but nothing really changes. Aside from being told that Mom's been bailed as suspected and assured that any contact with us will land her straight back inside. Dad's still in custody, he has bigger issues than just possession it seems, but I zoned out when the officer was explaining it. They're both going away and will be until I'm old enough to live my own life. If it's five years to twenty-five years, it really makes no difference to me now. Our relationship was ruined years ago because of all this.

It's Tuesday afternoon and I'm walking back from the park with the kids after getting them out for some sun when I walk up the street to find a familiar car sitting in the driveway. I walk up beside it, telling Austin and Sofia to head inside while I bump Cooper's stroller up the steps.

"Jada, what are you doing here?" I don't mean it to come out accusatory, but it does, and I wince. "I mean, it's good to see you."

"You too, Poppy. How are you doing?"

"Oh, you know," I mutter, unstrapping Cooper and lifting him into my arms.

"I'll just go grab his bottle."

We both watch as my aunt disappears inside.

"You're a real cutie," Jada coos at Cooper. "Seems like a lifetime ago having babies this young around."

An awkward silence falls between us as Cooper giggles at Jada.

"Harley is missing you," she finally says.

"It's only been a few days."

"She's worried you're not going to come back."

"Well, I probably won't," I say on a sigh.

"Poppy," she says, her serious tone making me turn to look at her. "I know things are complicated and confusing right now, but if you want to come back and go to school, there is a place for you at my house."

My chin drops in shock.

"I know you've got a lot of things to think about right now and a lot of things are up in the air, but I'd never forgive myself if I didn't at least offer you the chance of keeping just one thing normal in your life. I know how hard starting over at a new school can be, especially on top of everything else."

"Wow," I breathe. "I really didn't see that coming."

She chuckles at me as Auntie Trish comes back.

"You want to feed him?" I offer to Jada, although I soon regret the offer when I glance at her pristine black pantsuit.

But she surprises me when her face lights up. "Yes, I'd love to. It's been so long since I held a baby."

I pass him over and she gets him settled before Auntie Trish hands over his bottle. Cooper greedily sucks it into his mouth the second Jada has it anywhere near, making her laugh.

The three of us chat about the weather and other nonsense subjects while avoiding the huge elephant that's staring at us.

I can only assume that Jada's already told Auntie Trish about the offer she just made me but neither of them bring it up.

Jada stays for another thirty minutes before announcing that she needs to get back.

She turns to me, a serious yet kind expression on her face. "Think about what I said, the offer is open should you want it. Oh and, Harley wanted me to let you know that there's a party at Ethan's Friday night and she'd love for you to come. You can stay at ours as long as you need."

"Thank you, I really appreciate it," I say, feeling totally blown away by her offer.

We wave her off before Auntie Trish goes to put Cooper down for a nap while the squeals of Austin and Sofia sound out from the house where they're playing.

"She's nice," Auntie Trish says when she finally joins me once more. "I'm glad you accepted her arrival better than her son." She laughs.

"Jada is an incredible mom. Harley, Zayn, and Letty are lucky to have her."

"She was serious with what she said. If you feel like you need to go back, then she's willing to make that happen."

"I know," I say, still trying to get my head around it.

"I'll leave you to it. You don't need to make any decisions right away, like she said, there's a lot up in the air right now. A lot of answers we don't have. Just take it one step at a time. School and the future can wait."

28

Poppy

Jada's offer and her mention of Harley wanting me to go back this weekend spun around my head all night. But no matter how much time passed, I was no closer to finding an answer.

Would it be easier to go back to Rosewood and return to school Monday as if nothing happened? Sure. But do I want to? I have no idea.

Going back means dealing with Zayn, and worse, Preston. I still have no idea if my suspicion about this all being down to him is warranted or not, but it still niggles away at me.

Uncle Evan and Auntie Trish's home phone rang during dinner last night, and the second she discovered it was Jake checking up on me, seeing as I was still refusing to deal with the many missed calls and messages on my cell, she immediately invited him to dinner tonight.

She's trying so hard to make things as normal as possible

for me, but as each hour passes, I'm realizing that there's a bigger hole opening up inside me.

Auntie Trish and Uncle Evan are incredible, but as much as I want this place to become home, it's never going to be.

The thought of Jake coming for the night perks me up and I even find myself showering and pulling on real clothes and some makeup.

"Poppy, you look lovely." Auntie Trish beams at me when I finally leave the safety of my room. I've been spending more and more time locked up in there while slowly handing over the role of mother of the kids to our aunt and uncle.

"Thank you. It feels good to be normal."

"One step at a time, Poppy."

I give her a sad smile before offering to help her in the kitchen. I can see she wants to argue about it, but after another look in my eyes, she concedes and allows me to take over vegetable chopping. It's the perfect kind of mind-numbing job I need until our guest arrives.

I'm pulling open the front door the second the rumble of an engine vibrates through the house.

"Hey," I say, smiling wider than I'm sure I have in days when Jake climbs from the car and walks over to me. "No Amalie?"

"Nah, she's having a girls' night with Cami, Rae, and Chelsea. You're stuck with just me, I'm afraid."

"Ugh, how will I cope?" I joke as he ruffles my hair like he used to do when we were kids.

"How you holding up?"

I consider lying but I'm pretty sure it would be pointless, Jake can read me better than that. "I have no idea. Everything is just... weird."

"You homesick yet?" he asks, probably knowing that I've never actually left Rosewood for any length of time before.

"Yeah. I never thought I would be, but I actually miss the

place. Jada offered for me to move in with her?" He stills at my words.

"Oh? Are you thinking about it?"

"Yeah, I guess. It would mean I could come back to school. Life could kind of carry on."

"I'd love to have you back, you know that. But you need to do what's going to make you happy. Life's too short to be miserable, Popsicle."

"Whoa, when did you get all wise and start seeing the positive side of things? Anything to do with a certain Brit?"

He laughs. "You know it. What's for dinner? It smells incredible."

We walk inside the house with me tucked under his arm and still unable to wipe the smile off my face. I know that Auntie Trish and Uncle Evan are my family, that the kids are my family. But there's something about being with Jake that just makes me feel safe, secure, loved in his own unique Jake way.

The seven of us sit around the dining room table and eat Auntie Trish's homemade pie as if we're a normal family. It's... nice. Normal.

Jake tells stories about what the team has been up to along with tales about him and Amalie moving into their new house and all the kinds of grown-up things I never expected him to do. But it seems that what they say is true, the right woman really can work wonders on a guy.

By the time we're full and the kids are sent to start getting ready for bed, Uncle Evan excuses himself to the living room after Jake and I insist that we'll do the cleaning. We're just about to get up and make a start when Auntie Trish stops us.

"That can wait, can I talk to you both first?"

I glance from her and to Jake who looks as confused as I feel before we agree and follow her down to her office.

She closes the door behind us and gestures for us to take a

seat on her couch while she wheels over her desk chair. I can't help feeling like one of the students she looks after at college. I feel like I'm about to get a speech about something important that might just help change my life.

"I don't think it's really my place to explain all of this to you both, but with the circumstances as they are, I think it's only fair that you finally learned the truth."

Auntie Trish looks at me as a swarm of butterflies take flight in my stomach. What the hell is she about to tell us.

Jake reaches over and takes my hand, clearly sensing that something big is about to happen too.

"Poppy, my brother isn't your dad."

"What?" I gasp, sitting forward for a beat while that bit of information filters through my brain before falling back on the couch in shock.

"So who is?" Jake asks as my head spins.

"Yours, Jake." His hand tightens on mine as the silence in the small room becomes deafening. "So... you're saying that we have... the same dad?"

Jake looks at me for a second before turning back to Auntie Trish.

"But I've never met my dad."

"Not that you would remember, no. But he was here when both of you were born."

"Fuck," Jake mutters, running his hand down his face. "Where is he? What happened to him?"

"He went to prison when you were only one."

"And what about after that?"

Auntie Trish looks down at her hands for a beat. "I'm really sorry. He fell into the wrong crowd, prison only made it worse. He's not..."

"He's dead?" Jake asks bluntly. "Of course he is," he mutters to himself. I don't think Auntie Trish hears, but I do.

Scooting closer, I wrap my arm around his shoulders. "I'm sorry, Jake."

"Nothing to be sorry about." He drops a kiss to my head.

"You knew him?" I ask Auntie Trish.

"We all went to school together," she says, repeating her words from the other night. "He was your mom's boyfriend all through high school. Childhood sweethearts that everyone thought would go the distance."

"What happened?"

"Your mom," she says with a sigh, looking to Jake. "From as early as I can remember they had their fierce sisterly rivalry going on. Everything was a challenge, just like your dad was. In the end, he didn't stand a chance. When Kate first announced she was pregnant, she didn't say who the dad was, but it soon came out. It was a mess, as you can probably imagine. But your mom took him back and a year later, announced she was pregnant with you," she explains, looking at me.

"So why keep it a secret?"

"Your dad was gone by then and Will and your mom had got together while she was pregnant, so they just decided to raise you as theirs and let Kate get on with her life. For whatever reason I still don't fully understand, they thought it was for the best."

"Wow," I breathe, falling back against the couch once more when Jake does.

"I know. I've thought you should have known for years, forever really. I know it wasn't really for me to say but..."

"Thank you. You did the right thing."

She smiles at both of us, but it doesn't meet her eyes.

"I'll leave you two to mull all this over. Call me if you need me. Jake, you're welcome to stay as long as you like."

She leaves the room, pulling the door closed behind her. The click of the lock cutting through the silent room.

"Well, I guess that explains a lot," Jake whispers, still staring ahead as if it's not really sunk in yet.

"Yeah. I always wondered why my mom treated you the way she did, how she could shove you out in that trailer. I guess this answers all those questions."

"Yeah." He turns to me. I expect to find a haunted look on his face after all those revelations. After all, Jake just gained and lost a parent in the blink of an eye when he could really use a decent one, much like I could, I guess. But when our eyes lock, all I find staring back at me is happiness.

A shriek rips past my lips when I'm suddenly pulled into his arms.

"You're my fucking sister," he says as if it's the most incredible thing he's ever heard. "I've got a sister."

I can't help but laugh into his chest at the awe in his voice. Rosewood's king, bad-boy Jake Thorn is totally bowled over by the fact I'm his sister. Me.

When he finally releases me, I find he's still got the smile on his face but also that his eyes are full of unshed tears.

"You know what this means?" he asks me excitedly.

"Uh..." I hesitate, trying to figure out where he might be going with this.

"You're Poppy Thorn."

"Huh, I guess I am."

"Has a good ring to it, right."

"It does. Although realistically, it couldn't be any worse than Poppy Poore. What was my mother thinking giving me his name?" I'm not sure it's totally appropriate to joke about it yet but when I meet Jake's eyes, both of us burst out laughing.

It feels so good after the past week of drama to just laugh. Even if it is at my own expense.

"You should totally change that, you know?"

Our laughter eventually fades off into the distance and sadly, my reality comes creeping back in.

"What are you going to do, Pops?"

My heart clenches painfully in my chest at the concern in his eyes. Suddenly, Jada's offer doesn't seem so crazy. Yes, I'd be leaving Austin, Sofia, and Cooper here, but I'd be leaving them in a loving home where they're going to get the care they deserve, and I could be with my friends, my brother. I shake my head, still not quite able to process everything. I could return to school and pick up where I left off, there would be no starting over and being the new kid.

"I think... I think I might come back."

"Really?" he asks, hope filling his features.

"Yeah. Rosewood is my home." Reaching for his hand, I squeeze. "It's where my family is."

"You could move in with us," he blurts, clearly not thinking straight.

"No, Jake. I appreciate the offer. But that's yours and Amalie's house. If Jada is serious, and I think she is, then I'll be okay there."

"But—"

"It's okay, Jake," I say, cutting him off. "I know you only want to look out for me, and that means the world to me, it really does. But I'll be okay there. We can hang out whenever, it's not like you don't ever go to the Hunter's."

He nods, knowing that I'm right.

"Pops, can I ask you something?"

"S-sure," I say, although I'm not entirely sure I'm happy with where this could be going.

"Preston Hellburn."

I rip my eyes from his, not wanting to go down this road but also knowing that it's inevitable if I'm actually going to go back. He's going to be waiting for me.

"Hunter's right, isn't he?"

"Jake," I breathe. "He's just playing a stupid game. He's trying to get to you through me."

"I don't give a shit, Poppy. No one messes with my family. I don't give a shit who his dad is or how much money they've got. This shit ends before you start back at Rosewood. You got it?"

All I can do is nod. I can't lie, seeing Jake so fired up kinda scares me.

"Please don't do anything stupid. I can't lose you, Jake." My voice trembles at the end as my emotions get the better of me.

"I'm not going anywhere, Poppy." He pulls me into his arms once more. "But I do need you to tell me what he's been doing. Not tonight, but soon. That motherfucker is going to regret the day he ever laid a finger on you, Popsicle."

Although my stomach is heavy with dread, hearing Jake say he's going to fight for me is a huge relief. I've carried the burden of Preston around with me for long enough. It's time it comes to an end.

"Harley invited me to a party Friday night."

"Ethan's. You should come. Let your hair down. You deserve it."

"Will he be there?"

"He'll find his ass kicked to the curb if he tries to be."

"Okay. Yeah. I'll talk to Jada and see if I can come back Friday. Maybe even come back to school Monday?"

"Yes. You belong in Rosewood, Pops."

"I know."

"This place is great an' all, I know the kids will be happy here, but it's not your home."

I nod at him. "You should probably get back. Amalie will wonder where you've gone to."

"Are you kidding, they were going shopping and then for pizza, they'll be hours. I should probably head off though, let you get some rest. You look exhausted."

"I am," I say, thinking of just how little sleep I've got since being here. Something has settled inside me now I've made this decision and I wonder if it's enough to help me get some sleep.

We push from the couch but before we get to the door, Jake's voice stops me. "I can't believe you're my sister," he says, his voice laced with disbelief.

"I can. Deep down, I think a part of me has always known. We were never just cousins, Jake. Something always ran deeper than that."

"Yeah, you're right. It did."

I can't help it, when I finally crawl in bed later that night after talking to Auntie Trish and Uncle Evan, and calling Jada, I fall asleep with a wide smile on my face. Things might be well and truly fucked up, but there might just be light at the end of the tunnel for all of us.

This doesn't mean the thought of walking into Zayn's house and looking him in the eye again doesn't fill me with dread.

29

Zayn

"Harley, get your ass out here or you're going to have to find your own way there," I shout through her door where both my sister and Ruby are getting ready for tonight's party.

I'm not sure what the occasion is but it's Ethan's first party of the year and everyone seems to be going a little crazy for it.

"All right, keep your panties on," Harley snaps, ripping the door open and marching past me in a minuscule dress.

"What the fuck are you wearing? I can see your ass."

"It's a dress, *Dad,* and no, you can't... quite."

"You should be fucking glad I'm not Dad because there is no way he'd ever let you out of the house looking like that."

"Well, then I guess it's a good thing he's not here." She storms off down the stairs, Ruby emerges soon after, dressed similarly only in a pair of shorts that do show off her ass.

I stuff down my protective brotherly instinct and keep my

lips sealed about her outfit and trail behind them, shaking my head in frustration.

Mom's in the kitchen making herself some dinner as I pass.

"Please try to be sensible tonight," she calls to the three of us, but the girls are already halfway out the door so they don't even hear her. "Keep an eye on those two, and please, don't let me find some random girl in the house in the morning."

"I'll see what I can do." I salute her and head out to my car.

I don't have any intention of hooking up with anyone tonight. I fully intend on being able to drive those two back before they get themselves in any trouble.

The drive to Ethan's is short and by the time I find somewhere to park, I'm already regretting agreeing to this. The temptation to just drop Harley and Ruby off and then disappear is strong, but not wanting anything to happen to them in their nonexistent outfits, I reluctantly follow. They immediately go in search of drinks and the squad, whereas I go for Ethan's den, hoping to find the others in there away from the rest of the party.

I'm in luck because when I push through the door, I find Ethan and Rae, Jake and Amalie, Mason and Camila, and Shane and Chelsea littered around the couches.

"The party is out there, man," Ethan says with a smile, nodding to the door I just walked through.

I lift my can of Coke and fall down onto an empty bean bag. "Meh, I'm not really feeling it. I was just my sister's chaperone."

"Zayn Hunter not out partying and trying to get inside a cheer slut's panties, what the hell is happening?" Ethan barks. The others laugh along with him, apart from Shane and Jake.

Shane just has an amused, knowing smirk on his face while Jake stares daggers into me.

"What?" I mouth at him, feeling like I'm missing something.

His lips part to respond but Amalie notices and slaps his shoulder, causing him to shake his head and lift his drink to his lips.

"Well, okay then."

Now I want to be here even less than I did before, and that's really saying something.

Two hours later, I find myself in the kitchen with the team while they line up shots and dish out names for tonight's tagging.

I want to leave, I have no interest in their games tonight but the sight of Harley over Justin's shoulder grinding up against some guy I don't recognize in that ridiculous dress has me staying put.

I'm too busy watching her antics to notice the guys' attention turn to me. But that's all forgotten when Harley lets out a loud shriek that pierces through the booming music. Everyone looks her way but I'm quicker, I'm already in the room and ready to take down the guy she was with. But the second I see her run across the room on drunk unsteady legs, everything changes.

"You're here," Harley cries, throwing herself at Poppy who stands stock still in the entrance to the living room. Her eyes locked on me.

Relief, desire, and frustration engulf me as I run my eyes down the length of her. Her hair is curled and hanging in loose curls around her shoulders, her makeup is heavier than usual but flawless, and her body. Fuck. I bite down on the inside of my cheek as I take in her loose-fitted tank and the short skirt she's got wrapped around her waist.

My cock swells, my fists clench with my need to go over there and drag her out of the room so that no other guy can look at her, but the moment she rips her eyes from mine and embraces my sister, I know I can't.

Fueled by my anger, I storm out of the room and toward the pool area where there's another huge crowd of kids.

Someone, no idea who, hands me a joint and I happily take it as I fall down on the lounger.

The crowd inside continues to dance and enjoy themselves while I sit here stewing.

Why's she here? Did she take up Mom's offer? Is she staying or is this just a flying visit?

Before long, the blunt is taken by someone else and my need for a drink begins to get the better of me.

Pushing from the lounger, I make my way to the kitchen, telling myself I'm just going to grab a soda, although my need to drown everything out right now with something stronger nags at me.

I'm almost at the kitchen when her voice has a shiver racing down my spine.

"Zayn?"

I still, desperate to turn around but not wanting to look into her eyes again if she's going to dismiss me as easily as she did the last time I saw her.

"What?" I bark, without looking back, figuring it's the easiest way to deal with the situation unless we want to make a huge scene.

"We need to get Harley home."

Her words ruin whatever promises I'd just made to myself, and I find myself turning her way in an instant. Both Poppy and Ruby are holding on to a passed-out Harley.

"Fucking hell," I mutter, stepping up to them and scooping my sister up into my arms. "Let's go." I pin Ruby with a look, she might still be standing but she's in no better state.

I don't look to see if they fall in line behind me as I march from Ethan's house, I don't need to. I know her eyes are drilling into my back.

I place Harley into the back of my truck before helping Ruby inside. I don't bother assisting Poppy, instead, I just walk to the driver's side and rip the door open.

We've barely pulled away from where I'd parked when I look back to find Ruby passed out behind me.

"Why are you here?" I ask, my voice rougher, my question harsher than I was intending.

"It's good to see you too," she sasses.

"I'm sorry, but the last time I saw you, you slammed a door in my face. Apologies if I'm not all that welcoming right now." I focus on my anger, it helps my attempt to ignore how badly I want to pull her into my arms right now and never let go.

"I'm sorry," she whispers, refusing to look at me and instead keeps her eyes out the windshield.

"You're sorry for slamming the door or accusing me of going after a cheer slut the second you left?"

"Uh... both, I guess. I wasn't—I'm not—in a great place right now."

My grip on the wheel tightens, my knuckles turning white. I don't want to make her life any harder right now but fuck... having her turn me away like that. I won't lie, it was brutal.

I know I fucked up the night before letting Laurie get close, but nothing happened. I try to ignore the little voice in the back of my head that screams what I might have done had Ruby not been there. I hate that it's right. I could so easily have done something stupid that night.

I pull up outside my house and jump from the car before she has a chance to say anything, not that I'm sure she wants to.

I lift Harley into my arms once again as Poppy wakes Ruby enough for her to stagger inside.

After depositing them on Harley's bed, we both back out of the room, closing the door shut behind us.

"So what now?" Poppy asks, making me still where I was making my way to the stairs.

"Now? I need a fucking drink."

I take two steps but I don't get to descend.

"Zayn, please. We need to talk."

"Talk?" I balk. "That's what I came to do the other day. I—"

"Please, Zayn. I need…"

Blowing out a long breath, I turn around. My eyes lock on to her sad, lost ones and I cave. Only when I move for her, she retreats until she's at one of our guest bedroom doors. She pushes it open and walks inside.

I stalk toward her, my pulse thundering around my body with my need for her.

"Poppy, don't run from me."

"Zayn, we just need to…" She swallows nervously as I close the door, shutting us off from the rest of the house. "T-talk."

"I know."

She bumps up against the wall, but I don't stop. I don't stop until I'm pressed right up against her body with her heat burning into me.

"And we will talk. Right after we—"

My hand slides into her hair as my lips crash down to hers.

Fuck, I've missed this.

She stills for a few seconds, and I start to think she's going to push me away. I lean into her, my cock pressing against her stomach, trying to show her just how much I need her, and she finally caves and parts her lips for me.

A groan rumbles up my throat as her tongue glides against mine and she hooks her leg up around my waist.

Gripping on to the back of her thighs, I lift her, pinning her to the wall with my hips and pressing myself against her core.

"Zayn," she moans when I rip my lips from hers and begin kissing down her neck.

"Missed you, Pops," I breathe against her skin, causing goose bumps to break out.

Her nails scratch at my scalp as I get lower. "We shouldn't." Any attempt to actually stop me fails the second I push the straps of her top from her shoulders. "Oh God."

"You're right, Pops. We probably shouldn't. But doesn't that just make it so much hotter."

The fabric passes her nipples and I hungrily suck one into my mouth as she cries out, her head hitting the wall behind her.

"You need to be quiet," I warn, going for the other side.

"Your... your mom is o-out."

"Oh, now you tell me."

Spinning her from the wall, I throw her down on the guest bed, watching her bounce as she settles.

She props herself up on her elbows as I rip my shirt off and drop to my knees at the end of the bed.

"Well, now you've given me permission to make you scream." I reach for her hips, finding the lace of her panties and ripping them from her body before latching on to her clit.

"Zayn," she cries, her back arching, her hands twisting in the sheets beneath her. "Oh God. Oh God. Fuck."

Pushing two fingers inside her, I circle her clit before grazing it with my teeth.

"Come for me, Poppy. Show me how much you missed this."

Bending my fingers just so, she moans as I hit the spot before upping the ante on her clit.

"Come, Pops."

"Zayn," she cries, her muscles tightening around me and her body convulsing with her pleasure.

I don't stop until she's ridden out every last second, before standing, wiping my mouth with the back of my hand and dropping my pants and boxers to the floor and climbing between her legs.

Leaning over her, I capture her lips, allowing her to taste herself on me. She moans, her nails scratching down my back.

"I," I say, dropping a kiss to her lips. "Missed." Kiss. "You."

"Zayn." My name rips from her lips as half a demand for more and a warning.

"Shush, baby. Let me take care of you." Reaching down for my pants, I find a condom in my wallet and rip it open.

Poppy watches my every move with her bottom lip sucked into her mouth.

Part of me expects her to tell me to leave, that this shouldn't happen. But she never does.

Instead, the second I sweep my cock through her folds, her hips roll and she immediately sucks me deeper once I push into her.

"So fucking tight," I murmur against her lips as I slowly slide into her, inch by glorious inch.

Her hands burn a trail down my back before her nails scratch all the way back up.

"Fuck, yes," I grunt, dropping my head to the crook of her neck once I'm fully seated.

My speed increases and she meets me thrust for thrust as I chase the release we both need.

Dropping my hand down her body, I press my thumb against her clit and she detonates beneath me dragging me over the edge right along with her.

After pulling the condom off, I fall down on my back beside her and tangle my fingers with hers as our hearts return to normal and our skin cools.

"We shouldn't have done that." Her words are like a bucket of ice that is thrown over me.

Rolling onto my side, I turn to look at her. Tears pool in

her eyes once more but she refuses to let them drop, or even look at me as she continues staring at the ceiling.

"If this is going to work, then this," she says, gesturing between us. "Can't happen."

I look around the room and gasp when I find her suitcase sitting open on the other side of the room.

"You're coming back?"

"Yeah but—"

"Don't do this, Poppy. Don't shut this down because you're scared. I'm scared too. Fucking terrified actually. But this," I say, scooting closer to her and wrapping my arm around her waist. "But this is right. This is how it's meant to be."

"Jake's not my cousin, he's my brother," she blurts.

"Uh... what?" I ask, my brows pulled together in confusion.

"My dad... well, he wasn't my dad. I've come back for him, for Harley and Rubes. To finish school so I can finally get the fuck out of here for good." She swallows before turning to look at me. "I didn't come back for this. You need to leave."

30

———

Poppy

I force the words out past the huge lump in my throat, but as much as it kills me to say them. I know I'm right.

I can't move in here, attempt to restart my life while Zayn and I continue with this dirty little secret we started.

It's never going to work. We'll get caught and it'll ruin everything. Jake won't have it. Harley will hate me for lying to her.

The best thing that can happen now, is that both of us forget it even happened in the first place.

This is time for a fresh start, for all of us.

I can't watch as he swipes his clothes angrily from the floor and storms to the door.

He's still naked and my eyes beg for me to look over at him, but I can't. One look and he'll know I'm lying. That the last thing I want right now is for him to walk away.

But it's for the best.

With the silence around me threatening to engulf me. Zayn crashes about in his room for a minute or two, before the door is ripped open once more, he storms down the stairs before the force of the front door slamming rattles the entire house.

It's not until he's left, taking a piece of me with him, that I allow myself to break.

Curling in on myself, I hug the pillow that vaguely smells like him to my chest.

I must cry myself to sleep because the next thing I know, I come to, still naked and still hugging the damn pillow. My eyes feel puffy from the crying and my throat is dry.

He didn't come back last night, that I'm pretty sure of. Where did he go? Back to the party? What did he do?

Before I've processed the thought, I sit up in bed, wrap the sheets around my body and reach for my cell, intent on torturing myself by scrolling through social media for evidence of what he got up to. Did I send him straight into the arms of a willing cheer slut? A shiver rolls down my spine at the thought and my stomach churns.

I did the right thing. I did the right thing, I tell myself over and over. But it doesn't matter how many times I hear myself say the words, my heart doesn't listen. It just continues to ache knowing I sent one of the best parts of my life away.

I knew he was going to be angry, rightly so, I did slam a door in his face. But I thought he... my thoughts trail off. I only believed what the evidence was showing me. What else could I do?

Trust him.

Irritated with the little voice inside my head, I climb out of bed, glad that I didn't drink last night, having a hangover would only have made today worse than it already is. My body aches as I move, and when I look down at my hips, I find the faintest of bruises from Zayn's tight grip.

A lump crawls up my throat and my hand comes up to cover my mouth as I attempt to keep myself together.

Coming here was the right decision. I knew that the second Jada drove me into town. Something settled inside me, and even walking into this house, I felt more at home than I did any time I was in Auntie Trish's.

Jake wanted to come and get me and drive me back himself. He wasn't happy when I told him no, but he'd already been out twice in the past week. It was Friday night, he should have been out enjoying himself, although I did swear him to secrecy.

I wanted to surprise Harley and Ruby and not have to worry about the fact that Zayn knew I was coming. In hindsight, was that the best idea I've ever had? Probably not.

The feeling that washed through me the second our eyes locked in Ethan's house is one I'll probably never forget. The regret, the need, the pull. It was all stronger than I expected, and it nearly knocked me on my ass. Add in the anger that filled his features and pulled his muscles tight and I knew I'd made a mistake.

Shaking the memories from my head, I pull off a robe that's hanging on the back of the door and head for the bathroom.

Aside from a toothbrush, I don't have any of my own toiletries. Jada offered to take me to my house today to pick up some stuff but I refused her offer, she's already done too much for me.

That house has been my home for my entire life, how can it so suddenly turn into somewhere I hate?

The image of Austin and Sofia's tear-filled eyes as I said goodbye yesterday fills my mind. They didn't want me to go, I'd expected that, but I hadn't appreciated just how much their trembling bottom lips would rip me apart.

I know I'm doing the right thing for them though. They

can have a life in Maddison with Auntie Trish and Uncle Evan, that me, our parents, never could have offered them. The best thing that can happen for them now is for both our parents to go down and they never have to worry about them.

I shower with Harley's products, hoping that if I have the water hot enough and use enough soap that all my regrets will wash straight down the drain. It's wishful thinking because when I step out and wrap myself in a towel, I feel as if the weight of the world that's on my shoulders has only gotten heavier.

I just need to get through the weekend and get back to school. Get back to normal. Everything will be okay.

There's noise coming from downstairs as I walk back to my bedroom and the scent of coffee wafts up. Needing a huge mug of whatever Jada is brewing down there, I quickly pull on some clothes and go in search of some caffeine.

"Hey, sweetie. How was the party?" Jada asks, looking up from her tablet the second I join her.

"Um... it was...." I blow out a breath.

"That good?"

"Harley and Ruby got drunk. Zayn had to bring us all back," I say without thinking. Jada's cool, and with my own parents, not ones to ever really give a shit about anything, I forget that Harley might not want her mother knowing some things.

"Did they?" she asks, her eyes rolling.

"They were just excited to see me. Got a little carried away."

She nods, probably wondering why I'm so alert this morning if they were so trashed.

"You didn't want to celebrate being home?"

"Not really. I don't really drink."

Jada chuckles. "I knew there was a reason I liked you. Want to try to rub off on my kids a little while you're here?"

My cheeks burn as I think about just how closely I've been rubbing up against one of her kids.

"Help yourself to coffee. Anything. You know where most things are by now, don't hesitate to take whatever you need. This is your home now."

I make myself a coffee and join her.

"I don't know how to thank you for all of this."

"Don't be silly. I'm just happy to be able to help."

"I really appreciate it."

"I know, sweetie." She reaches out and squeezes my hand in support.

"Whatever you need, Poppy. Just ask. My door is always open." She smiles at me before going to make herself another coffee. "If you need me, I'll be in my office."

She wanders off with her fresh mug and my eyes follow her, wondering if I can be like her when I grow up. She has everything together. A great life, job, kids, house. She makes everything look so easy, although I can't help wondering if that's true or if she's just a great actress.

I only know a little about the Hunter's previous life, but it doesn't sound all that great. Letty, Zayn, and Harley should be really proud of her though. She took her happiness into her own hands and made herself the life she wanted.

I can only hope that I can do that one day for myself.

Feeling like I should probably start my first day here by pulling my weight, I hop down from the stool and set about finding ingredients to make pancakes. If the smell doesn't lure the girls from bed then I'll go up there and drag them out soon.

The need for coffee and sugar must have been enough because just as I'm flipping the first batch of pancakes onto a plate, footsteps sound out before two very sleepy, hungover heads appear in the kitchen doorway.

"It wasn't a dream. You're really here," Harley says,

beelining straight for me and pulling me into her arms. "I'm sorry, I got a little over-excited last night," she whispers into my ear.

"It's okay."

Seconds later, another set of arms wrap around both of us and I stand for long minutes accepting their support. I don't think I appreciated just how much I missed them in the week I was gone. They've both always been my main support network, and without them, I was drowning.

I know it was my own fault and I just should have picked up my cell, but it was easier said than done.

"Are you hungry?" I ask once they've released me.

"Starved. I'll get the coffee. Rubes, get the plates."

Not ten minutes later, Jada has rejoined us and we're sitting around the table stuffing our faces and chatting about life, mostly anything that doesn't involve my sudden arrival or my parents. I'm grateful they keep it light and keep me distracted from reality.

The second Jada has finished, she disappears to her office once more, leaving the three of us to chat about school and what I've missed.

Everything comes crashing down around my feet though when there's a rumble of an engine outside seconds before the front door slams shut.

I hold my breath waiting for him to walk around the corner, but no matter how much I think I can prepare myself for seeing him, when he emerges, it knocks the wind right out of me.

He looks a mess. His eyes are dark and bloodshot, his clothes are a crumpled mess.

"What the hell happened to you?" Harley asks, voicing the question that I'm sure is on all our lips.

"Nothing," he mutters, his angry eyes locked on mine as he makes his way to the coffee machine.

"I thought you brought us home."

"I did. Then I went back out. Problem?" he snaps.

"Um... no."

Ripping my eyes away from him, needing to sever the connection in the hope no one surrounding us notices, I stare down at my half-eaten plate of pancakes, my previous appetite suddenly gone.

"What are you all eating?" he asks, leaning back against the counter with his mug in hand.

"Poppy made pancakes. They were incredible."

"Oh, did she?" His eyes turn on me but I don't look up, instead I leave them to drill into the side of my head. "Didn't think to make any for me?"

"I would have if you were here."

"Well..."

Risking a glance up, I find him gesturing to himself.

"Here I am."

"Zayn, stop being a prick. Get your own breakfast," Harley snaps.

"It's okay, I can make more."

I push my chair out to do so, but Harley's hand lands on my shoulder. "No. Don't follow his rude demands. Enjoy your breakfast. He's big enough and ugly enough to sort himself out."

"But—" I look between Harley and Zayn, knowing that she is right but feeling that incredible pull toward him like always, despite what I said last night.

In the end, I side with Harley, refusing to bow down to Zayn when he's acting like he owns the place.

"You know where the fridge is. Excuse me," I mutter, pushing my chair out behind me and running for the stairs.

I manage to keep my sob in until I'm safely inside my bedroom. It rips from me the second I rest back against the door.

I'm not sure I can do this. Maybe coming here and believing I could live under the same roof as him was the stupidest thing I ever could have done.

My cell vibrates on the nightstand and distracts me from my meltdown.

Thinking it's probably Harley already asking if I'm okay, I rush over. But when I get there and take in the preview, my body turns to ice.

Unknown: Welcome home. Let the games begin...

My hands tremble as I stare down at his words. I haven't heard or even really seen him in over a week. I might have my suspicions about him being involved but other than that, he's been far from my mind. A part of me I think might have hoped that this was over. But it seems that his threat is still very, very real.

I look over my shoulder as someone runs up the stairs. I don't need to open the door to know it's Zayn. I can feel it.

I reach out to take my cell. I should show him. He'll know what to do about it. But I can't. I remember the way he looked at me downstairs. It was almost like I didn't even exist to him. I can't send him away one minute and then need him the next.

If I'm going to stand by my word, then I need to deal with my own issues. Even if they terrify me.

Squaring my shoulders, I delete his message and set about getting ready for my day, not that I have a clue what I'm doing, but I refuse to hide in here because of him.

I'm better than that. Stronger than that.

I'm putting my mascara on when a knock sounds out on my door. For a second my heart jumps into my throat thinking that it could be Zayn, but then I hear the girly chatter on the other side and I blow out a long breath, although I'm not sure if it's relief or disappointment.

"Come in," I call, shocked that they even waited long enough for me to respond. They don't usually have those kinds of boundaries.

They both pile in and dive on the bed.

"So what's the plan for the weekend then?" Harley asks, ignoring the elephant in the room that was me running from downstairs. I'm not sure why she lets me off, but I appreciate it.

"No idea."

"Ooh, we should go and get mani-pedis," Ruby pipes up.

"I'm easy. I do need to go back home though to get a few things."

"Okay well, why don't we swing by your place, grab what you need then we'll head for the nail place?"

"What about a spa? We could go all out," Ruby says, excitedly jumping up and down on the bed.

"Um... I can't really afford that," I say quietly.

"Oh, don't be silly. We've got you."

I shake my head, an uncomfortable feeling twisting my stomach. It's already too much that I'm living here and relying on the Hunters as much as I am. I don't need them paying for luxuries for me too. "No, I can't."

"Pops," Harley sighs.

"No," I say, holding my hand to stop her argument. "I need to focus. I need to get back to school, get a job, and start thinking about my future. You two go to the spa, but I can't waste a day or the money doing that."

They look between themselves, I can almost hear the words that are right on the tips of their tongues.

Thankfully both their cells beep, cutting off anything they were going to say.

They both pull them out and stare down.

"Ugh, Chelsea is calling us for a meeting at her place."

"On a Saturday?"

"Yup. Championships are approaching and she is like a dog with a bone."

"I guess you'd better go then."

They both complain as they climb from the bed, probably more to do with their lingering hangovers than the fact they need to go practice. I smile to myself wondering if Chelsea's demands might have something to do with the state of some of her squad last night, if her actions are really no more than a punishment for their actions.

"What are you smiling about?"

"Nothing. Can I... um... borrow your car?" I hate to ask, but I really don't want to walk or pay for an Uber to get to my house, and I really don't want to ask Zayn.

"Of course. Rubes can drive us. Let me go grab my key."

She disappears leaving me with Ruby.

"You know," she starts. "He really didn't do anything at the party last weekend." She pins me with a look I don't need.

"It doesn't matter."

"Doesn't it?"

"It's done, Rubes. It's over. It doesn't need talking about again."

She studies me for a few seconds as Harley's footsteps get closer once more.

"Sure, whatever you say." She rolls her eyes at me but ensures I can't comment because Harley throws her key over.

"Ready?" she asks Ruby.

"No, but let's go."

"We'll see you later, Pops. Be good."

I laugh at them. When aren't I good?

When you were fucking her brother behind her back.

Pushing the thought aside, I grab my purse, stuff my cell into it and pull on my sneakers.

The house is quiet as I make my way through, I have no

idea where Zayn went, and I'm sure Jada is in her office as usual.

I unlock Harley's car and slide into the driver's seat. It's been a while since I've driven, I can only hope it's like riding a bike.

Just as I'm about to back out, movement in the second floor window catches my eye. I shouldn't look, I know that, but my eyes have a mind of their own and in a beat, I find them locked on a pair of dark angry ones.

He's standing at the window topless with all his olive skin and taut muscles on display. My body reacts like it always does but I force myself to ignore it. I've got to stand by my words, it's the right thing to do.

Ripping my gaze from his, I go back to what I should be doing, and drive away. Although I soon realize that despite the fact I've put some space between us, he's still in my head, driving me fucking crazy.

Pulling up to outside the house I've called home for all my life is weird. I've never really felt a huge connection to the place, but it's even less now. It's just a building.

I'm not sure what I was expecting coming back here. Maybe to feel like I was coming home, maybe some kind of nostalgia. But there's nothing.

It's weird the feeling of not belonging anywhere. I didn't belong at Auntie Trish and Uncle Evan's, I'm not sure I really belong at the Hunter's, but I don't belong here either. I don't even want to be here. There are too many memories. Too much that haunts me.

Pushing the door wide, I climb from the car, my eyes darting around the front yard.

My skin tingles with awareness as if I'm being watched. But as I look around, I don't find anyone or see any movement.

Setting my apprehension aside, I walk up to the front door

and slide my key into the lock just like I've done a million times before.

The house is cold as I walk inside and I can't help but wonder what's going to happen with it when my parents are unable to come back. Others keep saying *if* to me, but I'm more realistic than that. I stand by my words the day I was told about all this. They're both guilty.

Ignoring the downstairs, for now, I make my way up to my bedroom. Only, I don't push my door open first. Instead, I walk into Sofia's room. Her scent surrounds me and I look at everything she's left behind. Her entire life is in this room. She's got baby photos on the wall, toys from over the years, shelves full of books. I drop down onto her bed and pull one of her stuffed toys into my arms.

Tears burn my eyes as I think about the fact we're now apart.

Should I have come here? Should I have stayed with them?

The decision to come here seemed so right when I was in Maddison and missing everything about this place but now I'm here, now I've already ruined whatever relationship I had with Zayn. I'm starting to wonder.

Am I just making a huge mess of everything?

Pulling my cell from my pocket, I find Auntie Trish's number, swallow down my emotion, and hit call.

"Hey, sweetie. How is it being back?"

"I-it's weird," I admit, the emotion I thought I'd banished coming back full force and I fight not to allow a sob to erupt. "How are the kids doing? I miss them."

"Would you like to talk to them?"

"Yes, please."

"Hang on, I'll grab them and put you on speaker."

I wait as she calls for both Austin and Sofia and in only a few minutes I hear their sweet little voices through the phone.

"Poppy," they both sing simultaneously. Their excitement makes my heart ache.

"Hey, you guys. How are you?"

"Good. Auntie Trish is taking us out to buy new toys later. How cool is that?"

"That's very cool, bud. Do you know what you want?"

Austin chats away about this new game he wants and I'm pleasantly surprised it doesn't involve killing anyone.

"Do you want me to send the console to you?" I ask, thinking of the old one they have sitting in Austin's bedroom.

"No, it's okay. Evan is beside himself at being able to buy a new one."

"They don't need a new one, you don't need to spend that much."

"It's okay, Poppy. We're not going to spoil them. But we want this place to be their home. Especially if it's going to be long term." She knows as well as I do that it's going to be.

"What about you, Sof? What are you going to get?"

She's silent for a beat. "I... I don't know. I don't think I need anything."

My heart breaks for my poor little sister. "Aw, well, I'm sure you'll find something once you're there. What about that new baby that you showed me on the TV?" I ask, thinking of the one she excitedly pointed out a few weeks ago.

"Maybe. But I've got Sarah," she says, referencing her beloved doll that is usually attached to her hip.

"Well, I'm sure you'll figure it out. How's Cooper?"

"Ugh, he doesn't stop crying."

"Why?" I ask, a little too quickly.

"It's okay, sweetie. I think he's just starting to teethe. He's just had a bit of a temperature. It's nothing to worry about, I'm sure. I've got a doctor's appointment for them on Monday to get them checked out and registered here."

"That's good."

"We're really all okay," Austin says.

"I know you are. I just miss you."

"We miss you too. But we want you to be happy."

"Aw, bud. I'm so sorry about all of this."

Everyone falls silent and I can imagine Austin shrugging in the way he does when our parents did something they shouldn't have and he just dealt with it.

"Are you excited to go and see your new school?" I ask, trying to turn the conversation to something a little less depressing.

"Yeah, Auntie Trish says it's got this amazing playground."

I should hope so for the cost of the tuition. I still can't believe that Auntie Trish and Uncle Evan are willing to enroll them both into the prep school, but I'm equally thrilled for the two of them. They're going to get an incredible education and great start in life despite the past few years. As shitty as this situation is, it could well be the best thing that ever happened to the three of them.

"That sounds awesome." I can tell they're starting to lose interest so I say my goodbyes and allow them to go back to whatever they were playing before I interrupted.

"They're really happy, Poppy. You don't need to worry about them."

"I can't help it. I've been the only one doing so for so long now that it's kind of ingrained."

"I know, and they will never forget what you did for them. You're way more than just a sister to them. Anyway, how was the party last night? Was it good to see your friends again?"

"Ugh, yeah... it was good." The party was... meh. I was desperate to get back and see everyone but I wasn't expecting to be so nervous and that ruined it for me. I should have just had a drink and enjoyed myself, but being in the same house as Zayn turned me into a nervous wreck and I couldn't relax at all. Then Harley and Ruby got trashed and that kind of ruined everything. "It's nice to be with friends though. I think it might just take a bit of time to get used to this new normal."

"That's to be expected, Poppy. None of what you're going through right now is easy. Just take each day as it comes. Hopefully, we'll get news sooner rather than later and we can all try to restart our lives."

"We can only hope. I should go, I've got a few things I need to do. I'll get more of the kids' stuff packed up for you soon."

"There's no rush, Poppy. They've got everything they need for now."

"Thank you, Auntie Trish."

"I'd do anything for all of you, you know that."

"I really appreciate it. Just hearing their voices, I know how happy they are."

"They're going to have a good life here, and you're welcome anytime. You've got your key. This house is your home too, Poppy."

"I know," I choke out. "Thank you."

"You're welcome. Speak soon."

We hang up and I spend a few more minutes with Sofia's teddy clutched to my chest before I push from the bed and make my way to my room.

Opening my closet, I pull out a couple of old bags and place them on the bed next to the teddy before turning around and making quick work of rummaging through my things.

I don't pack everything. I don't need or want everything. I have no idea what's going on, but there's going to be time to come back and go through the rest over the coming weeks and months I'm sure.

The last thing I want to take with me is something I'm not sure I'm going to find. My parents have never been the kind of people to keep all our important documents in any kind of sensible place.

I'm sitting on the floor rummaging through the disaster that is the filing cabinet my parents abandoned years ago hoping to find a piece of paper to confirm everything that Auntie Trish told Jake and I last week.

I've never seen my birth certificate. I've had no reason to. I was brought up believing that my parents were my parents so I didn't really need to go snooping, but now, I'm more than intrigued to see what it says.

I find the kids' ones first in a nice folder before discovering mine right at the bottom of the drawer screwed up at the back.

Gently pulling it out, I smooth the paper out before looking down at what it says.

My breath catches at seeing it before me.

Poppy Anastasia Thorn

My hand flies to my mouth as I suck in a deep breath. I didn't not believe Auntie Trish but there was a small amount of suspicion after that revelation. It all just seemed too good to be true. I'd always felt a deeper connection to Jake. I put it down to the fact that he was my family and treated like crap for no reason. I just wanted to help him, to save him. But it turns out it really was more than that.

Pulling out my cell, I snap a photo of the creased paper before sending it to Jake.

He reads it almost instantly and starts typing, only when a new message comes through, it's not from Jake.

My hands tremble as I stare at the name on the notification sitting proudly in the middle of the screen.

This shouldn't be happening.

She shouldn't be contacting me.

Standing, I pace back and forth a few times as I try to decide what to do. I should delete it without even looking. That's what I've been told to do should either of them try to contact me.

But can I do that?

She might be useless most of the time, but at the end of the day, she's still my mom.

"Fuck," I breathe, swiping the screen and tapping on her name.

Mom: I'm so sorry, baby. I've done nothing but let you down.

Shit.

My thumb moves as if I'm going to reply but then the little bouncing dots start and I halt, wanting to see what she's going to say next.

I wait a few seconds but I soon get to find out.

Mom: I've screwed everything up. I've ruined your life. Your brothers' and sister's lives. You're better off without me.

Every part of me wants to reply, to tell her that everything is going to be okay. But equally, I'm desperate to follow the rules of her bail and not contact her.

They didn't allow her back here for fear she might not be able to stay away. Good move, it seems. I'd originally thought that she'd probably like the freedom, but then I guess she always had d-*dad* previously. Now she's got no one.

Before I get to make a decision, another message comes.

Mom: It all ends today. Everything. I'm going back to where all this started and I'm going to end everything for good. I just needed you to know that I love you and I never wanted it to come to this. I'm sorry.

My eyes widen as I stare at her words. Thinking I've read it wrong, I read and reread her message but every time the same words taunt me.

It all ends today.

End everything for good.

"Fuck, fuck, fuck," I chant, spinning on the spot, not knowing what to do.

Without too much thought, my thumbs start flying over the screen.

Poppy: Where are you? I'll come now. Please. Please don't do anything stupid.

My hands tremble as I send the message and my eyes burn with tears. Surely she doesn't mean it. She's just being dramatic, wanting attention. It sure wouldn't be the first time. But she's never sounded quite this serious.

"Fuck," I bark when I see that my message has been read but she's not typing. "Oh my God. Oh my God."

My ass hits the chair before I realized that I was going to sit down as I continue staring at my screen long after it's gone dark.

I run her words over and over in my head but no matter how many seconds tick by, I don't get any closer to figuring out what to do.

Poppy: Mom please, don't do this. Let me help you. Tell me where you are.

This time when it's read, the dots start bouncing and I breathe a sigh of relief.

Mom: I'm going back to where it all began, where the mistakes started.

"That's not fucking helpful," I scream into the silence of the house.

Screenshotting our conversation, I send it to Jake. I notice that he's still not replied to my previous message and that this new one doesn't show as read before I lock my cell, drop it into my pocket, and collect the bags I'd left in the hallway.

I'm throwing everything into Harley's trunk when an idea slams into me.

Auntie Trish said that they all met at school. Her, Mom, Kate, our dad, Will.

"Fuck." I race to the driver's side and after fumbling with the seat belt, I turn the engine over and slam my foot down on the accelerator sending gravel flying into the air behind me.

My heart is in my throat as I pull the car to a stop in the school parking lot. There are a couple of others here, but I don't see anyone.

Jesus. What the fuck am I doing? I'm probably way off the mark here.

I climb from the car and begin walking around the campus.

I check my cell again, despite the fact it's not gone off and I find that I haven't received anything else from Mom and that Jake's still not read the messages.

My legs pick up the pace as I convince myself that I'm going to find something, anything that's going to help.

I find myself breaking into a run as I come toward the gym building. Just like everywhere else, it's deserted.

I come to a stop, place my hands on my knees, and drag in some much needed air into my lungs.

This is crazy. She's not here.

Standing, I look up to the sky wishing that she hadn't put me in this position when something on the roof catches my eye.

She wouldn't. Would she?

I look around, not even knowing how to get up there.

I race around the building hoping to find the answer but there is no ladder or anything to climb on, I do, however, find the main door slightly ajar when I get to it.

Assuming it's how she'd have gotten in, I pull it open and step inside.

Not being sporty in any way, I'm not exactly familiar with this building so my eyes flick from left to right trying to find the answer. And I finally do when I find another half open door.

Looking back over my shoulder, I pull it wider and step through.

My heart thunders in my chest and my blood races past my ears as I make my way up the stairs behind the door.

At the top, I find another door and after sucking in a long, calming breath, I reach out a shaky hand and push it open.

The sun blinds me for a second after the darkness of the building and I squint as my eyes water.

My vision might be blurry, but I don't see anyone.

I almost laugh to myself when I realize that I've been drawn into this wild goose chase for someone who doesn't want to be found. It must have just been a bird or something I saw. She's not here.

I'm about to turn to go back to the car and return to the Hunter's when something hard connects with my head and everything goes black.

31

———

Zayn

I shouldn't have gone back to the party last night, and I really shouldn't have swiped the first bottle I found and drunk it all before finding another.

I couldn't help it.

Her words, her rejection, were on repeat in my head and I needed them gone.

I had no idea she was coming back, let alone moving in. I know Mom had broached the subject with me and asked if I'd be okay with it, but I didn't expect her to turn up just like that.

It knocked me for six and I couldn't resist taking everything I've been desperate for since she disappeared from my life.

Just for those few minutes, everything was right again. My world was back as it should be with my girl in my arms. Until she shattered it all over again.

I should have listened to her. Allowed her to talk before I

claimed her as mine once more because now I've had another taste of her, felt her soft curves beneath my hands, and the burning heat of her pussy, there's no way I'm going to allow her to follow through with her words.

She's mine. End of.

She might think we're a bad idea while we're living under the same roof. But I fully intend to prove her wrong and show her just how good things could be while we're living in the same house.

I have a fleeting concern about Poppy, and whether Mom will allow her to stay once they learn the truth. But it's unlikely she'll kick her out. Not after all the effort Mom's gone to ensure she can stay here.

I remain at the window long after she's disappeared down the street in Harley's car trying to figure out how I'm going to fix this.

I should be pissed still. But now the alcohol has started to disappear from my system, determination takes its place.

I need to talk to Jake. Fuck Harley and Mom. If what she told me is true then it's time he learned the truth.

Marching back to my room, I drop my boxers before walking into my bathroom to have the shower I was intending on having before I heard her close the door and walk down the hall.

The second I'm out, I shoot Jake a message, but it doesn't matter that he doesn't read it. I know exactly where he is.

Swiping my keys from the dresser, I head out toward the other side of town where Ethan's gym is.

I've been here a few times with him in the past. It's the fanciest one in town, hence why we all make use of his guest passes.

The young girl on the reception desk soon lets me past once I flash her my panty-melting smile.

"Yo," Ethan calls out. "How's the hangover, man?"

"Yeah, I've felt better," I mutter, turning to where Jake is pounding the treadmill. "Can we talk?"

Frown lines form on his brow before he hits the buttons in front of him and slows the belt to a stop.

Stepping off, he grabs the towel that was hanging over the rail and wipes his face.

"Sure, what's up?"

I nod over to the bench at the other side of the gym and we both turn away from Ethan.

"It's fine. I didn't want to know what you were going to talk about anyway."

Jake flips him off over his shoulder before grabbing his water bottle and cell from the floor and following me over.

"What's up?" he asks, swiping at his cell and opening the messages he's got waiting for him.

"I need to talk to you about Poppy."

"Go on…" he encourages, shooting a glare in my direction.

"She told me that she's your sister."

"Yeah, man. How fucking mental is that?"

"Uh… yeah. How'd that happen, anyway?" I ask. I was desperate to find out more last night but Poppy didn't exactly give me a chance.

"Seems *daddy* wasn't able to keep it in his pants and was fucking around with both our moms."

"Whoa. Why didn't they tell you?"

"Fuck knows. They're all fucked-up. Are you really surprised by all this?"

"I… uh… guess not." I don't know all that much about Jake's mom and his past, it's something he keeps close to his chest, but I do know that she's no longer around.

"So what did you want to… fuck," he barks, bringing his cell a little closer to his face.

"What's wrong?"

"Uh… fuck. I need to go."

"Go? But I need to..."

"Talk about Poppy, I know. You should probably come with."

He's up from the bench before I have a chance to register his words.

"Savage, we're out," he calls across the gym and practically runs for the door.

"Jake, what the hell is going on?" I call after him, racing through the door he just swung open so hard it crashed back against the wall with a loud thud. As I catch up with him, I notice his shoulders are pulled tight and his fists are clenched at his sides.

"Hellburn," he barks at me. "Anything new?"

"N-no, not that I'm aware of."

"Good. Hopefully that motherfucker got the message."

"What did you do?"

"Nothing much. It's still a work in progress."

"He's still alive, you need to work quicker," I mutter, remembering how terrified Poppy was after their last encounter.

"I told you that we'll end him, and we will. We just need to be smarter than him."

"What's going on?" I ask when he comes to a stop at my truck.

"This," he tosses me his cell and I only just manage to stop it from crashing to the floor.

Flipping it over, I stare down at the screenshot that's filling the screen.

"What the..."

"It's from Poppy," he says, although it's really not necessary seeing as I can see her name at the fucking top. "They're from her mom." Again, obvious.

"She shouldn't be contacting her."

"No, and she really shouldn't be sending fucking suicide

notes."

At his words, I focus on the messages.

"Fuck."

"Yeah, let's fucking go."

We climb in the car as Jake hits call on his cell and presses it to his ear. His grip on it is so tight his knuckles go white.

"It's just ringing."

"Where am I supposed to be going exactly?" I ask, sitting with the engine running and no fucking clue what we're supposed to be doing right now.

"School."

"School?"

"Yes, now fucking drive, Hunter."

"Yeah, okay." I put my truck in drive and speed out of the parking lot.

"Why school?" I ask once we're out on the main road.

"Just a hunch." His words are clipped and the way he sits in my passenger seat with his fists clenching and unclenching stops me from saying the words I wanted to. I don't think now is the time to admit to what's been going on.

We're on the other side of town to Rosewood High and seeing as it's Saturday, the traffic is busier than usual.

"Fucking hell," Jake complains when I stop at another light.

"What? I can hardly jump it."

"Can't you?"

"Jake, it'll be fine. We don't even know they're there."

He blows out a breath before saying words that turn my blood to ice.

"You really think that's really her mom?"

"T-that's what it said, wasn't it?"

"Yeah but... I don't know. Something doesn't feel right. Wendy is... a head case but sending those kinds of messages to Poppy. I don't know. It just doesn't sit right with me."

"W-what are you saying?" I ask, needing to know that we're on the same page here.

"Oh come on, you don't think this has Hellburn's name all over it."

"But how'd he..." I trail off as I realize that the details don't really matter because he's right. "Fuck." Slamming my foot on the accelerator, I do as he suggested before and jump the next few lights in my need to get to the school quicker.

"She's here. Look," I say, pointing to Harley's car that's parked haphazardly in one of the bays.

"Come on." We take off running, our eyes scanning all over trying to figure out where we're going to find her.

Time seems to slow as we run around looking for evidence. If it weren't for Harley's car sitting in the lot then I'd say it was a lost cause but I know she's here somewhere.

"Call her," I demand before Jake pulls his cell out and does as I suggest.

We stand with our chests heaving as we wait. After two seconds a cell starts ringing... above us.

I tilt my chin up, my eyes running up the bricks of the gym. "Up there," I say but when I look down I realize it wasn't necessary because Jake is already halfway to the entrance.

The door crashes back against the wall before he disappears inside. Picking up the pace, I run after him, my heart in my throat and dread lacing through my veins.

If this is as we suspect, what the hell is he playing at?

I'm not focusing on where I'm going by the time I get to the top of the stairs, being blinded by the last afternoon sun doesn't help and I almost crash into the back of Jake where he's frozen at the top of the stairs.

"Ah look, the cavalry has arrived. Are you ready to party?" His cold, evil voice sends a shiver down my spine before I get a look at the terrified set of eyes that bounce between me and Jake begging us for help.

32

Poppy

My head really fucking hurts is my first thought as I come to. The sun burns through my closed eyelids as I try to remember where I am and what the hell happened.

I try to pry my eyes open, but they resist.

Attempting to move my arms, I find them pinned together behind my back. I try my legs but find the same thing.

What the fuck is going on?

"Ah, good. My little toy is waking up."

Every single muscle in my body locks up at the sound of his voice seconds before everything that's happened this afternoon slams into me.

Being at the house.

The messages from Mom.

I'm at school on the gym roof.

But why is he here?

Finally, I find the strength to drag my eyelids open and the first thing I see is him, sitting on the edge of a chair in front of where I'm laid out on the rough roof, staring down at me like I'm a piece of shit.

"Where's my mom?" I manage to force out past the giant lump in my throat.

He laughs like a fucking maniac.

"Oh, Poppy, Poppy, Poppy. You've always been so easy to play."

I narrow my eyes at him but it just makes him laugh harder.

"You mean this?" He pulls Mom's cell from his pocket and throws it at me. It hits my shoulder before crashing to the floor beside me.

"How'd you get that?"

"I've been inside your house more times than you can probably imagine. It wasn't hard," he sneers, sending fear lacing down my spine.

"It-it was you wasn't it? You called the police?"

A wicked smile pulls at his lips, confirming what I already knew.

"I thought it was brilliant. I made you a promise, and I sat back and watched as I achieved it and you were carted off out of Rosewood like the piece of trash that you are."

"You think getting my parents locked up has ruined my life?" I ask, my own laugh falling from my lips despite the fact that any of this is funny.

His eyes hold mine for a few seconds and I use the time to try to sit up but the second I'm almost up, he pushes from his chair and his booted foot comes flying toward my stomach.

All the air is forced from my lungs with the force of the hit.

"Stay down there, bitch."

"Fuck you, Preston. You're not going to get away with this."

"Really?" he asks, an accomplished smile pulling at his lips. "Who do you think is going to find you up here? I hate to break it to you, Poppy. But no one is coming to your rescue this time. There is no Zayn, no Jake. There is no one but me and you."

"Fuck you."

Reaching out, his fingers grip my hoodie and I'm pulled from the ground as if I weigh nothing more than a feather before the knuckles of his other hand connect with my eye socket.

"Watch your fucking mouth, Poore."

I smile at him and he snarls, baring his teeth.

"Seems you didn't do your research very well, Hellburn," I spit, earning myself another punch, only this time it's to my jaw and the coppery taste of blood instantly fills my mouth.

"I've ruined your family. Your life. You have nothing."

"My parents were shit. Taking them away means nothing. They were nothing," I seethe, using the words he's spat at me time and time again.

"But—"

I shake my head at him. "Looks like you should have spent a little more time stalking me, asshole. I guess I should be thanking you though."

His brows pull together, waiting for what I could possibly want to thank him for.

"If you didn't *ruin* my life, then I wouldn't have discovered the truth."

"What the fuck are you talking about?"

"I'm not Poppy Poore. The sad and pathetic girl you seem to think I am with nothing to lose but who holds the keys to the one thing you really want." His eyes narrow. "I know for a fact that no matter what you do to me, you'll never get what you want. You'll never make captain, you'll never own the school because no matter how important you think you are,

Rosewood is run by Thorns. And I, you piece of shit, am not Poppy Poore, I'm Poppy fucking Thorn. And we always win."

I don't see his fist coming this time and I go flying back toward the asphalt when he releases me.

My head ricochets off the rough roof as a blinding pain races down my spine from the hit.

"Motherfucker," I grunt.

"You're lying," he states as if he really believes that.

"Whatever, Preston. I don't have anything to prove to anyone, especially not you. He'll be here. There will be only one loser here."

"No," he states again, his eyes beginning to get a little wild as he's losing his control of reality. "No one is coming for you, Poore. You are mine."

He drops down to his haunches, his fingers threading through my hair and tugs so hard that I think he's going to pull it from my scalp.

I have no choice but to roll onto my back when he encourages me to do so.

One of his legs lifts over my body until he's pinning me to the floor with his hips.

"You. Are. Mine," he repeats, his voice more harrowing than I think I've ever heard it before.

He reaches behind his back and produces his knife that he had in the closet last week.

I swallow harshly as fear races through me, my stomach somersaulting uncomfortably, making me think I'm about to puke up my pancakes.

Lifting the knife, he runs the blade straight up the front of my hoodie. The fabric parts in an instant leaving me lying beneath him in just my black lace bra.

The point of the blade connects with my collarbone before he trails it down between the valley of my breasts and down to my belly button.

"The fun we're going to have, *Thorn*," he seethes. "You know, that's even more perfect. I'll know that when I fuck you up, I'll be fucking him over at the same time. I thought it was good that you were that motherfucker's cousin. But his sister. It couldn't be fucking better."

"What the fuck is wrong with you?" I don't mean for the words to come out loud and when I see his eyes darken with anger, I instantly regret that I couldn't keep the question inside.

"Me? What the fuck is wrong with me? I'm fed up with that motherfucker walking around like he owns the fucking place. He owns nothing. He has nothing. He is nothing. Just like you. Pointless. Worthless. Nothing," he spits.

"This school, the team. All of it should be mine. And he is going to learn that when he finds you broken, begging for your fucking life."

Not that I've ever allowed him to see it, but I've always been scared of Preston. I learned a long time ago that he's unhinged. But no previous experience compares to this.

He's lost all control and the longer this goes on the crazier he's getting, to the point that I'm starting to believe that I'm not going to get off this roof alive.

My arms ache where they're pinned behind my back, the loose asphalt cutting into my skin. I try to move but all I achieve is to rub myself against him.

His lips curl in delight.

"I'm going to love fucking you up."

Placing the knife beside me, his hands drop to the button on my waistband.

He pops it open and wraps his hands around the fabric ready to pull.

I should be screaming, demanding that he stop but I already know it's pointless.

I might have warned him that Jake is coming, but the

reality is that he's probably not. If he doesn't read that message and put two and two together as I did then I'm going to end up dying here.

He lifts his weight off me ready to remove my jeans when something catches his eye behind me.

His chin drops and he stills for a beat.

"Ah look, the cavalry has arrived. Are you ready to party?"

My head tilts so I can see who he's talking about, praying that Jake really is on the same wavelength as me and I find the most incredible sight.

Not only is Jake standing there staring daggers into Preston with his fists clenched tightly at his sides, but behind him, looking equally as furious, is Zayn.

I look between the two of them, waiting for them to move, to discover what they're going to do.

Time seems to grind to a halt as the four of us stare at each other, waiting to see what the other is going to do.

"Let her go," Jake barks, dragging his eyes from mine and drilling into Preston.

Zayn, however, doesn't take his eyes off me. Concern fills them. I understand why, everything hurts right now, I can only imagine how I must look.

"It's okay," he mouths but I just shake my head. Something tells me that this is far from over just because they've managed to find me.

I'm so glad I sent Jake that screenshot, if I hadn't... a shudder rips through me. It's not worth thinking about.

Preston's grip tightens on the fabric that's still hanging over my shoulders and I'm hauled to my feet. He presses his front against my back and wraps an arm around my waist, while the other holds the knife he'd previously discarded to my throat. The cold blade presses against my skin and I fight my need to swallow knowing that any movement is going to cause it to cut right through. I saw how easily it sliced my hoodie. Skin is going to be no problem.

I almost expect to find a gun pointing at us, the way he's using me for protection but when I drag my eyes up, I don't find any weapons. Just two angry guys' wide shoulders, puffed out chests, and curled fists.

I wouldn't want to be Preston when they get their hands on him.

"Give me what I want, and you can have the slut."

"She's not a..." Zayn barks.

"Never," Jake calls, their words melting into one. "Just let her go."

"Firstly, I think we both know that your sister means more to you than any stupid football team," Preston spits, his lips brushing my ear and turning my stomach with how close he is. "And secondly, you really need to learn what a little slut your sister is. Right, Zayn?"

Zayn's teeth grind making his jaw pop but he doesn't say anything. Jake doesn't react, making me wonder if he's actually hearing anything Preston is saying right now or if he's lost in his own red haze of anger.

"Or do I need to show you the evidence?" His hand slides up my bare stomach before roughly grasping my breast. He squeezes so tight I can't help a whimper fall from my lips, before he tugs at the lace so hard it rips, exposing me to both of them.

He drops the knife, running it over my collarbone and down to my breast. I whimper again, only I'm not sure if it's the relief that the knife is no longer at my throat or with fear that he could be about to plunge it into my chest.

He circles my nipple and I do everything I can not to react.

"Aw, see how she loves it. She's just begging for me to suck her into my mouth."

Closing my eyes, I allow my head to fall back on his

shoulder. But it's not in pleasure. It's survival. I can't look at the reaction on Zayn's face right now as he watches Preston take what he thinks should be his.

"Let her fucking go," Jake repeats. "Tell me what you want. We'll figure something out, just let her go."

"Nah, not yet. I think we should have some fun first. See how far she'll go to protect you."

The knife leaves me but not before it's sliced through the other cup of my bra. His other hand continues to run over my exposed flesh. His touch burns, sending disgust straight through me. He makes me feel dirty, used, and I hate it.

He trails it down my stomach, hooking it into the waistband on my jeans. The blade cuts into my stomach and I wince in pain.

"Fuck you," I spit.

"She's feisty, I'll give her that. I do love it when they fight back, it really gets me hard."

I gag when I feel him press his cock into my ass, my eyes flying open and landing straight on Zayn.

Fury covers his face as he watches Preston touch me but the longer this goes on, the more my head pounds and the easier it's becoming to step away from my own body and just allow it to happen.

I should fight, I know that. But I don't think I have anything left.

Suddenly we're moving, my feet are being dragged across the asphalt until we're on the edge of the building.

"What are you fucking doing?" Jake barks, taking two giant steps and closing the space between us.

"Come any closer and we both go over. And I'll make sure your beloved sister is my cushion when we hit the concrete below."

Oh my God. Oh my God.

I'm going to die today and it's going to happen while I'm in this monster's arms. My body trembles with fear despite the fact I'm fighting like hell not to show him that I'm scared of him or his threats.

My heart races to the point I have no chance of breathing fast enough to drag in the air I need, and fear like I've never experienced before washes through me like a wave.

"Preston, please," Jake's voice is almost begging. I stare into his wide eyes as he tries to reason with Preston, but I don't think anyone but me realizes just how unreasonable he is. "We can come to some agreement, don't do this."

"I want the team. I want everything."

"Fine."

"What?" I bark. "Jake, no."

"I don't give a shit, Poppy. *You* are what matters here. I need you safe more than I need anything else."

Jake whispers something to Zayn but as much as I strain to hear, I can't make out any of the words.

"It's rude to whisper," Preston shouts. "Please, share your findings with the group."

Jake and Zayn share a look. Preston's grip on me tightens before everything happens at once and I start to fall.

33

Zayn

"We're faster than him," Jake whispers to me.

On the field, this is true but I'm not sure I want to test the theory right now while Poppy's life hangs in the balance. If she goes over then... My stomach turns over at the thought. There's no way anyone would survive a fall from this building. We have to get her.

"We can't risk it."

"You got a better idea? This isn't going to end unless we end it. He's fucking deranged."

He doesn't need to say the words, I can fucking see the reality right in front of me. I had a good idea of what was going on with Preston and Poppy, but I never could have imagined it would have led to this.

I drop my eyes to his feet. His heels are hanging right over the edge. The smallest of movements is going to send them both crashing to their deaths.

My heart races, my skin is covered in a sheen of sweat as the tension of this situation gets too much to cope with.

"Preston, please." It's the first time Poppy has spoken since we arrived and the fear within her voice damn near kills me. I need to get her out of this. She's already been through hell. She doesn't deserve this.

"I was jealous of you all, you know that. The perfect lives, the perfect friends, the perfect prospects." Jake scoffs beside me.

"You clearly didn't look hard enough because our lives are shit, Hellburn. You're the one with the money, the influential daddy, while we were scrambling to stay afloat."

I look to Jake, his eyes hold Preston's but the second he realizes he has my attention, his hand moves, urging me forward.

"You're the one with the power."

"I have nothing. This is high school. The team and the position you so desperately want mean nothing in the grand scheme of things. It's not worth risking your life for."

When I don't move as instructed, Jake glances at me. His eyes widening.

"Bullshit," Preston snaps before launching into a speech about Jake's position, just showing how delusional he really is.

But I don't hear any of the words because without putting another thought into it, I race forward.

But he sees it coming and he leans back.

The scream that rips from Poppy's throat as she realizes what's happening is one that I'm sure will haunt me for the rest of my life.

I'm in front of them before they've really started to fall and when I reach out, I manage to grip onto Poppy's arm.

Her eyes are wide in fear, her skin as white as a sheet.

"Fuck." Jake is at my side in a heartbeat and manages to get her other arm. "We've got you. It's okay. We've got you."

Preston's arms are locked around Poppy's waist but as we start to pull her up, his hands slip and he lets go.

Without his weight, Poppy flies toward us. I gather her up in my arms as her body trembles with the ferocity of her sobs.

Jake and I stand there still looking over the edge of the building and down to where Preston is now in a heap on the concrete.

"Fuck," he breathes, lifting his hands to his hair. "Fuck. Fuck." He takes a step back, spinning away from the horrifying scene as the events of the past few seconds hit me.

He just let go. He's...

I don't get to dwell on it because Poppy begins to wail against my chest.

"It's okay. It's okay," I whisper into her hair, moving us both back from the edge.

"You're safe, Poppy. He's gone. It's okay," Jake says, marching over and pulling her from my arms.

I feel cold, lost, the second she's gone but I know it would be wrong of me to fight him on this right now.

"Call 9-1-1," he instructs.

I stare at the two of them for a beat, relieved that Poppy has someone to support her right now, that she has some family but equally hating that it's not me with my arms wrapped around her. Before I drag my cell from my pocket, I reach behind me and pull my hoodie from my body.

"What are you... oh." Stepping up to the two of them, I gently pull Poppy's ruined clothes from her arms before tugging my own over her head. Jake releases her long enough to cover her up before he walks back to the wall and slides down to the floor, keeping Poppy cradled to him the whole time.

I make the call and in what feels like only minutes the sound of sirens and the flashing lights surround us.

Officer's footsteps race up the stairs before two surround

us, staring down at where we're sitting back against the wall, Jake still with Poppy in his arms. She's not so much as looked up let alone said anything.

"Is she okay? Is she hurt?"

"Uh... I don't think so. Just traumatized."

"Okay, well the paramedics are on their way. I think it's probably best we get her checked over while we get to the bottom of what's happened here."

As if on cue, two paramedics appear behind them and encourage Jake to release Poppy. He's clearly not happy about it but after a little coaxing, he allows them to get on with their job.

They take her weight and direct her to the stairs.

"Where are you going?" he asks in a panic.

"Just to the ambulance so we can lie her down."

"Can we follow? Please? She's my sister," Jake begs the officers. "I need to be with her."

I've never heard him so vulnerable and lost and I hate it. "You go and I'll tell them everything I can."

The officers agree and Jake takes off after Poppy.

The next hour passes in a blur as I'm forced to recount the events of the afternoon, from how we found her here to what happened when we arrived and how it resulted with Preston dead on school grounds.

Even as I retell the story, I still don't really believe I've just lived through it. It's like something you see on TV, it's not something that happens in real life.

Only it has. This is very, very real.

I'm finally allowed to come down from the roof after walking the officers through everything, along with what I know about Preston's previous abuse toward Poppy.

As I say the words, guilt floods me. I should have done more to stop all of this from happening. I should have taken him out before this, I should have done what I promised Poppy I wouldn't do and called a couple of guys from Harrow Creek and dealt with it once and for all. It never should have got to this.

"Zayn," Mom calls, jumping from her car and running toward me. "Are you okay?" she cries, pulling me into her arms and holding me tight.

"Yeah, Mom. I'm fine."

"Where's Poppy?"

"Over there." I nod to where she's sitting in the back of a police car answering questions.

"She's okay?"

"Physically yeah. She managed to convince the paramedics not to take her to the hospital."

"Good. That's good. I'm gonna..." She gestures toward the car and marches over, pulling the door open and dropping down.

"Your mom's a bit of a whirlwind," Jake says, walking over with two cans of energy drinks in his hand. I have no clue where he's found them but I'm more than grateful as he hands one over.

"She loves all this. It's her job."

"I thought she spent her time getting kids out of juvie."

"Yeah, let's just hope there's no juvie involved in this one," I say, cracking the can open and downing half in one go. "If you didn't read into that screenshot—"

"Can we not?"

"Sure."

"Why didn't you tell me it was this bad?"

"I didn't know he was that deranged. I had no idea it was going to escalate this far. Plus, Poppy never actually told me any details. She refused, told me she could deal with him. I wasn't going to force it out of her."

He's silent for a beat. "You gonna tell me the truth yet?"

"The truth?" I ask, half choking on a mouthful of my drink.

"Yeah. There's something going on with you two, isn't there?" He drops down on the curb at our feet, bringing his knees up and resting his forearms on them.

"Uh..." I hesitate, dropping to sit beside him.

"Just tell me, Zayn. Your answer can't be any worse than anything that's happened here this afternoon."

"Um... yeah, it has."

"Fuck," he barks, his body locking up with tension.

"How long?"

"What?"

"How long has it been going on?"

"Couple of weeks, but—"

"You should have fucking told me."

"I know. But there's nothing to tell now, I don't think. She called it quits."

"You serious?"

"Yeah."

"You're fucking delusional, Hunter." As he says those words, the back of the police car opens and Poppy's legs appear before she climbs from the car.

My mom races around and pulls her into her side.

She looks tired, so fucking tired. But she's still beautiful.

A soft smile pulls at my lips when she looks up and finds Jake and I waiting for her.

"Let's go home," Mom says, looking between the two of us.

"You go with Poppy," I say to Jake. "I'll meet you back at home."

He nods, quickly rushing to Poppy's side and taking her from Mom to help her into the car.

My heart aches to watch her walk away from me but she needs Jake right now, not me. As much as that might hurt, I need to accept her wishes and take a step back.

34

Poppy

Jake's hand holds mine as we make our way through town toward the Hunter's house. It's the only thing that keeps me grounded, stops me from falling headfirst into the nightmare that was this afternoon.

How could I have been so stupid to believe that Mom was sending me those messages? I should have seen the warning signs. But even now, I know that I wouldn't have done anything differently. No matter the past, no matter how terrible of a parent she has been, I'll always jump when she says to. It's just ingrained in me.

It's my ultimate weakness. If only I'd realized that before Preston did.

A sob rips from my throat at the thought of Preston. Jake's hand tightens in mine and I feel him look over at me but my eyes remain on the headrest in front of me. I can't cope with seeing the sympathy in his eyes right now.

I didn't see him fall. I didn't see his body in a crumpled mess on the ground. By the time I got down there, the police had already set up barriers and covered the area. But I have a good enough imagination and that's enough to keep the image burned into my mind.

I didn't want him to die. I might have hated him, but I never would have wished that on him.

Why did he let go? Zayn and Jake could have got to him.

Why did he decide that was how this was all going to end?

To continue punishing me.

It might all be over for him now. But I've got to live with this for the rest of my life.

I may not have pushed him or caused what happened today in any way. But right now, the guilt is pressing down on me so hard that I'm struggling to breathe.

"You're safe, Poppy. It's over," Jake soothes, but as comforting as his voice is, I can't help wishing for another.

I glance in Jada's side-view mirror at the car that's following behind us and I suck in a breath.

Why was he there today? Why did he have to be the one to save me when I'm trying so fucking hard to put a wall up between us.

Without knowing it, he's just come in and bulldozed it because all I want right now is to be in his arms, to hear him tell me that I'm safe and ultimately, to make me forget. He's the only one who can do that.

No one says anything else the whole way back. There aren't any words to say.

I told the officers everything I knew. But only Preston knew the real reason for all of this and he's no longer able to tell his side of the story.

I shake my head, trying to get it to register that today actually happened.

Preston is gone. His threat is gone.

I can walk back into school without having to look over my shoulder wondering when the next attack is going to come.

That might be true, but all of this is going to bring me something I really don't want.

Attention.

Now I'm not just Jake Thorn's cousin who'd rather hide in the shadows. Now I'm Jake Thorn's sister and I'm responsible for the death of one of my classmates.

Silently we all climb from the car, Jake has me in his arms again the second he's jogged around to me and I welcome his warmth, his support, but I can't help thinking that I need to get away from all of this.

Jada lets us in and she immediately turns toward the kitchen, Jake follows, pulling me with him and in only seconds Zayn jogs up behind us.

"Coffee?" Jada asks, turning to look at us, her face full of concern and sympathy when her eyes find mine.

"I'm... um... I'm going to go and lie down."

Everyone watches me as I back out of the room. I can tell that both Jake and Zayn want to argue or demand they come with me. But I need to be alone. I need silence and solitude. I just need... I don't really know what I need, but it's not all of them looking at me with pity in their eyes.

Jake's lips part but I cut him off before he says a word.

"I'm okay, really. I'm just exhausted."

He nods and thankfully, allows me to walk out of the room.

It's not until I'm at the top of the stairs that I hear their voices but although I can't hear their words, my skin tingles with awareness knowing they're talking about me.

My eyes lock on my bedroom door and I step toward it, knowing I'm going to find what I need inside, but when I get flush with Zayn's room, my body takes on a life of its own and I reach out to open the door.

The second I slip inside, his scent hits me and I instantly feel better. I don't know why I've come in here until I spot his jersey left in a pile on his chair. Walking over, I swipe it up and bring the fabric to my nose. I breathe him in deeply and allow myself to get lost in him despite the fact he's not here with me.

Their voices filter through to me once more and I quickly dart for the door, not wanting to get caught snooping, not that I think Zayn would have an issue with finding me in his room.

I've seen the pain in his eyes while Jake's supported me this afternoon. He wanted to be the one to hold me, to try to help me put the pieces back together. Finding me here right now would give him everything he wants.

But I can't. I can't allow myself to go there again. I need to stay strong. To remember the reasons why I sent him away last night.

What's happened today doesn't change anything. It can't.

With his jersey held tight in my hand, I close his door once more and finally make my way down to the bathroom.

I rip Zayn's hoodie from me, before stripping out of the rest of my ruined clothes. I don't even look at my ripped bra. I don't need more images in my head reminding me what he did. How he shamed me. Used me. Abused me.

Turning the shower on as hot as it'll go, I step under the water, hoping it'll wash the memories of his touch from my body along with the evidence he's left that today really happened.

Once I've scrubbed every inch of my skin until it's red and raw, I step out and wrap myself with the towel waiting for me.

I don't want to look in the mirror. I don't want to see what he did to me. But my need to clean everything away has me reaching for a wipe and gently cleaning the cuts and bruises he left me with.

Tears burn my eyes and emotions clogs my throat. My body wants me to break but I refuse to do so yet.

Dragging on Zayn's jersey, I pad to my room, closing the door behind me and diving for the bed. I pull the covers back and slide under them, pulling them right up until I'm surrounded by darkness.

It's then that the tears I've been holding inside me come.

I cover my mouth as I sob and allow my tears to soak the pillow beneath me.

The sound of the door opening sometime later drags me from my fitful sleep. It's not until my brain starts to wake that I realize the images within it aren't from a nightmare. Today really did happen.

"Hey, Sis. It's just me."

He can't see me because I'm still totally cocooned under the duvet but my lips twitch up at the corners.

"How are you doing?"

The temptation to stay hidden and allow him to think I'm still sleeping is strong but I don't. Feeling brave, I pull the sheets down a little until the cool air hits my face. I blink a couple of times, my eyes sore from crying until the blurry image of Jake sitting on the edge of the bed comes into view.

He's still got deep frown lines on his brow and concern filling his eyes. I wish he could just look at me like this is any other normal day and that I didn't almost die a few hours ago.

"Yeah, you know."

He reaches out and brushes his hand over my hair.

"You're so fucking brave, you know that?"

I shrug, I don't think I did anything anyone wouldn't have done today. There was nothing I could do other than be the pawn in his sick games.

"Amalie wanted to come and see you, but I said that you probably weren't up for it. I hope that's okay."

I nod because he's right. I'm really not up for it right now.

"Just tell her that I'm okay."

"I will." He smiles down at me. "That photo you sent me before…" He trails off, not wanting to go there. "That was pretty epic."

I have to wrack my brain for a few seconds to recall what he's talking about. I can't seem to think about anything that doesn't involve being up on that roof.

The birth certificate.

I smile with him and it makes his eyes soften.

"I'm Poppy Thorn," I whisper.

"You are. I still can't believe it. Do you know how many times I wished I had a brother or sister over the years?"

I shake my head. I always assumed he was fine on his own.

"I'm so fucking glad it's you." He cups my cheeks, his eyes getting a little watery.

"She's gone," I blurt out, causing his brows to pull together. "She died today?"

"W-who did?"

"Poppy Poore. She's done. She's fed up of being the pawn in his games, of watching her back, of hiding."

The smile that lights up his face makes my chest swell.

"When I walk out of this room tomorrow, I'm Poppy Thorn."

"Hell yes, you are."

"I'm going to get Jada to do whatever she needs to go to get my name changed, it shouldn't be too hard seeing as it's my actual name. I'm done with my past and allowing people to drag me down. It's time for a fresh start."

"That sounds like a plan, Popsicle. Can I ask you one question though?"

"Sure."

"What are you going to do about Zayn?"

My breath catches at hearing his name. "Um…"

"I know, Pops."

"You're not angry?"

"Let's just say I'm not overly thrilled, but I could never be angry with you."

"It doesn't matter. It's nothing. I don't need to do anything about him."

"Are you sure about that?"

"Positive. It was never meant to be anything more than a bit of fun." Jake winces at my words but it's the truth. Even now, I still find it hard to believe that the whole thing wasn't a game or a joke to him. It sure started off that way.

"Do I need to remind him what happens when he messes with you?"

I can't help but laugh at the serious look on his face. It feels good. "No, it's okay. I'll let you know if that changes though."

"I'm going to let you rest and go home to attempt to convince Amalie that you're okay. Call me if you need me, yeah?"

"I will."

Lowering down, he drops his lips to my head, lingering a second longer than necessary.

"I wish you'd told me about all of this when it started, Pops. But I understand why you didn't, and I really appreciate your loyalty."

"Always, Jake."

He pushes from the bed and walks to the door.

"Pops?"

"Yeah?"

"All that stuff you said about Zayn. It would be much more believable if you said it while you weren't wearing his number." He winks at me, a smirk pulling at his lips before he slips through the door, closing it behind him and I tug the covers up higher over my body.

35

Zayn

I stay in the kitchen with Mom while Jake heads upstairs to check on Poppy before he goes home.

"You okay, Son?" she asks, her eyes searching mine.

"Yeah," I say, dropping my head to my hands. "Today was... yeah," I breathe, not really knowing what to say about it.

"Poppy was really lucky that Jake figured out where she was."

"I know, I dread to think..." A violent shudder runs down my spine. It's bad enough that I can't get the image of him lying lifeless on the concrete ground out of my head, but thinking about Poppy being laid beside him. I can't... I just can't. "Is everything going to be okay with the police and everything?"

"Yeah. They need to come back and talk to you all again but there shouldn't be an issue."

"That's good. Poppy doesn't need any more on her plate."

Silence settles between us before Mom disappears to her office after telling me that we'll order takeout when Harley's home.

I agree but right now, I don't think I could stomach eating anything.

Jake's footsteps on the stairs has me pulling my head up just as he appears in the doorway.

He smiles at me sadly. "Is she okay?"

"She will be. She's stronger than we give her credit for."

"Trust me, I know."

"Okay, I'm out. Call me if anything happens."

"Of course. Mom thinks we might need to talk to the police again."

"Sure, whatever they need." He turns to leave but stops before he disappears. "Look after her, Hunter. She might not want to admit it, but she needs you." It pains him to say that, I can see it in his eyes.

"I will. You don't need to worry about her."

"I'd better fucking not. You know that if you hurt her, I'll come for you."

"I wouldn't expect anything else, Thorn."

He nods at me before disappearing.

Every muscle in my body screams for me to go up and check on her but I don't. She wanted space, so I need to respect that.

I'm not going to stay away forever though because I fully intend on standing by that promise, I just made Jake. I'm not going to let anyone, or anything hurt her again.

Harley appeared not long after Jake left, and Mom and I told her what happened before she went running up the stairs to see that Poppy was okay with her own eyes.

She spoke to Harley, but she refused to come down for dinner and the food Harley took up was untouched.

Trish also dropped everything the second Mom called her to explain what had happened and she spent a couple of hours here to see with her own eyes that Poppy was okay, but even she couldn't lure her out of the bedroom or make her eat anything.

I wanted to take charge, to storm in there and demand she eats something, but I know it'll just end up with her chewing me out.

Restraint isn't one of my strong suits. But I'm really fucking trying.

Before heading to bed, I cave to my need to check on her despite the fact I know she's okay because both Mom and Harley have been in to see her and spoken to her, so I knock on her door.

I wait for a beat, but unable to walk away, I twist the handle and poke my head inside.

She's got the covers pulled right up to her neck, her eyes are closed and her lips slightly parted.

Something aches in my chest at the sight of her. My need to step inside and crawl in beside her is almost too much to bear. But knowing I can't, I silently slip from the room and close the door behind me.

I shower, hoping that the memories of today will disappear down the drain with the dirty water but as I lie in bed staring at the ceiling and running the events of the day through my mind, I realize it was wishful thinking.

The room is in darkness and the house is in silence. Harley and Mom went to bed hours ago.

I toss and turn for hours, the image I've conjured up of her lying lifeless beside Preston earlier won't leave.

I'm almost at the point of getting back up and putting the

TV on or something seeing as sleep refuses to claim me when my door cracks open.

The hallway is in darkness so there's no extra light, but I don't need it. I already know who it is.

She doesn't say anything, Instead, she just lifts the covers once she's at the bed and she slides in beside me.

Turning on my side, I watch as she moves right up to me, her eyes catching the little light that's creeping through the curtains.

"Pop—" My word is cut off when her lips press to mine.

I hesitate for a second, not because I'm not willing, just because I'm so shocked.

My lips part when her tongue teases them, accepting her kiss. My arm snakes around her waist, pulling her up against my body.

No words are spoken as we devour each other. Her hands run over the bare skin of my back as I roll her onto hers and lock her ankles behind my waist.

Ripping my lips from hers, I kiss across her jaw and down her neck. My hands skim up her thighs until I get to the fabric covering her. Wrapping my fingers around it, I start pulling it up her body but I pause when I notice the color of it.

"Poppy?" I ask when I realize she's wearing my jersey. My cock twitches with my need for her. "Were you in bed wrapped in only my number?"

"Zayn, please. Make it stop."

"Fuck, Poppy. Anything."

She pushes up from the bed, making it easier for me to pull the fabric free from her body. The second I drop it over the side of the bed, I lower my hands to her breasts.

"I just want to remember your touch. Please, Zayn." Her words rip me open. I hate that she's suffering because of him. That he even had the power to hurt her in the first place.

Lowering her back to the bed, I brush my lips down her

neck, over her collarbones, and down to her breasts. I kiss, lick and nip over every inch of her skin. I suck her nipples into my mouth until her back arches off and she moans my name.

"Zayn, more," she begs, her nails scratching across my scalp as I lick down her stomach, dipping my tongue into her belly button.

Finding the edge of her panties, I wrap my fingers around them and tug.

The sound of them ripping fills my room along with her shocked gasp.

Pushing her thighs wide, I lower myself to my belly before running one finger through her folds.

"Fuck, you're soaked."

"Zayn." Her voice holds a warning, one that I'm more than happy to hear.

"You want my mouth, baby."

"Please, Zayn. Please."

Leaning forward, I run the tip of my tongue up the length of her. Her legs tremble as her nails scratch with her need for more.

I focus on her clit, licking the little bundle of nerves over and over until she's writhing beneath me, lifting her hips from the bed, trying to get more friction.

Lifting my other hand, I circle her tight entrance. Her muscles try sucking me in, making my teeth grind wishing that it was my cock getting ready to sink deep inside her body.

"More, more, more," she chants.

Unable to ignore her demands, I push two fingers deep inside her, immediately bending them so that I'll hit that magical spot inside her that will make her scream.

I up the pressure with my tongue and in only a few seconds her pussy clamps down on my fingers as she cries out her release.

I watch as her back arches on my bed and her fingers grip the sheets beneath her as she loses herself to her pleasure.

Her release lasts for a few long seconds and I don't pull away from her until she's coming back down from her high.

"More?" I ask, wiping my mouth with the back of my hand.

"So much more."

Smiling, I lower myself over her, sweeping my tongue into her mouth and allowing her to taste herself.

Taking my cock in hand, I rub it against her swollen clit.

"Oh God," she moans.

"I need you so fucking bad," I admit on a groan. "I've missed you so fucking much."

"You only had me last night," she whispers as I drop lower, teasing her entrance with the head of my cock.

"That's not what I meant, and you know it."

"Do it," she demands when I push in ever so slightly, my eyes rolling back at the sensation of feeling her skin on skin.

"But—"

"I'm covered. I went and... ooooooh," she cries out when I see where she's going and sink deep inside her in one quick thrust. "Oh God."

"So fucking good. Fuck, you feel like heaven."

Her nails rake down my back before she grabs on to my ass, pushing me deeper.

"Oh shit, Pops."

"Fuck me, Zayn. Make me feel it for days."

A growl rumbles up my throat as I pull almost all the way back out before slamming back inside her. She shoots up the bed with my force. The headboard rattles against the wall but I don't pay it any mind as I repeat my previous action.

"I'm. Fucking. Addicted. To. You," I groan between thrusts.

One of my hands wraps around her hip, holding her to me, my fingertips digging into her skin enough that she'll have bruises tomorrow but as I watch her throw her head back in ecstasy, I can't bring myself to care while she's losing herself to the pleasure. If anything, knowing that I'm going to leave marks just makes me harder for her.

Skimming my other hand up her stomach, I pinch her nipples hard, making her cry out and for her pussy to clamp down on me every time I cause a bite of pain.

"You like that, baby?"

"Yes, Zayn. More. Give me everything."

"Fuck."

Lifting my hand higher, I wrap it around her throat. She immediately lowers her chin and her wide eyes lock on to mine, but they're not filled with panic. Just desire, heat and lust.

"You fucking slay me, Poppy." My fingers tighten around her throat, her pulse hammering against my thumb. "You're mine," I grate out as my balls begin to draw up. "Mine."

"Zayn, shit. Fuck." She tilts her hips, so her clit hit my pelvis, pushing her closer to her own release.

"Say it," I demand. "Tell me who you belong to."

"You, Zayn. You. I'm yours."

Releasing her hip, I press my thumb to her clit as I slam into her once more.

She screams out her releases as her pussy pulls my cock deeper than I thought possible.

"Fuck, Poppy. So good, so fucking good." Tingles explode around my body, and I'm just about to fall over the edge when the door swings open.

"What the... Poppy?" Harley squeals, her hand flying to her eyes to stop her from seeing what's happening.

Poppy tenses beneath me, but I fall headfirst into pleasure.

"Oh my God. Oh my God," I vaguely hear my sister mutter as I lose myself to my girl, my cock jerking violently and filling her with jets of my cum. Marking her, making her mine for good.

Once I get control of my body back, I glance over to the door to find it closed, and Harley nowhere in sight. I start to wonder if I imagined it until I look down to Poppy to find her with my jersey bunched up against her chest, trying to hide.

"Get rid of that. I'm not done with you yet." I swipe it away and throw it across the room.

Still buried inside her and my semi already starting to grow once more, I flip us so she's sitting astride my lap.

"Zayn, stop." I catch her wrists before she can climb off me.

"Too late, Pops. This is happening and there's nothing you can say right now that will stop me from giving you everything you need."

My hands land on her hip and I rock her on my length.

"You're not playing fair," she whispers, her head falling back in pleasure.

"Did I ever say that I played fair?" I ask with a smirk.

Her chin drops and her eyes run up the length of my body until she finds my eyes.

"You're done running from me, Poppy. I know you're scared. Hell, I'm scared too. But I need this. I need you."

"But—"

I press two fingers to her lips, cutting off whatever she's going to say.

"There's nothing you can say that's going to stop this from happening. You're mine, Poppy Thorn. You just said so yourself."

She still wants to fight it, I can tell by the tense set of her shoulders, but her eyes give her away. She wants this as badly as I do.

"But Harley," she whispers in spite of my fingers. "Your mom."

I shrug. "I don't care, Poppy. They're going to have to get used to it because you're it for me."

"Zayn," she sighs.

"No, hear me out. I could have lost you today. Do you have any fucking idea how terrifying it was watching you fall? If I didn't get to you in time. Fuck," I bark, startling her as that image I've been battling with all afternoon slams into me once more.

Gathering her up in my arms, I pull her down onto my chest and hold her tight.

"I'm not letting you walk away ever again. I love you, Pops."

She gasps at my admission. I thought saying those words that I realized were true quite some time ago would be scary, but after the events of today, nothing seems as daunting anymore.

Is this an ideal situation? No, probably not with her without a home or parents and us living under the same roof. But it's us. It's meant to be and somehow, we'll figure it out.

Twisting my lips to her ear when she's still not said anything or even moved, I whisper, "I'm going to fuck you again, now."

A shudder rips through her and she turns to look at me. Her eyes are filled with unshed tears.

"Zayn—"

"Shhh, not now. Just let me give you this. We've got all the time in the world to talk."

I rock into her again and a low moan rumbles up her throat.

"I can't even tell you how good this feels," I tell her, pulling her down onto me harder, needing to feel every inch of her against me.

"So good," she mutters into the crook of my neck as her hips roll with mine.

I fuck her until she passes out. I know she's hurting after the events of the day, but I can't lie, being buried in her for hours, having our bodies laced together, for that long, it's the best night of my life.

As gently as I can, I slip out from beneath her, cover her so she doesn't get cold, and pad toward my bathroom. I hate washing her scent off me, but the thought of being able to slide into bed with her again soon makes it a little easier.

I have a quick shower before pulling on a pair of sweats and slipping silently from the room.

I knock on Harley's door and after a second she barks, "What?"

Laughing to myself, I push the door open and walk inside.

The second she sees me, she climbs from the bed, stands before me at full height ready to fight.

"What the fuck, Zayn? Don't you think she'd been through enough today? She really doesn't need to be fucked and chucked by you. You know she was a virgin, right? No, you probably didn't, probably didn't give a shit either. You can't just go around taking whoever you want and ruining all my friends. It's not fair, Zayn." Her index finger pokes me harshly in the chest as she continues to rant.

"Harley. Harley..." I repeat, waiting for her to run out of steam.

"What?" she snaps, placing her hands on her waist and popping a hip out in frustration.

"It's not like that with us."

"Us?" She laughs but it's anything but amused. "There's a fucking us?"

"I'm..." I hesitate, not really wanting to tell my sister this only an hour or so after telling Poppy but I can't see any other way out of this. "I'm in love with her."

"What?" she screeches at a pitch I'm sure only dogs are meant to hear. "Can you even hear yourself right now?" She shakes her head and walks to the other side of the room, disbelief oozing from her. "You really expect me to believe that shit?"

"Yeah, actually. I do because it's true."

"But—"

"Harley, this isn't the first time."

Her shoulders drop and I hate that I'm doing this, but she needs to know the truth. Jake does and he was mostly okay with it, she needs to understand too.

"You've been going behind my back?" she asks, her brows pulling together and her bottom lip quivering. "You've both been lying to me?"

I don't say anything. What can I say other than yes, we have?

"Zayn, for fuck's sake. I told you to stay away from my friends, damn it."

"I know, but I couldn't. I've wanted Poppy for..." She looks up at me, her eyes widening in curiosity,

"For?" she prompts.

"For a long time. Since before the first time I even kissed her," I admit.

She thinks for a second. "Your birthday party?"

I nod. "Yeah."

"But you were horrible to her that night."

"I know, and I've regretted it ever since. Then New Year's Eve, she was my tag and things just..."

She gasps in horror. "You used her in another game?"

"Yeah, well... yeah. I wasn't about to pass up the chance."

"But you hate each other. You've fought like cats and dogs for years."

I shrug. She's not lying. But we didn't hate each other for

the reason she thought. We hated each other because we couldn't accept how we really felt.

"You know what they say, Har. Hate sex is always the best."

"I wouldn't fucking know, asshole. Fuck it. I'm giving one of the guys from the team my V-card. Justin maybe, or Rich. Maybe both at once. See how you fucking feel."

"Harley," I growl, not amused in the slightest about her suggestion. "You go near them and I'll cut their dicks off and feed it to them."

"You're such a hypocrite."

"Are you in love with Justin or Rich?"

"Well, no, but…"

"There is no but here, Har. I love her. Love. Her. She's it for me."

"But—"

I smile at her.

"Fucking hell, Zayn." She tugs on her hair, spinning on the spot as she tries to accept that this is happening. "Where is she now?"

"Asleep in my bed."

"Well… you'd better get back. We don't want her waking up alone after everything."

I back up toward the door, not needing to be told twice to go back to my girl, especially when she's naked in my bed.

"Har?" I ask. "Don't be too hard on her. It's been killing her not to tell you. She didn't want to disappoint you."

"Damn you, Zayn Hunter. Damn you." As I close the door behind me, I don't miss the smile that twitches at her lips. "You'd better be the best boyfriend to ever walk the planet because if you hurt her, you're going to be the one choking on your own dick."

I can't help laughing as I push my bedroom door open, although it falls the second my eyes land on a pair of gray ones.

Poppy pulls the sheets back, revealing her naked body and inviting me back into bed.

My joggers are on the floor in a second and in the next she's in my arms, her lips on mine where they belong.

"I love you too, Zayn," she whispers, making my entire world tilt a few degrees.

36

Poppy

The weight of Zayn's arm resting over my waist presses me into the mattress, and despite everything, I wake with a smile on my face.

I told myself over and over last night that coming in here was a bad idea, but as I laid in my own bed, all I could think about was being in his arms. I craved the feeling of safety he brings me. I needed him and the longer I put it off, the more desperate I became until I found myself slipping from my own bed and into his.

Part of me expected him to send me away after how I've treated him, but thankfully, that wasn't what happened because it seemed that he needed me as much as I needed him.

My eyes flutter open and my breath catches when I find his dark, hungry eyes staring back at me.

"Morning, baby."

My cheeks heat as memories from our late-night antics slam into me. I'll be amazed if I'm able to walk away from this bed this morning after the number of orgasms he gave me.

"Good night, huh?" he says, running his knuckles across my heated cheek.

"I mean, it was okay."

His brows rise in amusement.

"Okay?"

"Maybe I need a reminder." I push against his chest and attempt to roll him onto his back, but he doesn't move. "What? What's wrong?" I ask, trying not to allow the hurt that wants to coil around my heart at his obvious rejection.

Dropping my hand, I skim over the muscles of his stomach, they jump at my contact until I wrap my hand around his length. His eyes shutter for a beat before he recovers, wrapping his own hand around me and stopping my movement.

"Talk to me, Poppy," he pleads, looking so deep into my eyes I swear he's staring straight into my soul.

"I was thinking actions spoke louder."

"Not right now." He lifts my hand from him and drops it around his waist before bringing his hand up to cup my jaw.

"How are you feeling?"

"Frustrated," I huff.

He chuckles, knocking his nose against mine. "Don't worry, I'll only be able to deny you for so long. But I want to know where your head is at first. Yesterday was..."

"A head fuck."

"Yeah, you could say that. I thought I was going to lose you, Pops," he says on a sigh.

"But you didn't. I'm right here."

"I know, and I couldn't be more grateful. Why did you change your mind... about me, us?"

"I..." I hesitate, trying to find the right words. "I needed you, Zayn. Jake was holding me, supporting me, and it meant so much to have him there, that he figured it out in the first place. But all I wanted was you." His breath catches at my admission.

"For real?"

"Yeah, for real."

"How did..." He blows out a breath.

"How'd I end up on the school roof?"

"Yeah. Start there."

I tell him about what Auntie Trish said to us about our parents meeting at school and how his messages took me back to that conversation, and thankfully, it seems that it did to Jake too.

"When did he steal your mom's cell?"

I shrug. "I don't know. He made out like he'd been at the house a few times. I guess that's how he knew about the drugs."

"Wait," he says. "He was the one who called the police on your parents."

"Seems so. He very proudly said about how he 'ruined my life'. He must be the worst stalker ever if he couldn't see that my life was shit."

"Jesus, Pops."

I shrug. "It is what it is. It's done now."

"I know but... fuck." He scrubs a hand down his face. "I can't believe he'd stoop to that level."

"I don't think any of us knew the real Preston. He was screwed up in so many ways."

The doorbell rings through the house, pausing Zayn's response.

"Poppy," Jada calls up the stairs. "The police are here to see you."

"Fuuuuck," Zayn groans much to my amusement.

"Regretting turning me down now?" I ask, quirking a brow at him.

"Fucking cockblockers," he mutters as we both swing our legs over the edge of his bed. "Here," he says, throwing me his jersey. "Wear this."

"I'm not sure..." My argument is halted when I get a look at the expression on his face. After a beat, my eyes drop down his naked body, following the lines of his cut abs down to the V that drops to his very hard cock.

My mouth waters as I stare at him.

"How quick do you think I could..."

"From the way you're looking at me right now, I'd say pretty damn fast. But that's probably not fast enough for the officers that are waiting for you downstairs."

"Shit, you're right." Dragging his jersey over my head, I push to stand. "I'll make it up to you later," I say over my shoulder as I walk to his door.

I make quick work of running to my room and pulling on a pair of panties and dragging some leggings up my legs.

As I make my way to the stairs, Zayn appears wearing a pair of sweats and a tight V-neck shirt.

"What are you doing?" I ask when he throws his arm over my shoulders and walks down the stairs with me.

"Coming with you."

"But your mom," I say, trying to push his arm from me.

"She knows."

"What?" I ask in horror, turning to him.

"Well, she's not said it in so many words, but she knows you mean more to me than I've ever let on."

"How?"

"I have no idea. Mother's intuition or some shit."

"I wouldn't know anything about that," I say sadly.

"You're about to learn. Nothing gets past Jada Hunter."

"Oh God. Was moving here a really bad idea?" I ask with a laugh.

"I guess that depends if you consider falling asleep every night with me a bad thing."

"Zayn, I've got my own roo—Officer, hi," I say as we round the corner and find Jada standing with a male and female office in the hallway.

Jada's eyes turn to both of us before she notices Zayn's arm over my shoulder.

This time when I push it away, he allows it to drop.

"Shall we?" she says, pointing through to the dining room. "Would you like coffee?"

"No, we're fine, thank you. Poppy, I'm Detective Archer and this is my colleague, Detective Jones. We've been looking into yesterday's incident and we're discovered a few things we'd like to speak to you about."

"Okay," I say skeptically, pulling out a chair and taking a seat as the officers do so.

"We went to Mr. Hellburn's house this morning," Detective Archer starts as Zayn drops into the chair beside me, lacing his fingers with mine. "Were you aware that Preston had an obsession with you?"

"Well, like I said yesterday, he'd been tormenting me for a while."

"Okay, but I think this might run deeper than you realized."

"Oh?"

Detective Jones pulls out some photographs and slides them across the table.

"Oh my God," I gasp, as both Zayn and Jada's breath catches.

"These are from his bedroom wall."

I stare at the images before me. There is picture after picture of me pinned to his bedroom wall. Many of which have been taken in my house along with others I recognize like him with his hand around my throat in the school's closet the other week.

"It seems he's had some interest in you for a while. Were you aware these images had been taken?"

"N-no. Jesus, this is scary," I mutter, taking in the evidence of his obsession.

"What did his dad say?" Zayn asks.

"He had no idea. But from what we gather, he wasn't around much of the time."

The detectives ask me more questions, but it seems that the evidence speaks for itself really and by the time they leave, they seem pretty confident that all of this is Preston's doing.

Jada sees them out, and after a brief chat, she closes the door behind them.

"Well that was dramatic," Harley says from behind where Zayn and I are still sitting at the dining table.

I spin around, my eyes wide as I take her in, leaning against the doorframe.

With everything that had happened, I'd forgotten about her late-night interruption.

"Zayn?" she asks.

"Yeah?"

"Fuck off, yeah?"

Zayn chuckles, but his sister's presence doesn't stop him from wrapping his hand around the back of my neck and dropping his lips to mine.

"Ugh, please," Harley whines before he releases me and walks up to her.

"It's like you don't want me to be happy, Sis." He rustles her hair and manages to dodge her fists when she tries to punch him in the stomach. "I'll be in my room," he says, shooting me a heated stare before disappearing around the door.

"You missy, have some explaining to do." She places her hand on her hip and pins me with a stare.

"You fancy going for pancakes?"

She opens her mouth as if she's about to rip me a new one but clearly thinks better of it.

"Yeah, actually. Let's go."

"I just need to tell Za—"

"No," she huffs. "If you go in there, I'm never getting you back. Sneak past his room, put on..." Her gaze drops to his jersey before she rolls her eyes. "Some of your own clothes and send him a message. You're mine for the rest of the day. He had you all night, it seems."

My cheeks burn bright red at her tone.

"Oh don't give me that innocent look, Thorn." Her eyes narrow but her lips twitch into a smile that I can't help but return. "I'm going to need the details, but I should warn you that if you so much as remind me that it was my brother you were banging, you might end up wearing your pancakes."

"I'll see what I can do. Call Ruby. See if she can meet us?"

"Sure. Be quick, and do not make me come up to find him doing... you know. I still need to bleach my eyes from last night."

As predicted, I don't manage to get past Zayn's bedroom door without him coming to find out why I didn't walk inside and come good on my promise from earlier. Instead, I forced him to sit on the end of my bed while I got ready to go out with his sister. He wasn't happy about it, but I think he kinda understood when I reminded him that she caught him balls deep inside me last night. That's not an image any little sister needs of her brother and best friend.

"Go out with the guys or something. Go and do something normal, hell knows we deserve it after yesterday," I say, dabbing at the tender bruises around my eyes and jaw in an attempt to cover them up.

"Poppy, are you ready?" Harley calls up the stairs.

"Yeah, hang on."

I turn to look at Zayn who sits with his muscles pulled tight and his eyes trained on me.

"Stop looking so worried. For the first time in... ever, I can go out without having to look over my shoulder. He's gone."

"I know, I just... worry."

"Aw, bad-boy Hunter is going all soft," I tease, stepping into his spread thighs and cupping his rough jaw in my hands.

"Trust me, Pops. There's nothing soft about me."

I glance down at his tented sweats and laugh.

"You might want to take care of that before you meet the guys. I'll see you later, yeah?" I lower down and brush my lips against his. His fingers curl around my hip but I manage to slip out of his hold before he can distract me too much.

"Finally," Harley huffs when I hit the bottom step.

"I just got dressed and tried to fix this," I say, pointing at my face.

"It makes you look like a badass. It's kinda hot."

"It's very hot. Stay away from my girl, Har. She doesn't swing that way."

"Shut the fuck up," Harley barks up the stairs before threading her arm through mine and pulling me toward the front door.

It's not until I step out that I remember I left her car at school.

"Shit, your..." I pause when I spot it parked outside the house. "How'd that get back here?"

"Jake and the guys sorted it. Seriously, I can't believe he's your brother."

"That's the most normal of the things that have happened in the past couple of weeks."

"Yeah but still, you're Jake Thorn's sister. You do realize

how high up the social scale that's pushed you at school right."

"And you know I don't care about any of that stuff."

"I know, just be aware that people will probably treat you differently."

"Yeah, they'll be more obvious about trying to use me to get to the top instead of keeping it hidden."

"That wasn't quite what I meant," Harley says with a wince as we drop into her car.

"Well, whatever happens. I've got your back."

I turn to her before she puts the car in reverse. "You're not mad?"

"I..." she starts but cuts herself off. "I was... then Zayn came to talk to me."

"He did? When?"

"He said you'd fallen asleep."

"Oh."

"When he talked about you, about how much you meant to him. He looked... he looked different. Happy. He told me that..." She turns to look at me, her eyes soft and full of emotions. "He said he loved you."

"He told you that?"

"Shit, hasn't he told you?" she asks in a panic, thinking that she's just put her foot in it.

"Yeah, he has. I still can't quite get my head around it though."

"Why? It's the most normal thing out of everything that's happened," she says with a laugh, repeating my earlier words back to me.

"Playboy Zayn Hunter making declarations of love, that shit isn't normal," I say.

"Fucking hell, you've whipped him, haven't you?"

"There's been no whipping, but I can confirm the school gossip because your brother has mad skills in the bed—"

"Stop, stop, please. I take back what I said earlier. I don't want any details. You're going to have to tell that shit to Ruby."

I bark out a laugh as she hurries to reverse out of the drive and heads toward the oceanfront for Aces.

Usually, I'd avoid the place, but today, despite the gossip that I'm sure is rife around town, I want to walk in there with my head held high.

I've done nothing wrong here. I'm the survivor in all of this. It's about time people learned the truth about what's been going on in the hope it stops someone else suffering like I have.

Ruby is already waiting for us when we walk toward Aces. The second she spots us, she flies at me, wrapping her arms around my shoulders and holding me tightly.

"I'm so glad you're okay," she breathes in my ear.

"I'm good, Rubes," I say, accepting her embrace.

The three of us walk inside as if this is just a normal day, and I guess it is to everyone else. No one looks up, no one narrows their eyes at me or gives me any indication that they know what happened yesterday. I'm sure they must, I can't imagine something as dramatic as that has been kept under wraps in a gossip-hungry town like Rosewood, but I'm grateful that I'm not under the spotlight right now.

The second our asses hit the booth, Bill is there, ready to take our orders. Unlike everyone else, he studies me for a second too long, taking in the bruises that I tried to cover.

"It's good to see you, Poppy. Breakfast is on the house."

"Oh, no, no, we can't."

"You can, and you'll enjoy it," he says with a wink and a laugh. "Brave girl like you deserves nothing less."

That is all he, or anyone else, says throughout our entire visit.

It's almost... normal.

"So…" Harley announces, although not loudly enough for anyone else to hear. "She's banging Zayn."

Ruby's chin drops but a smile tugs at her lips. "I know."

Harley turns her narrowed stare on our best friend. "You know," she seethes. "You knew and you didn't tell me?"

"Not my story to tell, Har." Ruby looks at me and winks.

"But… but…. Ugh, I still can't believe it."

"You should, you walked in on the evidence," I deadpan.

"You did not?" Ruby screeches, earning a few curious looks from the other diners around us.

Harley drops her head into her hands. "I did," she mutters. "And I'm afraid I'm never going to unsee it."

"At least Zayn's got a banging body. It could have been worse, it could have been your parents," Ruby helpfully points out.

Harley's head pops up, her eyes wide. "Well, yeah, that would have been a shock seeing as they can't stand to be in the same room as each other these days. Speaking of…" She turns her eyes to me. "You coming for your first visit to the Creek?"

"Uh…"

"Don't tell me you don't know it's Zayn's eighteenth."

"Of course I know," I argue. It's been three years since he turned my world upside down in that damn closet, I've never forgotten the date. "It had just slipped my mind with everything."

Harley's face drops slightly but thankfully she doesn't say anything.

"Okay, so we need to go and see Dad before the party so you can come, yeah? I know he'll want to meet you."

"Uh…"

"You're coming," she states as Bill brings over three giant plates of breakfast for us.

I can see the questions on the very tip of Ruby's tongue, the entire time we sit there, but she doesn't ask. I assume she knows most of what happened yesterday through Harley anyway. Instead, we just hang out, talk about school and all the gossip, that doesn't involve me, that I've missed while we stuff our faces with Bill's epic breakfast.

"So are you coming back tomorrow?" Ruby asks when we walk out of the diner and come to a stop at the railing to look out over to the ocean beyond.

My stomach knots at the thought of walking back down those hallways where the ghost used to be who haunted me.

Memories from yesterday, the feeling of him letting go and knowing that while Jake and Zayn were pulling me to safety that he was falling to his death threaten to consume me, but I manage to swallow it down and push the image aside.

"Uh... I don't know. I need to talk to Jada, see what she's organized."

"Well, I hope you're back," she says, pulling me into a hug. "It's not the same without you."

———

Zayn's car isn't in the driveway when we get back.

"Looks like I get you to myself for a little while."

"Is this really weird for you?" I ask as we walk to the house.

"It's not normal."

"Nothing is normal anymore, Har."

"I'm just worried I'm going to lose you," she says, coming to a stop at the front door.

"Har, I live in your house. You're not going to lose me."

"But you're going to spend all your time with him."

"I'm not, I promise. You're still my best friend, Har-Har. Your brother is not going to change that."

I pull her in for a hug and hold her tight.

"If he so much as hurts a hair on your head then I'll kill him. You know that, right?"

"I wouldn't expect anything less."

Eventually, we pull apart, both a little emotional, and step inside.

"Girls, how was breakfast?" Jada asks.

"Amazing. Just what the doctor ordered," Harley says, bouncing into the room.

"Poppy, can we talk?" Jada asks, flicking her eyes over to her daughter. "It's okay. Harley can stay."

"O-okay." I take a seat beside Jada while Harley makes us all coffee.

"I've spoken to Principal Hartmann, he's happy for you to return whenever you're ready." I nod. The concern in her eyes is telling me that she wants to say more about me returning to school. "I've also lined up some appointments for you."

"Appointments?" I ask, narrowing my eyes. I swear, if she starts talking about birth control, I'm going to want the ground to swallow me up.

Thankfully, I think, she goes down a different route.

"I've managed to squeeze you in with the best counselor I know."

"A counselor?"

"Yeah. I know you think everything is okay, but Poppy, you've just been through something huge. You can put on a brave face all you want, sweetheart, but I'm afraid that you're not dealing with everything that's happened."

I open my mouth to argue, but I soon realize that I don't really have one because she's right.

"Also, I think it's time we had a conversation about my son, don't you?"

"And that's my cue to leave," Harley announces, leaving me with her mother to have the most awkward conversation of my life.

37

Zayn

Poppy's body trembles in my hold. We all tried to tell her that she didn't need to do this yet, but she was adamant she wanted life to go back to normal—whatever normal is now—as soon as possible.

After a week of sitting at home and attending the counseling sessions that Mom organized for her, she was determined that this was happening.

Mom, Harley, and I are worried, but we could hardly lock her up in the house and refuse to let her out today. We've just got to trust that she knows what she's doing and that she's ready for this.

"It's not too late to change your mind," I say as we walk toward the benches where the team and the squad are gathered.

She turns to look up at me and despite the fear, I can feel it racing through her, her face is full of determination.

"No, I'm doing this. I'm not sitting at home wondering what they're all saying about me any longer. I'm facing it head-on."

I smile down at her, my chest aching with everything I feel for her. She's so strong. What she's been through over the past few weeks would break a weaker person, but she's standing tall with her head held high.

As we get closer, both Harley and Ruby smile over at us. Harley wanted to bring Poppy to school like they used to, but I point-blank refused, much to her irritation.

One by one, everyone starts to notice our approach. Shock covers most of their faces. Poppy was probably the last person they were expecting to see back at school today, let alone pressed against my side like she is.

"Guys," I nod to the team, and Jake, when we come to a stop before them all. "You know my girl, right?"

"What's up, Poppy?" Shane says, a shit-eating grin spreading across his face.

Poppy stiffens in my hold, but she soon relaxes when she realizes that he's just asking the same question he would any other day.

"Shane's known the whole time," I whisper in her ears.

"Oh."

"While we're making announcements," Jake says, standing up on the picnic bench he was previously sitting on.

All eyes turn on him as Poppy attempts to curl in my side, obviously guessing what's about to happen.

"I know you all know what's happened recently, but I just want to clear something up." His voice booms across the quad.

"Stop him, please."

"Baby, you know better than anyone that Jake will do as he pleases no matter what."

"Great."

"Well, hear this bit of gossip straight from me. That girl right there." He points directly at Poppy as she curls in even tighter to my side. "She's one of the strongest girls you'll ever meet. She also just so happens to be my sister. So anything you have to say to her, you had better be prepared to say it to me as well, because there is no longer just one Thorn in this school, there are two, and you will treat her with the respect she deserves."

"Jake," she barks. "Get the fuck down."

"Oh and..." he continues. "She's taken, so don't even think about it." He pins each member of the team with a look. "Unless you want both Hunter and me to beat your asses into next week."

Eyes turn on the two of us. I pull Poppy in front of me and drop my lips to the top of her head and wink at Jake.

When Poppy left with Harley to get breakfast last Sunday morning, I headed straight to Jake and Amalie's new place to tell him the truth, well after Mom collared me to talk about how she wasn't ready to be a grandmother yet.

I was fully prepared to leave with a black eye and split lip to rival my girl's, but I was pleasantly surprised when all I got from him was a harsh warning to treat her properly and to never hurt her. I'm not sure if I need to thank Amalie for him not going full throttle on me or if he had already accepted that I'd fallen head over heels for his sister.

Jake jumps down from the bench, walks over and holds his fist out to me.

I bump it before pulling Poppy from her hiding place.

"Was that really necessary?" she spits.

"Yep. Anyone says anything to you, you tell me, yeah?"

"I don't think anyone's that stupid." He raises a brow. He doesn't need to say the words, we all know that if that were actually true then we wouldn't have just lived the nightmare we have.

Poppy lets out a sad sigh. "Thank you," she whispers to Jake. "I appreciate you having my back."

"Always, Sis. It's me and you now." He drops a kiss to her forehead before going back to join the guys.

"Walk me to class?" she asks, looking up at me with her huge gray eyes.

"I'd love to. Want me to carry your books too?"

"You're such a goof. Come on," she says with a laugh, lacing her fingers through mine and pulling me toward her locker.

As expected, eyes follow us through the hallways as quiet whispers fill the space.

"Just ignore them," I say to Poppy.

"I am," she says with her head held high.

"I'm so fucking proud of you," I tell her, stepping into her body and pressing her up against the wall outside her first class of the day.

"Miss Thorn, Mr. Hunter, I'm not sure that's the way to start the day, is it?" Hartmann barks down the hall when spots us.

"S-sorry, sir," Poppy stutters, pressing her palms against my chest and trying to push me away. Her cheeks flame red and she refuses to look at him.

"You're going to get me in so much trouble," she whispers to me, still trying to put some space between us.

"Speak for yourself. I'm so hard for you right now."

"Zayn," she half warns, half moans. "You need to go to class."

"Well, it's your fault if Miss Peterson thinks it's for her."

"You're gross. She's like... five years past retirement."

"What can I say?" I shrug. "The older generation loves me."

"You're a nightmare." She shakes her head at me, a smile playing on her lips.

"Love you, Pops."

"I love you too," she says quietly as I start backing away from her.

I blow her a kiss before rounding the corner and bumping straight into Rich and Justin who immediately set about ripping into me for my declaration. Assholes.

———

Thanks to Jake's warning, almost all the gossip had died out by the end of the week. Although it's been impossible to ignore the weird atmosphere around school knowing that we'd lost one of our own. He might have turned out to be even crazier than any of us had imagined, but he was still someone most of us had grown up with. It was weird, and I hate that a person who threatened the life of someone I love is able to leave that much of a hole behind. But I guess it is what it is, the best thing we can do now is look to the future.

"Are you sure you want to come? I would understand if you wanted to stay here," I say to Poppy who's sitting in my passenger seat while Harley's been relegated to the back.

"Of course. If you want me there," she adds hesitantly.

Reaching over, I lace my fingers with hers. "Of course. It's just not exactly the kind of place you belong."

"I want to see where you all grew up. I'm sure it's not as bad as you make out to be."

"Have you two about finished?" My sister sulks from the back.

"We should go before the toddler has a tantrum."

"Fuck you, Zayn. I don't think I like you all loved up and shit."

"We need to find you a boyfriend," Poppy suggests.

"It's okay. I already told Zayn that I was going to fuck Justin or Rich. I might even get them to double team me at the party tonight."

I can't help the growl that rumbles up my throat at her words. "Shut the fuck up, Harley."

"What? Tit for tat. You fuck my friend, I fuck yours."

"I'm not just fucking your friend though, am I?"

"As amusing as this little argument is, I'm right here, you know?" Poppy points out beside me with a smug grin on her face. "Harley," she says, turning to look at my sister. "Don't give it up to those assholes. Pick someone decent who's not been around half the school."

"Like you did?" she asks sarcastically.

"Fair point. Forget I said anything, screw who you like."

"Poppy," I gasp. "You're meant to be on my side."

"Sorry, babe. Chicks before dicks."

My chin drops as Harley barks a laugh behind me.

"Charming."

"Seriously though, Har. Don't just give it up to get back at us. Make it special."

"Maybe I don't want special," she sulks, staring out the window. "I just want... I don't know what I want."

"You will when you find him."

As we head farther out of town, thankfully the conversation turns away from my little sister's virginity and to safer subjects, mostly about tonight's party. Mom wasn't all that thrilled to let me throw another after the mess my New Year's one caused, but she didn't really have a leg to stand on seeing as she allowed Letty to have one, and as I pointed out, I'm only going to turn eighteen once.

In the end, she conceded and has booked herself into a hotel for the night with the strict instructions that by the time she returns tomorrow afternoon that the house will look exactly like it did when she left it. I told her it would, obviously, but we'll see how that goes.

As we get closer to Harrow Creek, the scenery begins to change. Gone are the big houses and perfect front yards from our side of Rosewood, and in their place are trailers and beat-up old cars.

When I was young, I thought this was how everyone lived. I had no idea that just a few miles away there were houses with pools and home gyms and all the other luxuries that come along with having money.

"Regretting it yet?" I ask Poppy when her and Harley's conversation comes to an end.

"Never," she says, reaching over and squeezing my hand in reassurance. "I don't care where you come from, Zayn, so stop worrying."

I smile at her, but it doesn't reach my eyes. I don't want to be ashamed of this place, but I can't help it. I know it made me the person I am today, but I don't have great memories of the place, and I'm more than happy to be away from the kinds of people who live here, and I'd more than happily never introduce Poppy to most of them.

The gravel at the entrance to our trailer park crunches under my truck's tires and we make our way toward our old home.

I glance over to see Poppy's eyes flitting around everything.

"You know, it's not as bad as you made it out to be."

"Appearances can be deceiving."

As I pull up out the front of Dad's trailer, movement in my rearview mirror catches my eye, but when I look up, I don't find anyone there.

"Ready to meet Dad?" Harley asks.

"I am," Poppy says eagerly, pushing the door open and jumping out.

I do the same and walk around the car to join them. It's not until we're all standing together that the person who was behind us shows his face.

"Shit," I mutter, my arm instinctively reaching out, my hand wrapping around Harley's so I can pull her behind me.

"Zayn, why the fuck are you... oh," she says, clearly looking over my shoulder and seeing the same thing I am. "What the hell is he doing here? I thought he left."

"Me too."

My eyes hold his angry ones as hate crackles between us.

"Um... what the hell is going on?" Poppy asks hesitantly. "Who is that?"

"No one you need to know," I bark, as Harley says, "Kane. He doesn't like us very much."

"You don't say," she whispers, clearly sensing the hostility coming off him in waves.

"Let's get inside and get out of here as soon as possible."

Ripping my stare from his, I spin around and gently push both Poppy and Harley toward the door. The last thing I want to do today is get into it with Kane and everything that happened.

"Happy Birthday," Dad shouts loudly as we walk up to the door. He jumps down the steps and pulls me in for a hug. "I can't believe you're a man now. I swear it was only yesterday you were toddling around in diapers. And you were—"

"Dad," I say, cutting off whatever embarrassing memory I'm sure was about to fall from his lips. "This is Poppy."

His eyes leave mine in favor of my girl.

"Harley's friend, right?" he asks, proving that he does listen to Harley's stories when we visit.

"Yeah, but she's..." Harley starts.

"Also, my girlfriend," I state proudly, wrapping my arm around her waist and pulling her into my side.

"Girlfriend?" Dad asks, his eyes wide. We might live in

different towns now, but he's more than aware—mostly thanks to Harley—about my... ways.

"Yep. Girlfriend. Now are you going to invite us in or what?"

"Oh... yeah. Poppy," he says, turning to my girl, his eyes still as wide as saucers. "It's good to meet you at last. Harley talks about all the time, unlike this one who's just blindsided me."

"It's good to meet you too, Mr. Hunter."

"Oh, please. Call me Rob."

"Okay, will do. And don't be too hard on him, this is all new territory for him."

"Hey," I complain, following behind as we all pile inside. As I reach out to pull the door closed behind us, my eyes lock with Kane's once more. His narrow in anger but all I can do is smile. I had nothing to do with the beef he has with my family, although hell knows I'll do everything in my power to protect them if he decides he wants his revenge.

Shaking my head at him, I close the door and turn toward the living area of the trailer I used to call home.

"Whoa, Dad," I say, taking in all the banners and balloons.

"What? I couldn't let my boy's day go by without doing anything special. Here," he says, pushing a gift over the table toward me.

I take a seat beside Poppy and rip open the paper.

"This is stunning." I stare down at the Rolex in my hand. "How did you afford this?"

"That doesn't matter. Happy Birthday, Son."

"Thanks, Dad."

"Right, cake!"

38

Poppy

I've seen Rob in pictures a few times over the years, I know what to expect looks-wise, although I wasn't quite prepared for seeing another set of Zayn's eyes staring back at me. While Zayn mostly has his mom's African American features, his eyes are all his father's. And the way they light up when they looked into mine that first time warmed my heart.

I've heard stories about this place, most of which Harley and Zayn have been reluctant to tell me about, but so far, aside from the creepy guy who was staring at us outside, it seems... fine.

Okay, so there are none of the fancy houses and well-tended yards I'm sure the two of them have become accustomed to over the past few years, but it's not so bad, at least not on the surface. They gave me the impression we were driving into the center of Hell or something.

I sit back and watch as the three of them banter together while Rob cuts up the cake he bought for his son's birthday.

"So what are the plans for the big day then after visiting your old man?"

"Party!"

"Your mom's allowing that after the last one?"

"Of course."

"Jeez, you always did have her wrapped around your little finger."

"What can I say?" Zayn says with a shrug.

We chat away for over two hours before Zayn stands and announces that we need to get back. His dad's face drops and my heart aches for him that he's got to keep watching his kids walk away when he clearly cares about them so much. It makes me wonder why he would have chosen to keep this life when he could have had a better one in Rosewood. But I guess not everything is about money, and this place is where his heart is.

When we emerge from the trailer, there's no one hanging around outside this time. That doesn't stop the three of us from looking around for him though. I have no idea who he is, but just with one look, he sent a shudder of fear racing down my spine that I remember all too well.

We all say goodbye to Rob, Zayn thanks him once again for his gift and we climb into the car.

"So... thoughts?" Harley asks, leaning forward in her seat.

"It was nice?"

"Nice?"

"Yeah. From what the two of you had said, I thought it was going to be awful."

"It is."

"Well, on the surface it seemed fine. Apart from that guy, who was he?"

"No one," Zayn spits, his grip on the wheel tightening the

second I so much as mention him. "And if you ever see him in Rosewood, run the other way."

His eyes meet Harley's in the rearview mirror, and she sinks back into her seat. The weird vibe going on between them doesn't make me any less suspicious about this guy.

The ride back is quieter than the journey to Harrow Creek, but it doesn't bother me. I'm more than happy to curl up on the seat and get lost in my own head. After spending a few hours with Marley, the counselor Jada set up for me, this week, things are beginning to get easier to think about.

I think I'll probably always feel to blame for what happened with Preston, I'm not sure that will ever go away, but already it's getting easier to bear. We've talked about my parents at length and although I already knew that what had happened was probably for the best, I'm really starting to understand it now.

Zayn and I spent last Saturday with Auntie Trish and the kids, and we had the best day. Seeing them so happy, the wide smiles on their faces made my entire year. They've had too much to deal with in their short lives and to see them lose the responsibility and just be kids for once meant everything to me. And just to be able to be their sister and not worry about also being a parent felt incredible.

"I can't believe Mom is letting you do this," Harley mutters as we pull up outside the house to already find her gone.

"You should be thanking me, Har. I'm leading the way to ensure you also get a party next year. You won't even have your style cramped by me or Letty, seeing as we'll be at college."

The mention of him not being here in just a few months makes my stomach twist uncomfortably. But I plaster a smile on my face when he turns to look at me after killing the engine because I don't want to dampen his excitement about college. I know through Harley that he's talked about UCLA for years. I don't want to be the one to ruin that for him.

"Ready to do this?"

"Hell yes," Harley barks. "But I'm stealing your girl to get ready."

"But—"

"I don't give a shit," she snaps, cutting off whatever argument that was about to fall from his lips. "Anyway, you'll probably be thanking me later. She's my birthday present to you."

Zayn's eyes narrow at his sister. "You can't give me my own girlfriend for my birthday." The way he says girlfriend sends a tingle racing through my body just like it did when he introduced me to his dad as such.

"I can, I am, and you will enjoy it. Come on, girl. We've got work to do," Harley says, shouldering open the door.

"Wish me luck," I say, turning to Zayn right as another car pulls up beside him.

Reaching out, he wraps the back of his hand around my neck and pulls me closer.

"You'll be fine. But if you can escape, come find me. I've just about forgotten the gift you gave me this morning?" he murmurs against my lips.

"Oh yeah?"

"Yeah." Taking control of my hand, he presses my palm against his crotch and I gasp when I find him hard and ready.

"Zayn," I moan, my own body heating up knowing just how turned on he is.

"Do you know how badly I want to pull you over the console and fuck you right here in my truck?"

"Oh God," I whimper. His tongue takes advantage of the opening and sweeps past my lips, searching out my own.

I lose myself in his kiss, leaning forward and wrapping my own hand around the nape of his neck to try to close the space between us.

That is until a fist rains down hell on the window beside

my head and I shriek in fear jumping back from Zayn as if I've been burned.

Turning to the window, I find Harley staring daggers at the two of us with her hands on her hips.

"I should probably..." I point over my shoulder.

"I'll be there in a few minutes," he says, sitting back in his seat and making a show of rearranging himself.

"Down boy," Harley shouts into the car the second I push the door open.

"Fucking cockblock."

"Yeah, yeah, whatever. Come on, time to get sexed up... just not in *that* way."

Harley and Ruby each take one of my arms and physically drag me toward the house as if I'm about to run back to Zayn and finish what we started any second.

"Damn, that was hot," Ruby mutters. "I need a guy."

"Weren't you sucking face with Jamie last weekend?" Harley helpfully points out. Zayn and I might not have been at last weekend's party, but I sure heard all about it.

"Yeah, but that was as far as it got. He ended up so drunk he passed out on me."

I snort a laugh while Harley announces, "Wow, you must be one hell of a lay, Rubes."

"Wouldn't know. Talking about getting laid." Both of them turn their eyes on me.

"I'm not telling you shit."

"Ow, come on. Is he as good as everyone claims?"

"I've got no complaints."

"My ear, my ears," Harley cries dramatically as we climb the stairs.

"Chill out I'm not going to tell you just how big he is." I hold my hands out, totally exaggerating, much to Ruby's amusement and Harley's horror. Releasing me, she darts up the stairs and toward her room.

"She's going to kill you."

"She'll get used to it," I mutter, following behind where she ran like her ass was on fire.

"You've got two choices," Harley says the second we step into the room.

My stomach drops the second I look up and lock eyes on the two dresses she's holding up in front of me. Both contain hardly any fabric and don't look like anywhere near covering any part of me up.

"Um... I hope you're not expecting me to wear one of those."

"Sure am. Now pick. Red or purple?"

"Or my jeans and a tank?"

"Nope. It's Zayn's birthday. Don't you want him to enjoy himself?" She winks at me.

"I thought you wanted to keep us apart."

"Yeah, well, I might kind of like seeing him all happy and shit," she whispers, averting her eyes.

"I'm sorry, what was that?"

"I like seeing him happy, okay. You too. You both deserve it."

"Aw, Har. Are you going all soft?"

"Whatever. Red or purple?"

I run my eyes over the lack of fabric on each and after noticing that the actual sides of the red dress are missing, I opt for purple.

"I hate you for this, you know that right."

"Oh, sweetie. You won't when he locks eyes on you. You'll be thanking her. Now, get your ass in the shower then we've got work to do."

With a huff, I follow orders and make quick work of scrubbing and shaving my body, ready for my man's big night.

———

"Holy shit," I mutter, staring at myself in the mirror. This isn't the first time that Harley and Ruby have given me a makeover, but this is the first time I've ever looked quite like this.

"You like?"

"I... I... yeah. I look... wow."

"Exactly. Zayn is going to lose his mind."

I stare at my dark smoky eyes before dropping my gaze to my dark lips, the low cut of the strapless dress, and my cleavage that's on show above and down to my almost fully exposed legs.

A tingle of excitement races through me and pushes away my nerves about other people seeing this much of me. I don't care about them, but I sure as hell want Zayn to look at me because what Ruby said is right. He is going to lose his mind.

"I need your help with something tonight," I tell them both. They lean in and listen to my plan before smiles form on their lips and they eagerly agree.

After sucking in a deep breath, I hold my head up high and pull open Harley's door.

The party is already in full swing downstairs and has been for quite some time while we had our own little party for three in Harley's room along with a bottle of vodka or two.

Ruby can barely walk in a straight line with the amount she's drunk already. Harley and I share a concerned look. This is becoming more and more of a habit for her, and I'm beginning to worry that she's relying on it too much to deal with everything that happened over Halloween with her stepbrother. I hate that she's still dwelling on it all this time later.

Harley falls back, supporting Ruby so she doesn't go crashing down the stairs as we make our way to join the party.

All eyes turn on us as we emerge, or should I say, eyes turn on me.

My skin tingles as everyone stares at me, their chins drop and their eyes almost pop out of their heads.

"Uh... Zayn," Justin calls. "You need to get out here, man."

A weird silence falls over the house for a beat before Zayn emerges from his den.

"Yeah, what... fuuuuuck," he groans when his eyes fall on me. "All right, party's over. You all know where the door is," he calls, marching straight over to me.

"Pops, you look... wow."

"I got attacked by your sister," I say with a shrug.

His hand grazes along my jaw before his fingers grip on to the back of my neck.

Our eyes lock and everyone around us disappears as if they don't exist.

"Fuck, you're beautiful."

His lips brush against mine gently before his tongue sweeps into my mouth.

My body sags against his as his arms wrap around my body, holding me up.

"My bedroom. Now," he grates, his breath hitting my ear and sending a shudder through my entire body.

My core aches to do exactly what he just suggested, but it's his birthday party. Plus, I've got a plan.

"Later," I say, pressing my palms against his chest in an attempt to push him back.

"But..."

"I'll make sure it's worth your while later."

He finally pulls his face from my neck and looks into my eyes.

"You can't hang out down here dressed like that."

"Sure I can," I sass, walking around him, making sure I put as much sway as possible into my hips. "Come dance with me?" I hold my hand out as I walk toward the living room where the speakers have been set up.

In a heartbeat, his hand is slipping into mine and we're joining the crowd who are already grinding away to the beat of the music.

He keeps my back to his front, wraps his arms around my waist, and pulls me back against him. His length presses against my ass and I can't help but grind against him, teasing him.

"You're such trouble," he groans in my ear as his hand splays across my stomach.

"You love it."

"I love you."

A wide smile spreads across my face as I continue moving. After a few minutes, I turn to look back at him, only for him to capture my lips with a knee-weakening kiss.

I spin in his arms and throw mine over his shoulders, teasing his hairline with my nails. I smile into our kiss as he shudders under my touch.

I have no idea how many songs play or how much time passes, but then equally I don't care either. All I do know is that when Harley calls my name, it's way before I'm ready to release him.

"Pops. Now would be a really great time," she says, reminding me that I asked her to help out with something earlier. I'm surprised she agreed knowing where it's probably going to lead, but I know she's a romantic at heart and couldn't really refuse.

"Oh yeah. Sorry, I need to..." I point to Harley with a wince.

"But—" he starts to argue, but I cut him off.

"We've got all night. Enjoy your party. Go smoke a blunt with the guys and relax a little."

"While you're walking around in that dress? Not a chance."

I laugh at him as I walk toward Harley and leave Zayn behind.

39

Zayn

I bite down on the inside of my cheek, watching Poppy's ass sway in that sinful fucking dress as she walks over to my sister.

Fucking cockblock.

Leaving the makeshift dance floor behind, I head out to the garden to do as she just suggested.

I find most of the guys out here passing a blunt around that Ethan probably supplied them with.

I drop down onto one between Justin and Jake and Amalie.

"You let her up for air, huh?" Justin asks, his voice full of amusement.

"Sadly," I mutter, snatching the joint from his fingers.

"She looks hot," Amalie points out, making Jake growl. "Oh calm down, caveman. She's almost eighteen, you can't keep up the protective big brother routine forever."

"Try me," he mutters. "What did she get you for your birthday?" Jake asks, trying to change the subject.

"Uh..." I hesitate, my cock swelling once more as I think about the wake-up call I had from her this morning. "N-nothing yet."

Amalie chuckles, giving me a knowing wink before she kisses Jake on the cheek and climbs from the lounger, heading inside.

"I can't believe this is all going to be over soon," Jake says, looking around at all the people in my backyard and spilling out from inside the house. I swallow harshly at the reality of what's coming for all of us. High school is almost done and we're all going to be heading off around the country as we start the rest of our lives. It doesn't seem all that long ago we started at Rosewood High thinking it would last forever.

We've achieved everything we dreamed of this year by winning the division and the state championships, but it's almost time to move on to new teams, new friends, new futures.

UCLA has always been my dream. I remember Mom showing me images of the campus when I was a kid. It was where she always wanted to go, and I've wanted it ever since. Only, the past few weeks, everything's changed for me. My vision for the future is suddenly totally different. I've just no idea what everyone else is going to think about it, but then, it's not their life, it's mine.

"There's still plenty of time for this. Plus, we'll all be back. Rosewood is our home."

"I guess so," Jake says, tipping his beer to his lips. Not so long ago, he was desperate to get out of this place, it's amazing how one person can change so much.

"Zayn," Harley calls. "Can you help me with something?"

"What, Har?" I bark, assuming that it's probably to carry a

passed-out Ruby upstairs, she wasn't looking exactly sober when I last saw her so I have no idea what state she's in now.

She doesn't say anything, stands with her hand on her hip by the door waiting for me.

"What?" I snap again when I get to her.

"Do you know where the karaoke machine is?"

I sigh. "Really? That's what you wanted me for? It's in the closet in my den. Are we done?"

"No, could you come and get it? It's too heavy for me."

"Jesus. I knew I shouldn't have invited you tonight," I mutter, following her inside, swiping a bottle of beer from the kitchen as I pass.

I've drained it by the time we walk through the door into my den. I expect to find the rest of the team in here on the Xbox or at least with a few of the squad grinding down on their lap, but when I look up, all I find is an empty room.

"What the hell?" I mutter to myself as Harley comes to a stop in the middle of the room and gestures toward the closet.

What the fuck did her last slave die of?

With a sigh, I pull the closet door open and step inside, my hand running down the wall for the switch that I know is there somewhere. But before my hand finds it, the door slams behind me and I sense someone step up to me, a beat before her scent fills my nose.

Her body presses against my back and my breath catches in anticipation.

"You want to play seven minutes in heaven?" she breathes in my ear making my skin tingle with awareness and my cock to jerk in my pants.

"Fuck yeah." Before I even know I've moved, I've got her backed up against the wall, the entire length of my hard body pressed up against her soft one.

"Happy Birthday," she breathes.

"You planned this." It's not a question because suddenly

Harley's random request and the empty room make total sense.

"I thought it was fitting. I also thought," she says, brushing her lips against mine. "That we could go all the way this time."

"Oh, hell yeah." I slam my lips down on hers in a bruising kiss. My need from earlier comes back full force and mixes with the alcohol and makes me forget any restraint I might usually have.

I soon realize I'm not the only one feeling that way because Poppy's hands slide under my shirt, lifting it and encouraging me to pull it off.

I do so without hesitation, dropping it onto the floor somewhere behind me.

"Poppy," I groan as she drops her lips to my collarbone and then lower, kissing across my chest, circling my nipples with her tongue before tracing the lines of my abs.

Her fingers make quick work of my pants and before I know it, she's pushing the fabric down my hips until they're pinning my legs at my knees.

Sliding down the wall, she stops on her haunches when her mouth is in line with my cock.

"Fuck, Pops," I grunt when her delicate fingers wrap around my length before she starts pumping slowly.

Reaching forward, I rest my forearm on the wall before me and stare down at her.

I can't see much in the darkness, but I can make out her silhouette to know exactly when she leans forward to lick at the head of my cock.

It jerks in her tight grasp as the sensation engulfs me before she leans forward further and sucks me deep into her mouth.

"Oh fuck. Fuck," I bark, already beginning to lose control despite the fact she's barely touched me.

Everything is heightened in the dark plus the knowledge that she's been planning this for who knows how long.

Her hand moves along with the burning heat of her mouth and the teasing touch of her tongue and in an embarrassingly short amount of time, my cock jerks deep in her mouth and I come down her throat.

She doesn't stop sucking or licking until I've finished.

Twisting my fingers in her hair, I gently lift her to her feet, and once again slam my lips to hers.

"Fuck, you're amazing," I murmur into her kiss.

My hands slide up her bare thighs, pushing her short dress up over her ass.

"Poppy?" I half ask, half warn when I find her bare of panties. "Tell me you haven't been walking around in front of all those assholes like this."

"Now, that would be telling," she teases before a squeal rips past her lips as I lift her, wrap her legs around my waist and pin her to the wall with my hips. My cock is already hard for her again and it teases her bare pussy. "Zayn," she moans, her needy voice almost my undoing.

Cupping her face in my hands, I kiss her once more. Tilting her head to the side so I can slide my tongue deep into her mouth, lapping at hers, showing her just how much she means to me, how much this right now means to me.

My hands drop over her shoulders and down her arms until I cup her breast in my hands, rubbing my fingertips over her already peaked nipples.

Gripping the fabric of the strapless dress, I pull it down so the whole thing is gathered around her waist and find exactly what I was expecting.

"Fuck, you're killing me," I grate out, taking her bare breasts in my hand and making her head fall back against the wall when I pinch her nipples hard between my thumb and forefinger.

"Zayn, please," she begs.

"What, Pops? Tell me what you need."

"You, Zayn. I need you to... argh," she cries out when I surge forward, filling her to the hilt in one smooth thrust. "Oh God, yes," she cries, making me understand why she thought to clear out the room.

Her nails scratch down my back until she clamps on to my shoulders as I grip her hips and start to pound into her.

Our slick skin moves together seamlessly as we chase our releases, and as she gets closer her cries and pleas for more only get louder. She doesn't drink very often, and when she does, it's still not much, but fuck does it help loosen her up even more than she is usually.

Pulling her bottom half from the wall, I change the angle to ensure my pelvis rubs at her clit with every thrust.

"Yes, yes, yes," she chants as I watch her full tits bounce with the force of my thrusts.

"Fuck," I grate out, my fingers digging into her ass as I try to get deeper, try to ensure she feels this for days, hoping that I make my mark on her, making her mine forever.

"Come, Poppy," I demand when I start to lose control of my own impending release.

Bringing one hand around to her front, I pinch her clit and send her flying over the edge.

"Zayn," she cries out as her pussy squeezes me impossibly tight, giving me no choice but to lose myself alongside her. My cock jerks, shooting jets of cum inside her. Making her mine.

Continuing to hold her up, I drop my head to her shoulder, trying to catch my breath.

"I applied to Maddison Kings," I blurt, not even realizing that I said the words out loud until she tenses in my hold.

"You what?" she asks, her voice quiet and unsure.

Pulling my head up, I stare into her lust blown eyes.

"I've applied to Maddison Kings," I repeat, sounding a little more confident this time.

"But... why? You want to go to UCLA. You've always wanted to go to UCLA. I don't..." She shakes her head, cute frown lines forming on her brow.

"Everything's changed now, Pops," I say, rubbing my thumb over her creased skin before cupping her cheek.

"But—"

"Nothing's set in stone, it's up for discussion but I wanted it to be an option."

"But... UCLA," she repeats, concern still filling her features.

"Yeah, but there's something else I want more."

Her eyes hold mine, hope shining in them for what I might be alluding to and my heart swells.

"I love you, Poppy Thorn. I don't want to move halfway across the country if it means leaving you behind. Maddison Kings is a good school, they have a good team and excellent programs. I could go for a year, and then maybe you could join me. We could get our own place off-campus together. You'd be close to your brother's and sister. Sorry, I—" I go to apologize, thinking that from the look on her face that I might have got a little carried away.

"You've really thought about this, haven't you?"

"You're it for me, Pops. I want to be wherever you are."

"And what if I want to be wherever you are?"

"Then I could do a year at Maddison and transfer to wherever you want to go."

"Oh, Zayn. I love you."

"I love you too," I mumble against her lips as she presses hers to mine and sweeps her tongue into my mouth.

I'm just about ready to fuck her once again when there's an almighty crash from outside our closet.

"What the hell?"

Poppy wriggles in my hold and I reluctantly place her back down on her feet.

There's another loud noise, this time something smashing before a cry sounds out.

"Fuck," Poppy barks, clearly recognizing the voice as she rushes to right her dress before flying out of the closet.

I make quick work of pulling my boxers and pants back up before following her out.

"Ruby," Poppy cries, running toward where she's sitting on the floor, her arms wrapped around her knees as she continues to cry.

Glancing around the room, I find liquid coating the far wall with shattered glass all over the floor beneath.

"What's wrong? What's happened? Are you hurt?" Poppy asks in a panic, dropping to her knees beside her friend and tucks her hair from her face.

"He... he's coming back. I can't see him again, Poppy. I can't. I can't live with him again. I won't survive it."

Meet Ashton in FAZE & FURY now!

ACKNOWLEDGMENTS

Wow, I don't really know what to say. Poppy and Zayn's story sure was a wild ride. I enjoyed discovering who they both were so much and finding out just how strong Poppy was.

I hope you enjoyed reading their journey as much as I did writing it.

I can't believe this is the fifth book in the series already. It's almost been a year since I released Thorn. These boys have taken me on journey's that I really wasn't expecting, but I wouldn't have it any other way.

There are only two more to go, assuming I manage to stop adding more books.

Ruby's story is next, make sure you've picked up FAZE the prequel to her and Ashton's story, FURY. I'm so excited to dive back into the two of them.

As always, I've got so many people to thank for helping me to write Hunter.

Sam, for putting up with me and my demands every day. For being at the other end of my messages when I need to throw ideas around and for falling in love with Zayn —and hating Preston—right alongside me.

Michelle, for once again alpha reading and giving me abuse where needed.

My team of beta readers, thank you for dropping everything to pick up Hunter and to give me your honest feedback.

Ellie, at My Brother's Editor, for once again making my words make sense, and Darlene and Athena at Sisters Get Lit(erary) Author Services for polishing everything up.

To all the bloggers and bookstagrammers who've supported me with this series. Your shares and support means everything.

And finally, to you for getting this far on this journey with me. Thank you so much, I couldn't do this without your support.

Until next time,

Tracy xo

ABOUT THE AUTHOR

Tracy Lorraine is a new adult and contemporary romance author. Tracy has recently-ish turned thirty and lives in a cute Cotswold village in England with her husband, baby girl and lovable but slightly crazy dog. Having always been a bookaholic with her head stuck in her Kindle Tracy decided to try her hand at a story idea she dreamt up and hasn't looked back since.

Be the first to find out about new releases and offers. Sign up to my newsletter here.

If you want to know what I'm up to and see teasers and snippets of what I'm working on, then you need to be in my Facebook group Tracy's Angels.

Keep up to date with Tracy's books at
www.tracylorraine.com

ALSO BY TRACY LORRAINE

Falling Series

Falling for Ryan: Part One #1

Falling for Ryan: Part Two #2

Falling for Jax #3

Falling for Daniel (An Falling Series Novella)

Falling for Ruben #4

Falling for Fin #5

Falling for Lucas #6

Falling for Caleb #7

Falling for Declan #8

Falling For Liam #9

Forbidden Series

Falling for the Forbidden #1

Losing the Forbidden #2

Fighting for the Forbidden #3

Craving Redemption #4

Demanding Redemption #5

Avoiding Temptation #6

Chasing Temptation #7

Rebel Ink Series

Hate You #1

Trick You #2

Defy You #3

Play You #4

Inked (A Rebel Ink/Driven Crossover)

Rosewood High Series

Thorn #1

Paine #2

Savage #3

Fierce #4

Hunter #5

Faze (#6 Prequel)

Fury #6

Legend #7

Maddison Kings University Series

TMYM: Prequel

TRYS #1

TDYW #2

TBYS #3

TVYC #4

TDYD #5

Ruined Series

Ruined Plans #1

Ruined by Lies #2

Ruined Promises #3

Never Forget Series

Never Forget Him #1

Never Forget Us #2

Everywhere & Nowhere #3

FAZE SPEAK PEEK
CHAPTER ONE

Ashton

Looking around the lavish house that I have never wanted to visit, anger races through my veins.

This is the last place in the world I wanted to be.

I should be home in the shitty apartment that Mom and I live in back in Seattle, but I'm not. I'm in *his* house, the asshole that ruined both of our lives.

It's been over five years since he walked away, leaving us with fuck all, just the bitter taste of his betrayal.

Mom said it was fine, that it was for the best. But it's all bullshit. She's tried to put a brave face on, tried to convince me that their relationship really was over and that he didn't shatter all of her hopes and dreams for the future.

But I know her better than she thinks. I see the shadows in her eyes. The coldness, the loneliness, that set in after he left. I also don't miss the number of bottles that sit in our recycling on a weekly basis. They seem to be multiplying week by week, and I have no fucking idea how to help her.

Getting suspended from school again for fighting probably wasn't the best thing to do to help, but that prick has had it coming for a long time.

I think of Jonathon fucking Parker and the way he looked down at us all like he was something fucking special.

My fists curl once again as if he's in touching distance. If I could take him out all over again I would.

My busted knuckles split open, the sting of pain a reminder I don't need of where I am right now.

He'd asked me time and time again over the years to come and visit his new home, his new family. But every time I refused. I had no interest in meeting the bitch that took him away from us or the girl who he got to play daddy for while he mostly forgot that I existed.

My teeth grind as I think about everything I lost the day he walked away. My best fucking friend. That's what I lost.

But this time was different. It wasn't him asking me to come. It was Mom. And as much as I wanted to refuse her request, I couldn't. One look into her tired, stressed eyes and I knew she needed the break probably as much as I did.

I haven't made it easy for her the past few years. I've been suspended more times than I can remember. I've been on my last warning at that shithole of a school for months, but the principal is a fucking pussy, so I doubt he'll ever actually kick me out. It'll give him too much paperwork to do, and we all know how much he hates doing any actual work.

"Please, Ash. Go and spend the week with him. Clear your head. It can be a fresh start when you get back." Her words ring out in my mind as if she's standing next to me having the conversation.

I couldn't say no to her. I've never been able to. Having experienced how much hurt he's caused her. I'd hate to do the same. I know I'm a constant disappointment to her, but no matter how I try not to be, it happens, nonetheless.

My temper always gets the better of me. My hate gets the better of me. My fury gets the better of me. It's only right that it does. It is my name, after all. The one and only thing I have that still connects me to the man who spends his days under this roof.

The perfect all-American family home. Wrap-around porch, the huge kitchen with an island in the center, the pristine garden and the glistening pool. It's a million miles away from the place Mom and I call home now.

I stand at the window waiting for her to pull up. Lisa, my stepmom, excitedly told me that I could expect her any time now before both her and Dad disappeared not long after picking me up from the airport. I can't fucking wait to meet my stepsister. It's been a long time coming, that's for sure.

I've seen the odd photo of her when I've needed to torture myself and looked at his Facebook. Every single time all it's done is to add to the anger that lives inside me as I see images of them together playing happy family.

He should be doing that with us. His real family. Not his replacements.

My teeth grind right as a little blue car pulls up in front of the house.

I lean toward the window a little, trying to get a better view of her before we're face to face. I need to get a read on her, try to make a game plan.

I know nothing about her aside from the fact she played a part in ruining my life. That he chose her and her mother over me and mine. His son and wife. The ones whose best intentions he should have had at heart.

Disappointment settles in my stomach when she doesn't immediately get out of the car. Instead, she looks down, I guess at her cell.

After a few minutes, she looks up at the house and blows out a long breath.

Is she nervous? Apprehensive about meeting me?

If she's not, she fucking should be.

This house, that I can only assume is her sanctuary, her home, is about to become the place of living nightmares because my darling stepsister has never met someone like me before, I can fucking guarantee it.

After what feels like a lifetime, she pushes the door open and a pair of legs emerge before she stands.

Her head barely appears above the door. She's so small, so breakable. I rub my hands together as my plan for my time here floats around in my head.

You ruined my life, I'm about to turn yours upside down, you motherfucker.

The second she slams the door, a smile twitches at the corners of my mouth.

She's wearing the smallest pair of shorts, that I can only imagine are cut high across her ass, and a crop top that shows off her tiny waist and more than ample tits.

Oh yeah, she's definitely rocking something I can work with.

Walking to the other side of the room, I wait out of sight for her to let herself in.

She does so quickly, but it's not until I hear her purse hit the table that I step from my hiding space.